Retaliation

DAEMONS & LUMENS SERIES

S. D. PAINE

When you are not fed love on a silver spoon, you learn to lick knives.
-Lauren Eden

To the ones who always wanted to be the villain of their own story.
Let your daemons out to play.

AUTHOR NOTE

This book contains dark themes and the characters make questionable decisions. Tropes and triggers include graphic violence, torture, bdsm-related scenes, and explicit intimate scenes.

For more information about this book and future books in the series, visit my website and sign-up for my newsletter! www.sdpaineauthor.com

BOOK ONE PLAYLIST

Find me on Spotify to listen to the Retaliation Playlist!

Wolves by Sam Tinnesz

Closer by Nine Inch Nails

Let It Burn by ZZ Ward

Odds of Even by Marilyn Manson

Monster by PVRIS

Sarcophagus by Do Not Resurrect

Running Up That Hill by Placebo

Bad Things by I Prevail

Masterpiece by Motionless in White

Happy by Mudvayne

Cinderella's Dead by Emmeline

Dating the Devil by Davina Michelle

Seven Devils by Florence

Necessary Evil by Motionless in White

Suffocate Bad Omens and Kayzo

Monster by Paramore

Easy to Love Bryce Savage

FOMO by Ready Set Fall

Sleeptalk by Dayseeker

Just Pretend by Bad Omens

Granite by Sleep Token

Hurricane by I Prevail

Werewolf by Motionless in White

Seen a Ghost by Lose Control

Heaven Knows by Pretty Reckless
Lost by Bring Me the Horizon
Twisted by Missio
All the Good Girls Go to Hell by Billie Eilish
Play With Fire by Sam Tinnesz
Silence by Marshmallow (feat. Khalid)
A Little Wicked by Valeria Boussard

THE V.I.P. LIST

Seraphina Valdis Bronwen - Undercover as Sara Braun
Tabitha "Tibby" Marsden - Tech wizard and friend of Sara

Andras Blackbyrn - Prince of the Obscuritas, son of Laszlo
Typhon "Ty" Radnor - Prince of the Obscuritas, son of Darren
Leviathan "Levi" Delano - Prince of the Obscuritas, son of Samuel
Devon "Dev" Parrish - Prince of the Obscuritas, son of Ezekiel

Laszlo Blackbyrn - King of the Obscuritas, Leader
Darren Radnor - King of the Obscuritas, Enforcer
Samuel Delano - King of the Obscuritas, Seducer
Ezekiel Parrish - King of the Obscuritas, Technician, Deceased

Aurora Valdis Bronwen - Mother of Lailah, Seraphina, and Michaela, Murdered by The Obscuritas
Joseph Bronwen - Husband of Aurora, Father of Lailah, Seraphina, and Michaela, MIA
Lailah Valdis Bronwen - oldest daughter of Aurora and Joseph, Murdered by The Obscuritas
Michaela Valdis Bronwen - youngest daughter of Aurora and Joseph, MIA

PAWNS & PLAYERS

Ryan Lancing - Lead Bartender at Noircoeur
James "J" Azer - Gym Manager, close friend of Ty
Dominique - Owner of Noircoeur, Obscuritas member
Otis Redford - Operations Manager of Noircoeur, Obscuritas member

Josie and Lottie Hayes - Twins, Dancers at Noircoeur, friends of Sara Braun

Jade Dawlish - Professional boxer, employed at Ty's gym, allegiance unknown

Audrey Kingston - Student at Law School, attends classes with Sara Braun

Xavier Saladino - Fireman at firehouse, member of unnamed gang, allegiance unknown

IMPORTANT PLACES

Noircoeur - Burlesque Club beneath restaurant downtown Boston, owned by The Obscuritas

The Towne House - Home of Andras, Typhon and Leviathan, located near Harvard University

The Haven - Local pub owned by Devon, lives in apartment above

Vespertine Hall - Estate located just outside city of Boston, owned by The Obscuritas

P4 Fitness - Gym owned by Typhon, located near The Towne House

WORDS & PHRASES

The Obcuritas - Exclusive cult seeking otherworldly power

Umbra Noctis - Shadows of Night, secret sect of The Obscuritas created by the Princes

Daemons - monstrous creatures of myths and legends, varying degrees of magic/power relating to the elements

Lumens - ethereal creatures of myths and legends, varying degrees of magic/power relating to the elements

Diabla - Spanish, (she) devil
Mi diosa - Spanish, my goddess
Belle femme - beautiful woman

Tu es magnifique, mon amour. - You are beautiful, my love.
Veux-tu me baiser ce soir, pompier? - Do you want to fuck me tonight, firefighter?
Merci, bébé. - Thanks, baby.
Tu es magnifique, mon ange. - You are beautiful, my angel.

CHAPTER ONE

Sara

Oh fuck me, I'm about to die.

I scrambled back, ducking behind a maroon wing-backed chair as the next gunshot rang out, the bullet narrowly missing my head. Despite the fact I'd spiked this motherfucker's drink with enough sleeping pills to knock out a whale, he was still standing. Sort of. Furniture crashed as he wobbled around the room, shouting for my death. I peeked over the chair and ducked back down just as quickly when he fired the gun again. The bullet whizzed by where my forehead had been seconds before, exploding into the drywall behind me. I guess they didn't call him Bullseye for nothing. Thankfully the Rohypnol slowed his reflexes enough for me to dodge his shots. The bulky asshole lunged for the chair, and I darted behind a bookshelf. He roared his fury, his words slurring as he hounded after me. Thank the gods I wore my combat boots tonight instead of my heels. The shoes didn't match my dress, but whatever. Comfort over fashion. Kill or be killed.

The sizable mansion ten minutes outside of Boston was pretty much destroyed. I'd managed to cut down the majority of The Obscuritas cult henchmen while they sat around their fancy dinner table getting drunk on their uber-rich employer's fancy liquor. The last few goons had been holed up in the study smoking cigars, exactly where I anticipated them to be. But damn if Bullseye didn't go along with my plan, favoring his smokes over the drugged booze—hence the sloppy shootout. I had one weapon left and I had to make this final strike count.

"Alright, I'm coming out! Don't shoot yet!" I made my voice quiver with fear like a frightened little girl. A naturally soft voice had its perks.

More incoherent words tumbled from his lips. I was very confident he said something like "*Sure Sara, come on out and let's be friends.*"

I slid the knife from my boot and sucked in a steadying breath, quieting my mind and sinking into the darkness inside me, preparing to pounce on my prey. My eyes snapped open, and I sprinted around the bookshelf and threw the blade seconds before Bullseye could pull the trigger. The knife buried to the hilt in his left eye. He dropped a heartbeat later, and I let out a sigh of relief.

Bullseye, motherfucker. I snorted at my own joke, then winced as pain shot through my ribs. Definitely bruised, possibly broken. But I healed quickly—like inhumanly quickly—so at least I had that going for me.

I looked around at the other dead bodies, but none of them were important enough to remember. I didn't mind killing them. Actually, I enjoyed it. My body sang with adrenaline and arousal at what I'd just done. Fucked up, maybe, but I didn't linger on that thought. Avoiding emotions like guilt and feeding on ones like rage worked well for me over the last decade. Besides, they were all predators. Karma was bound to catch up with them.

And tonight, *I* was their karma.

Bullseye, aka Big Fugly Douchebag, was one of the top assassins working for The Obscuritas, and he had a vile kink for torturing women. Rule Number One, never trust grown men in creepy cults. Unfortunately, the core members of The Obscuritas were much more than creepy. They were vile murderers with fucked up rituals. And they would pay for taking my family from me and fucking up every good thing I had ever known.

My dagger slid from Bulleye's eye socket easily. I wiped his filthy blood off the blade with his jacket. Blood dripped down my arm from a nasty cut, so I tore a piece of fabric from the dead guy's shirt and tied it around the wound, knotting it with my teeth. I picked my way through the broken glass and overturned furniture toward the front door, sucking in fresh, wintry air soon as I opened it. The wind whipped my hair around my face. I was still getting used to the silvery blue color of it, but I couldn't risk anyone recognizing my signature copper locks. The brown-colored contacts itched my eyes, and I was more than ready for comfy clothes and a steaming hot shower to wash away this day.

I stepped over the dead guy on the doorstep and walked toward my Buell motorcycle, one of my few prized possessions. Many hours were spent modifying and painting the bike to make it my own. Riding was a freedom unlike anything else. For that stretch of time, I was free from my thoughts and the darkness attempting to swallow me whole.

"Come in, Nova," a voice cracked in my ear, and I winced from all the gunshots still ringing in my brain.

"Here, Tib—"

She cut me off quickly. "Code names, Nova."

I rolled my eyes. "Here, Zenith."

"Injuries?" The *click, click, click* of her keyboard echoed in my ear as I made my way down the long driveway.

"Minor," I grunted, holding my ribs and eyeing the cut on my arm.

"Casualties?" She popped a gum bubble in my ear.

I snorted. "Many. Full house tonight. Including one very dead Bullseye."

"I saw. Really going for that deadly double entendre, eh?" Zenith popped another bubble.

I snorted a laugh. "I suppose I did. Felt good too. Did you get anything from them?"

Tibby let out an evil laugh. "Of course. Despite your failure to keep them from blowing their entire system to hell, I was able to extract some information before they crashed the network."

I smirked to myself. "Your skills are inferior to none, queen." I hesitated, but couldn't help asking my next question. "Anything on my family?"

The silence verified what I already knew. If Tibby had found them, she would have told me right away.

"Sorry, friend. Not yet."

I swallowed down my emotions and sighed. "See you later, Zenith."

Another bubble popped in my ear. "Peace out, Nova."

I strapped on my helmet, tucking my hair inside, and revved the Buell's engine. My motorcycle was great for quick getaways, even if it was a freezing January night in Massachusetts. I zipped down the dead-end street and away from the bloody mess, not feeling the cold biting at my skin quite like most people did. I kept the lights off as I eased out onto the main road. Tibby hacked into the cameras and diverted the feed when I first arrived at the house, but I couldn't risk someone seeing me leave.

Tabitha Marsden, aka Tibby, aka Zenith, was pretty much my one and only friend. We'd met in a shelter for homeless teens. She was hiding out in the States after leaving London where she put her abusive stepfather in a coma. And I was… well I was a mess with nothing and no one. A few friendship bracelets and several bottles of vodka later and voila. Tech hackers, thieves, and murderers.

I'd stolen a few pieces of jewelry, all the cash in the safe, and one particularly badass-looking medieval club-like weapon from the mansion to throw off anyone who came hunting for the murderer. Not that anyone would be looking for me specifically. No one even knew I was alive.

I didn't linger on that thought, not feeling up for a pity party tonight. I had plans in place. Things were finally coming together after almost two years of solid detective work on my part and a bit of tech sleuthing by Tibby. The Osbcuritas would pay. Starting with their Princes.

I pulled my bike into one of the employee parking spots behind the local pub, The Haven. I'd made friends with the bar owner and, as of two months ago, occupied the apartment above it. I'd finally found a solid lead on the men I sought and, lucky me, all four of them currently lived in the same city. Devon

Parrish was my first mark, an Obscuritas Prince masquerading as a "lowly" bar owner. Of the four men I tracked, he was the only one not strutting about the town, flaunting his wealth. Then again, I'd found out only six months ago his father, Ezekiel Parrish, one of the four Obscuritas Kings, was dead, and Dev didn't seem to stay in touch with any of the other Princes. Tibby couldn't find any details about his father's death other than the headstone Dev had purchased. The mystery of it just screamed "secretly murdered by the cult leaders."

I locked up my bike and used the fire escape to enter the apartment. The only other way in was via the stairs through the bar, and since I didn't fancy Devon knowing all my comings and goings, the fire escape was preferable. I shoved open the window and crawled through, cursing as my bloodied arm bumped into the rusty stove. The small kitchen was barely big enough for a child. Lucky for me, I was only 5'3" and although I wouldn't consider myself thin, seeing as I lived in the gym when I wasn't committing crimes against cult leaders, I could slip in and out of small spaces easily enough. My older sister, Lailah, had been gifted with legs for days and supermodel looks. I grimaced, unwrapping my arm and shaking the thoughts of my murdered sister from my mind. I tried not to think about her. Unless I was killing people, and then her broken body was all I could see before the rage took over. Sometimes I even blacked out from the fury of it, coming to on my bedroom floor with broken things scattered around me. I kept very little furniture these days.

I flicked on a lamp as I grabbed a towel from the hall closet and tugged off my boots, heading for the bathroom. My arm no longer bled freely, and the cut wasn't too deep. I hissed in pain as I rubbed a cotton swab with peroxide over it, cleaning it out before it closed up full of dirt and grime.

I wasn't entirely sure how my healing abilities worked, so it was better to be safe and clean the wound. The first time it happened, I was ten years old. I remembered my mother's face like it was yesterday because everything changed after that stupid day.

"Momma!" I cried out as I ran to her, my knee bleeding freely. Lailah and I had been playing in the yard when I fell from the trampoline. We were pretending to fly.

Our mother was beautiful, like an angel. Her auburn hair fell around her shoulders in waves as she ran toward me. "My sweet princess. What happened?"

I sniffed, my face wet with tears. "We were trying to fly. I fell and landed on one of Michaela's toys. Look at my knee!"

We both looked down at the bloody mess. Mother had come prepared with a cloth. She wiped it away gently, but the cut was already healing. I stared, confused. I looked up at her, and her eyes held something I didn't understand at the time. Fear.

My eyes burned with angry tears as I shook the memory out of my head. I turned the shower handle all the way to the left, needing the scalding hot water to cleanse my body and clear my mind. I stripped out of my bloody clothes and tossed them into a trash bag stashed in the bathroom closet. I'd need to pick up a few more shifts at the club to replace all my ruined clothes. Even though Tibby kept us rich with stolen money and offshore accounts, I needed to maintain a believable, low profile for now. I chose the underground burlesque club for two reasons: to observe drunk, rich idiots willing to spill their secrets and to sing.

The scalding water soothed my mind and washed away the grime from the evening's events. I lathered my skin with my favorite lavender and mint soap and scrubbed my body as I replayed the fight in my mind. While taking out Bullseye had been incredibly satisfying, tonight didn't go as planned. He'd made me instantly, and I didn't have time to interrogate anyone before the shooting started. Bullseye wasn't a completely useless assassin and somehow saw the devil in my eyes when I walked into that mansion. I needed to change tactics. None of the lower level cult members were giving me what I needed. So lucky me, I'd be starting law school next week.

Andras Blackbyrn was currently attending Harvard Law School's elite master's program. And with a bit of tech magic, Tibby had me enrolled as a student. We shopped online and purchased anything that screamed "slutty student." I didn't entirely hate it. I could really rock a tiny plaid skirt. Based on his dating history, Andras preferred his women blonde, young and pliable. I wasn't changing my hair again, though. The long, silvery blue locks were staying. I couldn't risk him recognizing me with a more neutral color. Not that he would. I hadn't seen the sons of The Obscuritas leaders since we were children.

I was only thirteen when they came for my sister, and the Princes were only a couple years my senior at the time. Lailah, my beautiful and bold older sister, was seventeen when she was murdered; sacrificed for some stupid ritual I still didn't understand. Tibby and I scoured the dark web for details, but found very little. The Obscuritas clearly had their own tech wizard to keep their dirty secrets hidden.

The details of the night my family was murdered only came back to me in small pieces, like my mind was trying to protect me from the horrors. We drove a very long way in the middle of the night. My sisters slept in the car, but I felt uneasy. Something wasn't right. When we pulled down a long, wooded drive, my father cursed. I could just barely see my mother take his hand in the dark, whispering reassurances.

I remembered my father giving Michaela, my younger sister, and I something gross to drink before we got out of the car. It made my limbs heavy and my mind clouded. Michaela was even more affected and she quickly fell into a deep sleep, so he had to carry her. He stuffed us into a large wardrobe before The Obscuritas arrived, but I could still hear everything when the ritual began. Beyond the door to the wardrobe, Lailah cried out for our parents, and my father quietly sobbed as he leaned against the door. Why wasn't he trying to save them? Why didn't he go to Lailah when she cried out for him?

I wanted to scream, but then my mother began shouting words in a language I didn't know. The house rocked and shook as the chanting grew louder, and I peaked out of a crack in the closet door, my curiosity getting the best of me. Thunder boomed as the storm built, and lightning flashed through the windows. It all ended so quickly, and suddenly my father was carrying us away. The shock of deathly silence assaulted my ears, and I could feel my heart pounding rapidly. My eyes landed on the men lying unconscious on the floor all around the house.

I saw my sister, bound and prone inside a chalked pentagram on the wood floor. Her throat was cut, her blue eyes glassy and terrified. My mother lay on the other side of the chalked surface, her eyes closed and her face pale. Her fingers only just grazed the tip of the chalky symbols. I barely registered the four boys passed out in the circle with Lailah. And then we were gone, driving away from my murdered mother and sister. A piece of my heart broke away and got left behind with them that night. The beginning of the end.

For almost eight years, I plotted my revenge. It didn't matter if the Princes hadn't actively participated in the ritual then or not. My insider information told me they were taking over as the cult leaders as soon as Andras graduated in May. Something big was coming. More and more members of the cult were traveling into town each week.

I lingered in the hot water for a few more minutes, keeping my hair dry, before deciding I needed a drink and loud music to drown out my dark thoughts. I quickly dried off and slipped into a pair of fleece-lined leggings and an oversized black sweater with Ghostface on it. I rearranged my hair in a messy knot and coated my lashes with mascara, finishing with my signature blood-red lipstick and leaving my freckles on display. Perks of being a natural ginger—fair skin and a few freckles. I pulled on some cozy socks and boots, grabbed my keys and cash, then headed down the stairs into the noisy dive bar.

The Haven was a favorite for locals and far enough off the beaten path to avoid cringe-worthy college boys and tourists. Dim lights and sticky bar stools dominated the space. Nirvana played loudly from the digital jukebox, the only new-age piece of technology in the place. I slipped onto a stool at the far end of the bar and waited for Devon to make his way to me. I watched him work, appreciating the fitted T-shirt riding up as he flipped a bottle of whiskey into the air and smoothly poured four shots. Devon's scruffy beard dominated his face, hiding his unruffled and easy smile, which he only gifted to his regulars and myself. Otherwise, he was permanently in grumpy mode. I called him grumpy-sunshine. Not that anyone would notice, but I'd been watching him for some time now. He had a soft side, a good side. Dev wasn't evil on the inside like I hoped he'd be.

He passed out two of the whiskey shots and grabbed the other two, turning toward me with that sweet smile, the skin around his light-green eyes crinkling as he dropped the shot in front of me. It was impossible not to be captured by his gaze, the amazonite color of his eyes contrasting against his dark-brown skin and shaggy, dark hair. My stomach fluttered and heat flooded my body, heading south fast. *Down, girl.*

"Hey, beautiful." His smile widened, and I couldn't help smiling back.

I wanted to point out that he was the beautiful one here, but that was a little too bold for tonight. I wanted him close but not too close.

"Hey, Dev." I picked up the shot, clinking the glass to his and knocking it back. "Looks like a busy Saturday for you."

"It's been steady. Mostly regulars. Nothing too exciting. How's your night been?" He leaned against the back of the bar, crossing his arms and giving me an eyeful of his muscular, tattooed arms.

He was just so pretty to look at. It was a shame he'd have

to die with the others. I told myself his hot bartender vibe was the only thing I'd be missing, even if it wasn't entirely true.

"Nothing exciting in my life, as usual." I shrugged, keeping the details of my life vague as always. He never asked for them anyway.

Devon Parrish was going to be the hardest of the four to take out. He seemed normal, well-adjusted, and very much my type of bad boy turned good guy. But he was one of them. His father had been one of them. And for what they did to my family, they all had to pay the price. No matter how deep those piercing eyes stared into my revenge-riddled heart.

I tried not to dwell on the knowledge that in two months of semi-close contact with Dev, I'd felt more alive than I had in the last eight years, which was impressive since we hadn't even kissed. Sure, I'd been with men before, but it never meant anything to me, it was always a job. I faked the smiles, faked the orgasms. Besides, how could you feel anything for anyone when you were already dead inside?

"Sticking around for a bit?" He leaned toward me, muscular arms stretching his shirt sleeves.

I caught a whiff of his whiskey and sage scent and inhaled deeply, finding it oddly relaxing. I dipped my head and winked playfully. "I could be persuaded."

Dev grinned and poured a double shot of Jack into a glass. I grazed his fingers as I took the glass, a spark of heat passing between us. It was always like that, but for the two months since I started renting his apartment upstairs, I hadn't acted on the urges to drag him into my bed. And I would not be sharing how many times I used my vibrator and thought of his hands on my body. I could tell he was into me, but he was so damn private, he'd never really made a move beyond our little bar bantering. As he pulled back, I noticed a new tattoo on his wrist. His arms were covered in tattoos, but this one looked fresh—and strange.

I nodded toward his outstretched arm. "Did you get a new tattoo?"

He frowned, looking at his wrist. "No. I've had this for a while now."

"Are you sure? It looks new."

Was he lying? The ink was clearly brighter than the rest of the tattoos on his arm.

Dev shook his head, his bright eyes avoiding mine. "Nah. It's just the bar lights playing tricks."

He was definitely lying, but I wasn't about to ruin my cover by going all detective on him now.

I shrugged casually and smiled. "Yeah, for sure. It's cool. I'm a sucker for tattoos."

"Don't move, beautiful." He winked, and my insides heated.

Beards, tattoos, and cute smiles really looked good on him. I'd tracked his movements, and he never brought women back to his place. I saw him leave at the end of his shift with a female or two, but never back to his apartment upstairs, which was across from mine. We both kept our sanctuaries firmly in the no guests zone.

I watched Dev work, wondering if he'd be rough and let his bad boy loose in bed. The way he tossed kegs and shoved the drunks around, I could definitely see it. Okay fine, he was hot, and I could definitely see myself pinned against the bar, his beard tickling my throat as he trailed kisses down my neck. Maybe I just needed to get laid; like well and truly fucked by someone who could make my blood boil and finally give my body the sexual release it needed. Maybe one little night of—fingers crossed—real pleasure would be worth it? My plans wouldn't change. He'd still die with the others. Who said I couldn't make him moan my name before I cut his throat?

I clenched my thighs and gulped down the whiskey. Mina was feeling extra feisty today, and I was having a difficult time keeping her in check. *Bitch been real quiet for years now and you perk up for an enemy?* And yes, I named my vagina. I called her Mina, after the character in the novel *Dracula*. Even though Lucy was presented as the slutty one, Mina was all lust and danger when she gave into the darkness.

"Hey there, girlie," a deep voice slurred into my ear, making me jerk back.

I looked up into a pair of glassy, familiar eyes. I scooted away as a pudgy, old man sat down on the stool next to mine.

"Hey, Jackson." I rolled my eyes at him, a regular at The Haven.

Jackson also managed a garage not far from here. He let me self-service my bike there for free because of my sweet-as-pie smile, so I tolerated a little drunken flirting. While he wasn't unattractive, he was pushing sixty, and I wasn't generally interested in men old enough to be my father. He was also married, so not really my type. Oh, and of course, the whole bit where he belonged to the cult that destroyed my family.

"How's the little blue bird doing tonight?" He leaned into my personal space, tugging my silvery blue hair.

His stale beer breath made me want to vomit. His eyes dipped down my body, and I held back a shiver. Just, no. If I wasn't trying to maintain a low profile, I'd smash his head into the bar until his nose cracked. I sipped my drink, imagining it instead.

"Just fine, thanks." I pulled Jackson's grimy hand out of my hair and turned away from him to continue watching Dev work. I noted his frown from the other end of the bar as he glanced our way.

Jackson, who clearly could not take a hint, tugged the arm of my sweater. "You're looking lonely tonight, blue bird."

I pulled my arm out of his grasp with a tight smile. "I'm not. Thanks, though."

He leaned in closer, grabbing my arm, and I winced where his grip connected with the cut from earlier. "Come on—"

"Jackson," Dev's gruff voice cut in, and I turned to see him standing behind us, his shadow bearing down on Jackson. He glared down at the drunk mechanic. "Time to go home, man."

He gripped Jackson's wrist and twisted until he let go of my arm with a little cry of pain. A tattoo on Jackson's arm caught my eye, and I nearly choked on my tongue. He had a simple design of the letter *O*, the mark of The Obscuritas. It was easy enough to overlook, but I'd seen enough of them on the lackeys I'd taken down already to notice it. I let my gaze search up and down Dev's muscular arms for the same mark, but I couldn't see it among his many other tattoos. Fuck, I loved tattoos.

"I'm just talkin' to her, Dev. It's no big thing." Jackson smiled broadly and stood, nearly tipping over.

Dev caught him, towering over the man by several inches.

"The conversation is over. Go home, Jackson. Home to your *wife*." Dev enunciated the last word.

I wrinkled my nose. Fucking cheaters. He deserved his death for that alone.

Jackson huffed and stumbled off. Dev stood with his arms crossed, watching him until he pushed through the exit. His sea-green eyes turned back to me, concern etched on his face as his gaze slid down my body.

"You okay, beautiful?"

I nodded and smiled. "Yeah. He's pretty harmless."

Dev grimaced, his muscular arms tense and itching for a fight. "He's a drunk and a douchebag."

I smirked. "Well that too. I'm good, though. Thanks, Dev."

He reached out and gave my shoulder a gentle squeeze, heating my skin beneath the soft material of my horror movie sweater. Dev nodded to the image. "We should catch a movie sometime. Haven't seen a good thriller in ages."

"My favorite genre." I smiled, tugging at Ghostface printed on it. "You pick the day, I'll bring the popcorn."

Dev leaned down, dropping his mouth close to my ear and making me shiver for a whole new reason. "It's a date then."

He stepped back smoothly and wound his way through the customers, picking up empty bottles and chatting casually with the patrons. I didn't know what to think about his last comment. A date? Dev had *never* asked me on a date. Why now? Did he know who I was? Was I overthinking this? Fuck. I'd have Tibby look into his latest movements to see if anything changed.

I downed the last of my whiskey and watched him work.

Maybe this was a good thing. Devon Parrish had no contact with the other three Obscuritas sons, as far as I could tell. But if I could get into his apartment, maybe I could find something new. The sons were easy enough to find, but the four men truly responsible for destroying my family were like ghosts. I found Vespertine Hall about two months ago. The place was a fortress, but there was no evidence of anyone actually living there, just a massive mansion about two hours outside of town where The Obscuritas held their secret meetings and fancy parties. So where were the leaders of The Obscuritas staying now?

Dev might be hiding information that could help, and if going on a date with him brought me closer to my end game, so be it. Speaking of the devil's son, Dev sauntered over, flipped the whiskey bottle, and filled my glass once more. He popped open the fruit box and dropped a sticky, blood-red cherry into the glass.

"What's that for?" I batted my eyelashes up at him.

"A dive bar's Manhattan." He winked with a smirk, and my pussy purred with desire.

Fuck. I should probably play with a toy or two on my own *before* going anywhere near Dev's apartment or he'd have me parting my legs faster than a whore in heat. *Get it together, Sara. Since when do you get so turned on?*

"So fancy." I winked back, pulling out the cherry and pushing it between my lips. I watched his hungry eyes track the movement. I sucked the tart fruit into my mouth, enjoying the bite of whiskey coating it. "Delicious."

Dev's eyes heated as his gaze locked with mine. His hands gripped the edge of the bar, and his biceps bulged as he leaned toward me, bringing his lips close enough to taste. I licked mine slowly, my skin feeling hot everywhere his eyes roamed.

"That's what I think you'd taste like, Sara Braun."

"Oh?" I whispered, my whiskey brain melting any real words before they could form coherently in my mind.

"Oh yeah." Dev shoved off the bar and went back to slinging drinks.

What was his deal tonight? He was never so forward with me. I needed to get out of this bar fast before I dropped my panties and let him get a taste right here in front of everyone.

The whiskey was warming my insides as quickly as Dev's flirting, and I stood slowly, needing some air. I felt Dev's eyes tracking me as I walked toward the front door and pushed out into the street. Multiple patrons followed as the local bars began to close for the night. January in New England was always cold, and the chilly air bit into my face, cooling my skin. I walked toward the alley leading around back to the fire escape, figuring I'd just tuck in for the night. If I was going to take Dev up on his offer, I needed to be sober and in control of the situation. Maintaining my plans was required to do what needed to be done. For my sisters, for my parents, for myself. The Obscuritas deserved all the pain I had planned for them.

Someone shuffled in the dark behind me, and I turned my head, the liquor slowing my movements just enough that I stumbled and fell into the rough arms of the shadow behind me.

"Hey, blue bird. I've been waiting for you," Jackson took me by surprise, grabbing my arms and shoving me against the wall.

"Fuck, Jackson. You scared the shit out of me." I tried to laugh and push him back, but he wouldn't budge.

His sagging dad bod pressed into mine, and his rank beer breath filled the air between us as he looked down at me. I couldn't see much of his face in the dark but I knew this was not good.

"It's time to pay up, little birdie," he slurred, gripping my waist and pressing into me as the cold bricks bit into my back. Fuck he smelled awful.

I needed to think fast. He was on my list just for being a creep, but not worth my time tonight.

"Okay, Jackson. How about tomorrow, though, at your shop?" I lowered my voice to a seductive whisper. "You know I've always wanted to test out that '70 Chevelle tucked away in your garage."

His hands tightened around my waist, and I fought the instinct to punch him in the nose. I couldn't murder a local in the alley next to my apartment. Too many questions. Too many nosy cops, and all my plans would go to shit. I refused to let some lecherous drunk ruin everything I had planned. But I could use my body as a weapon to lure him in. I learned very early on how easily men turned into vile animals at the sight of a beautiful female body. Only then, I was too young to realize I could say no, and by the time I did, it was too late. But this old prick, I was more than prepared to handle.

"I'm going to fuck the shit out of you against that car, blue bird," Jackson slurred.

I wanted to gag, but I forced it down and wrapped my fingers around his flabby arms and smiled coyly instead.

"Tomorrow night then, okay? I'll come after hours. Let me get my beauty sleep tonight, though, yeah?" I teased, giving him a little shove, and he finally stumbled back.

"I'll be waiting." Jackson shoved me against the wall again and brought his sloppy mouth down to mine.

I wanted to puke but let him kiss me instead. If you could even call it a kiss. He groaned like this was something magical, and I stared up into the sky, waiting for it to end and methodically planning his demise.

"Okay, big boy," I teased, breaking the kiss and faking a ragged breath. "Let's save the rest for tomorrow."

Jackson staggered back and grunted like a drunk ape. How was this guy even married? I'd probably be doing his wife a favor by killing him. He stumbled away down the alley, and I deftly backed into the shadows to wait for him to leave. The fucker was so drunk he might not even remember our play date. But I would be there, and he'd regret forcing himself on me. You picked the wrong girl, Jackson. My head felt clearer now that the ugly fucker had officially killed my buzz and my libido. I climbed up the fire escape and into my apartment. I tugged out of my clothes and put on an oversized t-shirt. I washed my face then brushed my teeth twice to get the yuck Jackson left behind out of my mouth.

I padded barefoot into my bedroom, if you could call it that. It was just a room with a bed, no personal touches anywhere. I didn't even own a dresser or nightstands, just a bed with a shitty iron headboard and a small lamp on the floor. I didn't care about furniture, and it wasn't worth the money to decorate when I destroyed it so often after my nightmares. And besides, I had my own fully furnished room at the apartment I shared with Tibby downtown. When I slept there, the nightmares stayed away too. Here in this sad little apartment, weapons were more important. The most expensive furniture I owned here was the gun safe hidden behind a false wall in my bedroom closet. Another reason why Dev could never come to my place. As my landlord, he'd easily find the new addition Tibby and I added to the closet. Although he didn't seem like a snooper.

I pulled the covers around me like a cocoon and sighed, staring up at the peeling popcorn ceiling. What a fucking day. Started with murder, ended with assault.

"Ugh, gross. At least I'd make him pay for the shitty end to my day," I murmured to myself.

Well, it wasn't entirely shitty. I remembered a few good things from before Lailah died, before my life became focussed on revenge. I closed my eyes and forced my brain to focus on those memories instead. At least, I tried. Sleep usually brought me nightmares of the people I killed, so I avoided it often. It wasn't so much that I regretted killing them, what scared me most was that I felt nothing at all.

CHAPTER TWO

Sara

I slipped the handwritten note under Dev's door and scurried back into my apartment. I was taking a risk, I knew that. But I was getting restless. I needed to get The Obscuritas Princes under my thumb now. Dev had come by the apartment after he closed the bar, and I could barely keep my raging libido in check. What was with me these days? We talked about having a movie night, but that date with Dev would have to wait because tonight, I was hunting. Despite the strange desire I had to wrap myself in his arms, I needed to focus on the reasons I was here in the first place. I pulled out my phone and dialed Tibby's number.

"Reporting for duty, Nova," her big voice boomed into my earpiece.

"Why are you always shouting?" I grumbled, grabbing my backpack.

I stuffed it with extra leggings and my favorite blade, a small, unadorned dagger. I picked up the dainty chain that held my mother's key and placed it around my neck. I knew it was a keepsake I should hide away, but I felt safer with it on me. The skeleton key was one of the only things I had from my mother and father, from my life before. I closed my eyes, taking in a deep breath, remembering that day.

"My fierce little warrior," Joseph Bronwen whispered, tucking a hair behind my ear, his face grim. "I have to go away now. I'm taking your sister somewhere safe. And you will be safe here."

Tears burned my eyes. "Why can't I go with you?"

"It's not safe for us to be together," my father whispered.

We sat in the back pews of a church in some small town we stopped at after driving for hours. I wasn't even sure what state we were in. My father cupped my face, wiping away my tears.

"You are stronger than all of us, Seraphina. I must go and hide your sister from the men who killed Lailah."

"Where's mom?" I whispered for the hundredth time.

"She's keeping us all safe," my father responded for the hundredth time, a lie we both knew he had to tell. He wouldn't say anything else about the night before last, and I pretended not to know she was dead. Joseph pulled out an old skeleton key made of gold. "This is for you, Seraphina. When the time is right, you will find what you need from…from your mother's family. Can you keep it safe for her until then?"

I nodded, accepting the key but uncertain about the rest. I didn't know a thing about my mother's family. Only that they were very far away.

"Don't show it to anyone, it's yours alone, okay?" Joseph whispered, his voice serious.

"I'll keep it safe until mom comes back for it."

I kept my eyes on the key. I didn't want to look up and see the truth in my father's eyes. My mother wasn't coming back. And I wouldn't see him or my sister, Michaela, ever again. I knew it deep in my bones. Something was waking up inside me. I couldn't understand it but I knew everything was changing.

"Sara?" Tibby's voice cut through my trip down memory lane. "You there?"

I shook my head, forcing the memories out of my mind. "I'm here."

"What's the plan tonight?" Tibby asked, the keys of her keyboard clicking in the background.

"I plan to scare the shit out of the local drunk, pump him for information, kill him, then let out my frustration at missing my date with Dev by singing at the club." Those last words escaped my traitorous mouth before I even knew what happened as I shoved open my window and slid down the fire escape.

Tibby's typing stopped short. "Your what now? Date? With *Dev?*"

"Did I not mention that?" I smirked, straddling my bike and grateful she couldn't see my burning cheeks. "He sort of asked me out last night. And I figured it would be a good chance to do some recon."

Tibby scoffed. "Recon, yeah? Will you be reconning on his dick or…?"

I barked a laugh, and my stomach dropped. "If I have to take one for the team, I will."

"And what a chore that would be. It's a damn shame I couldn't find a single dick pic of that man on the internet. What a prude."

I snorted a laugh. "Like he could even give me an actual orgasm. You know it's all for show."

Tibby mumbled something unintelligible, and I knew she didn't believe me. I rolled my eyes, starting the ignition on my bike and moving down the alley, away from the bar.

Tibby was a tech-savvy queen and found all the dirt on the four men I planned to murder for the crimes against my family. Dev was squeaky clean other than a few arrests for fighting. The charges were always dropped, though, and we figured The Obscuritas were behind that, even if Dev wasn't an active member.

"So, this guy Jackson is a member." Tibby snorted, typing away. "He's a lowlife. A cheater. I've caught him on cameras leaving casinos and clubs with new girls on the reg. His wife is honestly just as bad. Also a cheater. Sleeping with one of the other mechanics at his shop."

I gagged. "They can both rot for all I care. Maybe I can get some information out of her too."

"She spends a lot of time sending nudes to other men. Doesn't look like she's got any meaningful tattoos. I don't think she's a member."

I sped through the city, ignoring traffic lights, and parked my bike a block down from Jackson's garage. "Guess I better make this count then."

"Have fun. See you later, Nova."

"Save me a seat at the bar."

I ended the call and stayed in the shadows as I walked to the garage. I didn't need Tibby for this particular mission but I kept the earpiece in, just in case. The lights were off inside. I knew he was alone.

Jackson only had two cameras in the shop, and Tibby had already tapped into them to make sure his employees were long gone. I checked my phone. I had forty-five minutes before

I had to be at the club, which meant I had approximately seventeen minutes to fuck with this prick. I opened the front door, unlocked of course. What an idiot. I slipped inside and crept toward the Chevelle Jackson had tucked in the back. I said a silent prayer to the muscle car gods asking forgiveness for what I was about to do. Poor thing wouldn't make it out of this unscathed, but that was Jackson's fault.

I climbed onto the hood of the car and tossed my leather jacket on a toolbox. Jackson stumbled around in his office, making a ruckus as he ran into everything. I adjusted my black corset top, pushing up my cleavage, and leaned back on the cool metal. Beauty was a weapon, one I could use easily against vile men like the one I had in my sights.

"Oh, Jackson!" I sang out the words with a smile. "Time to come out and play."

He stumbled toward the back of the garage, knocking over tools as his steps faltered, likely trashed. He staggered into view, his eyes going wide and ogling my body. I fought the urge to vomit.

"Hello, blue birdie," Jackson slurred, leaning on the hood and staring directly at my tits.

I slid off the hood and cocked my hip, eying him with a shy smile. "Want to play a game?"

"Fuck yeah."

I grinned, batting my lashes and licking my lips. "Close your eyes, big boy."

Jackson leaned back against the passenger side of the car and closed his eyes. His hands moved to his pants, unbuckling his belt and dropping the dad jeans to his feet. I grabbed a pair of handcuffs and slid one around his wrist, attaching the other to the side mirror of the car.

"You're a wild bitch, ain't ya?" Jackson grunted, his eyes still closed.

"Can't help it. You got me all hot and bothered." I whispered the words, dropping my tone and trying not to laugh.

Was he really buying this shit? I noted his lack of a hard-on and figured too much whiskey was a regular issue. No wonder his wife was looking elsewhere to get hers.

"Tell me a secret, Jackson," I whispered as I pulled out my blade, the metal glittering in the dark.

I grabbed a piece of rope, tied it to Jackson's other wrist, and yanked. His eyes popped open, and he yelped.

"What the fuck?" Jackson's eyes bugged out of his skull at the sharp blade. His gaze darted wildly between the cuffed wrist and the arm I now yanked away, stretching him wider. "What the fuck are you doing?"

I tisked, shaking my head as I tugged the rope, stretching him further away from the car and straining his shoulders. He grunted in pain, and I smiled. "Tell me, Jackson. What exactly does a piece of shit like you do for The Obscuritas?"

His mouth clamped shut. At least he had some loyalty to his masters. I tugged the rope further, and he gritted his teeth.

"I dunno what you're talking about."

"I've seen the tattoo, asswipe. All the little lackeys have the same one. I need information. If I don't get it, I might have to start cutting you into tiny pieces."

"Fuck you. You're bluffing," he spat.

I pulled the rope tight, tying it off to a pole on the far side of the garage. I twirled the blade lazily and smiled.

"Sadly, I'm not. Let's see. Where to start? The ears? Hmmm… not the tongue. What about your dick? I doubt you use it much anyway." I stalked toward him. "Let's start with something a little smaller."

I soaked a rag in motor oil and stuffed it into his mouth before he could scream. Then I straightened his fisted hand and sliced off his pinky, my knife smoothly cutting through flesh and bone like soft butter. Jackson screamed and choked on the rag in his mouth as his blood dripped to the floor. I grinned again and tugged out the rag.

"You fucking bitch. They'll kill you." Saliva dripped from his mouth as he cursed at me.

I slid the blade along his chest, causing him to jerk back. "Perhaps. But right now, I'm going to kill you. Unless you give me what I want. Where have the founders been staying? I know it isn't at Vespertine Hall. So where are they hiding out?"

"I dunno. I swear." He slurred the words, and fear filled his glazed eyes.

Before Jackson could clamp his mouth shut, I stuffed the rag back in, then sliced off his other pinky, just to keep things symmetrical. His eyes watered as he tried to scream. I ripped the rag out and jumped back as he puked all over the garage floor.

"Gross. You're a fucking wimp, Jackson. How did they even let you into their little cult?"

Jackson panted, sucking in breaths as he cried. "Samuel Delano is my cousin."

Levi's father. I crossed my arms, raising an eyebrow. Tibby had done some research on Jackson to help me prepare for tonight, so I already knew he was a relative of Levi's.

"So? The founders aren't exactly sentimental. What would one of the Kings want with you?"

He gritted his teeth, and I grabbed the rag. "No, wait. I'm...I'm watching Devon Parrish."

"Why?" My head cocked curiously, and I traced my blade across his chest.

Jackson shook his head, sweat coating his skin. "I dunno. He's important to whatever is coming. They don't tell me much."

"Shocking. Where are the founders, Jackson?" I slapped him across the face. Hard. "Where are the fucking Kings?!" I screamed at him, my frustration building.

"I dunno. I swear. It's someplace out of state, I think. South, maybe. I heard Sam say something about going to North Carolina once or twice."

Interesting. I hadn't heard anything about a location in North Carolina, but that didn't mean it didn't exist. "Well, that was marginally useful." Jackson sighed heavily, and I laughed. "Unfortunately, you're still going to die."

His eyes went wide. "But I told you everything I know."

I nodded with a cruel smile. "You did. But I can't have you squealing to your friends. And you're a squealer, Jackson. I sliced off two little fingers, and you sang like a canary. And you stuck your tongue down my throat without permission. You're a lying, cheating piece of shit and you don't deserve any mercy from me."

"Fuck you! They'll find you and they'll kill you!" he screamed, tugging on the rope and the cuffs as blood dripped to the concrete floor from his mangled hands.

I stuffed the rag back into his mouth and dumped the gallon of oil onto the floor. Circling back toward Jackson, I sliced the rope, swiftly wrapping it around his neck and pulling tight as I slammed him to the ground. His head cracked against the concrete, and he groaned. I crouched down near his face as blood pooled from the wound.

"Not if I find them first, big boy," I whispered, pulling a Zippo from his pocket. "Enjoy hell."

I uncuffed his other hand and pocketed the handcuffs and my blade. I grabbed my jacket and the oil container, leaving a trickle in my wake. I flipped Jackson's lighter and tossed it to the ground. The oil burst into flames, along with everything else in the garage. Jackson's screams grew higher in pitch as his body began to burn.

I wish I could say it was music to my ears, but like everything else, the sounds faded away, sucked into the eternal darkness that lived inside me. I didn't care if he died. I didn't care if he lived either. I just didn't care.

The flames grew rapidly, and the heat licked against my skin. I stared into the fire and suddenly I heard them. The screams of my first victims, two innocent little girls. The sound pierced my ears, and my body froze. I wanted to reach out, to go to them, but I was stuck, staring into the fire I created and listening to them burn. They called to me, and my body lurched forward, toward the fire. They called to me, begged me to save them.

"*SERAPHINA!*" Tibby shouted my full name into the earpiece, and I choked on smoke.

I jumped away from the fire and shook the voices from my head. Fuck.

"Sara! What the fuck. Answer me dammit!" Tibby shouted as the sirens blared, drawing closer.

I turned and ran. "I'm okay." I choked out the words, my voice shaking.

"What the fuck just happened?" Her voice was panicked.

I shook my head again to clear it. "I just got caught in a memory. I don't know. I'm okay. I'm nearly back to my bike. See you soon."

Fire trucks arrived just as I turned the corner into the alley where my bike was hidden. I quickly shoved on my helmet before straddling the seat and speeding away. They wouldn't make it in time to save Jackson, at least. The gloves I wore made sure I left no fingerprints. No trace that I was ever there. Tibby hacked every camera in the area that could possibly tag me. Jackson's death would remain either unsolved or, more likely, declared accidental. From the alcohol in his blood and the lack of any stolen property, the cops would assume the drunk finally fucked himself, dying from his own stupidity. The Obscuritas would cover the rest, if they even looked into it.

I gunned the engine, speeding onto the highway toward downtown Boston. Yvonne's was a fairly well-known restaurant in town. What most people didn't know about was the burlesque club hidden beneath it. There was a secret entrance to the club, and only very few people were allowed in. Luckily for me, I'd made friends with some of the dancers and immediately got a job offer. But I wasn't there to dance. I preferred to sing. Singing at the club brought a tiny piece of my soul back to life. A tiny piece of my dark heart pulsed when I sang, when I listened to a beautiful melody. Music called to the part of me that died with my mother and sister.

When my father left me behind, my heart nearly cracked in half. But I would find him and Michaela, no matter the cost. They weren't dead, I just knew it, had to believe it. As much as it pained me to remember any of them, I pulled that spark of light out of the abyss again and again. I was a glutton for punishment and apparently a sucker for the biggest lie of all. Hope.

I found Tibby seated at the mahogany bar that dominated the back wall of the club. She wore a white crop top and skin-tight, black leather pants. Her bright-pink heels matched the color of her blunt bob wig. Her brown eyes glittered with mischief as she watched the new, muscular bartender mixing drinks.

Three stages flanked the wall opposite of the bar, with metal cages between the roped-off VIP booths along the adjacent walls. Women decorated in glitter and stage makeup danced in the cages, catching the greedy eyes of men and women alike. The women in cages were available for purchase for the night. I watched as one of the bouncers unlocked a cage and led Maxine into a VIP booth. The velvet curtain dropped back into place before I could see who was hiding behind it, but Tibby had cameras hidden in every booth. If someone worth knowing about was here, she'd tell me. The twins, Josie and Lottie, were currently on the main stage performing their aerial silks act. Dominique, La Noircoeur's owner, tried to get me into their act, but I refused. I enjoyed practicing with them, and after spending a few of my teen years living in a gymnastics center, I was the obvious choice. But I didn't learn gymnastics to be a performer. I learned to be a hunter.

The memories of my early teen years barreled into my mind. I ran away from the final foster house when I was fifteen. My heart had finally broken into irreparable pieces. I'd lost my virginity, lost my family, lost everything that was me. I slept on the streets or in abandoned buildings and rarely ate. On a particularly cold and rainy night in Myrtle Beach, I snuck into a gym near the boardwalk and tried to sleep in a bathroom, only to have the owner and gymnastics coach, Connor Rigby, discover me the following morning. Instead of kicking me out, he offered me a job. I manned the front desk and cleaned the equipment and locker rooms. He turned a storage room into a mini bedroom for me. Rigby was the first and only man I decided to trust again after my father abandoned me and took away my last living sister.

Rigby had two daughters of his own, one a gymnast, the other a semi-pro volleyball player. He coached competitive gymnastics and self-defense classes. After two months of work, I started taking the classes. Pushing my body to the absolute limit became sort of an obsession. And, like everything else in my life, the brief happiness turned to ash because I chose to trust another father figure, and he turned out to be a pedophile. So I burned his gym to the ground, with him inside it. Cold satisfaction turned to endless guilt when I realized too late his daughters were inside the building too. They weren't supposed to be there. That night, I became someone else. Someone cold, unfeeling, and set on vengeance. People were going to die on my quest for justice, and feelings got in the way. Innocent people, just like my sisters, like his daughters, would continue to die until someone stopped the evil men of The Obscuritas, and that someone was me.

A raucous round of applause pulled me out of the dark memories as I straddled the bar stool next to Tibby. I had about fifteen minutes before my own act.

Tibby slid a vodka tonic toward me, her face a mask of calm. "How'd it go?"

"Cried like a fucking baby." I smirked, sipping the cool liquid and letting it soak up the bad memories stuck in my head. "Bled out like a regular human."

Tibby was the only person who knew of my accelerated healing abilities. And so far, we hadn't found anyone else like me. As far as I knew, I wasn't hiding any other super powers.

Tibby grinned manically. "Not surprised. Too trashy to be anything else. I'm monitoring his wife to see if she does anything interesting once she finds out he's dead."

I nodded, scanning the room. "Good."

Tibby cleared her throat. "You good, Sara? You scared the shit out of me."

I gulped down the rest of my drink, enjoying the burn of liquor splashing against my throat. "I'm fine. Just got a little distracted."

She frowned, but let it go for now. "There's something else," she whispered. "The mansion burned to the ground."

"Interesting." I didn't burn the mansion, not intentionally, at least. And I couldn't remember seeing anything on fire when

I left.

Tibby rolled her eyes. "Not interesting. You just burned someone else to a crisp. Perhaps the police will see a connection. I know it wasn't us. I checked the cameras and didn't see anyone show up until the police arrived with Samuel Delano."

I shook my head. "The dark lord douche kings would never let that happen. Then the police would be looking into them as well." I felt eyes on me and scanned the room again for any overly attentive gazes turned our way.

"Someone is here to see you," Tibby raised an eyebrow, her eyes darting across the crowded tables.

I followed her gaze. Dev was sitting at a small table near the stage. I licked my lips, and Tibby snorted, but I couldn't help it. He looked delicious. He wore dark jeans and a white button-down shirt, the sleeves rolled up to reveal his tattoos. One hand rested on his thigh while the other stroked the short glass of whiskey on the table. His dark hair was swept back in a messy but stylized way. Dev watched the crowd, his bright-green eyes scanning the room with the preternatural ease of a predator. But he couldn't see me unless he turned around fully.

"What a strange coincidence," I purred with a devilish smile.

Tibby snorted a laugh. "Sure, like you didn't invite him."

I shrugged innocently. "I might have mentioned it in the note I slipped under his door earlier."

"And how is this part of your plan?" Tibby's eyebrows rose up into her pink hair. Her matching pink lips tipped up into a smile worthy of the Cheshire Cat.

"I had a feeling my little meeting earlier would be a bust, even with all the torturing bits. He was too low on the food chain. I need to aim higher." I dropped my voice, leaning closer to Tibby. "I saw a strange tattoo on Dev and I think I remember it. The men who murdered Lailah and my mother had similar markings. I know it was the founders who took her and I'd wager all four of the Princes have the same tattoos. It means something, and I'm going to find out what that is. Jackson said one of the founders talked about going to North Carolina. I need you to look into it. Weird money trails to big properties, strange deaths, anything out of the ordinary."

Tibby saluted me, leaning back. "Got it, boss lady."

I hopped off the stool, grabbing the fresh vodka tonic the bartender slid toward me. "Thanks, Ryan."

"Break a leg, Sara." He winked. He was cute, not much taller than me, but stacked with muscles. His blond hair was trimmed neatly, and he was always clean-shaven. A little too cleaned up for my tastes, but his British accent made all the other girls feral.

I gave a little salute as I walked away toward the dressing rooms.

"So, Ryan, is it?" Tibby turned on the charm. She was beautiful and feisty, just his type. And like Tibby, he had no problems bringing extra bodies into the bedroom for a good time. Where I liked to wallow in darkness alone, Tibby preferred to keep her demons at bay by surrounding herself with naked bodies and regaling me with stories of her multiple orgasms.

I ducked into my own little dressing room and stripped out of the black clothes. The faint scent of smoke clung to my clothes, and I stuffed them in a mint-scented trash bag to mask the smell. My hair didn't smell too bad, but I spritzed the strands with a scented dry shampoo just to be safe. I slipped a shimmering gold dress out of the garment bag and dropped it over my head. The sleeveless dress hugged my curves, pooling around my feet. The corset boning of the top half propped up my cleavage, and I deftly buttoned up the back. I pinned my blue locks and secured the Marilyn Monroe wig against my hair. I kept the brown contacts in and added bright-red lipstick, quickly touching up the winged eyeliner and false lashes. I leaned against the doorframe as I strapped the gold heels to my feet, humming the song I planned on singing to loosen my vocal chords. The silk gloves I saved for last, slipping them up my arms before opening the door.

Josie popped her bright-red head into my room with a smile. Her cropped hair was a new color almost every other week. "Need any help?"

I shook my head, standing tall in my four-inch heels. "Nope. Ready to rock."

"Go show them who runs the world, girl." Josie winked, shimmying her chest, and I laughed.

"Always." I grinned.

My stomach was full of excited butterflies, and my skin tingled with anticipation. I wasn't much for center stage, but dressed up like this, no one had a clue who I was. No one ever did. My voice might be well-known at the club, but I dressed in wigs, makeup, and contacts to hide the real me from the crowd. I pointedly ignored the extra nerves that might or might not have been because of the very sexy Obscuritas Prince in the crowd.

A rush of adrenaline spiked in my blood as I settled my

face into a seductive smile and sauntered onto the stage. The lights dimmed until only a golden light shone on my vintage microphone where the stand manager had placed it at center stage for me. The crowd buzzed with excitement as I stepped into the spotlight. A few low whistles pierced the hushed silence.

I looked up, keeping my gaze hooded and my lips slightly parted. I spotted Dev in the crowd. His eyes were wide with shock, and I gave him a wink. His gaze traveled from my gold heels to my blonde wig, and he smirked devilishly. My body heated under his undivided attention.

The low musical notes of the song began to play, and I pressed my lips close to the mic, running my hands down the curves of my hips. "As the mesmerizing Mae West once said," I whispered huskily into the mic. "Anything worth doing, is worth doing slowly."

The beat dropped and I sang out the first line of the song, letting the crowd fade away as I fell into the beauty of the music around me. "Ooh…oohhhh…" I sang out the lyrics to "A Guy What Takes His Time," drawing the audience in to feel what I wanted them to feel. Lust.

CHAPTER THREE

Devon

As Sara took the stage, my dick jumped to attention. I had to adjust my dark-washed jeans as I followed the curve of her swaying hips. She looked extra fuckable in that golden dress. Holy fuck. I barely recognized her when she walked into the spotlight. Her silvery blue hair was hidden away under the platinum blonde wig, which anyone would believe was real. Whoever was in charge of costumes for this club deserved a raise. She looked like Marilyn reincarnated with her soft curves and full, red lips. Her eyes glided across the room, a blend of innocence and seduction like the woman she now embodied.

I almost didn't come out tonight. But then she'd invited me to La Noircoeur. I knew the place, of course, given that The Obscuritas owned it. She mentioned working at a club, but I never would've guessed it was this one. When I arrived, I hunted for the royal assholes, but lower level Obscuritas members occupied all the VIP booths. The Kings and their little Princes rarely left their mansions to mingle with the general public. It set my teeth on edge being here, and if anyone else had asked, I would've said no.

Sara never once mentioned she could sing. And not just

sing, her voice was like a siren's song, clawing its way into my soul. It vibrated through me until my insides burned with desire. I could understand why the sailors were lured to their deaths, their souls burning with the need to be closer to the angel calling out to them. I wanted to lick every inch of her body and devour her melodic voice with my tongue. I fidgeted in my seat, unable to relieve the pressure of the blood pumping to my dick. I noted several other men in the crowd squirming and eyeing my girl hungrily. I wanted to punch their fucking faces in.

Jesus, Dev. Your girl? Sara barely acknowledged you most nights. I gulped down my whiskey to smother the possessive thoughts racing through my mind. But she did invite me here, so that had to mean something, right?

Sara's voice caressed the last line of the song as the music quieted, and her eyes locked on mine. I winked at her with a smirk, keeping my feelings aloof as possible. She blushed, and I ate up the pink color flushing her skin. The music ended, and the crowd jumped to their feet, whistling and tossing money on the stage. Someone even tossed a red rose at her feet. She turned to pick it up, giving everyone a look at her glorious ass in that tight, sparkling dress. I growled possessively, but the sound was drowned out by the wolf whistles and catcalls of other men. She sniffed the rose delicately and dipped her head in a curtsy, demure and sexy as fuck. Marilyn would have approved. Hell, Mae West, the song's original singer, would have also enjoyed that show.

Sara left the stage, and five women decorated in feathers and glitter pranced onto it for the next act. I gulped down my whiskey and headed for the bar. A woman with bright-pink hair winked at me, and I eyed her curiously. Did I know her? I didn't think so. As a bar owner, I had a solid memory for faces, and hers didn't register. I leaned across the bar and ordered a bottle of champagne.

"Enjoy the show?" Pinky asked with a smile. She was a pretty little thing, but my dick was firmly interested in one woman.

"I did." I gave her a smirk as the bartender popped the champagne bottle, passing it over with two empty glasses. "I'm off to offer my congratulations to Marilyn."

Pinky laughed, the sound like the tinkling of bells. "You do that."

I wasn't sure what she meant, so I smiled casually and nodded before walking toward the right side of the stage. Performers eyed me curiously as I passed dressing rooms but said nothing as I looked for my Marylin. I finally stopped at the door with her name on it and knocked.

"Come in," Sara called.

I placed the champagne bottle and glasses in one hand and opened the door. She turned toward me, her eyes going wide as she slipped one of her white silk gloves from her hand.

"Devon." She breathed my name in surprise, and my dick twitched at the sound.

I needed to hear her calling my name again with my mouth settled between her thighs.

"Well hello, Marilyn." I smirked, filling one of the glasses with champagne before handing it to her. "That was fucking amazing, Sara."

She smiled, her dark eyes twinkling a little at the compliment.

"Thank you."

I clinked my glass to hers and watched her throat hungrily as she gulped it down. "I didn't know you could sing."

She shrugged, moving to set down her glass and remove the other silk glove.

I slipped closer, stilling her hand. "Allow me."

I ran my fingers down the silk covering her forearm, and she shivered. I slowly pulled the fabric, releasing her hand. She took another sip of champagne and looked up at me through dark lashes.

"Singing is pretty much the only thing that makes me feel alive."

My eyes locked on hers, and my hand danced up her arm and across her collarbone. I gripped her chin roughly, forcing her to look up at me, so petite even in stilettos.

"Is that a challenge?"

Her pupils dilated, and she bit into her bottom lip. I tracked the movement with my thumb, and her cheeks flushed.

"It could be." She whispered the words, and I watched her cleavage rise and fall rapidly as her breathing quickened. She was the most beautiful creature I'd ever seen.

I traced my fingers down her neck, circling across her heaving breasts. I gulped down the last of my champagne and stepped further into her, forcing her to walk back against the vanity table. I set the glass down and braced my arms on either side of her, caging in her tiny frame. Her quick breaths mingled with mine as I brought my lips down close enough to meet hers.

"I want to fuck you like this, all dolled up," I whispered, and her lips parted in shock. I dropped my head, my tongue grazing her neck and tasting the sweetness of her skin. "And then I want to take you home and fuck you in the shower, all bare and just as beautiful."

Sara whimpered quietly as I nibbled her ear, and I couldn't hold back any longer. I grabbed her hips and pulled her close, crushing my lips to hers. Her mouth parted, inviting me in, and our tongues clashed as she moaned again, her breasts pressed against my chest. I gripped her tightly, bringing her closer, and she smiled into my kiss as my hard-on pressed into her stomach.

Red lipstick smeared her chin, and my dick twitched, aching for attention from those full lips.

"Turn around," I ordered, giving her chin a squeeze.

She smirked but listened, and the heady feeling of her obedience heated my veins. Sara faced the mirror, watching me as I unbuttoned the corset top and wrenched it down to reveal her full tits and peaked nipples. She gasped as I reached around and palmed her breasts, tweaking her perfect, pink buds. Her head fell back against my chest, and she moaned, bringing her hands up to meet mine and squeezing her own breasts like a greedy little slut.

My cock twitched at the sight of her coming undone before me. I licked and sucked along her bare neck. She squirmed, pushing her ass into my dick, and I released her with a growl. She turned and dropped to her knees in front of me. Her petite hands made quick work of my jeans, pulling them down with my boxer briefs and taking my very hard cock between her fingers. She looked up at me as she wrapped one hand around my cock, the other squeezing my thigh.

"You look good on your knees, beautiful." I ground out the

words. I needed her mouth on me right fucking now.

She smiled, rubbing her thumb across my slit and following the motion with her tongue. She took my cock into her mouth slowly, and I groaned as her lips wrapped around the head, her tongue sucking me in further.

"Fuck," I mumbled, wrapping a hand around the back of her neck and urging her deeper.

She hummed, taking me to the back of her throat before pulling out slowly. I looked down, and she grinned.

"Ever had your dick sucked by a singer, Dev?" she asked softly with a smile.

I shook my head, unable to form words at the sight of this goddess in front of me. She winked, her gaze locked on mine as she pumped my shaft and wrapped her lips around the head of my cock. She angled her head back, taking my length all the way to the back of her throat, and I shuddered with pleasure. Sara began to hum, and the vibrations pulsed through my cock as she licked and sucked and fucking sang around my dick. *Oh fuck.*

My hand tightened around the back of her neck, and I urged her on as she hummed her song, sending vibrations through me in waves. Holy shit, I was going to fucking explode.

"Stop," I commanded, and she looked up at me, pulling my swollen head from her mouth. "Stand up, beautiful."

She stood, her breasts heaving and her lipstick smeared across her face. I grabbed her roughly and kissed her, my tongue devouring the taste of my own pre-cum in her mouth. I broke the kiss and turned her back to face the mirror. I slipped my hands down her legs and brought the skirt of her dress up over her hips. She was bare beneath it, and blood pulsed to my cock as I gripped her plump ass.

"Are you wet for me, Sara?" I whispered against her neck, and she shivered.

"Yes," she whispered. "Dev."

I nearly came undone as she pleaded my name. I gripped one of her legs and bent it at the knee, propping it on the vanity tabletop in front of her. She closed her eyes and pushed her ass back into my dick.

"Eyes open, beautiful. I want you to watch what I'm going to do to you."

I dipped my fingers between her thighs and groaned. She was soaking wet. My fingers slid along her slick center, parting her lips as I nibbled her ear. I slid two fingers inside her, groaning as her pussy tightly clamped around them.

She whimpered, her hands kneading her breasts and tugging her nipples. "Dev. More."

I chuckled against her neck and slipped my fingers out, lining my cock with her drenched pussy. "As you wish, beautiful."

I slammed into her and groaned as she cried out. I pulled out a few inches, thrusting in again to the hilt and moaned. I wasn't going to last long. She felt like sin, and I wanted to drown in that feeling.

"Fuck, beautiful. You're so tight."

Her body shuddered with pleasure, and I thrust in harder, stretching her with my swelling cock. I reached around and tugged on her clit. Her mouth popped open, and her eyes locked with mine in the mirror. I thrust my hips faster, harder, circling the bundle of nerves between her legs as she cried out, bracing her hands on the mirror, her eyes locked with mine and filled with lust.

"Come for me, baby," I growled into her ear and bit down on her neck, enough to leave a mark without drawing blood.

She screamed my name, pressing her ass back to meet my thrusts. Her sweet pussy clenched my cock, and I groaned, gripping her hips tighter. I thrust in again and again, rubbing her clit and drawing out her orgasm.

"Oh fuck, Dev," she moaned.

I lost control, thrusting in once more to the hilt and spilling inside her. Her arms dropped to the vanity as her legs shook, and I wrapped an arm around her waist to keep her from falling forward.

I kissed her neck gently where my teeth left a mark. Sara tilted her head up to meet my gaze in the mirror with a lazy smile.

I winked at her. "I like this look on you."

"Yeah?" She smirked.

I straightened, letting my cock slide out as my seed dripped down her leg. "Yeah. But I'm still going to enjoy fisting your silvery blue hair in my hands later, beautiful."

Sara laughed, and the sound had me half hard already. "How could I refuse?"

I smirked back at her and grabbed a washcloth from her vanity, wiping up the mess between her thighs. I released her waist, and she slumped into a chair to take off her heels. I hiked my jeans and boxers back up and ran a hand through my hair. I eyed the knotted wig as she pulled out the pins. I was more than ready to give her that just-fucked look with her real hair later.

"I'll wait outside for you." I stepped out of the dressing room.

Performers grinned as they passed me. The music from the club was still loud back here, but I was sure a few of them heard Sara's screams as they walked by her door. She appeared a few minutes later with her blue hair braided back, dressed in black skinny jeans, a fitted red sweater, and sexy as fuck knee-high boots.

I grinned down at her, grabbing her ass. "I like this look on you even more, beautiful."

Sara smiled and palmed my half-hard dick through my jeans. "I can tell."

"We're leaving. Now." The words were more of a growl.

This woman made me feel feral. I grabbed her hand and headed out into the club. I kept her close, glaring at anyone who looked at her. But they didn't know who she was, now that Sara no longer wore the whole Marilyn costume. She was still sexy as fuck, though, and I noted several sets of lecherous eyes looking her way. *Mine.*

Pinky raised an eyebrow as we passed, and I smiled at her. She glanced at Sara, but my girl merely gave her a grin and looked away, unbothered by the attention. We stepped into the parking lot, and I slid my hand around her waist as I started toward my truck.

"I rode my bike here." Sara stopped, looking in the opposite direction.

I tugged her toward me. "I'll bring you back tomorrow to get it. Right now, I'm ready for round two."

Sara laughed. "Damn, Dev. Who knew you were so wild

under all those grouchy looks at the bar?"

I pulled her flush against my chest and squeezed her round ass. "I'm only grouchy when I'm not looking at you, beautiful."

Sara smiled, wrapping her arms around my neck and pulling me toward her. I was nearly a foot taller than her, and I snorted as she pressed up on her tiptoes to reach me. I gripped under her ass and lifted her off the ground. Her legs wrapped around my waist as she slammed her lips into mine, her tongue searching hungrily. I nipped her bottom lip, and she bit back.

"So feisty." I chuckled.

"Only for you," she teased.

I scoffed. I knew that was a lie. It had to be. This girl was all unfettered fire, but I was happy to burn up in the flames with her for as long as she would have me.

The things I was feeling for Sara were unlike anything else. It didn't make sense. How did we go from landlord and tenant to this? I wasn't sure I cared. After tonight, all I wanted was more of her. More of her sweet mouth and her delicious scent. More of her beautiful voice and sassy attitude. I would never get enough of her.

CHAPTER FOUR

Sara

I adjusted my tight, little plaid skirt for the hundredth time. The damn thing kept riding up my thighs as I walked. I paired the miniskirt with my favorite knee-high, suede boots and an off-the-shoulder, black sweater. I gulped down my steaming coffee, urging the caffeine to do its fucking job. Staying all night with Dev was not an option, so I snuck out of his apartment around 1 a.m. I barely slept all night and when I finally drifted off, the nightmares were awful. Hazy images of my sister screaming in pain and the sound of my mother chanting in a strange language, followed by terrible silence.

Father pulled Michaela and I from the wardrobe we were hidden inside. "Close your eyes, girls," he whispered.

Michaela listened, still sleepy from the drugs. I didn't. My eyes were wide-open as I stared at the bodies littering the floor. Some were bloodied and definitely looked dead with their glassy eyes and awkwardly positioned limbs. I noticed four younger boys, close to my age, maybe, lying near my sister. They didn't look dead, just sleeping. They were curled up, and their faces looked scared. Were they kidnapped too? Father turned my head away before we got close to where mother and Lailah were lying on the floor. But I knew they were dead. Stolen from us forever. I could feel it. Something was broken inside me now.

"Zenith, you there?" I whispered, pulling myself from the visions of the past and trying to keep my lips from moving too much. The earpiece was barely visible, and I didn't need anyone seeing me talking to myself.

"Always, Nova," Tibby tsked, typing away. "How was the rest of your weekend with Prince Number One? Or are we definitely calling him by his name now?"

I rolled my eyes, even as a blush crept across my face. Dev's behavior caught me so off guard. When he surprised me in my dressing room the other night, looking fucking edible and eyes smouldering, I couldn't resist. His touch was rougher than I expected, and his tongue, *gods*, he was good with his tongue. But I still couldn't give in. Couldn't fully lose control and let a man like that own my body. So I faked the orgasms. I wouldn't lie and say he was bad in bed. He was delicious in every way. But every time I came close to surrendering control, my brain shoved images of my past to the surface and I shut down. He believed the lies my body told. Dev fell asleep easily, and I slipped out of his arms without saying goodbye.

"Did you get *any* information out of him, you fucking slut?" Tibby scoffed, pulling me away from my filthy thoughts.

I barked a laugh, scaring a dude walking ahead of me. I passed him quickly before responding.

"Yes, bitch. He's going to some secret cult meeting this week. On Tuesday. He didn't actually say those words, but he lied. I could see it in his eyes when he made up some reasons he'd be busy this week. And Mo told me he was covering for

Dev on Tuesday night."

Mo was Dev's bouncer and fill-in bartender who I had wrapped around my little finger from day one; the perfect unwitting spy.

"Well done. Congrats to your lady bits for taking one for the team." Tibby clapped. "I've got a tracker on his car, so we'll be able to find him."

"You're welcome." I snorted.

Tibby stopped typing in my ear before responding. "You know, if you could see Dev right before he leaves for his cult meeting…I'd give you a teeny tiny device to slip on him, and we'd be able to listen in on their secret boyband talks as well."

I frowned. How was I supposed to see him before his meeting without looking suspicious?

"I'll think of something. Leave it at the club, and I'll grab it later."

"Right then, boss."

A gust of cold, New England wind tore through my thin sweater, and I curled my arms across my chest as wisps of hair snapped in my face.

"I'm heading into the building now, keep quiet," I whispered.

Tibby proceeded to sing "Say You'll Be There" by the Spice Girls loudly in my ear.

My hair was swept back in a fishtail braid, and I wore simple makeup, eyeliner, mascara, and a burgundy lipstick, for my first day of classes at Harvard. I was going for a dark and moody Elle Woods to entice Prince Number Two. I also switched my contacts to a light blue instead of brown. The green of my irises turned them more aqua, and I thought he'd enjoy that.

From what Tibby and I could find, Andras Blackbyrn liked submissives who always obeyed his orders. He frequented some interesting websites with all kinds of BDSM kinks. Not that I was shaming; you do you, dude. I'd be murdering him and his shitbag father for plenty of other reasons.

I edged my way into the classroom, scanning the crowd of students for Andras. I spotted him up ahead, walking toward the teacher's desk as the other students filed into the stadium seating. He was easy enough to spot, being 6'5" and taller than most people around him at any given time. His black hair was neatly trimmed and styled, and his facial hair was cut perfectly to highlight his chiseled jawline. He was entirely overdressed in a custom navy suit, but I'd expected that too. Andras was all business all the time.

Andras Blackbyrn was no stranger to the spotlight. He finished his undergrad in two years and was now the top dog in his class, set to follow in his father's footsteps as one of the most ruthless lawyers in the country. And not the good kind. Blackbyrn Law defended the bad guys, the very rich bad guys.

I slipped through the crowd and got close enough to bump into him, dropping my books at his feet. Andras turned, his rich, brown eyes locking with mine. His full lips were set into a grim line, and he arched an eyebrow as he watched me pick up the fallen books. I stood slowly, ensuring he got a nice view down my sweater of the lacy red bra I wore beneath. I blinked slowly, making my eyes round and innocent.

"Sorry," I stammered, keeping my voice soft and delicate.

Andras smirked, his eyes scanning my curves before returning to my face. "Hi, sweetheart. You must be lost. This class is for L.L.M. students only."

Nope. Fuck it. I couldn't do it. I narrowed my eyes and smirked back, giving his body the same slow once over he offered me. "Don't worry, *sweetheart*. I'm exactly where I need to be."

"Oh shit." Tibby laughed in my ear.

I stepped past him, bumping his shoulder once more, and sauntered to a seat in the very back. I felt his eyes on me the entire way, and heat crept up my neck from the attention. Well, I fucked that right up. But I couldn't help it. I wasn't the submissive type. Several other sets of eyes looked my way curiously, and I glared back at them.

"Fuck," I muttered under my breath.

"Yeah." Tibby snickered. "What a splendid way to start the semester. Fuck all our plans in the ass."

My eyes rolled before they locked on Andras. He was staring, his eyes narrowing on mine from across the room.

"There's been a slight change to the class," Andras called out, his deep voice commanding the room. "Professor Potter was diagnosed with an aggressive cancer over the winter break. I will be teaching this class for the remainder of the year."

Tibby burst out laughing in my ear, and I winced.

Andras returned his gaze to mine before he continued. "You may sit wherever you want today. Next class I'll have assigned seating for group projects."

"Fifty says you'll be in the front row next class." Tibby snorted.

I grimaced, forcing my mouth shut instead of snapping back like I wanted to. All the students were finally seated as Andras moved behind his podium to the right of the desk and surveyed us all.

"You're going to kick my ass next time you see me, aren't you?" Tibby snorted, and I smothered a laugh.

"Something amusing in the back row?" Andras called out, his piercing eyes locked on me once more.

"Nope," I responded, popping the *P* loudly. "Just so excited to get started."

Andras gripped the podium, his biceps stretching the fabric of his suit jacket. "Why don't you get started then, sweetheart. Stand up and tell us about yourself."

My lips parted, and a blush crept up my cheeks. He did not just call me that in front of the entire fucking class.

"Seriously?"

"Do I look like I'm joking?" He raised an eyebrow, and several students snickered.

I stood, forcing my shoulders back, and stared down at him from the back row. "What exactly do you want to know?"

"How about two truths and a lie." Andras's eyes twinkled, and his lips turned up slightly. "Let's see how good your poker face is."

I crossed my arms, holding his gaze and staring him down. Fuck this guy.

"Alright. My natural hair color is brown. I have thirteen tattoos. And I murdered a man last week." I said all three with a smile, blinking innocently and keeping my back ram-rod straight.

Andras grimaced as several students laughed. "Answer these next questions quickly. When did you first dye your hair?"

"When I was fifteen."

"What was your first tattoo?"

"Wings."

His lips parted slightly at that answer, and I arched an eyebrow.

He recovered fast, though. "How did the man die?"

"Bullet to the head."

Andras stepped back from the podium and removed his jacket. He turned back to me as he rolled his sleeves up his forearms, revealing multiple tattoos covering his dark skin. "Well. Ms....?"

"Braun. Sara Braun."

Andras nodded. "If I were your lawyer, I'd have a hell of a time trusting your words. Your inflection changed twice, indicating two lies, instead of two truths. You answered quickly enough. But the strange part was the lies in your second round of statements did not match your first."

My mouth popped open, and I squirmed under his hard gaze. He seemed to enjoy that.

"So, Ms. Braun, I can only assume you're a murderer, but the weapon was not a gun, you're not a brunette, and you do have wings, perhaps of an angel tattooed…I'm going to guess, across your back."

I laughed, keeping my voice as casual as possible when I responded. "Not exactly."

Andras narrowed his eyes before turning to the class.

"Luckily for Ms. Braun, we don't care whether or not she is a murderer. We care about beneficial evidence, creating doubt in court, and keeping our client out of prison. Perhaps it was a gun, perhaps not. As long as the weapon of choice remains a mystery, our case remains strong. Winning is not always about facts and hard evidence. It's about perception." He glanced back at me with a smirk, and my face heated. "Sit down, sweetheart. Your time in the spotlight is over."

I bit back a nasty retort as I slumped into my chair. What a fucking prick.

Tibby clapped in my ear. "I am having so much fun. I'm going to install cameras in that room so I can see your face every time that jackass calls you out. What a wonderful day."

I nearly jumped when the guy sitting next to me leaned over and whispered close to my ear. "For the record, you don't look like the murdering type to me."

His easy smile and dark-blue eyes danced with mischief as he winked at me, and I couldn't help but smile back. Why was he so familiar?

I winked in turn, leaning toward him. "Looks can be deceiving."

His responding smile made my insides melt. From what I could see, his skin was bronzed like he'd spent the last few hours basking in sunlight. His light-brown hair fell in waves around a chiseled jawline. The clothes he wore were simple—a navy T-shirt, fitted just enough for me to take note of his toned arms and chest, torn and stained dark jeans, and muddy, unlaced boots.

"So what do I look like then?" he whispered, his breath tickling my ear.

I let my eyes roam over his broad shoulders and squared jaw, marked with stubble from a few days without shaving. I inhaled slightly as he cocked his head, waiting for my answer.

He smelled like a campfire.

"You smell like a lit match, and your clothes are too dirty for a law student. I'm going with a logger. Got lost on your way down from Canada?"

He barked a laugh, and Andras snapped his head toward us, glaring.

"Ms. Braun, are you interrupting my class again?'

Oh *Christ*. "Um no—"

"My fault, *sir*," the logger cut me off. "Just couldn't help myself."

Andras stalked toward us, his eyes gleaming like a predator. He pressed his hands down on my desk, staring into my eyes like he could read every dark secret I held inside. He spoke without moving, and I swallowed audibly.

"You can help yourself out of my fucking classroom, Leviathan."

Holy shit. I clamped my mouth shut and forced my eyes not to widen in shock.

"Holy shit!" Tibby screeched in my ear. "Is that Levi Delano next to you? What the hell is he doing there?"

I pressed my lips together, unable to answer Tibby's questions as the keys on her keyboard clicked away. What *was* he doing here? Levi was a firefighter, not a college kid. He barely finished his associate's degree at community college before joining a firehouse in the city. And how the hell did I not even notice an Obscuritas Prince sitting next to me? I was way off my game this morning and too busy eye-fucking Andras to see the devil sitting next to me.

Levi turned, and I looked up as he stood. He loomed over

my desk, his shoulder brushing against Andras as he moved. He winked and gave my forearm a squeeze, his small touch scorching my skin and sending fire right between my legs. I clamped my thighs shut, and his gaze dropped, his nostrils flaring. *Was he smelling me?* Levi grinned broadly, and my insides fluttered. He sauntered down the stairs and out of the classroom, cupping his dick and smirking at Andras on his way out. Andras looked ready to murder him, and if it wasn't so terrifying, I'd be laughing.

Andras kept his face neutral as he walked back to the podium. He proceeded to call on me for literally everything for the next forty-five minutes of class. If Tibby wasn't in my ear rapidly feeding me answers, I'd be fucked. I kept my face as bland as possible, hoping he'd grow tired of picking on me, but failed spectacularly. The clock ticked the end of the hour. My shoulders slumped with relief when Andras finally dismissed us. I needed a fucking drink and gave zero shits that it was 11 a.m. Bars opened at 11 a.m. for a reason. Well, this was a damn good reason. I stuffed my notes into my bag and shuffled down the stairs. I felt Andras watching me so I quickly pressed into the crowd of students to avoid him. I couldn't take anymore bullshit today.

"Well, that was exciting," a pretty blonde whispered as we walked toward the exit.

I glanced at her. She'd been sitting on my other side for the lecture. Her long, straw-colored hair hung down her back, and her brown, doe eyes gave her an innocent look.

"Oh yeah?" I raised an eyebrow.

She grinned. "Andras Blackbyrn literally never shows

emotion or gives a student his attention like that. He's a TA in several classes."

"Wow, I feel so special," I deadpanned.

She laughed, and it was a pleasant sound. I decided I liked this girl. She looked out of place here, and I guessed there was more simmering beneath the surface of her babyface.

"You're not going to make any friends that way, though. I'll bet most of the girls in this lecture hate you now."

I rolled my eyes before reaching the exit. "They're welcome to him. Nice to meet you…?"

She held out her hand. "Audrey Kingston."

"See you next class then, Audrey." I shook her hand and smiled.

Tibby muttered information on the girl in my ear. Not a threat. Maybe a new insider. Her family was wealthy and potentially connected to the Blackbyrn family. Ergo, more evil cult people.

I stepped out of the room and yelped when a warm hand wrapped around my wrist and tugged me away from the other students. Levi stared down at me, a mischievous smirk on his face. He wasn't nearly as tall as Andras, but since I was only 5'3" I still had to tilt my head up to look fully into his face. And it really was a beautiful face. He had the aura of someone exotic, and I remembered his father's family was from Spain. His navy blue eyes smoldered, and it took all of my willpower not to melt at his feet. His calloused hand still held my wrist, and I finally recovered enough to speak, tugging it out of his grasp.

"Do you always snatch up women like that to get their attention?" I raised an eyebrow, and his cheeky grin widened.

"I'll let you punish me for it if you want, babe."

His voice was deep and gravelly, and I wanted to eat him up immediately. He pressed forward, and I stumbled back into the wall. His massive arms pressed on either side of my head, boxing me in. I could easily get out of this little cage but I wasn't quite ready to show the Princes my strength.

I crossed my arms, trying to appear stern beneath his fiery gaze. "I'm not sure you could handle it."

"Oh yeah?" Levi whispered, leaning in.

I clamped my legs together as my body betrayed me, responding to his husky words. He noticed and smirked down at me, his eyes trailing down my legs and back up to my face.

"I'm happy to die trying."

My cheeks turned red, and I stuttered out a laugh. "Damn dude. Things are heating up fast. Let a girl catch her breath, will you?"

"I promise not to burn you up. Although, I think you'd like it." His grin turned a little wicked, and my pulse thrummed. What was happening right now?

Pushing off the wall, I let my hands run down his hard chest and shoved him away from me. "I'm not afraid of a little heat, fire boy."

Levi chuckled and grabbed my waist as he moved into my personal space again. "Little heat? Babe, I'm a forest fire. I'm going to take you out this weekend. Why don't you come by the firehouse Friday night? I'll even let you ride the pole."

I laughed loudly. This guy was crazy, but his lazy smiles and heated gaze were doing things to my body, and I was already craving more. Besides, I needed information on his father.

Maybe this would work in my favor.

"Well I suppose I could make time for—" I yelped as a hard body shoved me back to the wall. I glared up at Andras as he stepped in front of me.

"Leviathan," Andras whispered his name like a threat, glaring down at me instead of the man he was trying to threaten.

I glared right back because fuck this asshole straight up the ass.

"Chill out, dude." Levi laughed leaning casually against the wall to my right.

I was starting to feel trapped but I forced myself not to panic. I was definitely not ready to take on two Princes. It would blow my cover completely. Tibby was suspiciously quiet in my ear as she listened in.

"Were you asking out *my* student?" Andras flicked his eyes to his friend. His emphasis on the "my" was a little too possessive for me.

"I'm not *your* student," I snapped. "I'm not *your* anything. This is Professor Potter's class. You're just filling in."

Levi laughed loudly. "Babe, you better be careful. Andras bites."

I glared up at the dark god in front of me. His eyes glittered dangerously, but I refused to back down. He took a step toward me, and I held my ground, our chests nearly touching.

"I'm going to let you in on a little secret, sweetheart," Andras whispered, and I shivered, his voice deep and dangerous as he brought his mouth down to my ear. "I own this town, and this law school and everyone in it. Which means you now belong to me, whether you like it or not."

I smirked, keeping my voice steady even as my pussy throbbed for this alpha asshole. I was clearly a glutton for punishment and dangerous men.

"Pass." I turned my gaze to Levi and smiled sweetly. "I'd love to visit the firehouse with you Friday and ride your pole."

Levi laughed, and I smirked just as Andras grabbed my chin roughly, turning my face back to his. His touch was cold, burning through my skin like dry ice.

"Leviathan has selective memory issues. We're attending a party Friday night."

Levi smirked. "Trouble focusing Andras? That's next week."

Andras's lips twitched as he held my gaze. "Why don't you join us?" His eyes and voice softened, drawing me in, but I knew he was a predator to his very core.

"Alright then." I pressed my chest up against Andras, tugging his tie loose. "But I'm going for Levi, not you." I shot Levi a wink, and he laughed again.

"Sounds good to me, babe. Come by the firehouse this weekend." Levi shoved off the wall. "Let's go, man. We've got places to be."

Andras glared down at me for another moment before releasing my chin and stepping back. "Well then. Give me your number. I'll text you the address."

He slipped his hand into his pocket and frowned. His phone wasn't there.

"Looking for this?" I held up his phone with a cheeky grin.

Fuck I loved that trick. Living on the streets really boosted a girl's life skills, like picking the pockets of rich idiots. I stepped back, typed in his passcode, and sent myself a text. I tossed back the phone, and Andras caught it with a growl.

"How the fuck did you get my passcode?" His voice was low and threatening, and the beast hidden beneath snarled out at me.

Levi stepped in and pressed a hand to Andras's shoulder.

I shrugged innocently. "Saw you type it in earlier. Should really stick to face recognition in public places, *professor*."

Levi laughed, slapping Andras on the arm. "Come on man, let's go before you get thrown in jail for murdering your hot new student. See you later, sweetness."

I waved casually and spun on my heel, leaving them behind before Andras could say anything else. I grinned to myself, feeling much better about how that ended. I had a feeling he was the type to always get in the last word.

"Fucking shit, Nova, that was insanely hot. I wasn't sure if you were going to get fucked or gutted in that hallway." Tibby whistled her approval. "I was hoping for the former. Damn those men are fine-ass creatures."

I laughed, finally far enough away from people to talk back to her without anyone eavesdropping. "You were watching?"

"Of course! Hacked the building's security cameras." She crunched a mouthful of food into my earpiece. "I made popcorn too."

"First, thank you for saving my ass with all those legal bullshit answers. Second, I'm going to kill you for the constant sassy commentary during class. And third, yes, they're hot as fuck, but they're still dead men walking."

My body might have been responding to these devils, but my plans were the same. My mind was locked on its need for revenge, and no amount of physical attraction could change that.

"Three down, one to go," Tibby said with a smile in her voice.

"Indeed. Tonight, I'm drinking myself into a coma at our place."

"No plans to meet up with Dev?" she teased.

I shook my head before remembering she couldn't see me. "I need a break from all the testosterone."

Her tinkling laugh made me smile. "Perfect. I'll pick up Chinese food, and we can watch kick-ass women in action movies for the rest of the day."

"Deal."

I pulled out the little earpiece and tucked it into my pocket. My bike was parked a few streets over, and I used the walk to relax in the silence for a bit. No, my plans hadn't changed, but today was draining. Andras was even more intense than I expected. And dealing with Levi on the fly like that, I could barely keep my own lady cat from pulsing with need when he smiled at me.

I didn't regret sleeping with Dev either. In fact, it surprised me that I enjoyed the sex as much as I did. But I needed to clear my head, to step away and remind myself what this was all really about. The Obscuritas were a disease that must be eradicated, and I was the only person willing to bring them down. So tonight, booze and girl bonding, tomorrow, another attack on the Princes.

I checked myself out in the mirror one last time. I was sluggish today from our girl's night last night. I sweat out most of my hangover this morning with a long run, ending at Ty's gym. He wasn't there, of course. Our meet-cute would come soon enough. But I was hoping to find out exactly what was hidden beneath the gym. We tracked his staff and the regular members. Once a week, every single one of them showed up and went into the basement for two hours. Seems like creepy cult shit to me.

Unfortunately, I hadn't quite sweet talked my way in the door with James. He was a tougher nut to crack than I expected.

Tibby shot me a text, letting me know Dev was about to leave for his stupid cult meeting, so I had maybe five minutes to get him distracted enough to plant the listening device. I hid a camera inside his apartment when I first moved into the building. Tibby's equipment was top level and wouldn't be detected. Besides, Dev was too trusting. I frowned a little at the thought but brushed it away. I didn't have time to feel guilty. I wouldn't have to murder them all if they hadn't started this war in the first place.

I adjusted my cleavage, making sure my boobs were pushed up in the fitted, black velvet dress. My icy blue hair fell in long waves. I painted my lips in my favorite burgundy lipstick and spritzed my Dirty French perfume. It smelled like black currants and warm amber, and even I thought it was irresistible.

I grabbed my jar of cherries and a bag of Jiffy Pop, dropping them into a grocery bag and sauntering over to Dev's apartment. Just as I was about to knock, the door opened, and Dev's eyes widened in surprise. His gaze turned lustful as he looked me over, giving me goosebumps. He looked exceptionally hot in black slacks and a navy button-down shirt. His hair was styled, and even his dress shoes looked fancy as shit for his little cult meeting.

"Holy shit," he stuttered. "Damn, beautiful. You look amazing."

I smiled coyly and cocked my hip. "Ya think?"

Dev swallowed, his Adam's apple bobbing as his eyes dipped to my chest. "Yeah, beautiful. But I'm always thinking about you."

I shrugged like I didn't care, even as his words sent a rush of pleasure straight to my belly.

"Well I thought I would just pop by and see if you were free for dinner tonight. I decided I couldn't wait to see you again." I stepped closer to him, leaning against the door frame, and he gazed down at me with a groan.

Dev frowned. "I've got somewhere to be tonight, beautiful."

His words said no, but I could see in his eyes what he really wanted. I smiled wickedly, tugging his belt loops to bring his body flush with mine.

I stood on my tiptoes and wrapped my free hand around his neck, discreetly planting the tiny listening device under his shirt collar. "Oh well. I guess I can wait until tomorrow."

Dev groaned, and I felt his cock twitch.

"Fuck it." He grabbed my waist and yanked me into the apartment.

I yelped in surprise as he tore the bag from my hand and gripped my ass, pulling me into his arms. I wrapped my legs around him as he kicked the door shut and shoved me up against it, his mouth devouring mine like it was our last night on Earth.

I really wasn't planning to sleep with Dev again; I thought he'd stick to his plans. But as his hard-on pressed into me and his tongue dipped eagerly into my mouth, I couldn't resist. I moaned greedily as his rough hand cupped my breast, wrenching my dress down and freeing my tits for his hungry mouth. My back arched as he licked and sucked my peaked nipples.

Dev carried me into his bedroom, tossing me down roughly, and I let out a gasp as my ass bounced on the mattress. My short dress rode up on my legs as he spread my thighs apart. I wasn't wearing any underwear, and Dev licked his lips as he gazed down at my bare pussy. I squirmed under his heated gaze, trying to scoot back toward the headboard, but his hands locked on the backs of my knees, and he yanked me to the end of the bed.

"Oh no, beautiful. You're not going anywhere. Not when you're so wet for me already. I'll take your sweet pussy over those cherries any day," he growled out, his head moving between my legs, and his teeth nipping my inner thigh.

He moved fast, his tongue licking up my center and flicking my clit. I moaned like a greedy slut as my hands threaded his dark hair and pulled him closer.

"Dev—" I stopped short when his phone started ringing loudly, and he growled in frustration.

"Don't move," he commanded, and I lay there, panting and needing his mouth on me again. Instead, he answered the phone, his free hand brushing along my thigh and drifting higher.

"What do you want?" he growled out, his fingers pinching my thighs playfully as his eyes locked with my own.

He slid his hand higher, slicking two fingers between my

pussy lips and rubbing slowly up and down, feeling my arousal. Blood flooded to my core as his fingers moved lazily between my legs. I started to squirm, but his hard gaze pinned me to the spot.

"I'm busy. Can't make it," he snapped, dipping a finger inside me and making me whimper, my back arching into his touch.

Holy shit I was about to have an honest-to-gods orgasm.

I could just make out the sound of someone shouting into the phone, but my senses were all mushed together as Dev curled two fingers inside my soaked pussy and found my G-spot. My skin tingled, and my body felt like it might explode with pleasure. I needed more. More. More.

"Dev. Please," I whispered, rocking my hips against his hand.

Ohmahgawd was I seriously begging right now? My thoughts scattered as his hands continued to toy with my body, and I lost myself in lust for this wicked man.

"Fuck off, Levi. I'll be there in twenty minutes," Dev growled, hanging up the phone and tossing it to the floor. His gaze locked with mine, and he grinned. "Now where was I?"

I huffed a laugh, and it turned into a moan as Dev brought his mouth down on my clit. His tongue teased the swollen bud. I choked down a whimper, refusing to beg.

He lifted his head slightly, and I looked down at him. "I really do have to go, beautiful. But I'm going to make you come on my face first."

"Oh fuck," I panted as his teeth grazed my clit.

My hips arched, thrusting my pussy closer to his mouth, and I fisted his hair in my hand, begging for more. He shoved a third finger inside me, and I moaned in pleasure as his tongue swirled around my clit while his fingers stretched and fucked my pussy. My body burned with desire, and my vision blurred as the orgasm built between my legs.

"Come for me, baby," Dev demanded as he sucked my clit into his mouth, and his fingers curled deep inside me.

When his teeth grazed that most sensitive spot I screamed his name, and my release shuddered through my body. His fingers twisted inside me, drawing out the orgasm as I tried and failed to breathe. It was too much. I saw stars, fireworks, all of it. My skin was on fire and the pleasure was mind blowing.

His fingers slowly slid out of me, and his wicked tongue licked up the mess between my legs like a dying man devouring his last meal. My thighs quivered with pleasure, and my body felt like a limp noodle. A very satisfied limp noodle. My mind was a broken thing, not even comprehending what had just happened.

"Fucking delicious." Dev smiled as he crawled up and kissed me.

I kissed him back eagerly, tasting my cum on his tongue.

"You screamed so loud for me this time, I think the entire neighborhood heard you."

"You really have to go?" I murmured changing the subject, my cheeks flaming as I realized how different the sounds I made were when the orgasm was real.

"Sorry, beautiful. Important meeting with some business partners." Dev stood and helped me up, gently tugging down my dress, his hands squeezing my ass to keep me from falling over. "I still want that movie night, though."

He brushed his thumb along my bottom lip, and I nodded,

unable to say no.

I walked with him back to the living room, and he grabbed the bag of cherries and popcorn from the floor. "I'm holding these hostage until our next date."

I laughed. "Fine then. I'll be back for those. We can finish where we left off."

Dev grabbed my waist and pulled me in for another soul-sucking kiss. I wrapped my arms around his neck and kissed him back with equal fire. He was just so irresistible. And now that my lady was desperate for more, would my trusty vibrator even be worth it? Or, maybe I'll bring the vibrator to our movie night. Yes, that was definitely going to happen. New kinks were being unlocked.

He pulled away first and kissed my knuckles before descending down the stairs through the bar. I went back to my apartment and quickly changed my clothes, calling Tibby.

She answered on the first ring. "I will say I am glad we only put a camera in his living room and not the bedroom. Although, from the noises you and the cult Prince were making, I'd say it was probably a good show. That was real, wasn't it?"

I gritted my teeth. "Maybe."

Tibby scoffed. "Damn, I knew it. Even got me reaching for my vibrator. I bet we could sell it, if you're interested?"

I rolled my eyes. "I think I'll keep my sex life to myself for now. Besides sharing it with you, of course. If you need to borrow the audio to spice things up, though, it's all yours."

"I think I'll just have my next group activities include some role play. Dev has some good lines."

I laughed aloud. "He really fucking does. His wild side

comes out in the bedroom. Whatever. It doesn't matter. I'm heading over. Keep tracking him, and I'll see you in fifteen." I kept my voice even, somewhat emotionless, so Tibby wouldn't catch my rapid heartbeat.

"Over and out, slut." She hung up the call.

I could pretend all I wanted, but something was happening with Dev. I *felt* things. Emotions I'd buried deep and thought I could no longer access. Somehow, between his dirty words and rough hands, his soft kisses and sinful tongue, something in me started to shine. I silently slammed the cage around my heart shut, forcing that shining spark to cower once more. That light was more terrifying than anything hiding in the deep dark. That light was happiness. It was hope. Two things I didn't deserve and could never want, especially from an Obscuritas Prince.

When I arrived at the downtown apartment Tibby and I shared, I immediately knew something was wrong. She was quiet, and the computer monitors were dark. I froze in the doorway.

"What happened?"

I dropped my bag to the floor and took a slow step toward her. There was an accident on the highway so it took me twice as long to get here. I missed something vital, and Tibby's grim face told me I didn't want to hear it.

"Tell me," I demanded, even as my voice shook.

"They have your father, the founders have him, I think. But, it sounded like he went to them willingly." Tibby whispered the words, and I fell to my knees as she continued. "I didn't get much before they went into a lower level of the manor and the audio cut out. It must be deep underground, and probably has signal blockers to keep whatever is down there secret."

"Michaela?" The word scraped out of me, leaving my insides raw and exposed. We'd been searching for my father and sister for years, and suddenly they were here, mere miles away from where I now knelt.

"I couldn't hear. They didn't mention her before the audio cut out. I don't know, Seraphina."

Tibby's use of my true name was too much. The computer lights winked too brightly, and I squeezed my eyes shut. I dropped into the darkness waiting inside me. I couldn't take this. The Obscuritas had my father, which meant they could have my sister too. The people who murdered Lailah and my mother now had the only two people left to me in this world. But he went willingly? Did they already have her? Was she being tortured? Assaulted? My throat burned with rage, and I started to shake.

Shame scorched through my body as I thought about what Dev had just done to me while my sister was out there, lost and alone.

"Seraphina," Tibby snapped, and my eyes flew open. "We need to do this the right way. If you storm in there now, when they're all together, you'll die. And so will your father and sister, if they're both even there."

I stood, pacing with pure rage. My blood boiled, and I pulled my knife from the sheath on my thigh, twirling it in my hands. "I can't just leave them there, Tabitha. I can't."

Tibby stood, stepping into my path and grabbing my arms,

a dangerous move when I was feeling murderous.

"Look at me. We aren't leaving them. But we need more information and a plan. We've come this far. This is the first true lead, and it sounds like they're alive, Sara. Let's work this out and bring them home, alright?" Tibby's eyes searched mine, the cool blue irises begging me to listen.

I let out a breath and nodded, a plan forming in my mind.

"Friday," I whispered, my voice coming back from the edge of madness. "Andras said they're having a party next Friday. Levi will be there. Ty will be at the gym tomorrow. Maybe I can get more details about who else will be attending. They'll be occupied. We can track any movements at Vespertine Hall so we know exactly where they are, and I can sneak away to get them out."

Tibby nodded. "Good plan. What about Dev?"

I couldn't think about Dev and the things he was making me feel. "He's one of them. He was there tonight, Tibby. If he was any kind of decent, he wouldn't let some cult leader assholes torture and murder innocent people. The plan hasn't changed. He will die with the others."

She looked like she had something to add but wisely kept those thoughts to herself. I was in no fucking mood to hear anything anyway. I stalked to the kitchen and pulled the vodka out of the freezer. I spun off the cap and poured the cold liquor down my throat. I needed to be drunk immediately or I'd run out of this apartment and set the whole fucking city on fire.

My phone buzzed with messages from Dev, but I ignored them.

Tibby's dinner for us arrived, but I was no longer hungry.

I carried the vodka into the living room and continued to swig from the bottle. My thoughts began to fade, and my eyes glazed. I kept drinking, needing the alcohol to soak my insides until I couldn't feel anything but the cold nothingness of sleep. But when I finally blacked out, the nightmares barreled in, locking my mind in an endless torture.

CHAPTER FIVE

Typhon

I pulled into the parking lot of my gym, parking next to a sleek Buell. I was more of a Harley guy myself, but the matte black bike was hot. The blacked-out look and A-line framing was beautiful. It looked expensive too, with additional mods for speed and elegance. Had to be a chick's bike for sure. The thought had me curious to find its owner. Weeknights were usually pretty relaxed around here, so I was certain I could pick out a new member. I swung my gym bag across my back and walked into the gym, heading straight for the back office.

Radnor's Gym was more than just a fitness center. When I bought the place three years ago, I added a boxing ring, CrossFit equipment, and a few gymnastics pieces like a balance beam and uneven bars. I wanted this to be a place where anyone could come, leave behind thoughts of the outside world, and get their adrenaline pumping. I offered deals to the young kids looking to get off the streets. I wanted Radnor's to be a place where people felt safe, something I never had when I was younger.

Of course, I also used the basement for Obscuritas meetings, but the general public didn't know about that. And it technically wasn't Obscuritas. When our fathers did what they did to us eight years ago, my brothers and I vowed to find a way to fight against them. We started small and only began actively recruiting others in the last three years. We call it Umbra Noctis. We were the *Shadows of Night,* always watching, waiting for our time to strike. We played our roles for The Obscuritas leaders—our fathers—and followed orders, all while gathering dissenters, readying for the moment we would finally take control.

My brothers and I couldn't live like this, not for much longer. The daemon inside me writhed, feeding on my anger. I shoved the fucker down, but until I had full control, I was a slave to The Obscuritas and the daemon within.

Inside my office, I dropped my gym bag to the floor, and James jumped out of my seat, smiling broadly.

"Hey boss." He nodded, taking a seat on the small couch in the corner instead. He propped his feet up on the coffee table and continued typing out a text. "Meeting is all set for later this week. About thirty potential recruits."

I grunted in approval. James was twenty-seven, roughly two years older than me, and three inches shorter. He was a CrossFit junkie and ripped after years of training. He was also my eyes and ears at the gym and my Number Two within Umbra Noctis. His bright-green tank stood out against his midnight toned skin, and I grunted a hello as he continued to text.

"Writing a novel over there?" I smirked, sitting behind my desk and switching on my laptop. I rarely used the thing, preferring to keep my personal emails on my private cell. Overlord Laszlo gave us cell phones, but we avoided using them, knowing he was always tracking our conversations. I didn't trust him not to hack into my network at the gym either.

"Just managing the bets." James grinned again, glancing at

the security camera screens behind me and quickly typing again.

"Bets on what?" I arched an eyebrow, turning around to the screens. I scanned the different monitors until my eyes locked on the boxing ring. There was a curvy, fit-as-fuck woman boxing with Dominic, another Umbra Noctis recruit. "Who the fuck is that?"

"The girl?"

"Obviously, fuckface."

James laughed, unafraid. He wasn't affected by my generally threatening personality like most people. "Sara Braun. She's been a regular for about a month."

I squinted at the screen. She was kicking Dominic's ass in the ring. She landed a kick to his stomach, and my dick twitched happily. Her toned legs were on full display in tiny shorts, and her tits bounced in a tight, red sports bra

"I've never seen her here before."

James shrugged. "Comes in randomly. Jade says she works at some club, which I definitely plan to visit once I find out where it is."

A possessive growl built in the back of my throat. *Why do I care?* "She's a fighter?"

James nodded, watching her intently on the screen. "She's an athlete. Messes around on the beam, deadlifts more than her own body weight. And tosses the guys around in the ring like a champ. Kicked my ass once."

I snorted, giving him a wink. "Not difficult."

I turned to see Dominic drop to the floor. Sara immediately straddled his waist and began pummeling his face. Fuck, watching her shot blood straight to my dick. Who was this girl?

Dominic tapped her leg, and she stopped, offering to help him up. He grinned as he panted, his nose bloodied.

"Damn that's hot." James whistled, standing up and texting again. "I'm headed out to collect my winnings. Night boss."

"See you later, J."

After James left, I watched him come into view on the camera. He said something to Sara, making her laugh, and my nostrils flared with annoyance. *Why am I annoyed?*

"Fuck this." I shoved out of the chair, determined to meet this fighter chick and get it over with. She was just another girl, who gave a shit if J flirted with her?

I pulled off my hoodie and dropped it on my chair, heading onto the floor in my black tank and gray sweatpants. My workout for the evening could wait now that someone too interesting to ignore was currently boxing in my gym. I pulled my hair into a bun on top of my head, absently wondering if she was attracted to guys with longer hair, then instantly rolling my eyes. *Fuck off, Ty, you idiot.*

I rearranged my face into a disinterested scowl and approached the ring. Dominic was leaning against a corner post, angled toward Sara. The security cameras did not do this girl justice. She was easily a foot shorter than me, maybe 5'3" at most, and her curvy waist was toned and glistening with sweat. My stomach dropped, and I bit my lip hard enough to bleed. I wanted to taste the adrenaline pulsing in her blood. She had long, icy blue hair, braided back with strands falling around her face. Dark lashes framed her dark-brown eyes, and she had full pink lips I wanted to ravage.

She smiled at something Dominic was saying, and I instantly

wanted to throttle him. Her eyes slid to mine suddenly, and my dick nearly stood at attention just from her piercing gaze. Heat rose in my body as she continued to watch me. My breathing became shallow, and I forced my face to remain calm as her dark eyes pierced my fucking soul. *Holy fucking shit.* The daemon inside me groaned with lust.

Dominic turned to see who caught Sara's eye, and his smile faltered. "Oh hey, boss."

I nodded, my eyes locked on Sara's. "Dom."

He straightened off the ropes awkwardly, and backed away from her. "Uh, this is Sara. She's a hell of a fighter."

"I've heard." I slid my eyes down her body as she laughed huskily, sending another pulse of blood to my dick.

"You boys talking about me? Never had a girl kick your ass in the ring before?" Sara tossed the braid off her shoulder and curled her wrapped fists on her hips.

Dom grinned at her. "None as good as you, babe."

I frowned at the little pet name, a growl building in my chest. My daemon wanted to rip out Dom's fucking tongue. This one was mine. I cleared my throat, stepping into the ring and towering over them both. Dom was fit, but not nearly as broad as me, and several inches shorter. He stepped back, wisely, sensing my mood. The girl, however, did not. Sara cocked her hip and continued to look up at me, unaffected. I wanted to wrap my fingers around her throat and show her exactly how terrifying I could be.

Her petite stature was dwarfed by my shadow as I stepped closer to her. "I'm Ty Radnor."

Sara smirked. "I've heard."

My dick twitched at her attitude. This girl needed to get her ass kicked. "Interested in another round? Since this is my place and all, let's see what you got, little girl." I grinned menacingly, and Sara's eyes narrowed. Oh boy, was she a fighter. Adrenaline pumped through my veins as I thought of her struggling beneath me, bruised and bloodied.

"Dude, you're easily over twice her size in height and weight," Dominic scoffed. "She has no chance."

I started to respond, but Sara cut me off. "I've fought bigger guys."

She was taunting me, and I let the daemon smile behind my eyes. *Hell yeah, babygirl. It's on.*

Dominic's eyes darted between us, and I grunted at him to get lost. He stepped out of the ring in a hurry and nodded at Sara. "See you around, babe."

I growled possessively, and he quickly exited the room without looking back.

Sara snorted a laugh. "What are you, some kind of animal?"

I turned toward her, leaning down close to her ear. "Yeah, babygirl. And my bite is even worse than my bark."

Sara pulled back, her eyes locking with mine in a challenge. "Bring it on then, monster man."

I quickly wrapped and taped my hands and got into position, stalking her slowly around the ring. I let the monster inside me loose, just enough for her to see the danger lurking behind my eyes. I was the predator, and she was the prey. There was nowhere for her to go, but instead of cowering, she glared back at me. Her eyes were fierce, and her full pink lips were set in a determined grimace.

"Your angry face is cute, pet," I taunted, stopping short to circle in the opposite direction.

She matched my pace, her eyes staying locked with mine even as her body responded to the change in direction.

Sara smirked. "And yours is hardly intimidating. J and Dom are far scarier."

I snarled at the challenge, unable to resist, and she laughed. "Careful, pet. You're asking for it."

"Come and get it then." She bared her teeth like a feral kitten, and I launched at her, feigning right, but she was quick.

Sara danced out of my reach, landing a quick punch to my ribs. I spun, throwing a punch to her left shoulder, but it glanced off as she jumped away, wobbling slightly from the force of my hit. I wasn't putting my full strength into it. At least not yet. She came at me like a wild cat, throwing quick punches and ducking and dancing around my own. My breaths became shallow, even as hers remained even. She moved like a panther on the hunt. Her muscles loose and her dark eyes hungry for violence. I was instantly curious where she learned to fight with such finesse. And why? What did this strange, beautiful girl have to fear, other than the monster in me now hungering for her destruction? Her gaze narrowed with suspicion as if she could hear my thoughts, and I grinned.

"Eager for my death, pet?" I licked my lips as her chest began to heave with labored breaths.

Blood rushed to my dick when she shot out a quick punch to my face, causing me to groan loudly. I felt her hand connect with my bottom lip and tasted blood. I grinned, letting it drip down my chin like a maniac. Most men pissed themselves when

I let my daemon show like this, but Sara tracked the blood as it dripped from my mouth, biting down on her full bottom lip.

"Red looks good on you, monster man. Is that all you've got for me?"

I smirked. *You asked for it, little girl.* I came at her quickly, throwing punches I knew she could deflect. I kicked out once and, as she spun away, slipped my hand in my pocket and whipped out a small knife. As she turned back, I slipped behind her and brought the knife to her neck. She stilled, and my dick twitched as her ass pressed against my thigh.

"A knife? Really?" She panted, her eyes looking up into mine. Fuck, I liked this look on her.

I brought my bloodied mouth down to her ear. "This is the real world. You've gotta fight dirty to win."

Before I could move, Sara brought her elbow back into my gut and shoved away from me. The knife sliced into her neck as she darted away, and she hissed in pain. I watched the blood drip from the shallow cut even as her eyes lit up with lust. My little pet liked the fight as much as I did.

"I like watching you bleed for me, pet." I chuckled.

She let out a little growl that had me close to coming in my fucking sweatpants. I brought the knife to my mouth and licked the edge, tasting her blood as her eyebrows shot up. The taste was like sin and made my own blood sizzle. The daemon inside me begged to be let out to play. *Who was this girl?*

She jumped toward me, but the movement was lazy, and I wrapped my hand around her throat and tossed her to the floor of the ring. Her back crashed into it, and she let out a woosh of breath. Sara wrapped her hands around my arm, but it was no use. I straddled her waist, my fingers tightening slightly.

I grinned and leaned in close, my blood dripping on her chest. "You lose, pet."

Sara went limp and smirked up at me. She wriggled her hips into mine, and I groaned at the friction against my fucking hard-on. I moved to adjust our position, and she immediately brought her knee up to my groin. Pain shot through me as she rolled us over, and suddenly I was beneath her, my knife in her hand and pressed under my chin. Her legs straddled my bruised balls, and my dick twitched with a mixture of pain and pleasure as she ground her body against mine.

She leaned down, her chest brushing mine, and I grabbed her waist. She dug the knife into my skin, and I grinned, catching her gaze. Her pupils dilated with desire, reflecting how I felt even as she pressed the tip of the knife into my skin. I tilted my head back, giving her further access to my throat.

"You lose," she hissed through clenched teeth.

"Finish me off then," I whispered.

She leaned down, and I slid my hands to her ass, squeezing it. She squirmed against my dick, making me groan even as the knife tore at my skin.

Sara sucked in a breath, her pupils fully blown as she watched me bleed. "Are you so eager to die?"

I gave her ass another squeeze. "Like this? With pleasure, pet. I'd steal a kiss as you cut open my throat, dying with the taste of you on my tongue."

"I'll keep that in mind." Sara laughed, her face a mask. She sat up, flipping the blade closed and tossing it to the ground.

Before I could move, she punched me hard in the stomach

and I flinched, releasing her. She stood smoothly and ducked out of the ring.

"Thanks for the dance, monster man."

I stood slowly, adjusting my sore and very blue balls. "Looking forward to the next one, Sara Braun."

She flipped me off, and I watched her ass hungrily as she sauntered to the women's locker room. I would have that woman screaming my name very soon.

CHAPTER SIX

Sara

My blood was still near boiling from my fight with Ty when I stepped out of the gym into the cool night air. I clamped my thighs together as I walked, cursing inwardly at my body for getting so hot and bothered by yet another fucking Obscuritas Prince. *Why* did they all have to be so enticing? Was I just a glutton for pain? It was difficult to remain indifferent when all four men now caused my fucking vagina to pant like a lioness in heat. Gods, this was infuriating. *Get it together, Mina.*

Ty's hot as sin looks weren't a surprise. I'd done my research on them all and *knew* they were all attractive before meeting them. But there were plenty of attractive guys in the world. Even James, his gym manager, was hot. When I sparred with Ty, though, it was like my insides caught fire, and I had to force myself to not crush his lips to mine. I knew he was into it too when his hard and admittedly massive dick pressed into me while I straddled him, holding the knife to his tattoo-covered throat. *Fucking hell.*

Thankfully, he was nowhere to be found when I slipped out of the gym. I had to sing at Noircoeur tonight, so I'd spent extra time in the locker rooms getting ready before slipping into my faux leather leggings and black jacket for the bike ride and ducking out of the gym in a hurry.

I didn't know what would happen if I saw him again, what I would say. My mind was jumbled, and I ignored three calls from Tibby before texting her to fuck off. I knew she tapped into his security cameras and saw everything, but I wasn't ready to talk about it.

I noted the lifted, black Bronco parked next to my streetbike. Of course it was Ty's. It screamed "bad guy" with the massive tires and blacked-out windows. I rounded the SUV and stopped short. Ty Radnor casually leaned against the hood, his eyes raking over my body, and I forced myself not to shiver under his gaze. His dirty blond hair was still tied up in a bun, and he wore a leather jacket over a fitted black t-shirt and dark jeans, his fully tattooed body now hidden away. His hazel eyes reflected the lights of the gym behind me, and he smirked.

"Hello, pet." Ty's mouth lifted slightly, his eyes feral.

I clamped my legs together, forcing my brain to ignore the blood rushing between my thighs at the sound of his deep voice. Fucking shit, why was my pussy such a traitorous slut?

I lifted my chin, meeting his gaze as I walked toward him. "Looking for another beating so soon, Ty?"

His jaw clenched when I said his name, and I could see I affected him as much as he did me. This was insanity. This fucker helped The Obsuritas destroy my family, and I was ready to rip his clothes off in the parking lot. I forced my eyes to narrow angrily, and he chuckled.

"Anytime, pet." He growled out the words, and I walked toward my bike just to give my legs something to do besides crumple at his feet. "Fancy a drink?"

"Sorry, monster man." I laughed, feeling better as his lips flattened at my flippant tone. "I've got somewhere to be tonight. Perhaps another time."

He stepped toward me, crowding me against the bike, his hands reaching out to rest on either side of me. I breathed in his leather and tobacco scent, his lips nearly brushing mine.

"And where's that?" He whispered the words, his eyes holding mine.

I swallowed, keeping my voice casual. "Noircoeur. I work there."

Ty arched an eyebrow. "You're a burlesque dancer?"

I smiled tauntingly. "That a problem?"

He shrugged, even as his eyes narrowed. "No."

Alright then, liar. "Well, I'm going to be late so, kindly back the fuck up."

Ty barked a laugh, and I smiled sweetly as he stood, towering over me. "I think I'll come see you dance then, little pet."

I rolled my eyes and looked away, not wanting him to see how much my body responded to his words. "I am not your *pet*, and do whatever the fuck you want."

He chuckled, and the gravelly sound of his voice had me biting down on my lip. "Whatever I want? You might want to choose your words more carefully, pet."

I turned away, pretending to be unaffected even as Mina screamed for me to fuck this dark and delicious creature. Images of my naked flesh pressed against his Bronco as he pounded into me flashed through my mind. Before he could see my flushed cheeks, I pulled the helmet over my face.

"See ya around, monster man."

My body was reacting too often to these dark princes, and I needed some space from this beast of a man. I forced myself not to look back as I spun out of the lot and away from Ty Radnor and his stupid, gorgeous, evil face.

I turned up my music, blasting out some boss bitch tune. Grace's version of "You Don't Own Me" filled my ears, and I belted out the lyrics into my helmet as I zipped down the highway into the city. Fuck these guys and their sexy smiles and piercing eyes and rough hands and just—fuck all of it. Okay, no, don't. Because apparently I was way too keen to fuck all of them.

I nearly upended my bike when I slammed to a halt in the parking lot, arriving at the club in a matter of minutes. I grabbed my backpack and pushed into the back entrance of Noircoeur. Tibby usually came to my performances, but I didn't feel like talking about any of my feelings about Ty, so I ducked directly into my dressing room instead of meeting her at the bar first.

There was a bottle of champagne and a single rose on my vanity. I looked around, but there was no note. Who sent this? It couldn't be Ty. He wasn't the type. I racked my brain until it clicked and I smiled. Devon. He'd brought me champagne last time. But how did he know I was working? I'd also ignored his texts today. After the bomb of my father and sister being in the hands of the monsters I was hunting dropped, I couldn't fake feelings of happiness or pleasure with that on my mind. Apparently, beating the shit out of Ty had helped, though. Whatever. I poured a glass of champagne and gulped it down. I couldn't get shitfaced before singing, but a couple glasses wouldn't hurt. I picked up my phone and texted our stage manager. Tonight, I was switching things up, something a little less retro and a little more intune with my current feelings.

A variety of dresses hung in my closet, but the black bodycon dress would fit my song of choice perfectly. The sweetheart neckline and soft fabric hugged my curves like a second skin. To complete the outfit, I pulled on a pair of black, leather, knee-high boots, then walked around the room, letting my feet adjust to the four-inch stiletto heels. The braid in my hair left it all kinky, and I used a two-inch curling iron to add some styled waves to the mess. It looked freshly fucked, which worked well with the outfit. Lastly, I chose bright-red matte lipstick over my usual burgundy pout and black eyeshadow for an extra smokey, badass look. I stared at my reflection.

This would be the first time I'd be on stage without a wig. Everyone would recognize me after this. It was pretty impossible to forget the icy blue hair. Well, fuck it. This performance deserved a little more of the girl hiding in the shadows. Let them see. I poured a second glass of champagne and walked out of the dressing room, toward the stage. Josie rounded the corner, her brown eyes going wide.

"Holy shit, Sara. No wig?" She smiled broadly as she flipped my hair, her body shimmering in glitter.

"Nope." I shook my head and rolled my shoulders back. "Switching things up tonight."

Josie clapped excitedly. "Hell yeah, girl. I'll be sure to grab a seat out there."

I saluted her with my glass and headed to stage left, waiting for my cue. The other girls on stage finished to a rowdy round of applause. The house was packed for a Wednesday night. My eyes closed as I took a deep breath, feeling the anxiety rushing out of me. This was my happy place. On stage, singing like the world could end at any moment. And I knew it could.

I heard my cue, smirking at the name I gave for tonight's introduction, Harley Quinn. I never used my real name, it was more fun this way, to be someone new each night. Not Sara Braun or Seraphina or the lonely girl with nothing and no one, but a character people could love and adore. I sauntered on stage with a smirk on my red lips and fire in my eyes. The catcalls came quickly, and I gave a little turn, resting a hand on my hip as I stopped in front of the microphone.

"This one goes out to all my ladies waiting for a real man to step the fuck up. Don't settle for less, bitches," I crooned into the microphone before downing the champagne. I tossed it to a table in front, and some guy surprisingly caught it. I kept my eyes up, not looking into the crowd. I didn't want to know who was watching, didn't care.

The music pounded out through the club's speakers, and I pressed my lips close to the microphone as I sang out the first line of the song. The words were desperate, begging for a man who could handle a woman with a dark side.

I heard Josie's wolf whistle in the crowd and grinned wickedly as I sang, feeling the words of the song in my bones. My fingers stroked the mic stand, and my hips swayed to the music as the words tumbled out of me. My voice belted out the last lyrics, forcing the audience to feel some type of way. The final notes rang out over a mesmerized crowd, and I blew a kiss and flipped off the audience as it ended.

The audience erupted into applause, men and women standing, whistling and yowling excitedly. I continued to stand there for a solid sixty seconds, my chin high and my hands on my hips, taking it in like a fucking queen. Intermission music began to play, and my heels clicked as I sauntered to the stairs in front of the stage. Several men jumped up to offer their arms as I descended into the crowd. None moved to touch me, as if I was above them all, though I felt their hungry gazes on every inch of my body. I spotted hot-pink hair at the bar and walked casually toward Tibby. Ryan, the bartender, slid a glass of champagne to me as I leaned next to her.

She sipped her drink with a smile. "That was fucking brilliant. You should dress like this always."

I laughed. "It felt fucking brilliant. I needed that."

Tibby nodded. "I know. Ty is here."

I snorted, rolling my eyes. "Not surprised. Dev?"

Tibby shook her head. "Actually, I haven't seen him. He was still working at the bar last I checked."

I slid my empty champagne glass back to the bartender, and he instantly moved to fill it.

"That was badass, Sara." Ryan winked, topping up the glass.

I grinned. "Thanks, Ryan. Glad you liked the show."

"Digging the blue hair too." His eyes roamed over my face. "It suits you."

A shadow appeared behind me, and I felt his muscular frame closing in as Ryan's eyes widened and he backed away.

"Hello, pet."

Tibby kept her body angled toward the bar, her face buried in her martini. I turned around and leaned back on the bar, my arms resting on the edge, and looked up into Ty's face. He wasn't exactly scowling, and I noted the curve of his lips and the glint of mischief in his hazel eyes. Strands of hair framed his face, and his bun was messy, like he'd stuck his head out the window on the highway.

"Hello, Ty," I said, giving him a smirk.

I licked my lips and enjoyed the hunger in his eyes as he tracked the movement of my tongue. His eyes dipped lower, taking in my curves on display in the tiny dress. I looked away, scanning the crowd as if his attention meant nothing. He stepped closer, and his rough hands grasped my chin, turning my face up to look into his own. My skin heated where his hand lingered.

"Not the performance I was expecting. You're looking every bit the vixen on that stage. Sing like one too. I like it."

I gave him a wink and leaned into his touch. "So did everybody else. Get in line, monster man."

Ty's hand trailed down my throat, and he squeezed gently, his lips turned up into a devilish grin. "You have no idea who you're taunting right now, little vixen. You should be very, very careful."

I pushed off the bar and further into the hand gripping my throat. His grip tightened, and, *fuck me,* did I like the feeling settling between my legs. I tilted my head to the side as I stared up into his fiery gaze.

"Or what? I'm not afraid of you, Typhon Radnor."

Ty's eyes flared at the use of his full name on my lips. I slid my hand over his dick, rubbing slightly at the hard length beneath his jeans.

"Besides. I think you like it rough."

Ty growled, letting me know I was, in fact, correct, and I grinned in triumph. Maybe I liked that too. I stepped back, and he released my throat, his fingers brushing against my cleavage. I was so hot and bothered I barely heard Ryan calling my name from behind the bar. Ty's head snapped up.

"What do you want?" he snapped at Ryan, stepping closer to me and leaning one arm against the bar. I turned toward Ryan, and felt Ty's free hand pressing into my lower back, showing his dominance. Ryan's wide eyes drifted down to mine.

I rolled my eyes and smiled. "Ignore the brute. What's up, Ryan?"

Ryan cleared his throat as Ty pinched my waist and snarled possessively, as if he had any claim to my attention.

"Uh. Otis asked if you'd sing again tonight. The crowd went nuts for you, and he said you can sing whatever you want."

My cheeks flushed with pleasure. I knew I had a decent voice, but it was still nice to receive high praises like that. I nodded. "Of course. I'd love to. Just give me like thirty to change costumes."

Ty leaned in behind me, his lips brushing against my ear and making me shiver. "What will you sing for me now, pet?"

I turned my head toward him, our lips nearly touching. "Who says the song will be for you?"

Ty gripped my waist, turning my body toward his, and gripped my chin tightly so I couldn't look away. "If you want to sing for another man, little vixen, point him out. He'll be dead before you finish the chorus."

I huffed a laugh even as my thighs clenched. "Well, that's not very nice."

He grinned, his muscles taut and his grip tight on my chin. "I don't play nice with others. And I don't like to share."

I rolled my eyes. "I don't belong to you, monster man. Or anyone else."

"Yes you do, pet. You'll figure that out soon enough." Ty shoved off the bar. "Better get backstage and ready for your next song, little vixen."

I chugged my champagne and flipped him off before turning my back to him and heading backstage. I heard his growl and felt his angry eyes following me as I walked away. I smiled and winked at several men and women along my path, just to piss him off a little extra. This was too much fun. The only problem was, I desperately wanted to get laid now, and no way in hell could I give in to Ty Radnor. I suppose I could go back to Dev, but wasn't that just trading one devil for another? My vibrator wasn't going to cut it after the orgasm Dev wrung from my body. Fuck, this was annoying. Maybe I could find a nice boy to screw? I could practically feel Mina laughing at me. No, a nice boy wasn't going to work either.

I shoved into my dressing room and stripped out of my boots and dress, rummaging through my costumes. What to wear? What to sing? Something provocative and very "damn the man." I pulled out a black, leather catsuit with a thick, gold zipper leading straight down to my navel. I slipped into it, tugging the supple leather up my legs. I pulled my arms through the sleeves and left the zipper undone to show off my kick-ass cleavage. The catsuit was skintight, and my lacy red bra matched my lips perfectly. I stepped back into my knee-high boots and zipped them up tight. The outfit was surprisingly comfy to move in. I slid tiny black cat ears into my hair, a nod to the OG Catwoman, my idol, Michelle Pfeiffer. Anyone who thinks she wasn't the fucking shit in *Batman Returns* should be shot on sight.

As I walked out of the dressing room, several dancers and performers commented on my first performance and rushed to find open seats for my next act. I stopped at the end of the stage and gave the stage manager a thumbs up. She winked and gave me a thumbs up in return. I chose a handheld mic for this song and stepped onto the stage, grinning like the cat who caught the canary. Tibby's wolf whistle cut through the silence and the crowd quickly joined her. The music queued up for Elle King's bad bitch anthem, "Baby Outlaw." I shimmied to the sound of the guitar and started into the song with fire in my veins.

I began to dance, using the entire stage and moving with the rhythm of the music. I leaned down and winked at the men and women sitting close to the stage, luring them in with my voice. At that moment, everyone in the club belonged to me. I couldn't see Ty, but I could feel his eyes locked on my body, following my moves like a stalker in the shadows. I scanned the heads of the crowd and found his hulking frame sitting at the bar. He was leaning forward, his arms resting on his knees while he tracked me across the stage like a predator. I gave him a pointed look as I sang out the chorus. Elle King's message rang out in defiance; she was a woman who didn't need a man to save her, she was strong enough to save herself. And so was I.

His mouth twitched as I sang out the words. I slid my eyes away from him and caught Tibby's gaze with a grin. She toasted me with her martini, and I tipped a salute. The crowd faded into the shadows as I got swept up in the song, letting the world know I was nobody's baby, and in the end, they'd be the poor souls dead at my feet. Fuck, I loved this song. I barely finished the final lyrics before the audience jumped to their feet, clapping and tossing money onto the stage. The stage manager jumped into action, picking up all the bills. I kicked up a heel and winked, blowing a kiss again before heading backstage, instead of into the crowd.

With the lights dimmed, I ran to my dressing room and grabbed my backpack before heading out the back door toward my bike. I zipped up the catsuit so my tits didn't fall out when I rode down the highway. The incredible high from that performance was too fucking awesome and this outfit was too hot not to show off. My bike jumped to life, and I kicked off the gravel, flying into the night and away from the club. Adrenaline rushed through me, and I sped down the side streets, feeling smug as fuck leaving Ty behind. I pulled up to a stop light next to a newer Camaro. The driver and his frat boy friend turned, and their mouths dropped when they took in my catsuit.

The frat boy in the passenger seat leaned toward me, and I flipped up my visor.

"Am I dreaming? Because holy shit you look like my favorite wet dream, baby." The guy driving laughed, licking his lips.

"Sorry, little boys," I taunted, loud enough for them to hear. "I don't think you could handle me."

When the light turned green, I flipped the visor back down and zoomed onto the highway. The Camaro followed, speeding between cars to keep up with me. I laughed again.

What a fucking night. I weaved between cars and was mildly impressed when they were able to keep up.

I felt a shadow come over me and turned, trying to look up and around, but nothing was there except for the endless night sky. A sharp wind slipped down beneath my catsuit and made me shiver. An uneasy feeling came over me, like something—or someone—was watching me. The Camaro zoomed next to me, and I gave the boys a little wave before taking off, deciding to lose them well before they could see my exit and follow me home. I quickly outpaced them and made it back to my dingy apartment. I parked in the back, as usual, and climbed the fire escape up to my place, carefully avoiding the holes in the grated steps. The window shoved open slowly, the track rusted and uneven, obviously decades old. I slipped inside and dropped my backpack onto the kitchen table. I flopped onto my bed and lifted my legs to remove the boots.

The adrenaline was slowly wearing off, and thoughts of my younger sister flooded into my head. Next Friday, I would get them back. At least two of the Princes would be at the party. Dev would be working at the bar. To make sure Ty was at the gym, I planned to offer him a rematch. With the four Princes occupied, I could sneak into Vespertine Hall, dispatch the low level guards, and free my father and sister. We could be together. And I could finally be reunited with the only family I had left.

The idea of seeing my father after so many years brought mixed emotions. The ache of his abandonment still stung after all these years. He said it was for our protection, but he took Michaela and he just…left. I didn't even get to say goodbye to my sister. Why? Why did I have to stay behind?

I went over the events leading up to that day. Lailah was so strangely calm. She played with me and Michaela, which was rare. Our mother was trying to hide her fear, but I could feel it. And our father followed her around the house, whispering and agitated until the day we packed up the car and left our home.

After Lailah and our mother were killed, my father drove us away without looking back. We drove for hours and hours until we finally stopped. And he left me all alone. I needed to know why. Why was my Lailah murdered? Why did The Obscuritas think murdering my sister was going to do something for them? Magical sacrifice to a higher power? Give me a fucking break.

I was an atheist and a skeptic of anything I couldn't prove with my own eyes, even in my younger years. So the idea of this cult murdering people for some magical power was insane and just made me want to kill them all quicker. Tibby still couldn't find exactly what The Obscuritas were trying to achieve. I couldn't remember much, having been hidden away for most of it. And until we had eyes or ears inside their little wicked rooms of magic, we were basically going in blind. Tibby found the blueprints for Vespertine Hall, though, so I at least had that for the party.

After a quick shower, I crawled into bed and curled up with my pillow. My heart beat slowly, and the silence felt heavy. Music helped me drown out the bad memories, so I grabbed my headphones and chose a soothing playlist. Even with all of the adrenaline spent and the semi-good night, the nightmares still came. They always came for me in the dark.

Chapter Seven

Devon

"Fucking hell." The words slipped out as Ty Radnor stalked into my bar, grinning like a maniac.

I shoved the last of my regulars out the front door and locked it behind them. I didn't need any bloodied bodies in my bar, especially not the paying customer kind.

"What the fuck are you doing here, Radnor?"

"I've missed you too, Parrish." Ty chuckled like the daemon he was. Even before this fucking mess, Ty was more daemon than man. "We have a…mutual friend, it seems."

"Oh yeah?"

I grabbed a bottle of Jack and two rocks glass from behind the bar as Ty dropped his massive frame onto a bar stool. It creaked under the weight of all that muscle. I pretended not to notice, even though it irritated me he would always be stronger than me.

"So, Dev. Who is renting your apartment upstairs?" Ty asked, his voice laced with danger and amusement, an unnerving combination.

I poured the whiskey and shot mine back before responding. "What's it to you?" I arched an eyebrow, unable to hide my surprise at his question.

Ty smirked, his eyes glinting dangerously. I could tell he knew the answer to his question, but I wasn't ready to give him any information on Sara. He pulled out his phone and pressed a few buttons before placing it on the bar top, the ringing echoing in the empty space as he switched it to speaker.

"Hello, brother," Levi answered on the second ring, his overly peppy tone already grating.

I poured another shot of whiskey.

"Levi." Ty gulped down his own whiskey before continuing. "Meet any incredibly attractive, sassy as fuck, blue-haired women lately?"

I nearly spit out the liquor, choking it down as I absorbed Ty's words. *What the fuck?*

Levi was silent for a beat. "Funny you should ask."

"What the fuck is going on?" I slammed my fists on the bar, and Ty arched an eyebrow at my outburst.

Levi laughed, and suddenly I heard Andras's stern, *I'm-Always-In-Charge* voice added to the call. "Why do you ask?"

"I think we have a problem." Ty tossed his empty glass into the air, catching it before it shattered on the dirty floor of my bar. "Sara Braun."

What do they want with her? My heart was racing, but I kept my face as neutral as possible. "How do you know Sara Braun?"

Ty cocked his head, assessing me before answering. "She's apparently a regular at my gym. I met her tonight."

Levi laughed again as Andras cursed into the phone, a very bad sign. He rarely let his emotions show, even with us. "She is also attending Harvard and in a class I'm teaching."

"What the fuck?" The words escaped my mouth before I

could stop myself.

I knew she was in school but had no idea she was attending Harvard. Had I even asked? I was fucking obsessed with her and starting to realize I didn't know much about her.

"How do you know her, Devon?" Andras demanded.

His voice reminded me of his father, and I bristled. Ty stared at me across the bar with a sinister smile. Of course he'd beat me to hell if I didn't answer.

I crossed my arms defensively. "She lives above my bar. Moved in two months ago."

"And is that all, brother?" Levi cut in, his mischievous tone seeping through the line.

I could feel my face flushing even as I clamped my mouth shut, and Ty growled, crushing the rocks glass in his fist and making a mess, not even registering the blood seeping between his fingers.

Ty stood quickly, knocking the stool back and glaring at me. "You fucked her, didn't you?"

These assholes could fuck right off. "Fuck you! It's none of your fucking business if I did. I don't give a shit if she goes to your gym or your fancy fucking college."

Levi's laughter was cut short as Andras growled at him. "Typhon, calm down. Devon, I don't give a shit if you think you're in love with her. She clearly has some ulterior motives. I do not believe in coincidences. She moved here two months ago and has now made herself known to all four of us?" He paused, but didn't give any of us a chance to respond. "And there's something else. Can any of you read her?"

My mouth snapped shut. I hadn't even tried. I hated hearing

people's thoughts. Part of leaving these assholes behind included ignoring all the stupid abilities we gained from the rituals.

"I couldn't read her," Ty growled.

Levi agreed, and I frowned.

Andras sighed. "Neither could I. We need answers. And we keep this quiet. No mention of her to our fathers."

"Dev, what color are her eyes?" Ty asked, and I turned to him, caught off guard.

I thought for a moment. "Dark brown. Why do you ask?"

He frowned. "I think she's wearing colored contacts."

Levi chuckled. "I think you're right. She had pretty turquoise eyes when I met her."

"God dammit," Andras hissed. "Ty, bring her to my place. Now."

They're going to kidnap her? I glared at the phone. "Are you fucking serious? You're going to kidnap a fucking woman? Are you insane?"

The line went quiet, and Ty squared up to me, waiting for instructions from Andras.

"Devon. I've left you out of Obscuritas business for nearly two years because of the death of your father. It's time to return to us. If we don't do this together, we're all fucked. And we don't need any distractions, especially ones we don't understand."

I ran my hands through my hair and down my face in defeat. I knew this day was coming, I just hoped it wouldn't. And now the one fucking girl I'd caught feelings for was somehow a part of all of it. I took a swig directly from the bottle of Jack and passed it to Ty, a peace offering. At least for now.

"Fine. I'm in. But we need a better plan than this. If the

woman living above my bar goes missing, people will talk. Police will get involved. She has friends at the club who will look for her."

"Perhaps." Andras's tone was clipped and deadly calm once more. "A new plan then. Track her, find out everything we can about her over the next few days. Once it's confirmed she is a potential threat, as I have no doubt, after the event next Friday, we take her."

I slammed my fist on the bar angrily, barely controlling the rage and fear I felt for my girl. "And what if she isn't some super spy and just a girl who happens to live in this city like millions of others? It's not like she's doing anything out of the ordinary. Going to school, working out at a gym, and living in an apartment are hardly strange behaviors, Andras. She's also not the only person we've met who has decent mental shields."

"All behavior is strange when it comes to us, Devon. What about Jackson's recent death? And the robbery where a professional clearly took out Bullseye?" Andras countered, his voice clipped and irritated like he was arguing with children. "One of the relics is missing."

I rolled my eyes. "Jackson was a drunk fool, and I fully believe he set his shop on fire himself, then was too drunk to get out before burning alive."

Andras sighed. "It's a possibility. His body is being autopsied by our people. And his toxicology came back already. We know he was drunk out of his mind, but it still seems suspicious. And when something feels wrong, it usually is."

Ty cracked his knuckles. "Something is strange about her. I could see darkness and cunning in her eyes. I don't believe for a second she doesn't have secrets of her own."

"She's coming by the firehouse this week," Levi cut in. "I'll see what else I can find out about her."

I could feel my face getting hot with jealousy. "Why is she going to the fucking firehouse?"

Levi laughed, and I could practically feel the smirk in his voice. "Because saying yes to me pissed off Andras something fierce."

Ty grinned darkly, and I narrowed my eyes at him. "She definitely enjoys taunting the devil. This is going to be fun."

I was fucking fuming, but there was nothing I could do about it. I had to act like everything was fine to Sara's face because Andras was right. It was too strange, her showing up and singling us out. But if she was…something, did that even matter? I was falling hard for the girl already, and my heart beat erratically at the thought of her spending time with any of them. I schooled my features and conceded to the stupid plan. Ty left the bar without another word. If she fucked Levi, I would give her up. I'd let the devils take her without a backward glance. Probably.

CHAPTER EIGHT

Sara

"Good morning, Nova," Tibby's chipper voice blared into my earpiece, and I cringed. It was too early for loud noises. I mean it was almost noon, but still. Too many whiskeys last night and my head was pounding. I prayed my weird super healing abilities would take away the hangover soon.

"No, it is not a good morning. Something is wrong with the Princes." I gulped down my coffee as I stripped out of my oversized T-shirt and stepped into the shower.

Tibby's voice immediately switched gears. "Why do you say that? There's been nothing out of the ordinary with their movements. Andras was snarky as ever in class."

I huffed, recalling his incessant questions as he picked on me for all the answers. I had to force myself to answer incorrectly a few times so he wasn't suspicious. The smug look on his face every time he corrected me had my fucking blood boiling while Tibby laughed in my ear. He'd given us assigned seats, forcing me to the front row, and I didn't entirely hate it. He was so goddamn beautiful. I soaped up my body as I remembered the way his muscles bulged in the Armani suit, tailored perfectly to fit his athletic form. He wasn't as broad as Ty or even Levi, but he was sculpted to perfection. I had to squeeze my thighs together to keep my horniness in check during his lectures and I swear his nostrils flared and his eyes dilated when he walked by, as if he could sense my arousal.

My hands dipped lower, and I brushed my fingers between my legs slowly, feeling a different kind of wet between my thighs.

"Hello? Wake up, Nova," Tibby shouted through the speaker of my phone, bringing me out of the very dirty daydream I was sinking into fast.

I quickly grabbed the shampoo and started aggressively washing my hair instead.

"Andras seemed mostly his asshole self, but Devon was all wrong last night. He wouldn't look me in the eye, and his smiles were tight. When I asked if he was okay, he just said he had a bad business meeting. Do you think he figured something out about me?"

Tibby typed faster, the clicking ringing like tiny shots firing in my brain, and I breathed through the pounding in my head.

"He's at the bar now, and I didn't see anything strange, but—"

"But what?" I cut in, my anxiety rising. If they figured out who I was before my plans had barely come together, I was fucked.

"Wednesday night, after Ty was at the club, I checked cameras the next day and there was some kind of glitch for the two inside Dev's bar. I'm not sure why. If someone tampered with them, they did an excellent job of hiding that fact. Right now, it's like they shorted out for all of twenty minutes, then went back to working like normal."

I mulled that over. The cameras Dev had in his bar weren't high quality. They could malfunction, as technology does, but because of who he is, I'm not so sure.

"I don't want to rule anything out. Keep checking to see if you can find out if the cameras were tampered with. I can set up one of our own cameras in the bar." I frowned, because, duh. Why didn't I do that in the first place? I was being lazy letting Tibby hack into his. I wouldn't make that mistake again.

"Yeah, that's probably smart. I'll leave a camera for you at the club. I'll be there tonight," Tibby added casually, her voice changing sultry.

I smiled, stepping out of the shower and drying off. "Got Ryan wrapped around your little finger now, do you?"

Tibby's Tinkerbell laugh carried through the speaker. "Obviously. Tonight I'm going for Josie."

I arched an eyebrow at my phone. "Josie? Since when?"

"Since now. She's hot. I'd like to get them both in my bed. Do you think she'd go for it?"

I laughed. "Josie is 100% into pussy. She has no interest in sucking or fucking a cock. But she is kinky. So maybe if you were in the middle…"

Tibby let out a sexual moan that made my skin flush. "That sounds fucking divine. Can you try real hard not to have any drama tonight so I can live out that fantasy?"

I grinned. "I'll do my best. I'm heading to the firehouse in a couple hours and plan to hit up the gym before going to the club."

"Did you hear what I just said?!" Tibby screeched. "I asked for no drama, and you just made plans with two of our deadliest targets. Can't you just stay home and read a book like a good girl?"

Well, she wasn't wrong. Maybe I'd skip the gym and go for a run. I needed the exercise, but I suppose I could avoid Ty this evening. "Fine," I conceded. "I'm still going to the firehouse, but I'll be your good little girl tonight and stay away from the Princes after that."

Tibby snorted. "You will never be anyone's good little girl, but I appreciate the effort."

Since this wasn't a fancy adventure, I opted for sexy but casual. I slipped into a pair of forest green leggings with mesh cutouts on the sides. I paired them with a black sweater that hung off my shoulders to show off the lacy straps of my dark-green bra. I left my hair loose and wavy and my makeup minimal—mascara and a fire engine–red lipstick. I smiled to myself in the mirror. The lipstick was hot, and I hoped it would draw in a few gazes and get Levi's blood pumping. My insides heated thinking about it, and I grimaced. *Sara you slut, get it together.*

I stomped my feet into my favorite boots and slipped out the fire escape. I didn't feel like dealing with Dev today. I couldn't avoid him forever because I needed to stay close, but after the mindblowing orgasm, my brain got all fuzzy around him, and I needed a clear head. Although, he wasn't messaging as much, and that was odd. Maybe Tibby was right and something was off. I slipped my tiny backpack over my shoulder, with a few cameras tucked away for me to plant at the firehouse. I didn't think Levi would honestly do any shady cult shit at his day job, but I needed eyes on the Princes at all times.

Levi's firehouse was about fifteen minutes from Dev's bar, and as usual, I saw that as a challenge. I zoomed between cars on the highway, enjoying the feel of the cold wind biting into my skin. Goosebumps littered my flesh as I sped through traffic and relished in the freedom I always found with my motorcycle rumbling between my legs. For a few minutes, nothing mattered and I let my mind go quiet, pretending my life wasn't a dumpster fire.

The ride took less than ten minutes. I jumped the short curb and parked right up on the sidewalk in front of the station like a jackass. Levi would love it. I didn't block the open doors for the trucks, I wasn't *that* big of an asshole. Curious looks from several firemen peppered my skin when I pulled off my helmet and placed it on the handlebars. I whipped my hair like a fucking supermodel and spun around, giving them a bright smile as I walked just inside the doorway of Engine 33.

"Hello, boys." I let my eyes linger on their faces, noting their reactions.

I knew them all, of course. Tibby and I went over every fireman to find connections we might be able to use. Only one of them was a low level member of The Obscuritas and he wasn't any of these men.

"Hello, gorgeous." The flirtatious voice made me turn. It belonged to a man named Derrick Stromwell. No criminal record and had a cat. *What a softie.* He was average height with stacked arms, but looked like he could use a couple more leg days. His bald head gleamed in the sunlight, and he smiled as he approached me. "Can we help you?"

I nodded, glancing around. "I was promised a tour of the firehouse today."

"Is that so?" Another man, Xavier Saladino, stepped up. Taller than Derrick and muscular all around. He had curly blond hair and pretty blue eyes. Also unaffiliated with The Obscuritas, but he was in a nasty gang. He could potentially be useful.

I looked up into his baby blues and nodded. "It is." I drew closer to him, and his eyes dilated as I tiptoed up to reach his ear and whispered. "I was promised a ride on a pole too."

Xavier let out a low chuckle, his cheeks coloring slightly as his eyes dragged over my body hungrily. "Well, baby, you've found the right man for the job."

I smiled and tilted my head to the side, my eyes widening innocently. "Oh yeah? Well—"

"Sara," a deep voice growled, and I jumped back with a start.

I nearly crashed into Xavier as Levi hovered behind me. He wore a black ribbed tank and dark washed jeans, his muscles and swirling tattoos on full display, as if it wasn't the middle of fucking winter. He looked fucking delicious too as his dark blue eyes lured me in.

"Levi! I was just getting to know all these hunky firefighters. I honestly thought I'd wandered onto the set of a *Magic Mike* movie."

Levi narrowed his eyes slightly before his face broke into a smile and he laughed. The sound of his laughter was infectious and the other men chuckled as the tension broke. "We sell calendars, *diabla*. I'll get you one before we leave today." Levi held out his arm for me like we were headed into a ballroom.

I smiled and threaded my arm through his, noting his use of the word "we." Apparently we had plans after this little tour. "And what month are you, Levi?"

He grinned and winked down at me. "July. Hottest month of the year for the hottest fireman of the house."

Xavier snorted a laugh. "You wish." His gaze turned to mine once more. "Nice to meet you Sara. If you want something to really get your blood burning, check out December. Have a seat on Santa's lap, and I'll make all your wishes come true."

I licked my lips, and Levi's biceps bulged as he gripped my arm tighter. He leaned down, and his lips brushed against my ear, making me shiver.

"Xavier's pretty eyes might get you all hot, but my tongue will be the one setting your body on fire, *diabla*."

My whole body heated at his words. Levi was bold, and I loved it. He grinned, and I smiled back, unable to stop myself from enjoying this crazy man.

"We'll see. Can I have my tour now, or will we just stand here trading fire related pick-up lines all day?"

The men laughed, and I felt their gazes trailing my ass as Levi guided me further into the station, pointing out the trucks and tools all neatly placed. These men were incredibly organized. Everything was shiny and clean. I plucked a pack of mints out of my bag, popping one in as I discreetly pulled out the tiny cameras. I asked Levi questions, and he told me facts about the firehouse, from its beginnings in the late 1800s to today. It was actually interesting, and I half-listened as I brushed my hands along the equipment lining the walls, placing cameras throughout. Levi guided me upstairs to their offices, kitchen, and sleeping rooms. We passed other men, and Levi briefly introduced me to them, always keeping a possessive hand around my waist. The others cocked eyebrows curiously but were apparently too scared of Levi to say anything more than a hello.

"Why are there no women at this station?" I arched an eyebrow in his direction, genuinely curious about his answer.

Levi frowned slightly. "We had two women working this Engine about three years ago. There was a horrible fire and both died. One of them was a close friend of Xavier's and the other was Derrick's wife. It was a difficult year for all of us, and since then, we just haven't had any."

"Oh. But men die in fires too, don't they?" I asked.

He nodded solemnly. "Yes. And none of us are against adding females to the crew. It just hasn't felt right yet, I suppose."

I tilted my head back to look up at him, squeezing his arm. "I understand. I'm sorry that happened. Where was the fire?"

Levi's eyes darkened, and I almost gasped at the rage I saw burning behind his eyes.

"A factory fire. Incredibly flammable substances."

His voice trembled with rage, and I wanted to ask more but I opted against it. Tibby could find out what happened, and I could tell Levi didn't want me to push for more information. I stopped him and pressed my hands to his chest. His eyes softened slightly as he gripped my waist.

"We don't have to talk about it. I'm sorry it happened."

He nodded, and the light returned to his face. It was odd, seeing the darkness lurking beneath the surface. I thought Ty was the monster, but something about the shadows in Levi's eyes made me question whether he was the one to watch out for. Levi turned us, grabbing my hand and guiding me to the end of the hall to continue the tour.

"This, Sara Braun, is the best room in the house. And it's all mine."

Levi led me up a short set of stairs and opened a dark wood door, ushering me in. The room was about the size of a small studio apartment with an en suite. It was divided into three areas, with a large wooden desk, small faded caramel-colored couch, and flat screen TV on one side. An updated but minimalist kitchenette was opposite the living room, and a king bed that belonged in a fancy hotel with dark-gray bedding and a mountain of pillows dominated the far corner. But the most beautiful part of the space was the wall of windows with a view of the streets below. The massive wall of glass looked out to the front of the firehouse. A few of the windows were open, letting in a wintry breeze and the sounds of the city thriving around us.

"Damn, Levi." I whistled, looking out at the world below us. I almost squealed when I turned to find an actual pole in the corner, a circular hole in the floor around it, just big enough to fit a person. "Oh my god, you *do* have a pole!"

Levi grinned. "Yeah, babe. I told you I'd let you ride it."

I laughed and looked down into the hole and almost got dizzy. The pole went all the way down to the first floor to the trucks. I could see some of the second floor sleeping room just below, with a similar cut out for the other firefighters to access the first floor easily when they needed to move.

I grinned. "This is pretty fucking cool. And I do really

wanna ride your pole."

Levi stalked up behind me, pressing his body into mine and gripped my waist, his fingers teasing along the top edge of my leggings and making my skin tingle. He leaned down and brushed his lips across my neck, and I shivered in his hold. "Which one, *diabla*?"

His words set fire to my veins, and I turned my head to the side, looking up at him, our lips nearly touching. I bit my bottom lip and swallowed, his eyes tracking the move like a hawk.

"Both." The word slipped out as my brain fogged with lust, and I was seconds away from jumping into this devil's arms. My very own diablo.

Levi's eyes glinted like the fiend he was, and he crushed his lips to mine. It wasn't a soft kiss. His lips bruised mine, and as I parted my own to let him in, his tongue dove into my mouth, claiming me with his rough kiss. I moaned, my hands gripping his forearms tightly as his fingers dug into my hips. He sucked my bottom lip into his mouth and bit down hard, making me gasp. He let go before breaking the skin and pulled away. I stared into his eyes, my mouth tingling and my pussy wet from a single fucking kiss.

"Time to go." Levi winked.

Before I could do anything, he shoved me at the pole, his body molding around my own, and suddenly we were flying down and down. I screamed, unable to do a single thing as Levi held my body hostage against his own, one arm around my waist and the other wrapped around the pole as we glided down to the first floor. His feet touched the floor first, and he kept mine a foot off the ground as he took the brunt of our weight easily. He dropped me lightly in front of him, and I turned around and punched him in the face, my knuckles smarting from the pain.

"Asshole!" I shouted, shoving him back as he grinned maniacally, his lip busted and bleeding.

Several of his men were laughing, egging me on to hit him again, but I doubted Levi would let me land another punch.

He chuckled darkly as he stalked toward me, and I backed up, my ass hitting the pole. He gripped the metal just above my head and smirked down at me. "You scream so prettily, *diabla*. Was that as good for you as it was for me?"

I narrowed my eyes at him as my chest heaved. "It didn't last very long. How disappointing."

He barked a laugh, bringing his body closer to mine, and I pressed my hands into his chest. But he was so strong, I'd have better luck fighting off a bear.

"I know you loved it. I can see the fire in your eyes. That was just foreplay. I've got something else planned for the main course."

"Oh yeah?" I rolled my eyes internally. *Nice, Sara, that's really all you've got?* But my thoughts were mush, melting for the man before me.

"Oh yeah. Let's go."

Levi stepped back and grabbed my hand, tugging me along to the doorway where I parked my bike. He let go as we drew closer and hitched a hoodie off of a hook on the wall. He lifted his arms to slip the navy sweatshirt over his head, causing the black tank to ride up and give me a teasing look of the cut abs and sculpted V-line dipping below his jeans. My mouth went dry and that slut Mina panted between my legs. Levi turned toward me, and it took me a second to register the words on his hoodie. I laughed out loud, the heady desire I was feeling sinking away. Levi wore a hoodie with white letters that read, *"Keep Calm And Let Me Save Your Kitty. (It's OK. I'm a firefighter)"*

"That is fucking hilarious, actually." I smiled at him, and his eyes twinkled with mischief. This boy was 100% trouble. "So where are we going?"

Levi mimed zipping his lips closed. "It's a surprise. You're going to have to let me drive."

He glanced at my bike, and I crossed my arms.

"No way, fire boy. Nobody drives my bike but me."

Levi pushed out his bottom lip and made his eyes go round like a sad puppy, and *gah* if Mina didn't like that too. "But you can't drive or it won't be a surprise. Just this once. I won't tell anyone."

He stared at me with those beautiful navy eyes, nearly as dark as his hoodie, and I folded like a sucker. "Fine. Just this once. If you hurt her, Levi…I'll be your worst nightmare."

Levi smirked, dropping his leg over the bike and patting the bitch seat behind him. "You can haunt me to the ends of the Earth, *diabla*."

I pushed my helmet over my head and used his shoulder to lift myself onto the bike. He pulled my thighs forward, forcing me to wrap my body around his, and I shivered as his hands lingered.

His teasing words sent my pussy into cardiac arrest as the bike roared to life and we took off down the street. I slid my hands lower and gripped his dick over his jeans. Two could play this game. He grunted over the rumbling of the engine, and his thick cock twitched as I massaged my hands over the hard length pressing against his jeans. Levi had no idea how much of a devil I truly was, and if he wanted to coax my demons to the surface, I would gladly play along.

CHAPTER NINE

Leviathan

I was instantly impressed with Sara's bike. The girl had taste, and I smirked to myself, imagining the hard-on Ty must've had when he first saw it. I enjoyed riding, but Ty was the motorcycle connoisseur of the group. My dick twitched as we took a sharp turn and her petite hands slipped lower, her fingers grazing the waistline of my jeans. My cock had been in a permanent semi since Sara walked into Andras's class earlier in the week. I noticed her immediately, the way she held his gaze when he tried to embarrass her in front of the entire class, I knew she was something special. She was no weakling.

Andras hated when I popped into his classes, but it was his own fault for getting so butt-hurt about it. It was too easy to ruffle his fancy feathers. Which is exactly why this plan of mine was fucking awesome. He might kill me. Devon too. I could feel how possessive he was over the girl when Andras demanded we kidnap her. If I had to guess, he might already be in love with her, and I honestly couldn't blame him. When I saw her flirting with Xavier at the firehouse, I almost killed him. Like ripped his limbs from his body with my bare fucking hands for making her lick her lips and smile up at him the way she had. My brain short-circuited, and one word exploded across my eyes as the darkness descended. *Mine.*

She looked fucking exquisite in leggings and chunky leather boots. And when I pressed her body to mine and she shrieked sliding down the pole, I almost came in my pants like a damn teenager. Ty was right, there was something about her that was drawing us in. Already, I could feel her beneath my skin like a drug, seeking out my destruction.

She couldn't see around my broad shoulders as I slipped my hand into my pocket and pulled out a tiny tracking device. I tucked it into the bike, somewhere it wouldn't be visible as Ty had instructed earlier today. We zipped across the Charles River, and her thighs squeezed tighter around my own as I easily maneuvered the bike through the afternoon traffic. We had just enough time to get to the university before Andras's three o'clock class.

I gripped her hand and slid it lower over my now fully hard cock. I twined my fingers in hers and guided her hand, rubbing over the denim material barely constraining my dick. Her other hand slid under my hoodie, her nails scraping across my abs and lighting a fire in my belly. Had a woman's touch ever affected me so much? I couldn't remember, couldn't picture a single woman's face let alone her touch with this she-devil wrapped around me.

We made it to our destination too soon. I was tempted to change my plans and cruise for hours, just to keep her to myself that much longer. I was quickly becoming addicted to this wild girl. I parked the bike in a small lot reserved for faculty, and Sara leaned away from me to look around. Before she could move, I braced my feet on the ground and twisted sideways, gripping her waist and pulling her around my body to sit in front of me. I slipped the helmet off her head and dropped it lightly to the ground as she smirked at me, curiosity dancing in her bright eyes. I held her waist tightly as she wrapped her legs around me.

"So what now, Levi? Why are we chillin' in a parking lot for Harvard faculty members?" Her lips twitched with amusement, and I was almost tempted to taste them. But not yet.

"We're going to taunt a friend," I whispered, wiggling my eyebrows. "It will be very dangerous."

She grinned like a villain, and I fell into the depths of her siren's gaze. "I laugh in the face of danger."

I gripped her face, and she sucked in a breath as I drew near enough to taste her. "We could die."

Something dark flitted across her face and disappeared before I could name it. "Death is an old friend. I'll introduce you."

I smirked. "We're well acquainted. Maybe we can have a three-way?"

She laughed, the somber moment passing into something lighter. "You couldn't handle that. Now back to the point. Are we sitting here all day, or can I go back to the firehouse and play with your friends?"

I growled, knowing full well she was goading me, but whatever. I would be having a severely threatening conversation with every man on my Engine telling them to keep their hands off Sara Braun on pain of death. I gripped her waist and easily lifted her off the bike before swinging my leg over and grabbing her hand, tugging her along toward the law school's office building. I had codes to all the doors and I set a fast pace, Sara skipping along behind me.

Andras was in class for the next hour, and I intended to make use of that time. He had motion sensor cameras in his office, and I hoped he would be mid-sentence when his phone buzzed and the feed pulled up to Sara screaming my name as I made her pussy weep all over his desk. My cock strained against my jeans thinking about all the terrible things I planned to do to Sara's body. No one said anything about keeping our hands, mouths, or cocks away from Sara when we decided to stalk her. And I knew that was only because my brothers wanted her as much as I did. Even if we did find out she was some kind of spy, would that make a difference? I was quickly becoming addicted to this alluring woman and I was certain there was something special about her.

We finally made it to Andras's office on the fifth floor. It was quiet at this end of the hall, unsurprising since his rooms took up most of the floor. When your families were as powerful as ours, you took what you wanted when you wanted it. Despite not actually being a full faculty member, Andras kicked everyone out of their offices and remade the floor into a massive suite for himself, complete with a kitchen, living room area, and a private office.

I opened the door, stepping into the living room, and Sara whistled as she looked around. Andras preferred the dark, and his decor reflected his OCD Gothic vibes. Everything was painted black, with dark curtains lining the floor to ceiling windows overlooking the campus. Gold chandeliers hung in the living room and kitchen.

"This is not what I would picture for a professor's office,"

Sara mused as she looked around, walking up to the dark oak double doors across the room. "What's in here?"

I stalked after her, my grin turning wicked. "This is Andras's private office. And we have a very limited window of time before he catches us."

Sara pressed her back into the door as I prowled over to her, my arms resting against the doors and caging her in. My fierce little devil.

"Catch us doing what?" she whispered, her chest heaving.

Sara knew exactly what was going to happen. I could see the lust in her eyes edging me on.

I slipped my hands behind her back, grazing her ass as I pulled down the handles and opened the doors. A massive oak desk dominated the office, the curtains were open just enough to let in the cloudy afternoon sun. Sara moved to run away from me, but I caught her throat in one hand and gripped her waist with the other. Her eyes widened in mock horror, but she didn't push me away. I nearly lost myself in her heady gaze as I walked her backward until her ass pressed into the desk.

"Andras likes to keep his office neat and tidy. He rarely lets anyone in here. And I want to cover this desk in your cum before he returns," I whispered, my lips brushing against her ear as my hands tightened and she gasped for air.

Her hand slid up to grip my forearm, her nails digging in, protesting against the lack of oxygen as I held her immobilized before me.

"Fuck, Levi," she whispered through shallow breaths. Then she grinned, the she-devil lurking beneath her skin rising up. She pressed in closer to me, gripping my cock and making me hiss as she squeezed. "Give it your best shot, fire boy."

I laughed darkly, my daemon taking over as my body burned with need for the goddess before me. "Hold on tight, *diabla*."

Sara panted for me, the desire I felt matched in her own gaze. "What does that mean, *diabla*?"

My smirk deepened. I leaned in and let my lips brush against hers. "It means devil. Because that's what you are. My sexy as fuck little devil."

CHAPTER TEN

Sara

Levi's grin was purely demonic as he picked me up and slammed my ass down on Andras's desk. I honestly had no intention of fucking around with Levi, at least not originally, and not today. The way my body responded to these princes of darkness was fucking torture of the worst kind. A few smoldering looks and scorching touches from this fiery man, and I was lost, my body craving more before my brain could catch up enough to stop it. I could hear a tiny voice in my mind telling me to press pause, but the voice was weak compared to the devil on my shoulder whispering wicked things as my pussy pulsed with need for his attention.

His rough hands released my throat and waist to slide beneath my sweater. I lifted my arms over my head for him to discard the clothing easily. His eyes lingered on my breasts, propped up prettily in the dark-green, lacy bra. Levi leaned over me slowly and dragged his tongue across my cleavage. My head rolled back, and I moaned as he nipped at my flesh. He slid one hand up my stomach and around my back, deft fingers quickly working the clasp and freeing my breasts. My nipples hardened instantly and ached for more physical touch. I moved to toy with them myself and relieve some tension, but he swatted my hands away.

"No touching. I'm exploring," he growled, his voice rough with desire and bringing goosebumps out all over my skin.

"Explore faster," I demanded, although it sounded more like begging. He chuckled, and the sound sent shivers down my spine.

Levi brought his mouth to my tits and sucked one of my nipples into his mouth, his rough fingers tweaking and teasing the other, making me moan for him. The feel of his mouth and hands all over my body was driving me insane. My thong was soaked, and everywhere the fabric touched, my skin tingled. My vision darkened, and I was on the verge of an orgasm already.

"Levi, take my fucking pants off." If he wasn't going to let me touch, I was damn well going to give him commands.

He smirked at me, grabbing my throat and bringing his lips crashing down on mine. "As you wish, *mi diosa*."

His words sent shivers straight to my clit, and I moaned as his rough hands tore the rest of my clothes away, leaving me completely exposed on Andras's desk. I squirmed as he looked on, admiring and ravenous. I ran my fingers down my stomach and to the edge of my pussy, spreading my lips for him.

"Like what you see?" The words slipped out of my mouth, and I barely had a moment to register how bold they were before his deep chuckle tickled against my inner thigh.

His fingers slid between mine, teasing my lips wider and making me gasp.

"You have the prettiest pussy I've ever seen, *mi diosa*. Tell me, do you squirt?"

My brain nearly short-circuited at his words, and I stuttered.

"I…I don't think so."

"Let's see if we can change that." He hummed against my sensitive flesh, nibbling my thigh and making my legs twitch. "I want your juices all over this desk for Andras to find."

"Fuck," I gasped as his mouth latched onto my clit and he slid two fingers inside me. He curled his fingers and fucked me slowly, edging me to the point of pain. "Levi. More. Please."

He grinned, his eyes dark with lust as his teeth grazed my clit. And fuck I had no more thoughts left as he began fucking me hard and fast with his fingers while his mouth teased and tortured my clit. I could feel the orgasm building like a tsunami inside me. I writhed and moaned, one hand gripping the desk and the other tangled in his dark hair. I needed to come so badly and fuck he felt glorious.

"Squirt for me, *diabla*," Levi commanded.

He sucked my clit into his mouth once more, and his fingers pushed further inside my pussy, hitting the magic spot over and over until I was screaming my release, unable to think beyond the feeling of his mouth and fingers. It felt different from any orgasm I had before, my body letting go completely, and I came hard, my juices coating his mouth as he lapped me up. He hummed in satisfaction as he slid his fingers out of me.

"What a mess you've made, *mi diosa*. Perfection."

I leaned up on my elbows with the little strength I had and stared down at him, my cheeks heating as I looked between my legs at the wet mess on the desk. "Oh my god."

Levi stood and leaned over me, his arms resting on the desk and caging me in. "Not god. Me."

I smirked up at him. "Yes. All you, Levi."

He grinned like a kid on Christmas as he pulled me up off the desk and dropped to his knees to slip my thong back up my legs. He gripped my thighs and buried his nose at the apex and groaned.

"I think I'm addicted to this pussy. I'd do just about anything to have the taste of you on my tongue forever."

I gripped his hair and pulled his head back, gazing down at him. My blood heated at the adoration in his eyes. I felt powerful. I had a monster on his knees before me, and the feelings growing inside me were unlike anything I'd ever known.

I didn't know how to respond because we didn't have forever. But a tiny little part of me wanted that. I wanted to kiss him then but I held back. Kissing felt wrong when I knew this wasn't real. I smirked at him instead and backed away, finding my clothes and dressing in silence. My knees were weak as I took a moment to clean myself up in Andras's bathroom. I refused to look at the girl in the mirror. I knew how she would look. Flushed with pleasure and even…happy.

Levi led me out of the office and back to my bike. I dropped him off at the firehouse and left in a hurry. I decided to ride for a while, needing to clear my head and get my shit together before I talked to Tibby.

CHAPTER ELEVEN

Sara

I took a sip from my glass of whiskey as I surveyed the items I would pack in my bag of tricks. I didn't know what I would need to get to my father, wherever he was being held at Vespertine Hall, so I was bringing a little bit of everything. All the items were laid out on the second bed in my hotel room. Tibby picked me up from the club earlier today, and I left my bike there for the evening. I wasn't taking any chances of Dev seeing me leaving for the party, and it wasn't like I could ride it in the gown I was wearing anyways. I hit the call button on my phone for Tibby.

"Greetings, Nova," she answered immediately.

"Are you sure about this, Zenith?" I sipped my drink to calm my nerves.

Tibby was coming to the party. We needed access to their tech, and so far Tibby failed to blast through their safeties. We had the blueprints for the manor and a plan to get her in with our gear. And while she was sneaking in, I'd be playing the bait, luring all eyes away from the tiny Brit scaling the walls.

"Yes, Nova." I felt Tibby's eyes roll through the phone. "I can do this. We won't get another shot like this either."

I nodded. "I know. I'm just not used to you taking risks. I

don't want to put you in danger."

Tibby snorted down the line. "You're constantly throwing yourself into danger. It's my turn to play. I can handle myself."

I grinned. "I know, Zenith. Just stick to the plan. Tap into their shit and then get the fuck out."

"Will do, boss."

Tibby hung up, and I knocked back the last of my drink. I dropped my sweats to the floor and pulled out the gown I planned to wear for the party. Andras texted the address to Vespertine Hall earlier today, unaware that I already knew exactly where I was going.

DoucheKing

Vespertine Hall, 191 Clyde Street.

This is a formal event.

Sara

Thank goodness my fairy godmother already
dropped off my gown.

DoucheKing

Cinderella, is that you?

Sara

Too bad I already know I won't be meeting
my Prince Charming.

DoucheKing

I happen to be quite charming when
the occasion calls for it.

Sara

Doubtful.

DoucheKing

You wound me, lady. Save me a dance?

Sara

Only if Prince Charming doesn't show up.

DoucheKing

If he does, I'll kill him and take you anyway.

See you soon, princess.

My blood heated thinking of this particular Obscuritas Prince. He might be charming to some, but he was an ass, just like his father. Probably a murderer too, and I needed to remember that before my stupid, horny pussy got any more dirty ideas. The head asshole had been particularly attentive this past week. Andras called on me constantly in class, trying to get one over me but not knowing I had Tibby in my ear. Dev was weirdly quiet, as if our recent hookups didn't happen. His behavior was off, and I couldn't figure out why. Maybe the Kings had called him back to the fold. Everyone knew you didn't just walk away from a cult like this. Not alive, anyway. Ty sparred with me at the gym this week but he also kept his distance; flirting and sending chills up and down my spine, but never crossing any lines outside the ring. Were the Princes ignoring me? Did they figure me out already? I shrugged, even with the little voice in the back of my head telling me to be weary. I didn't have time to figure out their mood swings. Tonight, I had to focus on my family.

After pouring myself another drink, I stepped into the gown, pulling the corseted top over my chest. I strained my arms to reach the tiny clasps at my back. I should've chosen something easier to get into but I was really going for the princess look tonight. The navy fabric glistened with glitter and lace, cinching my waist and flowing out around my feet in waves of silk. I went with dark-blue contacts, something different than what they'd seen before. I picked up the crown on my bed and stepped in front of my mirror.

"Very Ice Queen, Seraphina." I grinned, patting myself on the back.

The crown sparkled silver and blue, matching my hair and dress perfectly. I planned to take an Uber and I hand-picked my driver with Tibby's tech wizard magic. I tucked my earpiece into place and shoved up my skirts to wrap my knife holster around my thigh. I figured my purse would be searched, but I might get by with the hidden blade. If my big distraction worked, security would be very busy all night.

"All set, Nova?" Tibby called out via the earpiece.

"All set, Zenith. We play this smart. No dallying. And don't get caught," I growled at her and could feel the eye roll she was giving me in return.

"I got this. We got this. You just keep the horny kitty between your legs on lockdown. That slut is adDICKted to those Princes."

I nearly spit out my whiskey. "Fuck. She really is. We'll just have to find her another bad boy to make her purr."

I stepped out of the hotel room and headed downstairs. Before I reached the lobby, I turned to a side door leading to the alley. I dumped the clothes I didn't need and walked to the top of the street.

I opened my phone and pulled up the Uber app. The car pulled up quickly, and I scanned the plates, asking for him to repeat my name before getting in. Too many girls got into cars without verifying the driver was actually their Uber. Not that I couldn't take the scrawny guy behind the wheel, but I had important places to be tonight and no time to find a new dress if this one was suddenly stained with blood.

The ridiculously big estate wasn't far from the hotel I chose, and after about ten minutes, we found the private street leading up to the grand driveway. Several heavily armed men guarded the gates, checking cars for weapons and checking names against their lists. My Uber pulled up next to one of the burly security guys, and I rolled down my window.

"Sara Braun," I stated my name before he could ask, and he frowned, checking his list.

"Welcome, Miss Braun." He nodded, eyeing my driver. "Please follow the drive up to the main entrance and drop her off. Then follow the other cars to the gates on the far side of the estate to exit. There will be security stationed along the road to guide you."

I smirked. Yes, guide you or kill you if you tried anything crazy. Of course, Tibby and I knew about the guards and the two gates. But she wasn't using a gate. My little tech spy was currently scaling the fence along the other side of the estate. The top of the wrought-iron fencing was lined with high-voltage wire, but we had a plan.

My Uber pulled up to the front doors of one of the fanciest fucking mansions I'd ever seen. If castles existed in the States, this was a castle. The stone walls were lined with ivy, and beautiful stained glass windows decorated the front of the mansion. The turreted rooftop disappeared high into the night sky. Stars twinkled overhead as I gazed out the window of the car. A servant quickly came to the door and opened it, offering his hand to help me out. I smiled brightly, catching his eye and making him blush. I needed all eyes on me and not my Uber for now.

"Why thank you, Mr.…?" I gushed, squeezing his arm.

The guy was probably close to my age, maybe early twenties. His long, curly hair falling across his face.

"Oh, um Samuel Blackbyrn, ma'am. Miss. Mrs."

I laughed, tugging his arm so he would follow me up the grand staircase leading into the house and away from the Uber driving toward the gates. "Just Sara, sweet Samuel. I'm a nobody, just like you."

"You don't look like a nobody." He gulped, eyeing my dress with another blush.

I batted my lashes. "Thank you, Samuel. Oh, will you pause a sec. I need to check my lipstick before going inside."

I pulled open my tiny purse and passed him my phone and the bag before taking out a compact and a gold lipstick case. I twisted the top off and felt the mechanism click. I smiled as I reapplied my blood-red lipstick.

Tibby's giggle sounded lightly in my ear. "Three, two, one…"

"Done," I smiled, snapping the lipstick closed just as a loud boom sounded near the gates of the estate. Brightly colored fireworks shot into the air. People screamed and the security guards ran to the gates as the massive explosions fired into the air. I grabbed Samuel's arm and gasped as the loud fireworks covered the other boom of the electric fencing shutting off.

"Electric fence is down. I'm in. Rounding the west side

of the mansion now. Part one of our plan is complete," Tibby whispered, a little breathless as she ran.

"Oh I do love fireworks!" I exclaimed and clapped as others started doing the same.

Another security guard ran down the steps, barking orders into his earpiece as he went. "Secure the driver. Bring him to the lower level for questioning."

Okay, so maybe I set up the Uber driver. But he was, in fact, a slimy dickhead. Tibby found out he'd been snapping and selling very inappropriate photos of girls who were too drunk to notice as he drove them home. He had his own sleazy site on the dark web with hundreds of photos. So I really wasn't all that sad about planting fireworks in his car or feeling remotely guilty about the blast blowing him to bits. And if it didn't, the tiny device on his jacket would shock his heart and kill him instantly. One less creep in the world.

To make sure no one suspected me, I planted several tiny bombs on a few other cars after Tibby secured the guest list. It would look like a targeted attack against the rich and powerful. Something too wild for little old me to come up with.

"Well, I'm off to the party then. Thank you for the entertaining reception, Samuel." I winked at the guy as I took my purse back.

His mouth flopped open like a fish out of water. For being a Blackbyrn, he was rather dimwitted. Poor guy was going to get eaten alive by this shitty cult, unless I destroyed them all first.

CHAPTER TWELVE

Leviathan

I hated attending these fancy events. Andras and Devon at least fit the part; they both looked excellent dressed up. We all wore custom tuxes, similar styles, but they really looked the part. I fidgeted with my bowtie. It felt more like a noose. I pulled it loose, my skin hot as the memory of my father's torture flooded my mind.

Samuel Delano was a beast of a man, average height, but thick muscles all over. He trained almost as hard as Ty in the gym. My father was duty bound guard to Ezekiel Parrish, Dev's father, like Ty's father was to Laszlo Blackbyrn. While they were all the Kings of The Obscuritas, Laszlo and Ezekiel were the brains, and Darren and Samuel were the brawn. When Dev's father was killed, the dynamic shifted to Laszlo now being guarded twice as heavy. We knew as soon as we were told about Ezekiel's death that it was no accident. Part of Dev broke that night.

I looked over at him, his back to us as he gazed out of the window. If I were being honest, I missed my brother. We refused the dynamic of our fathers and instead vowed to be friends and equals in all things. We protected each other equally. When he cut us out, it was like a missing link, our circle was broken.

Having him around just these few days made my heart ache for that bond to be healed.

My phone rang, pulling me out of the emotional spiral, and I grimaced at the caller ID.

"Hello, father."

Samuel grunted. "Son. I assume you've heard about the recent death of Jackson?"

I rolled my eyes. "Of course. What of it?"

"Watch your tone, boy," Samuel growled down the line. "Jackson was tasked with keeping an eye on Devon Parrish. And now I hear Devon has rejoined the group."

I turned to Dev and frowned. "Not exactly."

"Did he murder Jackson?" Samuel asked, his voice deadly serious even as I laughed.

"No, father. We're looking into it. Whoever killed Jackson was clearly a professional. Andras has his best people on the case." I faced the others, their attention turning to me with curious eyes.

"Well figure it out, and quickly," Samuel shouted.

I pulled the phone away and pressed mute, ignoring his rant.

Andras raised an eyebrow as he sipped his vodka. "Why is he so angry tonight?"

I shrugged. "Who knows." I unmuted the phone. "Father, I have to go. We're needed at the party."

"Yeah, yeah," Samuel huffed. "We moved the prisoner earlier today. A tip came through that something might happen at Vespertine tonight. Stay alert. Keep your daemons close."

"Will do." I hung up, not giving a single shit if that pissed him off. "Well that was random."

Ty leaned forward in the armchair, his sleeves rolled up and his bowtie hanging loose around his thick neck. "Interesting. I also received a call from my father. He was equally vague."

Andras stalked across the room and began retying my bowtie. "Suspecting Devon is a strange accusation. If Father actually thought Devon killed that letch, Devon would be locked in a cell. He was testing you."

I frowned. "Testing me for what?"

Andras patted down the lapels of my jacket, and I swatted his hands away.

He rolled his eyes and picked up his drink again. "As cautious as we may be, our fathers are paranoid and suspicious. They know we don't truly obey their orders any longer. I think they're trying to decide if the four of us are planning a coupe."

Ty chuckled and sipped his whiskey. "Well, they're not wrong."

Devon stuffed his hands in his pockets. "I'm not planning shit."

Ty stood, his hulking frame dwarfing even Devon, who was almost as fit as me. "You're part of this Devon, whether you've accepted it or not."

I was unsettled about my father mentioning our daemons. More so because lately, I felt mine more keenly than ever. When the ritual was performed just over eight years ago, we had no idea what was actually happening. No idea there was a whole world of beings you'd never believe existed outside of the movies. There were two species, daemons and lumens. The daemons were typical of the kinds you see in movies. Horns, tails, wings, and massively powerful. The lumens were similar to what humans thought of as angels, although they could be just as deadly as the daemons. The ritual our father's performed bound daemons to our souls, the four of us. I remembered vividly that feeling of powerlessness as the daemon latched onto me.

Even now, the thing was restless and always eager for violence. We didn't understand at the time why our fathers did this to us, until they presented our relics. Our daemons were bound to an object of power, and with those objects, our fathers were granted power—without the nasty business of housing a daemon in their own bodies. We searched for our relics, but our fathers hid them away. Only Devon was able to take his back. When his father was killed, Dev recovered his relic, and our fathers could no longer control him.

An attendant knocked on the door, pulling me back to the present. "Sirs, the party has begun."

"We'll be down shortly," Andras snapped. "Ty, get dressed. You look homeless."

Ty grinned and downed his whiskey. "Why put the jacket on when I'll only be taking clothes off after our girl arrives."

I laughed, clapping him on the shoulder. "I cannot wait to see her again."

Thinking of her got my dick twitching. The images of her exquisite body squirming as I made her come all over Andras's desk will live in my mind for eternity. Or at least until I get her naked and moaning for me all over again.

Devon stomped out of the room all moody, and part of me felt bad. He fell hard for Sara, and the idea of us all sharing her was clearly upsetting him. I didn't want that. We were brothers. And I knew she belonged with all of us, he just couldn't see that yet.

We walked through the maze of hallways to the ballroom. Ty fixed his sleeves and put on the suit jacket but refused to do up his bowtie. Andras muttered curses at him as we walked, making me grin.

My mood shifted as we entered the ballroom, standing at the top of the staircase and surveying the party below. Something about tonight felt different. We were coming to the edge of a precipice, and whatever happened next would change our fates.

"Damnit," Andras cursed under his breath.

We didn't look at him, keeping our faces neutral as we slowly descended the steps.

"My father is here."

"Where?" Ty voiced the question as we all scanned the room.

Andras smiled as we passed the governor of Massachusetts. "I don't know. But I can feel him probing my mental shields."

I almost stumbled down the stairs when I caught sight of her. "Sara is here."

The others followed my gaze.

"Fuck, she looks delicious," Ty growled, and I completely agreed.

Sara looked as elegant as a queen in her deep-blue dress. The layers of silk and lace rippled like waves as she walked through the crowds. Her icy blue hair was curled down her back, and a sparkling crown adorned her pretty little head. I instantly had visions of her riding my cock wearing only that crown. Men and women alike admired our girl as she made her way to the bar and sipped a glass of champagne.

"Do not let my father anywhere near her," Andras muttered

under his breath.

"Agreed." Dev, Ty, and I nodded in unison. On this, we were in full agreement.

I grinned and clapped Ty on the shoulder. "Let the games begin, brother."

CHAPTER THIRTEEN

Sara

I stepped through the massive wooden doors leading into the house. The decor was giving me *Beauty and the Beast* and the "Forbidden West Wing" vibes. Candelabras lined the charcoal gray walls between portraits of snobby looking old men.

"Typical," I murmured, and Tibby laughed in my ear.

"Same goes for their upper floors." She laughed as her fingernails clicked away. "I'm in the attic. Their tech really is incredible. I should be able to break in, but it's going to take some time."

"Well I think I'll find some free snacks and booze while you work."

I passed several closed doors as I walked down the never-ending hallway. Servants stood with trays of appetizers and flutes of champagne along the way, and I ate at every opportunity. So far the snacks were decent. Nothing gross or uncooked, but damn, I was craving a cheeseburger. I could hear music playing and followed the other guests into a massive ballroom deep within the mansion. The room was gorgeous and almost blindingly bright after the dark-as-shit hallways. Chandeliers made of sparkling crystals hung from the ceiling. Massive floor to ceiling windows covered the entire back wall of the room, with several sets of French doors leading out to a garden beyond the mansion. Guests danced gracefully across the room in beautiful gowns and fashionable suits. It was like something out of a movie. I kept my shoulders back and chin held high as I moved through the room. A grand staircase dominated the far side of the room, and I nearly choked on my champagne when I saw them descending into the crowd.

"Oh fucking fuck," I mumbled to myself as much to Tibby. "Zenith…"

"Nova? What's going on?" Tibby whispered frantically as I stared at the four gods moving down the stairs. "Say fucking words Nova!"

I sipped my champagne and stepped casually closer to a dark corner of the room, hoping to go unnoticed. "They're all here together, looking ridiculously hot of course, but it's not the Princes I'm worried about. Laszlo Blackbyrn is here. Why is he here?"

I tried not to look directly at the offending piece of shit King as I sipped my drink.

"Shit." Tibby gasped, typing away on her computer. "I don't have time to monitor them and Laszlo tonight. You need to keep them all busy while I get what we need. If I sneak into their system too soon, we'll get caught. I need time, Nova. Maybe an hour. Once the lights go out, you'll have a very small window to get to the basement. Until then, I need distractions."

"Fuck. Alright. Here goes nothing."

I gulped down the remainder of my champagne and set the glass on a small table against the wall. I scanned the crowd. I needed to find the right dumb male for my next magic trick.

The orchestra began another slow song as I spotted the guy I needed. He was quite handsome and had several ladies standing nearby waiting for him to give them any amount of attention. He was hot, cocky, and stupid—exactly what I needed. I walked slowly toward him as he chatted up another man. Just before I reached the target, I turned my head, then proceeded to bump into him, wobbling on my heels as I let out a small gasp. I caught his arm before I fell, since his own slow-ass reflexes would have had me on my ass. His eyes widened, and his other hand dropped to my waist.

"Oh no," I muttered, batting my lashes. "I'm so sorry. How silly of me. I wasn't looking where I was walking."

He smiled, and it was a winning smile that could make your average girl swoon. But I wasn't an average girl, and my lady bits remained uninterested. "No apology necessary, doll. Are you okay? Did I hurt you?"

I smirked on the inside at the idea of this silly boy being able to do anything that could hurt me, not before I castrated him. I smiled shyly and shook my head. "Oh no, not at all. I was just admiring the room and not paying attention to where my feet were leading me. But I suppose I don't mind where I ended up."

"I don't mind it either. Would you like to dance?" He smiled again as he held out his hand.

I decided he looked like Hercules from the cartoon. Big, blond, and not much going on upstairs. Well, that wasn't fair to Hercules, he came through in the end. I didn't think this guy could make anyone come, period. He probably didn't even know what a clit was.

I dipped into a curtsy and smiled. "I would love to dance."

I let him lead me onto the dance floor with the other couples. He gripped my waist awkwardly as we began to dance. He wasn't a horrible dancer, but it was boring, just like him. My eyes scanned the crowd as he twirled me once to the music, and I nearly stumbled when I caught Andras's glare pointed at me. I smiled up at my prey, and he smiled right back, unaware of the danger he faced. The other three Princes flanked him, their eyes also trained on me. Well, my plan was working. My bare arms tingled as their gazes continued to burn into my skin, and I stepped in closer to my dumb Hercules, pressing my body to his. His eyes widened, and his hand roamed further down my back as we danced. I looked up at him and pouted my lips just as he licked his own.

"You're a lovely dancer," I whispered in my sexiest voice.

He smiled broadly, still watching my mouth. "And you are—"

"Clayton." The icy tone of the interrupting voice made Clayton stop dancing immediately.

I turned to face Andras, his cool gaze fixed on my dance partner. Fuck, he looked good in his tux, tailored perfectly to his toned body. He stood before us, casual and poised to strike all at once. His ice-cold eyes pierced my own, giving me a quick glance before turning his quiet fury on Clayton-Hercules.

"Oh, hey, Andras." Clayton smiled even as his eyes darted around like those of a mouse caught in the sights of a snake. His shoulders dipped, and Andras towered over him. This one was clearly a bitch boy.

"May I cut in?" Andras asked a question, but the words

sounded like a threat. He was such an entitled dick.

"I don't think the song is finished yet," I spoke up first, unable to let his bullshit continue, but Clayton, it seems, was a pansy.

He let go of me instantly. "Of course, Andras. Sir. Please do." The idiot backed away and quickly found a dance partner not currently attracting the attention of an Obscuritas Prince.

I crossed my arms and glared at Andras as he held out a hand to me. "Maybe I don't want to dance with you."

He smiled, and the devil looked back at me in his eyes. "I wasn't asking, sweetheart."

Andras pulled me in close, trapping my hand in his own as his other arm wrapped around my waist. The music changed to a dramatic beat, and we locked eyes. Andras began to dance, forcing me along with him. My body heated where his skin met mine, even as his cool gaze attempted to freeze me out. But I was born of fire and could handle men like him.

"Are you enjoying my party?" he asked, spinning me out and crushing me back to his chest.

I tilted my head back to meet his gaze. Even in three inch heels, he was almost a foot taller than me. "It's a little dull. The food is average." I kept my tone even and my face neutral.

Andras murmured in my ear as he leaned in closer, making me shiver. "You're a terrible liar, sweetheart."

"Whatever. The food is good. I'll give you that. But the rest is disappointing, just as I knew it would be." I shrugged as we turned about the room and I fought to keep my heart from beating too fiercely for this dark god. *Keep it together, Sara.*

Andras quirked a smile even as his eyes remained distant.

Analyzing. "Why did you come then, if you were so sure you'd be disappointed?"

"Curiosity, I suppose." I smirked. "Wanted to see how the filthy rich folk lived. Did you grow up in this house?"

Andras stared at me for several seconds before responding. "No. I didn't move to Boston until I was thirteen years old. Before then, I lived in Côte d'Ivoire."

My treacherous pussy pulsed hearing his accent as the French words coated his tongue. I swallowed, trying to rein her in. "Why did you leave?"

"My mother died. Among other things." Andras spoke the words, and his eyes widened for a second, his mask falling and returning to place so fast, I almost didn't notice it. Why did he tell me that?

"I'm sorry," I murmured, unable to keep the emotion from the words as I spoke them.

Andras nodded curtly. "It was a long time ago." He spun me out and pulled me back in, his eyes glinting with cold indifference. "You look ravishing in that gown."

I fought the urge to blush at his compliment and the way his hand gripped my waist more firmly. His cold mask was back, and so was mine. I rolled my eyes. "I prefer leggings and biker boots."

"My kind of woman," a gruff voice cut in.

I turned to see Ty standing nearby, his demon eyes raking over my body and making my insides melt. Fuck, he was so hot—and I was so, so fucked.

CHAPTER FOURTEEN

Andras

I let Typhon take Sara from me for the next dance. It was the right choice, as I was losing my patience with her. More than that, I wanted her. I craved her. When she walked into the ballroom in that stunning blue gown hugging her curves, and those mischievous eyes turned my way, I knew it was a mistake to have her here. The delicate diamond necklace around her slender neck made my dick throb all too quickly. I wanted to collar her, see my own sparkling choker around her throat, put her on her knees and make her mine. When she started dancing with that half-wit, Clayton, I lost it. And I never lose it.

I felt Leviathan's laughing eyes on me as I strode toward him and the bar, away from the dark angel calling all my daemons to the surface.

"Did you speak with security?" I snapped at him, but he only grinned. Levi was one of the only people who could irritate and defy me regularly without immediate punishment. He was just so goddamn genuine all the time. Even Devon cracked a few smiles for him.

He nodded, one hand in his pocket as he casually sipped a whiskey. "The firework fiasco is under control, but the fence is down. It should be up shortly, and I have extra men patrolling the grounds as well. Four other cars had explosives attached to them. The Uber driver is dead."

I raised an eyebrow as we both watched Sara and Typhon dance. "Who did he bring to the party?"

Levi smirked, his eyes twinkling and making my frown deepen.

"Curiouser and curiouser," I muttered, staring at the woman I was quickly becoming obsessed with. Not that I would tell any of them. "Where's Devon?"

Levi rolled his eyes as we walked toward the bar and away from the dancers. "Pouting in the corner and stalking her from the shadows."

I scoffed, taking a sip of my vodka and letting the cold liquid seep into my bones. I needed to cool the fire Sara Braun was stirring in my veins. "That idiot is half in love with her."

"He's not the only one," Levi mumbled under his breath, his eyes roaming over the *belle femme* waltzing like a queen on the dance floor. The shining tiara resting in her styled blue hair would look ridiculous and tacky on anyone else. But not her.

I rolled my eyes and faked a bored expression. "She's just another greedy pussy, Leviathan."

Levi growled, and I snapped my gaze to him in surprise.

"Watch it, Andras. Just because you're in denial doesn't mean I will tolerate you speaking about her like that. Besides, you know she isn't. The other two have been watching her. She hasn't fucked anyone else at Ty's gym, or entertained any man who flirted with her at Dev's bar. Our girl isn't fucking around with anyone else. I think you're just pissed she's not on her knees for you yet. *And* that I got her to squirt all over your desk."

I tried to punch Levi in the arm, but he shifted out of range and laughed, his obviously possessive daemon settling once more.

Before I could reprimand him for that little stunt, Levi's eyes narrowed and we exchanged a look, a sudden presence crowding behind me. I turned and greeted it with cool indifference.

"Hello, Father."

The bartender immediately slid a gin martini to Laszlo. He picked it up and took a sip before turning away from me. Laszlo walked along the garden-side wall, and I knew he wanted me to follow. I downed my vodka and kept my pace even as I followed him to a quiet alcove. Laszlo Blackbyrn was a massive man, almost as broad as Ty. The deep green of his custom suit paired nicely with his dark skin. He kept his hair short and styled. Laszlo never moved hastily, commanding a room with his threatening presence alone. People edged away from him as he walked, easily registering the monster hidden behind the handsome smile and fancy suit. He watched the dancers and sipped his martini, saying nothing for several moments before I couldn't stand the silence any longer.

"I didn't realize you were attending the ball tonight, Father."

He ignored me. A lesser man would be sweating in the silence, but I was used to this. Molded by him from boyhood into the ruthless creature I was now. I maintained my bored expression until he finally responded.

"Things are moving along quickly. We will need you boys in North Carolina before long." He uttered the words quietly enough that only I would hear.

My body tensed, knowing what would come next.

"So, you've found the girl you've been looking for?" I asked, keeping my voice even.

"Nearly. Her father will get her to come to us. And once she does, we will finish what we started. Finally." The tremor of excitement in his voice unnerved me. "Have you discovered any information about the recent deaths of some of our members?"

My jaw ticked with frustration. In the last two years, fifteen members of The Obscuritas had been murdered. Seven of those were in the last two months, counting Jackson Delano. "No, sir."

Laszlo sighed. "Disappointing. How has it come to be that one of my spies has discovered information when my fully trained son has not?"

My teeth grated, but I chose to ignore his comment. Laszlo was in a mood, and with Sara here, I didn't want to start a fight.

I adjusted my suit jacket and pretended to be uninterested. "What did you find?"

He turned slightly and raised a condescending eyebrow. "And why would I share information with a son who cannot find things out for himself?"

For fuck's sake. "We know Jackson was tortured and murdered. It was clearly a professional hit. The mansion as well. The staging was well thought out."

Laszlo grunted. "For a novice, it was adequate. This was not a team. This was a single being seeking retaliation."

The way he spoke made goosebumps rise beneath my jacket. "Being?"

He didn't respond. I glanced his way and watched as his gaze caught on something, or someone, and I nearly choked as I realized who he was watching.

"Who is that beauty Typhon is attempting to dance with?"

"No one important." I kept my voice even and uninterested. "She's a student in one of my classes. Leviathan invited her."

I chanced a look, and my heart stopped as his eyes grew hungry, watching them. Watching her.

"Typhon seems to be enthralled with her. His thoughts are quite loud and unguarded," he mused, sipping his drink.

I checked my mental shields, but they were still intact. While he could read almost anyone, the other Princes and I were able to block out my father's psychic attacks thanks to the gifts—as he liked to call them—the four of us gained from the ritual all those years ago. We also all gained the ability to read minds. Apparently, Ty was thinking more with his cock if his shields were lowered. But I wasn't worried for him. In fact, I surmised he was doing it on purpose as a distraction. I was worried my father would discover something about Sara Braun if he spent too long looking, and I was right.

His breath caught, and I knew what he would say next. "Interesting. Can any of you read her?"

I grimaced, unable to get out of this. "No."

He cocked his head, tracking her with more interest as alarm bells sounded in my brain. "How very interesting. Keep her close. Bring her to me next week."

I swallowed as my throat went dry. "Of course."

Laszlo nodded, pleased. He handed his empty glass to a passing server and disappeared into the crowd.

Levi came up behind me and gripped my arm hard. "Andras."

I kept my eyes on Ty and Sara as my father stalked across the room. "We will take her tonight. She's caught my father's eye."

"Fuck." Levi cursed under his breath. "He cannot get his

hands on her, Andras. She's unlike anyone I've ever met. Any woman we've ever known, and you know it."

He was right. The thought of handing her over to my father made my blood boil and rattled the icy cage around my heart. I wasn't ready to admit that to anyone else but I sure as fuck wouldn't be giving her to my father.

"We move forward with our plan then. Tonight, we kidnap Sara Braun."

CHAPTER FIFTEEN

Sara

I laughed as Ty made another obscene comment and twirled me across the floor. Our dancing was completely off from the music, but Ty didn't seem to care. People jumped out of our way as he flung me out and pulled me back into his massive arms. His hands roamed over my ass, and his teeth nibbled at my ear. I shivered but didn't stop him. This powerful monster was causing a scene, and that's exactly what I needed.

Out of the corner of my eye, I watched as Laszlo Blackbyrn walked away from his son.

"Who was that guy Andras just talked to?"

I heard Tibby typing in my ear as she realized what I said.

Ty didn't even look in their direction, but his lips twitched with annoyance. "His father."

I arched an eyebrow curiously, even though I agreed with his response. "Oh? Don't like him?"

Ty frowned and shrugged, his hands circling my waist. "You could say that."

"Fathers are just the worst, aren't they?" I said, and Ty grinned, nodding in agreement. The thought of their fathers and my own soured my mood, and I stepped out of Ty's muscular arms. "I need to go powder my nose. Thanks for the dance, monster man."

Ty's arm snapped out, and he grabbed my wrist. He brought it to his mouth, his eyes locking on mine as he kissed and nipped at my palm. My mouth went dry, and I clenched my legs at the heat in his gaze.

"I'll expect at least one more dance before the night ends, pet."

I smirked. "We'll see."

I pulled my hand away and dove into the crowd before he could follow.

"I don't know where Laszlo went," I whispered into the earpiece, but there was no response. "Tibby?"

Silence. I started to panic. My heels clicked against the floor as I pushed through the crowd and approached the hallway. It was too loud, and I couldn't hear the muted sounds coming from the earpiece. As I stepped into the shadows, ready to call for her again, strong arms grabbed me and slammed me into the wall. I gasped, caught off guard, and turned my gaze to the man painfully gripping my arms above my head.

"Dev. What the hell?"

His face was furious as he looked down at me. "Did you fuck them too?"

I opened my mouth to respond, but he cut me off.

"Don't fucking lie to me. I know you go to his gym. I know you went to the firehouse."

"Seems like you know everything then," I snapped, because fuck him. I struggled against his grip, and his hands tightened enough to bruise my wrists.

"Did. You. Fuck. Them?" His face dropped down level with

my own, and I felt his hot breath against my lips. My body responded to the pain with pleasure, and my brain struggled to find some clever response.

"No, Dev. I mean, Levi…something happened, but we didn't fuck. But even if I did, it's *my* body. *My* choice."

He snarled, and my eyes widened slightly at the fury I saw in his gaze. Before I could stop him, he leaned in and kissed me—hard—bruising my lips and marking me with his fury. Dev pulled away enough to stare into my eyes, into my soul.

"You're on your own then, Sara Braun." He released me and was gone, disappearing around a corner before I even had time to register what was happening. *Fuck.*

"Tibby?" I whispered, but got no response. The line was silent, as if she muted me. Something was seriously wrong. I was about to head upstairs and find her when her voice finally called back to me.

"Zenith, here," she spoke so quietly I could barely hear her. "Fuck that was close."

My heart nearly stuttered in my chest. "What the hell happened?"

"Laszlo. He came into the office. I caught him on the cameras and hid in a closet. He opened a hidden safe and emptied it of a few files and a small wooden box."

"Shit. That was too close." I stood in the shadows of the dimly lit hallway as my heart settled.

"No shit. You need to get out of there, Nova. Your father's not here. I got into the security cameras and went through the feed. He was here, though. Three days ago. Their cameras were shut off, and there's been no new feed since then."

I wanted to scream. I missed him by three days. Three fucking days. "Was he alive? My sister?"

Tibby typed away as she responded. "Just him. He wasn't chained up for long. They took him out of the cell, put him in a car, and drove off. It wasn't the Princes who grabbed him. Or Laszlo. But Ty and Levi's fathers were there. They…hurt him."

My blood boiled, and I rested my head against the wall, willing my nerves to settle. "Any audio?"

Tibby sighed. "No, but we might be able to read lips. I've got it all backed up. Time to go, Nova."

"Alright. See you soon."

I took off down the hall just as the lights went out. Shouts and screams from the ballroom echoed down the hall as Tibby whispered directions to the side of the house where we were set to meet. I hurried down a set of servant stairs and nearly ran her over as we arrived at the exit door at the same moment. I slipped off my heels and stepped into the boots Tibby handed me as she grabbed the hem of my dress and tied it up with a scrunchy. This would have to do for now.

"The power will come back on in three minutes," she murmured.

I didn't respond, we just ran. Tibby kept pace with me as we darted out into the night and toward the fence line. She pulled out a remote and within moments another car exploded on the far side of the estate. Shouts and screams carried on the wind as we sprinted for the fence. There was a small gate used by the staff that led out to the dumpsters, and Tibby tapped a few keys into her phone as we got close. The gate unlocked, and we slipped through, unnoticed. We didn't stop, not wasting a moment as the electric fencing zapped to life and the gate locked. We raced through the woods into a small clearing where Tibby had an unmarked SUV waiting. I jumped into the front passenger's seat as she darted around to the other side.

"Well, that was fun," Tibby grinned, her chest heaving as she tossed her backpack into the back seat.

I laughed breathlessly, bracing my hands against the dashboard as we raced over the uneven gravel and out to the road. "Mission accomplished—sort of. At least we know they have him somewhere. But if they were hurting him, it was likely for information about me or my sister."

Tibby nodded. "Yes. I'm in the system now. And even if they find my hack, their entire system will self-destruct before they can trace it back to me."

"Tibby you're a fucking genius." I gave her shoulder a squeeze as she sped down the highway.

She grinned. "I know. MI6 ain't got shit on me."

I laughed and whole-heartedly agreed. I pulled out her small laptop from her backpack to look through files linked to The Obscuritas. There had to be information somewhere that I could use to find my sister. Every time Tibby hacked her way into their computers, we found just enough information to keep going, but not enough to find my family. It was infuriating. I opened a folder and clicked on an unnamed file. A list of names appeared with rankings beside them. I noted Bullseye and some of the others I killed at that mansion a few weeks ago, followed by a name I did not expect.

"Tibby." I frowned, and she turned at the uncertainty in my voice. "Your father's name is on this list."

"What? Why?" Her voice was shaky, and her hands tightened on the steering wheel.

My frown deepened. "I don't know. We need to look into it more. Do you think he's one of them? Part of the cult? As far as I know, there's no connection, right?"

Her lips thinned out, and she shook her head. "No. I would know if that piece of shit was involved. It's got to be a mistake."

I looked at her, noting her nervousness, but didn't say anything. Her response confused me.

"That would be one hell of a coincidence if he wasn't, and I don't believe in those. We'll figure this out. Now that you've got us into their systems, we'll find out exactly what's going on with that piece of shit."

She shrugged. "I'm not worried about him. I'll look into it but I'm sure it's a mistake."

Her words sounded like a lie, but I knew how awful her stepfather was, and she hated talking about him. After deciding it was safer to stay separated for the night, we rode in silence for the remainder of the trip. Tibby dropped me off a couple blocks from my apartment, promising to meet me tomorrow.

I walked the rest of the way, tired and wired all at once. We were one step closer to finding my family, and it felt like a significant turning point. My skin buzzed with adrenaline, and I sent a wish out into the universe that something would finally work in my favor. Finding Tibby's stepdad in the mix was a surprise, but if I had to fly to England and kill him myself for what he did to her, I would. And if he was involved in the destruction of my own family, his death would be incredibly, agonizingly slow.

I could hear Tibby's voice blaring out of the earpiece that was on the floor. I had finally fallen asleep, and that bitch decided to ring me up? I squinted into the darkness searching for my phone. Why was she calling me at 3 a.m.? I snatched up the earpiece and shoved it in.

"What the fuck are you calling me for?" I grumbled, snuggling my cold pillow.

"Fucking fuck, Sara, get out of your apartment right now. Ty is in the bar with Dev, and they're coming for you," Tibby shouted hysterically into the microphone, and I bolted out of bed.

"Fuck. Fuck. Fuck!" I mumbled. I ran across my bedroom into the hallway, but the creak of boots on the stairs leading up to the apartments made me freeze.

Tibby's long nails clicked against her keyboard as she picked up the cameras we'd installed in the stairwell. "You won't make it to the fire escape in the kitchen."

I stepped silently back into my bedroom and shut the door, locking it, like that would make a difference. Underestimating how clever these Princes were would be a mistake. I sprinted to the closet and tore into my weapons, strapping a knife to my thigh. I grabbed a coil of rope and shoved my window open as far as it would go. The drop wasn't terribly far, but I didn't have time to heal a broken ankle. I tied the rope to the window and yelped as the front door crashed in.

"Fucking hell, Radnor," Dev yelled from inside my apartment. "Sara? Are you here?"

Did he honestly think I was just going to walk out there?

Booted footsteps stomped down the hall, and I stepped onto the windowsill. The cold wind bit into my bare thighs, but I didn't exactly have time to get dressed. Hopefully there wasn't anybody wandering the alleyway behind the apartment, or they'd get a nice view of my ass as I repelled down the side of the building.

"Come out, come out, pet. You've been very, very bad." Ty's words echoed down the hallway, the dark timber of his voice making the butterflies in my stomach do backflips.

The rope burned my hands as I slipped and slid down the side of the building. I landed with a thud and winced as the dirt and gravel bit into my ass. I heard the crash of my bedroom door and jumped up, sprinting down the alley.

"Give me a direction, Tibby," I panted, my lungs filling with the freezing wind as I ran. My feet ached already, and I ignored the bite of broken glass as I pushed my body to move faster. "I can't go to the club, they know about it."

"I've got a getaway car parked at Belmont Cemetery half a mile away." Tibby's voice was calm as she monitored my route. "Shit. Typhon Radnor is a scary mother fucker."

"What's happening?" The words wheezed out of me as I ran straight down Grove Street to the cemetery.

Other than my labored breathing, the night was quiet. The world slept as I ran for my fucking life.

"One sec, I'm pulling up cameras in the area," Tibby rasped out. "Dev is in his truck. He's not on Grove yet. I can't see Ty. I'm assuming he's in the truck with Dev."

I ran across the street, cutting off a swerving SUV. The

driver honked and yelled. I flipped him the bird as I jumped over a fence and into the cemetery. It was deathly quiet. *Ha. Pun intended.*

"I can't see you," Tibby whispered, like someone might hear her through the tiny earpiece.

"In the cemetery," I whispered back as the wind howled. "Where's the car?"

"The back edge of the parking lot by some fancy apartments. You should be able to see the buildings above the trees."

I turned north and caught sight of the buildings. "I see it."

"Dev is on Grove now. He's moving slowly, looking for you. There aren't many street cameras around there, but it doesn't look like Ty is with him. He may be chasing you on foot. Hurry up, bitch."

"Fuck off, I am," I hissed into the night. "I can't feel my fucking feet, and my hands are burning. If I see Ty, I'm going to beat the shit out of him for this."

"You could just shoot him instead. One down. Three to go."

"How did this even happen?" I cursed, stumbling over a flat tombstone.

Tibby huffed angrily. "I have no fucking clue. I've been monitoring their phones, no calls or texts referencing you either. I don't know what set them off. Something must've happened at the ball."

I darted down a dark pathway leading to the parking lot. I could see a boring black sedan in the corner, waiting for me. I'd head to our apartment and lie low. My plans to rescue my father and sister would need to be adjusted, although I didn't know if the guys connected those dots yet. I was about to wonder aloud when a shadow dropped behind me, and I turned, screaming as a massive thing dove down on me. Tibby shouted in my ear as the shadow creature grabbed me around the waist and lifted me clean off my feet. Rough lips brushed against my ear as the ground disappeared.

"Caught you, little vixen," Ty growled before covering my nose and mouth with a damp cloth.

I caught a whiff of chloroform. Then the world fell into darkness.

My sense of smell came back first. I waited for the scent of a damp basement to fill my nose, but everything smelled… normal. A little musky, like old cologne? I kept my body still, feeling out with my other senses before alerting anyone I was awake. My knife was gone. My arms were tied to something behind my head, but my legs were free. Was I on a bed? I heard whispers, voices, maybe in another room. Footsteps moved closer, and I kept my eyes shut, feigning sleep.

"You said she was awake."

I nearly flinched at Andras's harsh voice.

A dark chuckle told me Ty was in the room too. "She is. I can hear her little heart beating faster, can't you? Her blood gives off such a lovely scent when it's coursing with adrenaline. Open your eyes, pet."

"Fuck. You." I spit out the words, keeping my eyes closed in defiance.

Rough hands gripped my chin hard, yanking my head up

painfully, and my eyes snapped open, locking with the cold glare of a pissed off prick. Andras let his gaze roam down my body, but I refused to squirm under his assessment.

"Sorry I didn't dress up. I was in a bit of a hurry," I half-sneered, my lips still squished between his fingers.

"Let her go, Andras," Dev ordered from his position near the doorway.

I slid my eyes in his direction. He stood in the doorframe of what was definitely a bedroom. His arms were crossed, showing off his biceps in the fitted black T-shirt. His hair was disheveled, and his eyes searched mine with obvious distrust. Well, guess I burned that bridge to hell.

I turned my gaze back to Andras, who still squeezed my chin tightly, the only sign of rage slipping from behind a mask of cool indifference. He let go, and I licked my parched lips. The adrenaline was keeping the pain thumping in my hands and feet dulled for now. I dropped back down, scooting my body up the bed to give my strained arms some relief. I finally noticed Levi sitting in a chair on the opposite side of the bed from Andras. His forearms rested on his thighs as he watched me curiously. His eyes were filled with mirth, and I was pretty sure he was enjoying this.

"Like what you see, pretty boy?" I purred, and he grinned.

"Hell yes. Do you?" He cocked his head to the side, and I snorted a laugh.

"Maybe under different circumstances."

Levi stood from his chair and leaned over me, his lips close to mine as his eyes swept down my body, noting my peaked nipples through the thin T-shirt I'd been sleeping in.

"How can I make you more comfortable, *mi diosa?*" he whispered low, and images of his mouth on me flashed through my mind. *Get it together, Sara.*

I smiled. Then I headbutted him, my forehead connecting with his nose. I don't think it broke, but blood pissed out of it, and I grinned.

"That's so much better. Thanks, babe." Levi's words were muffled as he held his head back to avoid bleeding all over the floor.

Ty laughed loudly, and Dev sighed.

"That wasn't very nice, sweetheart," Andras mused, his lips lifting at the corners slightly as he fought to hide his smile.

I arched an eyebrow at him, refusing to back down from his cold stare. "And kidnapping me was what, a grand gesture of your affections?"

Ty chuckled again and tugged on my ankle, making my T-shirt ride up my thighs. "It is for me, pet. I enjoyed chasing you through that cemetery."

I tugged my ankle out of his grasp. "Let's lose the ropes then, monster man, and try for round two? I don't think you'd win again. You had to knock me out just to get me here."

He smirked like an asshole. "I just didn't want you screaming those pretty lungs hoarse, pet. Did you guys know our little captive can sing? Her voice is like a siren's song, luring sailors to their deaths."

"Have you been to the club?" Dev cut in, walking up to the bed.

Ty chuckled. "Did you think she was all yours, Parrish? Looks like she wasn't quite satisfied with you."

Dev punched Ty in the side so quickly, no one saw it coming. "Fuck you!"

Ty rounded on him with a snarl, but Andras cut them off. "Stop it. Now. I'm going to chain you both up in the basement if you don't chill. The. Fuck. Out."

Dev and Ty glared at each other. I thought I might just have an ally there, if I played this right. Dev was clearly upset with me, but not fully on board with this kidnapping plan. Andras was unbreakable, and I couldn't fully read him like the others. I got the feeling Ty would let me go, only to chase me down again. He was loyal to Andras, though. Levi was interested, but now that I'd tried to break his face, he'd probably keep his distance. This was not looking good.

Andras turned back to me, his arms crossed and his muscles stretching out his ironed, button-down shirt. His dark skin refracted the flickering candlelight around the room. No other lights were on for me to see anything beyond the hallway, and it was still dark beyond the bedroom windows. Even at this ridiculous hour, he looked ready for a business meeting. He stood over me, his dark eyes captivating my own.

"You're going to answer my questions, or things will get a lot worse for you, sweetheart."

"I'm pretty sure I can handle it," I drawled, smirking at him even as my heart raced.

Andras's smile was a thing of nightmares. There was nothing soft or inviting in his face. Only hard angles and an icy darkness that made me shiver with desire. I wanted to dive into his nightmares and see if they matched my own. His eyes dropped to my chest, and I could feel all four of the monsters in the room taking in my hard nipples brushing against my T-shirt. I shuffled, trying to scoot my legs back, which only pushed my T-shirt up further, revealing the black, lacy, bikini-style panties I wore. Desire reared its stupid head, making me shiver under the weight of their hungry stares.

Dev moved suddenly, tossing a blanket over my legs to cover me up, and I gave him a damsel in distress smile. Yes, Dev was going to be my way out of this, once I gained back his trust.

"You're no fun," Levi laughed, the blood still wet on his face from my headbutt.

"Sara Braun," Andras snapped his fingers in my face, and I glared up at him. "Devon might still have a soft spot for you, but I can assure you, I do not. I can make this very painful for you. One way or another."

I sneered back at him, even as I breathed an internal sigh of relief. He didn't know who I really was. He didn't know what I was after. This was good news.

I shrugged, twisting my arms and pouting. "Fine. I'll answer your questions."

Ty growled. "Too easy. Let me take her downstairs for a bit. I'll make sure our little siren sings the truth."

"Not yet," Andras commanded. "What are you doing in Boston?"

"Going to school, getting my master's at Harvard."

Andras arched an eyebrow. "And how does a girl with no family, living above a shitty bar, afford Harvard?"

I was 100% sure Andras already looked up my records to see the scholarship Tibby had procured for me, so I continued to tell the cover story we created.

"I got a full scholarship. Then I got a job at Noircoeur to pay for rent and everything else I needed."

Andras arched an eyebrow. "Why?"

I frowned. "Why what?"

His dark eyes narrowed as he clenched his jaw in irritation. "Why Harvard? Why law school?"

I sighed audibly, letting my face fall. "My parents and my sister were killed in a car accident. Drunk driver. He got away with it because he had a better lawyer. I decided the only way to honor them was to become an even better lawyer."

The room was silent, absorbing my story.

"She's not lying," Dev defended, and I hid my smile at how easily he believed my lies. "She told me about her family one night at the bar."

"Mmhhmm," Andras hummed, staring down at me.

But my story was air tight, Tibby had made sure of that. Andras stepped closer and leaned down, close to my face. His hand snapped out, gripping my jaw.

"Do not fucking move." His voice was deadly and threatening.

"Andras—"

He cut me off with a hiss. "Not one word."

His other hand reached toward my eyes, and the others started to protest. I remained still as his fingers deftly plucked the dark-colored contacts from my eyes. Andras stood back, glaring at me.

"Your eyes," Dev whispered, shaking his head. "That night I came by, I thought they looked different. And the guys confirmed it. But why?"

Andras went to the bathroom and trashed the contacts, washing his hands. "Yes, *Sara*. Tell them why."

I clamped my mouth shut and refused to look at any of them. I wasn't about to give away all my secrets, not when they didn't really know who I was yet. The way Andras said my name, though, made me uneasy.

"Typhon, put her in the hallway bathroom. Nail the window shut."

Andras leaned over and untied my wrists from the bedframe. Ty came forward with a pair of handcuffs and locked my wrists together.

Dev moved forward, but Andras stopped him with a look as Ty scooped me up, keeping my body wrapped in the blanket. He nuzzled into my neck, and I tried to pull away, but his grip was too strong.

"You smell like sin, pet," Ty whispered into my ear, and I nearly moaned as he flicked his tongue against the pulse in my neck. "Try to run again, and we'll get to play a new game."

I huffed, ignoring the way my pulse ticked up as he pulled my body close to his and smiling sweetly instead. "When I get out of these cuffs, I'll use them to slice your big, fat throat, monster man."

Ty chuckled, and I clamped my thighs together, mentally cursing out my horny as fuck body for enjoying the sound.

"Such pretty little threats you make, pet."

He kicked open the bathroom door and dropped me roughly into the tub. It was an average-sized bathroom with a small window over the toilet. Ty pulled out a hammer and several nails, smashing them into the edges, securing it so I couldn't escape. I was flattered, I suppose, that they thought my curvy ass would fit through such a tiny window. He turned back to me with a wink, then left me to sulk.

A few minutes later, Dev knocked on the door, like it fucking mattered, and came in to sit on the edge of the tub, tucking a pillow gently behind my head.

"Can I look at your feet? I saw they looked a little bloodied."

I narrowed my eyes at him. "Guess that's what happens when psychos break into your apartment at 3 a.m. and you're running for your life."

His light-green eyes softened as he frowned. "Why did you run? I would never hurt you."

"Then why did you break in like a burglar?" I retorted because fuck his pretty eyes and gentle touches when he was clearly helping *them*.

I pretended to wince in pain as he wiped a warm cloth against the pad of my foot, cleaning it. My hands were already healing from the rope burns, and I kept them tucked inside the blanket.

Dev grimaced, cleaning the cloth before switching to my other foot. "That wasn't my idea. Ty is a little eccentric."

"Do you answer to them, then?" I asked, curious to hear the lies he would tell.

He frowned, gazing back at me and searching my face. "We have a long history. It's not all good. But it's not something I can't run away from any longer."

"Why not?" I pressed further.

"Our fathers are old friends and they're...strict. They're powerful men, not just in Boston, but everywhere. It's not exactly easy to hide from them.”

Dev finished cleaning my feet, and I tucked them gingerly under the blanket.

“Maybe you’re not trying hard enough.”

He frowned at me, and I made my eyes round as I looked up at him. I had to give him something real, something to believe in.

“Dev, you were my first…my first real orgasm. I’ve never felt the way you made me feel that night.”

Dev smiled, and the light finally reached his ocean eyes. “I thought that last time was different.”

I nodded, because it was, and smiled back at him, pleading. “You could just whisk me out of here right now, and we’d be gone. Shadows in the night. And we could have nights like that one, over and over.”

He turned to face me fully, leaning against the tub. His muscles tightened, and I stared up at him. His heated gaze locked with mine, and I swallowed audibly.

“Would you run away with me, beautiful?”

I couldn’t bring myself to say yes, the lie catching in my throat, but he didn’t give me a chance to respond.

He frowned. “Was it just as good with Levi then? Did he make you come, Sara?”

I turned away from him. Because a tiny part of me was ashamed. Ashamed that I could give my body so freely to them both. The feelings growing inside me were foreign and uncomfortable. If I was being honest, I wanted all four Princes.

Dev stood, staring down at me with hurt and indecision clouding his pretty eyes. “That’s what I thought. You’re in deep shit now, Sara."

I watched him leave, the door clicking as he locked it from the outside. I leaned back on the pillow and sighed loudly.

"Nova?" Tibby's quiet voice whispered into the earpiece.

By some crazy fucking luck, they hadn't noticed the earpiece. It was flesh colored and tiny, but still. I coughed once.

"Fucking holy shit, Nova, I thought you were dead when your screams cut off earlier. What should I do? Should I call the police?"

I clicked my tongue twice for no. I couldn't risk talking yet. Couldn't risk anything until I knew where I was.

"You're still in Boston," Tibby answered my unspoken thoughts. "They brought you to a house Andras owns. Should I try to break in?"

I clicked my tongue twice. Dev and Ty would recognize Tibby from the club. If they saw her, they'd probably kill her.

"Fine. What if I tipped off a detective? Anonymously, of course. Not about you, but say there's crazy drugs at the house or something? Nova, I have to do something. I'm going crazy."

I clicked my tongue once. If the cops caused a distraction, maybe I could escape. I guess it was worth a shot.

"Are you hurt?" Tibby whispered.

I sighed and clicked my tongue twice. I was a survivor. This could be a good thing. My identity was still a secret, and I could use that to my advantage. Why they decided to kidnap me now, I didn't know, but I'd find out soon enough.

"I'm here, Nova," Tibby said quietly. "I'll be here. Always."

I clicked my tongue once in agreement. She was the only friend I had in the world. As the adrenaline finally fizzled out, my muscles ached. My eyes began to droop, heavy with exhaustion. I tried to fight it, afraid to close my eyes, but it was no use. I drifted into the darkness to the sound of Tibby's music playing softly in the background.

CHAPTER SIXTEEN

Andras

I paced my room, unable to even attempt sleep after the fucking mess this night had become. My body shook with adrenaline, the daemon raging inside me, begging to be unleashed. I recited the Latin alphabet under my breath, taking my time, sounding out the letters to calm my mind. Sara Braun was a very unexpected surprise. I plucked the blade from the leather sheath we found strapped to her toned, milky white thigh. It was an expensive weapon, but ordinary. I set it down and picked up the key we found hanging around her neck. It was old and familiar all at once. I could feel an echo of something in my mind. I sat on the floor and crossed my legs, slowing my breathing and focusing my thoughts. I sifted through my memories with the image of the skeleton key. There, many years ago at a bank downtown. A very old vault with very old keys.

I knew who she was, though, even without the key. This was a secret even my brothers did not know. They might very well hate me for keeping it all these years.

I pulled a hidden file from my desk drawer. The young girl in this picture looked nothing like the fiery woman locked in my bathroom. This girl, with ocean eyes and long auburn hair, she was an innocent, a pawn. Sara Braun was…well she was enthralling. She was a woman I wanted to worship as much as I wanted on her knees before me. My dick pulsed at the thought, and I continued my pacing. Such fantasies were highly unlikely. As much as I ached to tame her, I knew already that would be a near-impossible task.

My mind pulled memories from the depths of my soul, a carnival, over a decade ago. I was only thirteen then, two years before the ritual. Laszlo curated a team to investigate a family that was potentially the one he sought, and I was sent with them. By then, I was training with men ten years my senior, and while I didn't have the strength I had now, my mind was already sharp enough to understand what to do. We had to blend in and look for someone else who was attempting to do the same. Our team was made up of four men, and each had what looked like a watch but was actually a special kind of radar device to detect what The Obscuritas called "parahumans." These parahumans were stronger, faster, and often capable of incredible things. I wasn't a believer in magic and I'd never witnessed such things, but stories of their existence were passed down for generations in my family.

We split up at the carnival. I played a couple games and assessed the families. They were all humans, living naive lives, and I envied them. I envied their innocence, their…togetherness. I never had that. Laszlo raised me to be a soldier who would one day be a leader, just as ruthless as he was. I never knew my mother. She was ripped from my life before I could walk. I wasn't even allowed to mourn her death. It was the same for the others, except for Devon, of course.

I rounded a booth and stopped short when I saw her. She

laughed, and the bright, happy sound drew me in instantly. She was shooting a gun at balloons, missing her mark over and over. There were no adults with her, and I watched, entranced as she failed the rigged carnival game. She couldn't be more than eleven years old. My wrist buzzed as I walked closer, and I knew without looking it was responding to this girl. Because how could a soul shining so keenly be human? I didn't want to turn her in. I didn't want them to find her.

I watched until she finished her game. Our eyes locked as she turned to leave. She was smiling, and I couldn't help but smile back. Her round, teal-colored eyes captivated me. I knew then I would never forget them. She turned suddenly and ran away. I tried to follow, but the captain called out in the earpiece, announcing they found a woman and her daughter. Sweat coated the back of my neck as I walked through the crowds, debating what to do. I didn't want my father to have this girl. He would take away her light, her smile. When I joined the captain, I followed his gaze, and my knees nearly gave out. They found another parahuman. She was beautiful too, with long, blonde hair. Her daughter looked exactly like her, and it was not my mystery girl. The relief I felt made my stomach ache. The captain reported the sighting to my father, but I kept my own sighting a secret from everyone.

How I didn't recognize her instantly is absurd. When I took the contacts out, I knew it was the same girl. I think it hurt more that she didn't recognize me. But what would a parahuman like her care about a boy at a carnival? I was only human then.

For now, Sara Braun would stay as she was. I would tell my brothers what I knew, but not yet. I needed to form a new plan. While she was locked up safely in our care, my father couldn't get to her. And if I could use her to lure him and the other Kings out, we could end their reign once and for all. I shoved the file and the blade back into my desk. The sun was rising, and I changed into a pair of black gym shorts and a white T-shirt. Generally, I went to Radnor's to workout, but today I'd use our home gym, where we converted one of the larger rooms on the basement level. I stepped out into the hall, pausing in front of the bathroom Sara was currently locked inside. I sensed her heartbeat, steady and even, likely still asleep. My feelings were a mess, and I had the urge to look in on her, but forced the thoughts away.

The others could deal with her for now. Devon was already obsessed with her and he needed to be monitored. Yes, he'd pledged to work with us after the latest developments, but his feelings could impair his judgments. Feelings caused problems, and I sure as fuck didn't need any more of those.

I texted the others, letting them know I'd be in the gym for the next two hours. I didn't expect an answer, considering it was just now 5 a.m. Levi was off work the next three days. Between him and Ty, she'd be under our protection. I smirked at the word, protection. Sara Braun was surrounded by monsters, not heroes. She'd find that out soon enough.

After two solid hours in the gym and a long, cold shower, I picked out a simple suit to wear for classes and followed the voices of the others, finding them all in the kitchen. I stopped short at the sight before me. Sara was tied to a chair at the dining table, rope wrapped around her middle and separate ties strapping her ankles to the legs of the chair. Levi was sitting on one side, trying to force feed her a bagel. Devon was scowling on her other side, ignoring his own food.

"Good morning," I uttered the greeting under my breath, sweeping into the kitchen and ignoring Sara's lethal gaze.

She looked absolutely delicious tied up, and my cock stirred beneath my boxer briefs at the sight. I poured a cup of coffee and returned to the table, taking the head seat on the opposite end. The smirk on my face only angered our little prisoner further, and I struggled not to laugh.

I raised an eyebrow, indicating her position. "Enjoying your breakfast?"

Sara scowled, and my eyes traveled to her full, edible lips. "Oh yes. Because being strapped to a chair and force fed bagels is every girl's fucking dream."

Dev frowned into his coffee as I set my own on the table, arching a single eyebrow. "And why is our houseguest tied to a chair?"

Levi grinned. "Our girl managed to escape her cuffs and punched Ty in the face when he opened the door. It was hot as hell." He turned to Sara with a wink, caressing her lip with his thumb as he pressed a grape to her mouth. "Open up, babe."

I couldn't help but stare as her lips parted gently. Levi groaned, dipping the fruit between her plump lips, and she sucked his thumb in with it. Her eyes locked on mine, mischief dancing in the dark depths, just before she bit down, hard. Levi grunted in pain, ripping his thumb out, and a bark of laughter escaped me before I could stop it. Devon snorted a laugh as Levi sucked his sore thumb into his own mouth.

"Sucks for you, *diabla*. I like it rough," Levi growled as his eyes darkened.

I watched him wearily. Levi was a strange creature, easy going and unwaveringly loyal, no one would suspect the monster within. While Ty wore his beast on the outside, most people rarely saw Levi's daemon. But if they did, it would be the last thing they ever saw.

"Leviathan," I called his name casually, trying to draw his attention away from the dark angel at our table. "Where is Typhon?"

Levi's gaze hovered on Sara for another minute, and I cleared my throat.

He turned toward me with a smirk. "He's showering."

I nodded toward the stairs. "You should do the same. You stink and it's ruining my coffee. I'll stay with her until you both return."

Levi grinned, then winked at Sara before whistling a tune as he left the room. Dev watched him go, his eyes meeting mine with questions, and I shook my head. No need to frighten the little lamb in the lion's den just yet. I wanted to see how long she'd play out her innocence before I had to question her more forcefully. Perhaps I would let Ty take her to his playroom afterall. The thought made me ache, and my dick pulse with need. I just needed to get laid. Since Sara Braun bumped into me that first day, I wasn't able to fuck anyone else. I tried with another student—Audrey or something—after that first class, but the sex was dull, and I practically threw the girl out of my office. Then Levi went and had Sara squirting all over my fucking desk. I closed my eyes, remembering that moment when I was teaching and the cameras registered movement in my office. I pulled the feed to find Levi stripping Sara and feasting on her pussy like it was his last meal. It took all the willpower I possessed not to run out of the room to join them. I had to stand behind the podium for the rest of class to hide my raging erection.

When I did finally make it back, they were gone. The scent of her delicious cunt lingered on my desk all day. It was a beautiful agony I willingly endured.

"So, will I be spending my day strapped to this chair then, or...?"

Sara's sultry voice cut into my thoughts, and I turned my gaze back to her. She still wore the worn T-shirt from the night before, her tits squeezed between the ropes, and I forced my eyes to her face.

I sipped my coffee, studying her. "I rather like seeing you tied up. Don't you, Devon?"

He grimaced, but his face flushed, and I smirked knowingly. "I do believe he does. Haven't tried that yet, have you? Sweet, vanilla Devon Parrish."

"Fuck off, Andras," Devon growled as he stood to leave, only stopping when Sara spoke.

She straightened her shoulders, forcing her chin higher as she gifted us with a devilish smile. "Dev fucked me in my dressing room while I was dressed like Marilyn. And I came on his tongue right before your little club meeting. We'll get to the bondage soon enough."

Dev chuckled, about to sit back down. My dick twitched, and I nearly groaned at the vision of her as Marilyn, until something Sara said registered in my brain.

"And what club meeting might that be, angel?"

CHAPTER SEVENTEEN

Sara

Well suck me sideways, I fucked that up. Andras's voice was low and deadly when he realized my slip. He stood, walking slowly toward me, and my heart was about to jump into my throat. *Oh fuck. How did I manage to fuck this all up already?*

Andras stopped in front of me and rested his muscular arms on the edge of the table. "Well, sweetheart?"

"The phone was on speaker, Andras," Dev cut in, saving my gods-damned life. "When you and Levi called. I, uh, put the phone on speaker while she—"

"While his fingers were curled inside my tight, greedy pussy," I finished for him, recovering fast. I winked at Dev before turning back to Andras with an easy smirk on my face. "It was difficult to keep my moans quiet while you talked. I remember your voice."

Andras eyed me for an endless minute, his dark eyes boring into mine as he leaned in, his lips brushing my ear. "If you were laid out before me, with my fingers buried deep in your wet cunt, you wouldn't be hiding soft little moans. You'd be screaming my name straight down to the depths of hell."

I sucked in a breath and clamped my thighs as much as I

could with my fucking ankles tied to the legs of the chair. His words made me ache, and blood rushed to my clit like a fucking volcanic eruption. I swallowed, breaking his stare and refusing to look at Dev. His outburst trying to help me was confusing. He was so mad before but now seemed to be softening toward me. Dev was so hot and cold, he was going to give me whiplash.

Andras smirked as I squirmed and he inhaled my scent. "Are you wet for me, sweetheart?"

Fuck this, I decided another headbutt was in order. One for each prick in this house. I snapped my eyes to his, but before I could even move, his hand was wrapped around my throat. His fingers squeezed, and I gasped. My lungs begged for air, but I refused to be afraid of this particular monster.

"Not this time, Sara," Andras whispered, his tone sending a shudder through me. "Look at me."

I didn't want to look, but I couldn't help it. The command in his voice was so intense, I'd probably be kneeling if I wasn't tied to this fucking chair. My eyes slid up to his as his fingers squeezed my throat further. His eyes bore into mine, and I sucked in a breath. Something about the way he looked at me was unsettling. Like he knew something about me that even I didn't understand yet.

"As of this moment, you belong to us. Until I've decided otherwise, you'll remain here." His fingers loosened, and I sucked in a breath, looking away from his ridiculously perfect face.

"You can't fucking do that," I spat, the words hoarse as I sucked in oxygen.

Andras stood back, crossing his arms. "Actually, I can."

Levi and Ty chose that moment to return, stopping in the

doorway when they noticed the tension.

Ty's eyes moved to my neck, noting the red handprint. "Starting the fun without us, Andras?"

Andras smirked. "Sara is our new permanent house guest. Someone must be with her at all times. Understood?"

I scowled as Dev nodded along with the others. "What about my classes? My work? I'm supposed to sing tonight."

Andras studied my face, considering. "I'll let your teachers know you're taking a leave of absence. As for the singing, if you can behave yourself while I'm gone, perhaps we can accompany you to the club."

I furrowed my brows at him. "Why?"

"I want to hear this voice Ty and Dev have gone on about." Andras smiled, and I shivered as the devil looked down at me from behind his eyes.

"And who says I won't run and scream for help when we get there?"

Andras smirked, cocking his head to the side. "You won't."

"We own this town, pet," Ty added, rounding the table and caressing my face with his knuckles. "And now we own you too."

I jerked away from his touch. "No one owns me, fuckface."

Levi laughed, and the sound was anything but comforting. "Welcome home, *diabla*."

I turned to Dev, but he refused to meet my gaze. It seemed I was on my own in this house of monsters.

Andras left shortly after his ridiculous declaration, and I

glared at the three devils left before me. Dev's feelings about me were growing more unpredictable by the hour. One minute he was gently cleaning my torn feet, and the next he was ignoring me while his so-called "brother" choked me half to death. And so what if I liked it? Fucking fuck these guys.

"Now what?" Levi smiled, hopping on the island counter and eyeing me hungrily. "We've got our very own princess locked away in our castle. What should we do with her?"

Ty leaned over the table, his muscles straining beneath his fitted black tank. His hair was loose and wavy around his face, and he looked every bit the lion on the hunt. "I have a few ideas."

Dev slammed his hands down on the table, grinding his teeth. "We are not torturing Sara."

"I think she'll like it," Ty murmured, licking his lips as his eyes wandered to the ropes squeezing my tits and my very hard nipples.

"*She* is sitting right fucking here." I rolled my eyes. "Can we start with a shower?"

"Fuck yes." Levi clapped, and I had to laugh.

"As in the royal we, you dick. I need a shower. And clothes. Don't want a stinky house guest, do you?" I arched a brow, and they all looked around, unsure what to do next. "So when Andras isn't here do you all turn into a bunch of limp noodles? Can't make a decision without Daddy, eh?"

Three sets of angry eyes snapped in my direction, and my mouth popped open at the demons prowling just beneath the surface.

"Damn. What'd I say?"

Dev thrust his chair back and stood from the table without

looking at me. "I need to go check on the bar and get someone to manage for a couple days while I'm here. I'll grab a few things from her apartment. If there is a single fucking scratch on her when I come back, I will shoot your fucking dicks off."

I laughed and was rewarded with a ghost of a smile from Dev before he stormed out.

"And then there were two," I murmured the words, and Ty arched an eyebrow.

"Agatha Christie fan?" He smirked, and my mouth popped open. "What?"

I shrugged. "I just didn't realize you could read."

Levi barked a laugh, pulling a knife from his pocket and stalking toward me. I watched him, fairly confident he wasn't about to gut me. He slipped behind my chair and cut through the ropes. I groaned as my muscles ached from being tied up for so long. I stood, reaching my arms to the sky and stretching, pushing up on my tippy toes and shaking out the aches. I opened my eyes and smirked at the two beasts eyeing me hungrily. I was fully aware the T-shirt rode up my thighs, exposing my panties to them. If I could keep them thinking with their dicks all day, I might get out of here sooner than I thought.

"Alright, boys. Point me to a shower, please." I batted my eyes and smiled sweetly.

Levi offered his arm, and I took it.

I kissed his cheek playfully. "Such manners."

He winked and grinned down at me. "Happy to play the prince for you, my lady. Ty can be the big bad wolf trying to steal you away."

Ty chuckled, following behind us as Levi guided me toward

the stairs. "This is one story where the villains win in the end, pet. Just so you're prepared."

"Well this is one princess who doesn't need rescuing, mongrel. I'll be kicking all your asses before the day ends."

Ty smacked my ass, making me yelp. "Looking forward to it, babygirl."

Levi led me all the way to the top floor. I recognized it as Andras's room, from the night before. The bedroom was huge, with two walls of massive windows facing out to the concrete jungle beyond. We were definitely in the city. This townhouse was actually stunning, now that I could see it in the light of day, like millions of dollars stunning. I suppose being in a crazy cult with thousands of followers paid well. Levi ushered me into a massive bathroom with light-gray marble covering the floors and walls. A beautiful clawfoot tub sat beneath a bay window, and a zero entry shower dominated the far wall. This was less of a bathroom and more of a personal spa.

"Damn." I whistled, looking around. "A girl could definitely get used to this."

Ty pulled a fluffy charcoal robe from a closet and hooked it on the wall next to the shower. His eyes dragged across my body from my toes up to my face. He gave me a filthy grin and a dark chuckle that had my pussy pulsing. His eyes darkened as they followed the flush spreading across my skin, and he dragged his thumb across my bottom lip.

"Get cleaned up, pet. We'll be waiting."

Levi brushed my hair off my shoulders, fisting it in his hand and tugging lightly, bringing my attention back to him. "Need any help, babe? I could hold your hair up for you?"

I laughed even as my heart raced with thoughts of these monsters owning my body all at once. "I can handle it, but thanks for the gracious offer."

Levi gave my hair a little tug and smiled broadly. "Next time then."

"Yeah. Sure." I waved them away and shut the door.

I waited until I heard them walk away, then locked it. Of course, they could break it down, but it still felt better to have it locked. I peered out the windows near the sink and tub. We were on the top floor, and there was not a single thing I could use to scale this wall without falling to my death. And I didn't fancy dying just yet, so showering was my next best option. I turned on the water and flicked the switch for the exhaust fan to drown out any noise.

"Zenith?" I whispered, watching the door.

"Here, Nova. What an eventful morning you're having," Tibby snarked.

I rolled my eyes, pulling off my T-shirt and panties. "You could say that. I don't know how much alone time I'm going to get."

"We don't have much time anyway. The earpiece is dying. So unless I can come up with a way to get a new one to you, I'm going to lose you."

"Well fuck."

I stepped into the shower, tying my hair up to keep it out of the water. I only washed it about once a week and I'd just shampooed it two nights ago. Besides, until Dev came back with all my personal hair and makeup products, it wasn't worth the hour-long blowdry.

"Oh, I've got it!" Tibby shouted in my ear, making me jump. "If you can get them to let you go to work, I can slip a new ear piece in your dressing room."

I grinned. "Zenith, you're a genius."

Tibby snorted. "Obviously. I suppose you don't need any new contacts."

"Fuck I know. I thought Andras was going to gouge my eyes out. And he looked at me so strangely. He knows something, Zenith. I know he does. He's not going to keep me here without questioning me."

Tibby's fingers rapped against her keyboard. "Don't answer too many questions and avoid using your badass ninja skills. Be the damsel for now. And just keep them distracted. Make them focus on something else, like your tits."

I barked a laugh then clamped down on my mouth, watching the door. "I'll work on that. I'm almost done. How much battery life do we have?"

Tibby clicked away on her keyboard. "Not even an hour. Sorry, Nova. You'll be on your own for a bit. Don't die, okay?"

I sighed. "I'll do my best. See you tonight, hopefully."

"Make it happen, Nova." Tibby's voice was stern and pleading all at once. "Otherwise I'll send the cops."

I nodded, even though she couldn't see me. "I will."

I tugged the earpiece out and tossed it on top of my T-shirt. I'd have to stash it somewhere for now. I snagged a clean razor from the closet and decided to enjoy this alone time a little longer, humming to myself. The lyrics to Carly Simon's "Nobody Does it Better" poured out of me in a wave. It was one of my favorites. Her words always resonated strongly with me.

Feeling significantly more alive as I sang out the rest of the song, I stepped out of the shower, ready to take on whatever these Princes had in store for me. I shrugged into the robe and left my hair in a messy bun on top of my head. I picked up Andras's toothbrush with a grin and turned to the toilet. He deserved this, honestly.

There were no extra toothbrushes for me to use, so a clean finger and some mouthwash would have to do for now. Once my teeth were clean, I grabbed the dirty T-shirt and underwear. I slowly opened the closet door, but didn't need to bother. Everything in this house was updated and the door swung open without a sound. I tucked my earpiece into the back corner under several layers of fresh towels. I was certain Andras had a housekeeper. Someone like him wouldn't bother with laundry. But if a housekeeper found it, how would they know it's mine? I flattened out the towels, making sure everything looked the same before closing the closet door.

Dirty clothes in hand, I stepped out into the bedroom to find Ty sitting in an armchair and Levi lounging on Andras's massive king bed. Both men eyed my robe, and I could see the hunger in their gazes. I stuck out my tongue and stalked for the door to leave.

"Pretty siren, where do you think you're going?" Levi rolled to the side, resting his head on his arms. His blue eyes landed on my face, and he winked playfully. "Sing us another song."

I turned back, eyeing him before sliding my gaze to Ty who watched my every move like a predator preparing to pounce. "You'll have to earn it. Now, I'm getting a drink. Because if I have to sit in this house all fucking day, I might as well get drunk."

Ty stood, crowding toward me. "As you wish, pet. There's a fully stocked bar in the theater room."

I let Ty and Levi lead me through the house, descending down two flights of stairs into an open-concept area on the first floor. The room had a pool table and projector screen complete with oversized couches and lounge chairs. A premium stocked bar was tucked into the corner, and I headed straight for the good stuff. I pulled out Tito's and Dry Vermouth. A mini fridge, I was pleasantly surprised, held all kinds of garnishes, including my favorite blue cheese–stuffed olives. I popped one into my mouth and groaned. Fucking delicious.

I could feel the men watching me, but I didn't care. Tibby was right. I needed to keep them distracted. Maybe even get some information out of them, if I could. I stirred ice into my ingredients, then poured the cool liquid into a martini glass and dropped in two olives.

I took a sip and smiled. "Delicious."

"Indeed." Levi grinned, loitering on the far side of the bar as he watched my every move. "I'll take one too, *diabla*."

"And what do I get?" I asked playfully.

He stalked toward me, leaning over the bar. "Endless orgasms mixed with pain so pleasurable you'll beg for more?"

I laughed aloud, spinning away from him to grab another martini glass. I turned to Ty, watching us as he leaned against the pool table. "You too, monster man?"

"I'll just take the vodka on ice, little vixen."

How I got sucked into making all the drinks, I didn't know. But at least the men were sufficiently distracted. Who knows, maybe I could get them hammered before Dev or Andras came back and just book it out of here. I slid the martini across the bar to Levi, and his fingers lingered over mine as he took the glass.

I carried my own martini and Ty's rocks glass over to the pool table, setting his drink on a coaster. I had a healthy appreciation for pool tables, growing up in a variety of bars and hustling whenever I needed money. It was bad form to leave drinks directly on the tables, especially one as nice as this.

"Fancy a game, pet?" Ty asked, stepping close to grab his vodka. His glance trickled down to my cleavage peeking out of the fluffy robe.

"I'm a little rusty." I smiled, stepping around the table and sipping my martini.

"How about Strip Pool?" Levi chimed in.

"I'm literally wearing a single piece of clothing. Hardly fair," I tsked at him.

Levi shrugged. "I can give you clothes."

I bit my lower lip, pretending to debate. "Alright. Three pieces of clothing, minimum."

Levi grinned and took my hand. He dragged me into a bedroom directly across from the theater area. It was just as spacious as Andras's room, but with deep-blue walls and rich, redwood furniture. All the rooms in the house were surprisingly clean. Definitely a housekeeper.

"So do you all live here?" I asked, snooping around as he pulled out clothing.

"Dev hasn't for some time. Ty stays at the gym sometimes, and I have to sleep at the firehouse when I'm on duty. But yes, we all have rooms here." Levi laid out a pair of black sweatpants, a red tank top, a zip-up Nike hoodie, and a pair of black boxer briefs. "Alright, this is what I have to offer."

"I'll take it all. If we're playing this game, I'd better up my chances of winning."

Levi laughed. "Good luck, babe. Ty is a pool shark. You don't stand a chance."

"Hhmmm," I murmured, handing Levi my martini and turning back to the bed. I untied the robe and let it drop to the floor.

"Fuck," Levi rasped out.

I glanced over my shoulder and smirked. His eyes were fully glued to my ass, and I can't say I didn't like seeing him squirm.

"Your ass is fucking edible, *diabla*."

I pulled the tank top over my head. I tied it in a knot, leaving my stomach bare. I picked the boxers up next and stepped into them, bending slightly and smiling as Levi groaned. I turned in time to see his free hand adjust his semi.

I smirked, pulling the sweatpants up next and finally the hoodie, which I left mostly unzipped to display hints of skin. I walked toward Levi with a coy smile. I took my glass from him and leaned in close. "Close your mouth, dog."

I stepped back and headed for the door. Levi moved faster than I expected, slamming it shut and caging me in his arms. I stared up at him, seeing the danger lurking within. Levi was all smiles, but I knew there was more, something dark and needy inside him. His darkness called out to mine, and I was tempted to let them play.

"There's a devil lurking behind those midnight-blue eyes, Levi," I whispered. "Will I get to meet him?"

Levi's eyes sparked with mischief, and I licked my lips. His hand snapped out and caught my bottom lip, tugging it toward him. I held my breath, waiting to see what he would do. His rough hand freed my lip and jerked my head to the side. He brought his head down and growled as his tongue licked up my neck, flicking my ear. I shivered, releasing a breath.

"You don't want to meet my demon, babe. He'll burn you up from the inside out."

His low voice vibrated against my skin, and a soft moan escaped my lips before I could stop it. I felt him grin against my neck.

"I'm not afraid of a little heat," I whispered, turning my head back to meet his gaze.

Levi stepped back with a wink. "We'll see, *diabla*. Let's go play some pool."

I took a sip of my drink as I followed Levi out of his room. Ty's eyes stalked my movements like a panther preparing to pounce. My cheeks were flushed, and I went to the bar to fix a second drink to give me a chance to chill out. That was a little too intense. Tibby said distract the bad guys, not fuck them. *Damn you, horny pussy.* I finished prepping my second drink and topped off Levi's. I noted Ty's was still full. Or he'd refilled it while we were in the bedroom.

"So," I started, looking at Ty. "What are the rules?"

"We don't have to call shots, but if you take a shot and you miss, you lose a piece of clothing." Ty glanced down with a smirk. "I see you stocked up on layers."

I shrugged. "Can't make it that easy on you assholes. Besides, Levi tells me you're a skilled player."

Ty took a step toward me, his massive frame casting me in

shadow, and I stared up at him. "It's true. You'll be stripping for me soon, pet."

"Sure, sure. And what does the winner of the game get?" Both men glanced at each other, smirking, and I rolled my eyes. "Horny fucking assholes."

Levi grinned. "I got a little preview and I am eager for more. Can you blame me?"

I flipped him off. "If I win, you have to take me to the club tonight."

"And if we win?" Ty's deep voice settled in my bones like a cool breeze.

"A kiss," Levi answered before I could.

I considered it, then nodded. "Fine. A kiss."

The bastards grinned like this was the easiest win for them, but they'd be in for a surprise.

Ty racked the balls into the triangle, organizing the solids and stripes accordingly. He turned to me. "You want to try and break, babygirl?"

I smiled sweetly. "Sure. I'll try."

I set my martini glass on a side table and grabbed a pool stick. I chalked the end, then circled the table, lining up the cue ball. I leaned onto the table and lined up my shot. I snapped the stick out and the balls flew across the table. Two went in, a solid and a stripe. Not that it mattered, we weren't playing for that.

"Lucky break, I guess." I turned to the scowling men. "So do I get to make you strip when I get them in too?"

Levi shrugged with a laugh and kicked off his shoes. "Sounds good to me. Let's all get naked."

Ty growled at him but proceeded to take his shoes off as well. I grinned, then turned back to the table. The green was in a perfect position, so I leaned in and gently knocked it into the corner pocket, setting myself up for the yellow stripe in the opposite corner.

"Ty, socks," I commanded him, lining up my next shot. I hit the cue, and it knocked into the stripe perfectly. "Levi, your turn."

Levi grinned, even as his eyes darkened. He slapped Ty on the shoulder. "I think we're being hustled, brother."

"So it seems," Ty grumbled like a sore loser, gulping down his vodka.

I took a moment to assess my table. I set up two more shots, knocking both of my intended balls into the pockets. Levi wore a hoodie and a T-shirt beneath, but Ty was only wearing his muscle tank. He reached behind his head and tugged it off. I couldn't help myself as I gazed at his tatted abs. His abs had abs. Typhon Randor was the god of muscles, and I licked my lips, wondering what it would taste like to kiss my way across his chest. His body was a work of art between the layers of ink and ripped muscles.

"Like what you see, pet?" Ty growled, the sound rumbling in his chest.

"What? I like tattoos." I shrugged, sneaking another glance.

His back was covered in a pair of dark-green, bat-like wings. The attention to detail was incredible. I brushed my fingers across the ink as I walked around him, and a purr emanated from his throat. It sounded like a panther's, beautiful and deadly.

"I noticed. Where did you get your work done?" Ty leaned

casually against the table, that beautiful *V* dipping below his sweatpants and impossible not to ogle at.

Fuck. "Around. I moved a lot." Focus, Sara. I lined up the shot. It wasn't even that difficult of a shot, but my eyes strayed to the muscled monster before me, and the pool stick slipped, going wide. "Fuck."

Ty chuckled. "My turn."

"And you have to strip," Levi added, wagging his finger.

I rolled my eyes and unzipped the hoodie, dropping it to the floor. I sauntered to my martini glass and took a sip. "Go on then."

Ty smirked and dropped his gaze to the table, he lined up a shot and easily knocked in his ball. "Drop the pants, pet."

I crossed my arms. "Why not Levi?"

Ty snorted a laugh. "I've seen his dick out plenty of times."

"Oh yeah?" I set my elbows on the table, giving Ty a view of my tits.

Levi rested his arm against the table, looking down at me. "Oh yeah, *diabla*. Are you interested?"

"In what, exactly?" I arched an eyebrow and turned, leaning my ass against the pool table and letting Levi cage me in between his thick arms.

"Would it turn you on if I sucked his cock for you, *diabla*?" Levi's voice dropped to a lusty whisper. His shaggy hair fell over his navy eyes as he cocked his head and stared at me, waiting for a response.

Heat flooded through my body, and I shivered. I didn't know why, but the idea was a massive turn on.

Levi grinned. "Ty, I think she's into it."

"We're playing pool now, you horny prick. Get her off the table," Ty growled.

Levi grabbed my hips and jerked me away from the table. I fell into his arms, and my fingers traced down his solid chest. His hands dropped to the waist of my sweatpants and tugged hard, dropping the pants to the ground. "Rules are rules, babygirl."

I rolled my eyes, stepping out of the cozy sweatpants. Ty shot again and missed. He tugged his own pants down and tossed the pool stick to Levi, rounding the table toward me.

I dropped my hands to my hips and cocked my head, staring up at him. "What?"

"Just looking at my prize, pet." Ty smirked. He was a massive, sexy as hell male, and I couldn't help the dirty thoughts flooding my brain. I wanted him. Wanted to feel what it would be like to let him take control of my body.

"Ha. Not yet, monster man." I stepped away, keeping my dirty thoughts to myself.

Levi missed his first shot and ripped his T-shirt off as he cursed himself. His chest wasn't fully tatted up like Ty's, but beautiful, colorful designs dominated his arms and muscular back. Flames danced along his arms and down his shoulder blades, blending into a pair of red, scaly dragon wings.

"Damn that's cool, Levi. Or, hot I suppose."

"Thanks, babe." He winked, handing me the pool stick.

"Do you all have wings tattooed on your backs?" I asked curiously.

Ty and Levi exchanged a look.

"What? I know Dev does. Dark-gray, feathered wings, kind of like an angel. You both have wings. So, does Andras have them too? Some kind of cool kid club thing?"

Levi barked a laugh. "Yeah, *diabla*. Something like that. Why do you have wings?"

I shrugged. "Thought they'd look cool."

Ty growled. "No lying, pet. Or we might have to chain you up again."

I rolled my eyes. "I don't know why I got them. I woke up from a bunch of weird dreams and knew I needed them."

I studied the table for a minute, deciding what shot to take next and ignoring the heavy silence that followed my admission. There were only a few balls left. I could have both boys naked in three shots. Then a final shot to win. I picked up my martini glass and downed the delicious, cold liquor. I popped another olive in my mouth. I took all three shots in quick succession, then turned to my captors. Ty looked ready to murder someone, and Levi looked ready to fuck me.

"I think it's time for you to strip, boys," I said with a smile.

Levi dropped his pants and boxers at the same time, and I choked on my fucking spit. He was fucking huge, not incredibly long, but thick with a full head dripping a bead of pre-cum. I bit my lip, avoiding meeting his eyes as I turned to Ty. He smirked at me before dropping his black boxer briefs to the floor. His dick was not only massive, but tatted and pierced at the head too. My overeager curiosity wanted to find out more about those tattoos. Ty's hand moved to his dick, stroking it, and my eyes shot up to meet his.

"Enjoying the show, pet?" Ty's voice was rough with desire.

I swallowed, not trusting my own voice. I cleared my throat and turned back to the table, lining up the final shot.

Ty casually walked toward the end of the table, making sure his hard fucking cock was on display for me. I wondered what it would be like to fuck a pierced cock. I leaned down for my shot, only to feel Levi pressing up behind me, his dick rubbing into my ass.

I wiggled, making him groan. "Back up, boy. You're cheating."

Levi smacked my ass and moved back a step. I still had Ty's sexy as fuck nakedness to contend with, but I was getting out of this house tonight, so I had to win this fucking game.

"Corner pocket."

I trained my eyes on the eight ball, ignoring Ty's edible abs and focussing on my shot. I took a breath and snapped the stick into the cue ball. It hit the black ball perfectly and stopped just as the final ball rolled into the corner pocket.

Fuck. Yes. I stood up with a grin. "Looks like we're going to the club tonight, boys."

Levi pouted. "I still want a kiss."

I snorted. "You didn't win shit."

Ty slammed his fist on the table's edge. "One more round?"

I couldn't resist the challenge. "Fine. Someone else fix my drink. I'm milking this fucking win like a queen."

I slipped my discarded clothes back on and hopped into a bar stool along the wall to wait for them to return with fresh cocktails.

Ty only put his boxers and sweatpants back on, as did Levi. I drank in the beauty of their muscles and tattoos rippling as they walked. Levi passed me the martini, and I sipped it, needing the cold liquid to douse the heat building between my legs.

"Getting cocky, boys? No shirts? Even after you lost so spectacularly?" I smirked.

Ty grinned, and the look was frightening. I was certain lesser men would piss themselves after being on the receiving end of that look, but I just grinned right back.

"My turn to play, pet."

Shit. Levi laughed, and Ty rearranged the balls, breaking and scoring two. He quickly forced me back into boxers and a tank. Levi was now back in boxers as well. Ty finally missed a shot, and I took my turn. Ty left a shit table, and I missed the shot. I pulled my hair from my scrunchie and decided that counted as clothing. Levi laughed, and Ty shrugged, the cocky asshole prepared to win.

His next two shots went in, Levi lost his boxers to me, and then I lost my top to Levi. My hair was long enough to cover my breasts, but both men drank in my mostly naked body like it was liquid gold. My skin heated under their constant attention, and I kept my thighs firmly clenched.

Ty grinned. "You're squirming an awful lot, pet."

I leaned down on the table, and his eyes drifted as he shot, missing the ball.

"Fuck," he growled in frustration.

I sauntered toward him, taking the stick. "Boxers, now."

"Make me," he taunted, his eyes hooded.

I laid the stick on the table and hooked my fingers in the waist of the briefs. I pulled the band out and let it snap back. Ty flinched, his hands shooting out to grab my upper arms.

"Gotta play by the rules, monster man."

"Your turn then, pet," he taunted, releasing me.

He dropped the boxer, and I couldn't help sneaking a look. His dick looked even bigger than before, somehow, and I turned away, grabbing my pool stick. I lined up the shot, feeling Ty close behind me. I breathed out slowly, focusing. The ball shot out and into the pocket, and I grinned.

"Hell yeah. One left. I think I deserve two prizes now."

"We'll consider it," Levi said with a smile. He leaned against the table, stroking himself as I lined up the final shot.

Ty was still behind me, close but not touching. It was almost worse, knowing he was naked and so close. He groaned slightly just as I took my shot, and the cue went wide.

"Mother fucker."

He chuckled, and the sound rumbled through me. I spun around, pointing the end of the pool stick at his throat.

"You missed, babygirl. Looks like you've got one final piece of clothing to lose. And I get a chance to win that kiss."

Ty gripped the stick, tugging it from my hands. I glanced back, eyeing the shot Ty needed to make. I turned back to him, dropping the boxers to the floor. His eyes raked over my naked flesh, and I kept my thighs firmly together even as I bumped my ass up against the table.

"It's your shot then. But I'm not moving." I propped my arms against the table and stared into the eyes of a monster.

He smirked, licking his lips as he continued to stare. "Don't move, pet."

I held my breath as he leaned into me, his dick pressing into my abdomen as his arms wrapped around me to line up the shot. I wiggled, and he growled.

"Don't. Move."

There was no way he could make the shot, so I held still.

"Better not fuck this up, Ty." Levi smirked, his eyes drinking me in as he stroked his dick.

"Fuck off, asshole," Ty mumbled and took the shot.

I craned my neck to see the ball slide into the side pocket. Ty dropped the pool stick and hovered over me, his coarse fingers wrapped around my throat.

"Time for my prize."

"Just a kiss." I swallowed audibly, my body wanting him more than I cared to admit.

Ty leaned down, gripping my throat tightly as his tongue traced my lips. I didn't move, barely breathing as the beast within slowly came out to play. I parted my lips to say something, and his mouth crashed to mine, his tongue dipping into my mouth, tasting, devouring. I moaned into the kiss, and his dick twitched. My breasts smashed against his chest as I arched into his touch. Another hand traced down my spine.

"My turn," Levi growled.

He tugged my hair into his fist and pulled. I cried out as Ty released me enough to give Levi access. Levi's mouth crushed my own, eating up my cries of pain and whimpers of pleasure.

Ty traced his fingers along the curve of my breasts and down my hips as his friend kissed me so thoroughly the rest of the world fell away into nothingness. My lips were bruised and marked by them both. I felt Ty's fingers tracing a path down my stomach. He tugged playfully on the jeweled piercing at my navel, continuing down until his hands reached the apex of my thighs.

"Are you wet for us, little vixen?" Ty whispered into my ear.

Levi's lips left mine long enough for me to suck in a breath, my chest heaving.

"I thought this was just a kiss?" I rasped out.

"I never said it was a kiss on the mouth, did I?" Ty chuckled, and my pussy pulsed like the slut she was. "Open your legs, pet. I want my reward."

Levi tugged on my hair, forcing my head back to meet his mouth again as Ty dropped to his knees and shoved my legs apart. His fingers immediately dipped between my legs and he groaned.

"Fuck, little vixen. You're soaked."

I moaned as Ty continued to run his fingers between my legs. Levi's free hand moved to join him, his finger circling my clit.

"*Diabla*. You are wet for us. Your body craves us." He whispered the words against my lips.

I cried out as Ty dipped two fingers inside me and I writhed with pleasure, grinding my hips against his hand.

Ty chuckled, and the sound made me shiver. "Look at you, pet, fucking my fingers like a little slut."

Levi's fingers spread into a V, sliding along my outer lips as Ty's mouth came down on my clit. I dropped my head back and moaned wantonly, closing my eyes as Levi's tongue licked and teased my nipples. My hips bucked as their mouths and hands wrought pleasure throughout my body.

"Oh, fuck," I mumbled, thrusting my hips into their eager touches.

Ty's fingers curled deeper as he sucked my clit into his mouth. I cried out as the orgasm shuddered through me. I fisted Ty's hair in my hand as he continued to lick and suck and fuck me with his hand, drawing out my pleasure.

Levi's mouth came down hard on mine, drawing out the last of my cries. Ty removed his fingers then licked up between my thighs, eating up the cum seeping out of me.

Levi released me, giving Ty a shove. "I want a taste," he demanded, and Ty stepped aside.

"You taste like fucking ecstacy, pet. Taste yourself," Ty commanded, dipping his fingers into my mouth so I could taste too.

I sucked on his fingers, using my tongue to lap up my own juices, and watched his eyes heat with desire.

Levi propped my leg on his shoulder as he dropped to his knees and lapped up my drenched pussy. His hands slid between my legs and circled my ass. Levi pulled away from my body, and I whined, needing his mouth on me.

"I want you to come for me, *diabla*," he commanded.

Ty pulled his fingers from my mouth and gripped my chin. "Can you do that for him, pet? He wants a taste."

I whimpered, unable to form fucking words as Levi's tongue dove back inside me. One hand gripped my ass while the other dipped into my slick center before circling to my backside. He dipped the tip of his middle finger into my ass, teasing and circling as his tongue curled inside me. My legs began to shake with pleasure. Ty held my chin in place as my orgasm built up and up.

"Eyes on me, pet. I want to see your face when he ruins you," Ty growled, and I nearly came from his words.

Levi's finger moved faster, pressing further into my ass. He sucked my clit into his mouth, letting his teeth graze the sensitive bundle of nerves, the sensations sending my body over the edge. I screamed, staring into Ty's lust-filled, hazel eyes as I came. Levi moaned, the sound vibrating through me as he lapped up my pussy like a greedy dragon hoarding his treasure.

My legs felt weak, and my body vibrated with energy all at once. Levi slowly pulled his finger from my ass and dropped my leg to the floor. I lurched forward, and Ty propped my ass further onto the pool table, steadying me. I shivered, and Ty brushed his knuckles under my chin, turning my face up to look at his.

"All spent, pet?" His voice was teasing as he whispered the words, rubbing his thumb across my swollen bottom lip.

"I want more," I begged, reaching down to stroke his cock.

"Tell me what you need, little vixen." His words demanded an answer, and his eyes turned feral as I smiled up at him.

"Give me more, monster man. Make me feel alive."

Ty's hand wrapped around my throat with a snarl, and he shoved me flat onto the table. He grabbed my hips and pulled my ass to the edge, lining up his massive pierced cock with my entrance.

"Scream for me, pet."

Ty thrust inside me without warning, and I moaned loud enough for the neighbors to hear me. Holy fuck did I scream as his hard thrusts shoved his considerable length deeper inside me. My back arched, and my pussy stretched as he filled me. His Prince Albert piercing brushed against my G-spot as he drove in deeper, over and over. I moaned loudly, clawing at my nipples for some kind of release as he fucked me raw.

Levi's hands gripped my wrists, pulling my arms straight

behind my head. "No touching, *mi diosa*. The only pleasure you get comes from us."

"Fuck. Fine." I panted the words as my two delicious demons forced more pleasure from my body. I wrapped my legs around Ty's waist, digging my heels into his ass, and screamed for more.

Levi used one hand to hold my wrists in place and reached over with the other to tweak my nipples, making me moan like a greedy slut. Ty's calloused hand pressed down my stomach, his thumb circling my clit as he pounded into me. The orgasm rushed through me like a forest fire, and I screamed his name as he roared mine, spilling inside me with three deep thrusts of his cock.

Ty didn't even give me time to breathe before he pulled out of me, his seed dripping down my thigh as he flipped me over. He smacked my ass hard, and I moaned. My legs dropped to the floor, my toes barely connecting with the surface as I turned my head to see what was happening next. The thrill of having these two monsters worshiping my body with pain and pleasure was intoxicating. Levi came up behind me, gently caressing my ass where Ty's handprint lingered. He rubbed his thick cock between my drenched lips, coating his dick in the mess Ty left behind and making me whimper with need. His fingers slowly dipped inside me, and I begged for more. His fingers brushed over my ass, coating it with the mixture of mine and Ty's cum.

Ty chuckled. "Such a dirty little pet, begging for our cum."

"Brace yourself, babe," Levi whispered, as his cock slowly filled my ass.

I gasped, bracing my hands against the pool table, my toes scrambling to reach the floor. Levi spread my asscheeks and shoved deeper inside me.

"Fuck, *diabla*. You've got the sweetest ass I've ever fucked."

My arms buckled as he pulled out and back in slowly, stretching me. Ty came around the side of the table and wrapped his hand around my neck, holding me up when my arms started to shake. Levi growled and thrust in deeper, making me cry out even as Ty's fingers bruised my throat and he cut off my screams with a harsh kiss.

Levi pounded into me, groaning my name, and I was helpless in their arms. He reached a hand around and circled my clit with his slick fingers, making me moan into Ty's mouth. This was insanity. I'd received my first orgasm from Dev barely a couple weeks ago, and now my body was winding up for a fourth in the space of an hour. My body lit up for them, and I couldn't think straight as they took and took from me in a way I never knew I wanted.

My legs shook as Levi's pace increased and his fingers pinched my overly sensitive clit. I cried out in pleasure and pain as the orgasm tumbled through my body like a tidal wave, and Levi groaned my name, his cock pulsing as he spilled inside my ass. Ty nipped my bruised lips with a wicked smile.

"Fuck, *mi diosa*," Levi groaned, trailing kisses down my back as he wrapped an arm around my waist, holding me up gently. "You're a fucking goddess. A queen."

I whimpered as my body went limp, and Levi scooped me up in his arms. He carried me to the bathroom first, cleaning up the mess between my legs with a washcloth. Ty joined us with my hoodie and sweatpants, and I let the two men dress me. Levi whispered filthy and sweet words in my ear as he carried me to the plush sofa in front of the projector screen. He laid my weak and satisfied body down in the center of the couch as Ty pushed the matching ottoman against the edge, turning the couch into a sofa bed. They shrugged into their own sweatpants and curled up on either side of me. Ty flipped on the screen and started browsing through movie titles. My eyelids drooped.

"Need anything, babe?" Levi asked, kissing my cheek.

"Yeah," I mumbled, snuggling closer to them. "Pizza."

Ty chuckled as Levi pulled out his phone and placed an order for delivery. He barked a laugh, checking his messages.

"What?" I turned my head to see, but he tucked the phone away.

He turned toward me, nipping my nose. "Andras said to make sure you're hydrated after all that exercise."

My lips popped open in an *O* as my eyes narrowed. "Excuse me?"

Ty laughed, and the sound was almost not terrifying. "There are cameras all over this place, pet. Not our bedrooms. But definitely out here."

"Oh my god." I couldn't help but laugh. "Tell him I hope he enjoyed the show."

Ty chuckled as Levi snickered. We settled on a movie called *Savages* that came out a few years before. Blake Lively had her stunning body wrapped around two men as they worshiped her with their mouths and hands. My clit pulsed with desire, and Ty growled like he knew, like he could smell the desire building between my legs.

"Ready to be ravaged again so soon, little vixen?" He

chuckled, brushing his thumb roughly across my bruised lips.

I scoffed, wiggling against them under my blanket. "My lady bits have a mind of their own, I can't help it. Pizza first. Then… maybe. I do need to rest my voice before I have to sing later."

Ty's fingers brushed gently against my neck. "No more screaming then. Your tight little cunt will be rewarded after your performance, siren."

I shivered at his filthy words as Levi wrapped an arm around my waist, tugging me closer. I was too wired to sleep, even as my body lay completely spent and satisfied. This was definitely not part of my revenge plan, and I don't know what the fuck came over me. It was like something deep inside me, hiding in the darkness, called out to these monsters. My body almost didn't feel like my own as their devilish mouths and feral eyes drew me in. These feelings inside me were strange and chaotic. Was this like Stockholm Syndrome? Did women fall for their captures so quickly? No, this was something else. Something deeper was happening here, and I didn't understand it.

Levi left us long enough to get the pizza when it arrived, and Ty stole a filthy kiss, palming my breasts underneath my hoodie. Levi punched his arm playfully when he returned, and I sat up enough to devour several slices of sausage and bacon pizza. I moaned as the gooey cheesy goodness filled me up.

"Careful, pet," Ty growled and pinched my thigh. "I'm getting jealous of your food."

I tilted my head back, closing my eyes and moaning loudly. My eyes snapped open when Ty grabbed my arm and stole a savage bite from the thick slice of pizza in my hand.

"You animal!" I shoved him with my other hand, laughing.

Ty winked, licking his lips, and turned back to the movie. Levi eventually got up and gathered an ice bucket of beers for us. He even made popcorn as we started our second movie, *Baby Driver*. The action was intense, and the soundtrack was crazy good. It was also a few years old, but clearly I was behind on my pop culture, unless it was music of course.

Toward the end of the movie, Dev reappeared. He frowned, his eyes narrowing as he walked over to the three of us curled up on the sofa. The floor was littered with beer bottles and pizza boxes.

"Don't you three look…cozy." Dev shoved his hands in his pockets. "I expected to come back to blood covering the walls."

Ty chuckled. "All in good time, Dev."

"So you've just been lounging around, watching movies all day then?" His gaze locked on mine, and I blushed, heat creeping up my neck and across my face.

"Not exactly." I smiled smugly, owning it, because fuck that. "I beat these assholes in pool, which means I get to sing at the club tonight."

"Oh yeah?" Dev snorted a laugh, crossing his arms.

His fitted, forest-green T-shirt stretched around his muscular biceps, and I licked my lips. How was I so damn horny for these psychos?

"She did, little hustler," Levi added, pinching my arm. "Then Ty beat her, and we fucked the life out of her on the pool table. Andras has the video footage if you want to check it out."

"What the fuck?" Dev snarled, his eyes darkening with anger. But fuck him, he had no right to be pissed at me.

I smirked, cocking my head and taking a gulp of my beer.

"I wonder if I could sell the tapes and make some money?"

"No," all three men snarled at once, and I barked a laugh.

"What? You don't think they'd sell?" I eyed their angry faces.

"No, pet." Ty's whisper was dark and deadly as he gripped my chin. "You'd be a star. But your naked flesh is for our eyes only."

I huffed, batting his hand away. "My body, my choice, assholes."

Levi smiled like a serpent and shrugged. "Go on then and share the tape. I will enjoy plucking out the eyes of every man who watches it."

Dev shrugged in agreement, like this was totally okay, and Ty chuckled, sipping his beer. *Possessive monsters*, I thought, even as my insides curled with pleasure. In twenty-four hours, I'd somehow acquired two more devils willing to worship me like a queen. Would Andras be next? I wasn't so sure. There was heat between us, even with his cold stares and icy touch. I just needed to pull that fire out of him first. Perhaps once I did, and they were all kneeling before me, I could simply walk into Vespertine Hall and take what was mine without a fight.

It was an interesting thought, but highly unlikely. Andras's father was the leader of their stupid cult and in the end, they were all slaves to The Obscuritas founders. I needed to remember that, particularly when my horny pussy had other plans.

CHAPTER EIGHTEEN

Andras

I let the others persuade me into taking Sara to Noircoeur. I was curious enough to hear her sing that I allowed it. And I needed to get her out of the fucking house. If she wasn't acting like a brat and pouting about her new prison, she was stirring shit up between my brothers. Devon was pretending not to be furious about Sara fucking Typhon and Leviathan while those horny daemons followed her around like a pair of whipped puppies. She seemed to enjoy it, and I didn't trust her.

And to make matters worse, my dick was permanently half-hard with her at The Towne House. I watched the video of my brothers fucking the life out of her on our pool table more times than I cared to admit. I listened to her moan as I stroked my cock in the shower before we left for the club. My hands gripped the steering wheel of my Land Rover tight enough to break the damn vehicle. I pushed her naked flesh out of my mind and forced my body to relax before I killed us all in a deadly car accident.

Devon was sulking in the passenger seat while Levi and Ty pawed at Sara between them in the back. She laughed, a low sultry sound that made my dick twitch, and I narrowed my eyes on the road. What was it about this woman that captivated us so?

This was a first for Ty, especially. Levi was more of a lover, a pleaser, but Ty was rough and unforgiving. You'd be surprised to find him with the same woman more than once. Devon was a closed book but clearly infatuated with her. I could see his wrathful mask dissolving even as he tried to stay angry about having to share her. Because that's what was happening, wasn't it? The four of us, sharing one woman. It was insane. Why share one when there were plenty of beautiful women in the world for us to each find our own?

Sara remained a puzzle I could not solve, a strange light in our dark world. I could see she had her own darkness, but it was nothing compared to ours. I wondered what she would do when she saw us for the daemons we were. She would run away, of course. Who wouldn't?

Before I could think any further into it, we arrived. The Obscuritas owned Noircoeur, as well as Yvonne's, the restaurant it was hidden beneath. I had only visited once, and our fathers have never visited the place, which is why I allowed this little outing. Sara was safe enough to be seen here. My father left Boston as often as he could, preferring his estate in North Carolina. I hated that estate. Everything bad happened there. The first time I watched my father nearly beat Ty to death. The first time he forced me to do the same. Our fathers broke us, over and over again, until we were too fractured to fight back. But what he didn't intend for was the connection the four of us formed when our fathers destroyed us. And now we would rise against them, stronger than we ever were before. I hoped we were strong enough.

I drove the SUV up to the front door of the restaurant and

stopped. The attendant immediately jumped out of his booth, recognizing who I was instantly. He stammered, keeping his eyes lowered, as I stepped out of the vehicle and handed him the keys, threatening his life if anything should happen to my Land Rover.

Levi tugged Sara against him, and she didn't protest as they walked in front of Ty and Devon. I led the way toward the restaurant, the winter wind whipping around us.

Devon had gathered most of her things from the shitty apartment above his bar, so she had fresh clothes. I also had her motorcycle brought over and parked in our garage. I wanted her to feel comfortable at The Towne House, which was strange considering she was supposed to be our prisoner. But every time I thought of treating her as such I just…couldn't. The only thing he couldn't get into was the safe hidden in her closet. Sara refused to give us the code, so Ty and Devon ripped the thing out and hauled it into the basement. Perhaps I would let Ty torture her later and force her to open it. The daemon inside me perked up at the thought of her chained and vulnerable for us. I glanced back at her, seemingly incapable of having her out of my sight for more than a few minutes.

Tonight she wore ripped skinny jeans and a mesh black top, her lacy red bra visible through the open-weave sweater. I found her style more attractive than I cared to admit. The cropped leather jacket she wore over the top was hardly winter attire, and I had to resist the urge to lick the goosebumps rising on her skin.

The streets were less busy because of the weather, although indoor dining seemed busy enough for a Thursday night. A hostess pulled open the door of the restaurant, and I stepped inside, ignoring her and walking toward the VIP room in the back, where the door to Noircoeur was hidden.

"I usually sneak in the back entrance, you fancy fucks," Sara taunted, rolling her eyes at us, and Levi laughed.

I chose to ignore her. I rapped my knuckles on the door, and a bulky bouncer opened a small window at eye level. He registered who I was but looked unimpressed. Sara shoved in front of me, and I resisted the urge to shove her against the wall and spank her ass raw for her rude behavior. She stood on her tiptoes, her ass pressing back against my cock, and smiled at the bouncer.

"Hey, Beau. They're with me."

She waved in our general direction, and I pursed my lips in annoyance.

Beau's face softened. "Hey, crazy. It's busy down there."

He opened the door and stepped aside for her, and I immediately followed, making sure the bouncer understood who Sara belonged to.

"Awesome. I've got something new for tonight." She grinned and winked at Beau the Bouncer, who might wind up on a missing persons list if he didn't avert his fucking eyes.

I threaded her arm through mine before she could walk any further and slip away from us. She rolled her eyes, but didn't fight me, and my blood heated at her obedience. The others followed behind us. At the base of the stairs, there was another small landing and French doors with red, stained-glass windows. Two attendants opened the doors, their eyes widening when they registered exactly who was walking into the club.

Sara winked at the young men we passed, and I snarled at them until their attention returned to the four daemons walking at her side. I let my eyes sweep the crowd, looking unimpressed, even as I made note of any important faces. I knew Ty was doing the same behind me, always on alert for threats. My father made sure of that. Whether he wanted it or not, Ty was molded into my personal bodyguard, just as his father was to mine.

A perky girl in a pink wig rushed toward us, her tits bouncing in the small sequined one-piece she was wearing. I barely glanced at her, and she turned her attention to Sara.

"Hey, Josie." Sara smiled, giving the girl a half hug as I refused to let go of her arm.

"H-hey, girl," Josie stammered, her slanted brown eyes darting between the men crowding around Sara.

Sara turned toward me with a bored expression. "I'm assuming you've got a VIP booth here?"

I nodded curtly.

Sara rolled her eyes and made a gagging motion before turning back to the girl. "I can take care of them. Just have Ryan bring over a bottle of Ketel One on ice and a bottle of Jack. Five rocks glasses, stuffed olives, and cherries, please."

Josie nodded quickly and sprinted to the bar. Sara tugged on my arm, and I let her lead us to the VIP booth closest to the stage where she would be performing. The room was a rough U-shape, and the VIP booths lined the walls on either side of the main stage. Of course she would know which booth belonged to us.

Dev pulled back the velvet curtains to reveal two small

couches and an oversized lounge chair with a low glass table resting in the center. Ty settled into the chair, pulling Sara onto his lap. She wiggled her ass, and he growled, nipping her neck. Levi, Devon, and I moved to sit on the two smaller couches. A built young man came over with our drinks, expertly laying out the bottles of liquor, glasses, and garnishes Sara ordered. He wasn't exactly young, only a couple years behind me, by the looks of him. What I didn't like was his unfamiliar face. I knew everyone who worked here, but I did not recognize him. I made a mental note to look into his background later.

"Hey, Ryan." She smiled, leaning across the table to speak to him. "It's packed. Making good money tonight? "

Ryan smiled back but wisely stepped away from Sara as we all glared up at him. "Yeah, doing alright. It's a rowdy crowd. I'm sure they'll go nuts when you show up on stage. Break a leg out there, Sara."

Sara's smile turned devilish, and her turquoise eyes glanced my way before turning back to him. "Go find a seat! You won't want to miss this show."

Ryan laughed as he backed away from our booth. "Don't worry, I won't."

Four sets of eyes locked on Sara, and she squirmed under the attention before sticking out her tongue at me. I snapped my hand out and grabbed it, pulling her face toward mine while Ty gripped her waist.

"Behave, sweetheart. Or I'll take you back to The Towne House and chain you to the bathtub," I growled low enough so only she could hear.

I chuckled as her curses slurred with her tongue locked

between my fingers. I released it, wiping my fingers covered in her spit on her pants, and sat back with a smirk while she scowled at me.

"Someone make me a drink," Sara ordered, breaking eye contact first.

Levi sat forward, icing up a glass of vodka with a blue cheese olive. Dev leaned forward and picked a cherry out, dipping it in his whiskey and reaching out, pressing it to her lips.

"Open your mouth, devil girl," Devon teased, his eyes following her full lips.

Sara's scent changed as her eyes filled with lust, and my dick twitched. Her tongue curled around the cherry, sucking it from Dev's fingers. Ty rocked Sara's hips against his dick and groaned.

"Close the curtain, pet," Ty whispered for only us to hear. "I want to suck a cherry out of her sweet little cunt."

Sara laughed, wiggling against him. "I've got to go get dressed. I'm on in twenty minutes."

I grabbed Sara's drink and my own, offering her my arm as I stood. "Let's go then."

Sara rolled her eyes. "I can't even go to my dressing room without a bodyguard?"

"No." I chose not to elaborate because there was no room for argument. Even if she enjoyed riding my brothers' dicks, I didn't trust her to not run from us.

She huffed, and Ty grabbed her face, sticking his tongue down her throat. She moaned into his mouth.

He pulled away with a wink. "Be a good girl for Andras. We'll be watching."

Sara flipped him off and stormed out of our booth. I

followed after her, enjoying the view of her ass swaying angrily as she stormed down the hall to the side of the stage.

Her dressing room was larger than I expected, with a plush, velvet chaise in the corner and several racks of costumes, shoes, and accessories. I placed our drinks on her vanity, shoving aside her makeup as she tugged out a garment bag from her costume rack.

"And what will you be singing for us tonight, *belle femme*?" I sipped my vodka, watching her.

Her captivating eyes turned my way, and I swallowed thickly. This woman was going to be my end.

She grinned and braced her hands on her hips. "It's a surprise. Now go stand outside. I don't want you to see my costume yet."

I arched an eyebrow, and she pouted.

"Please, Andras? I actually enjoy singing. I'm not going anywhere but on that stage. At least not right now."

I shoved off the wall and stalked toward her, tipping her chin up to meet my gaze. She was so petite, her head barely reaching my shoulders. "If you run, I will find you, Sara Braun."

Her lips parted, and her tongue flicked across her lips, her pupils dilating with desire. "I know."

I smirked, releasing her and picking up my drink. "Good girl."

I stepped out of the dressing room before she could respond and shut the door. I returned to the others, their eyes curious as they watched me sit.

"You left her in the room alone?" Dev spoke up first, frowning at me.

I leaned back, resting my right ankle on my left knee and sipping the cold liquor. "She's not going anywhere. And if she does, it just gives Ty the opportunity to chase her."

Ty chuckled darkly, swigging whiskey from the bottle. "Fuck, I hope she runs."

"You're fucked up, man," Dev snapped at him, leaning back in his seat.

"We all are, Parrish. You're just in denial," Ty retorted, taking another swig from the bottle. "Let your daemon out, brother. He's bored."

Dev chucked a cherry at Ty, who caught it in his mouth with a grin. The lights dimmed, and a voice echoed through the speakers, announcing the next act.

"Please welcome our very own Singing Siren, Sara Braun."

The crowd went wild, whistling and clapping for our girl. The lights darkened completely, and I picked up the click of her heels as she walked on stage. The music burst to life, and a hazy pink spotlight shined down on Sara. My mouth went dry, and my dick hardened instantly. She wore a blonde, blunt bob wig and pin-up girl makeup. Her lips were a bright pink, matching the silver-and-pink corset she wore. The top cinched her waist and boosted her cleavage. Sara looked absolutely exquisite. Her round ass swayed in tight cheeky, pink bottoms, and her black stilettos clicked against the stage as she sashayed to the edge.

"Fucking hell," Dev whispered, his voice rough with desire.

I wholeheartedly agreed. Sara looked like the sweetest sin I wanted to devour. The music picked up, and her voice rang out to a coquettish tune. It was mildly familiar, and I turned to Levi, knowing how excited he must be. *Burlesque* was one of his favorite movies, and the song "But I Am a Good Girl" was one of his favorite scenes.

I couldn't help the laugh that escaped my lips, and the others joined me as she glanced our way, singing the next line directly to us. Unlike the song lyric, our Sara was no "good girl."

Oh, she was in trouble for sure.

Sara danced and moved her supple body to the beat as she sang out the words. The crowd whistled and howled. I grimaced, seeing all the men ogling her. Sara sauntered closer to the steps at the front of the stage and the damn bartender, Ryan, was instantly there, helping her down into the crowd. I felt my brothers go still beside me as we watched her move through the crowd, letting them paw at her as she sang.

I growled, the music drowning out the sound. "Our little angel is looking for punishment."

Ty grunted in agreement, and Levi laughed before he spoke. "*Mi diosa*. I'm in love."

Sara drifted through the crowd, pausing at our booth. She winked and turned, shaking her sweet, round ass in our faces. Levi reached out and pinched her plump cheeks and she yelped, adding it into the song, and the crowd roared with applause. She tiptoed back to the stairs, where Ryan helped her up onto the stage. She draped herself across a chair as the song came to an end, and the room leapt to its feet. Money and flowers littered the stage. Sara fanned herself and blinked innocently as I rearranged my growing hard-on. I was about to come in my fucking pants. *Oh yes, she would be punished.*

Sara skipped off the stage behind the curtains, and I stood with a growl.

"Mine."

I left the others adjusting their own swollen dicks and walked swiftly to her dressing room, noting the bouquet of red roses on her vanity. I slammed the door, and she turned with a shit-eating grin on her smart mouth. I snarled.

"Did you like it, baby?" Sara cooed, blinking up at me.

I grabbed her forearms, pulling her close. "You think you're cute, don't you, sweetheart?" I purred, my voice low and threatening.

She smiled back, unphased, and I think I loved her more for that.

"Just being the good little girl you wanted." She pouted.

I wrapped my hand around her throat. "Then you'll take your punishment like a good little girl too, sweetheart."

I turned her around swiftly and bent her over the vanity. Her arms darted out, bracing herself, and I slapped her ass. She cried out when I ripped her cheeky shorts down and slapped her ass twice more. I smoothed my hand over the red marks, making her moan for me. My fingers slid toward her glistening pussy, and I chuckled darkly.

I dipped a finger inside her sweet cunt. Sara responded instantly with pretty little moans and pushed her ass back into my hand. I added a second finger, curling the digit and finding her G-Spot with ease.

"Fuck, Andras," she whimpered.

I slid my fingers out, and she whined. I slapped my hand over her soaked pussy, my cock twitching when she screamed for me.

"Only good girls get orgasms, sweetheart," I taunted.

I pulled her up, turning her to face me. I unbuckled my belt and unzipped my pants, pulling my dick out and stroking it. Sara gasped, eyeing it greedily.

"On your knees."

Sara swallowed, and her eyes locked on mine as she dropped to her knees. "Don't fuck up my makeup. I have another song to sing, asshole."

I growled. "If I want you to go back on that stage covered in my fucking cum, you will."

Sara smirked up at me, tugging my cock into her dainty hands, twisting and stroking and making me groan. "Wanna bet?" she whispered.

I was about to protest when she sucked my cock into her mouth. The head of my dick touched the back of her throat, and she hummed, the vibrations making me shudder and my dick throb. *Holy fuck.*

I fisted my hand in her hair, taking back some semblance of control. I circled my hips, pulling back and thrusting into her mouth steadily. She closed her eyes, moaning. Her hands slid around my waist, and she dug her nails into my ass while I fucked her throat. I groaned loudly as her tongue danced along the tip of my cock, lapping up the pre-cum.

"Fuck, angel."

My grip on her hair tightened, and she whimpered on my dick. I lost control, thrusting into her mouth faster, harder, my dick swelling to the point of pain as I forced myself to hold back my release. Her mouth was mine to punish, and I would prolong my own torture just to see her pretty eyes water while I fucked her throat without mercy. She started humming the song she just sang on stage, and the vibration tipped me over the edge.

I thrust in once more, my cum spilling down the back of her throat. "Take it all, my good little slut."

My eyes rolled back in my head as she expertly swallowed down my cum. Sara pulled away slowly, her tongue licking up my still-hard cock as she sat back on her heels. I grabbed her arms and pulled her up from the floor.

I kissed her roughly, tasting my orgasm on her tongue. My cock throbbed again just thinking about her sweet red lips. She nipped at my lip, and I growled.

"Now do I get an orgasm?" She pouted, and I smirked.

"Oh no, angel." I dipped my fingers between her thighs, and she gasped. "You're going back on that stage with the taste of my cock in your mouth and your pussy pulsing with need for me. If you behave, I'll let you come later tonight."

Sara crossed her arms and attempted to look angry. "I don't need you to find my release, Andras. I can do that all by myself."

I grinned like the devil, and she backed up a step.

"No, sweetheart, you won't. Not unless you want me to let Typhon punish you instead. And I promise you, it will hurt. Now change into your next costume."

She slammed her hands on her hips. "You're not leaving?"

I pulled up my pants, secured the belt, and leaned against the wall. "No."

CHAPTER NINETEEN

Sara

I rolled my eyes for the millionth time. Andras really brought out the brat in me.

"Fine, then be useful. Untie me." I turned around as Andras stalked toward me, tugging on the strings of my corset.

"I'd prefer to tie you up," he muttered, his lips brushing against my neck.

I shivered, imagining myself tied up and at his mercy. I'd never in my life thought being tied up was attractive, nor did I trust anyone enough to do it. So why did the idea of letting Andras bind me sound so appealing?

Something was changing inside me, and I wasn't entirely sure if that was a good thing. My corset came loose, and I let it fall to the floor as I stepped behind my three-panel room divider to change. The dress I chose for my next song was new, and I finally had the perfect excuse to wear it. The floor-length gown was made of sparkling burgundy fabric. The halter neckline dipped low between my breasts, and the back was entirely open, the fabric sitting just above the curve of my ass. A long slit ran up my right leg, making it easier to walk in the form-fitting gown. I ran my fingers through my hair, letting the soft waves fall around my shoulders. I was going back to blue for this performance. I stepped out from behind the divider, and Andras looked up, his eyes going wide as he drank me in. He cleared his throat, and I twirled.

"What do you think?" I asked, trying my hardest to look nonchalant while his piercing eyes burned through my skin.

Andras stepped toward me, brushing the icy hair off my shoulder and making me shiver. "*Tu es magnifique, mon ange.*"

I stared up into his dark eyes, waiting for the punchline, but he simply stared right back. His fingers traced my jawline, my lips. My breathing grew shallow under the intensity of his gaze. As much as I loved the pain and roughness his hands offered, the light touches against my skin did things to my soul I was definitely not ready to acknowledge.

"Sometimes I think you are an angel, sent down to bring me to my knees. Is that what you are, *belle femme*?" His voice was low, barely above a whisper.

I swallowed audibly, unable to respond. So I deflected with humor and shrugged it off. "Perhaps. Speaking of getting on your knees, can you put my heels on? It's difficult to bend over in this gown."

Andras thankfully didn't call me out, but instead grabbed the gold strappy heels and knelt at my feet. He slipped the stilettos onto my feet, caressing my ankles. The dress slipped to the side, revealing my right leg up to my hip while my stiletto rested on his knee. Andras slid his hand up my thigh, moving slowly, bringing his lips to my skin. I slammed my hand to his chest as his hand nearly reached between my thighs.

"Don't start something you can't finish, Andras," I whispered, heat building in my core as my body burned for release.

He gazed up at me, and my breath caught at the beautiful god on his knees before me. His hand moved again, sliding between my thighs. Andras cursed, finding me bare beneath my gown as his fingers dipped inside my very fucking wet pussy. I clamped down around his fingers and moaned, grinding against his hand. My nails dug into his shoulder as his thumb circled my clit.

"Andras," I pleaded, throwing my head back and squeezing my breasts to relieve some of the tension. "Please."

"Only because you beg so prettily, angel," Andras hummed, his voice like velvet. "I like the sound of my name on your lips when you beg me. Do it again"

His fingers curled inside me, thrusting in and out, his thumb circling my clit. I moaned, saying his name over and over again and bucking my hips to match his rhythm. I was close. So close.

"Come for me, sweetheart," Andras growled the command as he sucked my clit into his mouth.

I cried out, the orgasm blasting through me. He gripped my thigh, thrusting his tongue inside me as I clamped down around his fingers and my legs shook.

Andras slid his fingers out of my pussy and sucked them into his mouth, making my face heat. "Delicious, just like angel cake."

I laughed and blushed like the virgin I most definitely wasn't, then nearly jumped out of my skin at the knock on my door.

"Five minutes, Sara!" the stage manager called out.

Andras stood, adjusted my dress, and dropped a gentle kiss on my lips. "I look forward to more time spent between your thighs, Sara Braun."

He stepped out of the room, leaving me reeling from the orgasm he finally took from my body.

I quickly reapplied my burgundy lipstick and powdered my face. I spritzed cucumber water down my throat to combat dry mouth. Then, I added the final prop, a pair of devil horns. I smirked to myself, and butterflies filled my belly at the thought of the four monsters waiting for me.

I stepped up to the curtain, giving the manager a thumbs up. There were three musicians on stage with me and no backtracks. This performance would be acoustic. My favorite vintage mic stood at center stage under a dark-purple spotlight. A fog machine produced wisps of gray smoke that coated the stage. I stepped out, gliding up to the mic. The crowd hushed, already mesmerized by the performance as the accompanists began to play. The music touched my soul, and I swayed to the sounds before I began to sing "I Put a Spell on You."

I channeled my inner Nina Simone and Annie Lennox as I sang, following the riffs of the musicians with my own voice. I loved the soul and blues both women brought to the song and I poured my heart into the words.

I finished out the song, and a heavy silence settled before the crowd erupted, clapping and whistling. I dipped slightly, as much as the dress would let me, waving and smiling at the people in the crowd. Shouts of encore caught my ears, but I wasn't prepared for anything else tonight, and my voice needed a break. The musicians began to play some instrumental tunes from the blues era. I waved and bowed, turning to go backstage.

"Sara!" A voice I recognized shouted my name.

Dev stood at the edge of the stage, near the stairs. He held out a hand, and I took it, letting him guide me down and through the crowd. I threaded my arm through his as he led me back to the table. I locked eyes with Tibby for all of three seconds. Enough to see her nod. My new gear must be in my dressing room by now.

Dev dropped my arm and pressed his hand to my back, his fingers brushing against my bare skin, as we approached the table. Ty wrapped his arm around my waist and pulled me down to perch on his knee. His fingers traced down my spine, and he leaned forward, trailing kisses across my shoulders.

"That was beautiful, little vixen," he murmured against my skin. "And you're keeping those horns for later."

Levi winked at me, his eyes dragging down my body hungrily. "Our very own siren, come to sing us all into submission."

I laughed. "Does that mean I'll get all four of you on your knees tonight?" I turned my gaze to Andras, and he smirked.

"Fuck, you even got the boss whipped already." Levi grinned, shoving Andras, who scowled but said nothing. "Where did you come from, *diabla*?"

I shrugged. "I was born of pain and suffering and very few moments of happiness, just like everyone else, I suppose."

"You're nothing like everyone else, beautiful," Dev countered, and I turned to him, catching his pretty eyes. Maybe he was coming around to the idea of me sleeping with the others. His face softened as he smiled, and my insides melted a little. His eyes were still guarded, but I had hope.

"Agreed," Andras added.

A waiter dropped off a bottle of champagne and five glasses

at our table, and Dev poured and passed them out.

Andras raised his glass first. "To my brothers. And the siren who's captivated us all."

My blood began to sing with emotion as the others saluted and drank the bubbly liquid. I sipped my drink, feeling dazed and powerful all at once. These feelings were foreign, a light-heartedness I didn't know my soul was still capable of. Even with Tibby, as much as I trusted her, there was still a barrier. There was always a barrier. After losing everyone I cared about, I couldn't drop that final wall. I didn't want to feel all those feelings if I cared so much for someone again only to lose them.

I wouldn't deny something was shifting with the Princes, but for now, lust was the only feeling I was willing to name. And yet, the thought of killing any of them was starting to become…uncomfortable. I gulped down more champagne and let Levi refill my glass. We quickly polished off the bottle, and Andras stood, commanding our attention.

"Time to go," he announced with authority and offered his hand to help me stand.

I ignored his hand and pouted. "Why are we leaving?"

Andras scanned the room, his lips tight. "Because, sweet-heart. If I have to watch one more male in this room undress you with his eyes, I'm going to burn this entire club to the ground with everyone in it."

"Oh, let's do that anyway." Levi grinned, rubbing his hands together.

I swatted him playfully. "No! I like this club."

Ty wrapped an arm around my waist from behind, bringing his mouth to my ear. "I can build you a new club, pet. One where you're the star."

"And let me guess, no one else is allowed in?" I rolled my eyes, and Ty nipped my ear with his teeth.

Dev smirked at my comment, but said nothing.

"As I thought. No thanks. I like singing for a real audience." I elbowed Ty in the gut but he refused to let me go. "Don't smother me, assholes. Or I might just disappear."

Levi shrugged and stood next to Andras. He crossed his arms and looked down at me with hunger in his eyes. "You could try. But we'd find you. We've got your scent now, Sara Braun. There's no escaping."

His words made my insides flutter, but I rolled my eyes again as if I was unaffected. "I need to change out of this costume if we're leaving."

Ty pinched my ass, making me jump.. "No, leave this on, pet. I want to peel it off you later."

The idea was incredibly appealing, but I shoved him away. "No! This is brand new and you monsters will ruin it."

"As if Andras won't buy you a thousand more dresses," Dev scoffed, and I grimaced.

"I don't want a thousand more dresses. I'm not your barbie doll or your whore. I bought this for me, and you're not fucking ruining it."

My fists balled as I glared at them. I backed away as Andras stepped toward me.

"We won't ruin your pretty dress, angel. And don't you ever call yourself a whore in my presence again. Only we are allowed to do so when your pretty cunt is milking our cocks. Grab whatever you need from your dressing room, but leave the gown on." His words were more than a command, and I could see in his face any argument would be futile.

I spun on my heels and flipped them off, ignoring the heat building between my thighs at his filthy words. Levi's loud laughter rumbled as I walked away. I was honestly surprised when none of them followed. I hurried into the room and locked the door. I scanned the vanity and found a small backpack that wasn't in here before. There was an earpiece in the front pocket, and I shoved it in.

"Zenith?"

"Nova." Tibby's voice was clipped.

"What's wrong?" I frowned. She was never short with me.

The noise of the club around her drifted through the ear piece.

"Everything. Our plans are so fucked." Her voice quivered with anger I'd only heard from her once or twice in the years we'd been friends.

"Why?"

"Because, *pet*," Tibby snarled the word, making me flinch. "Those men are targets, not fuckbuddies. What the hell are you doing?"

I crossed my arms, feeling defensive. "I know they're targets. But it's not that simple anymore. Getting to know them…it's not…they're like brothers. They care about each other more than anything. More than the stupid cult. They care about me too."

"Are you serious? So you care more about them and their new feelings for you than *you* care for *your* sisters?"

She might as well slap me across the face for the sting of her words. "Tib…Zenith. I-I don't know what to say."

She huffed in irritation. "Yeah. Me either."

This wasn't right. Tibby was never this short and harsh with me. "What's really going on? You're not telling me something."

Tibby sighed, and I heard a faint sniff. Was she trying not to cry? "My mother is dead. Self-inflicted, supposedly. And my stepdad woke up from his coma and he's now in the wind."

I sighed, running my hands through my hair. "Fuck. I'm sorry, Zenith."

This was all wrong. Her stepdad had been in a coma for months, and the doctors said nothing about him waking up. Tibby kept tabs on him at all times.

"Yeah." She sniffed, and I could hear the pent up emotions in her voice. "She was a terrible mother, but it still sucks. I have to find him, Nova."

"And we will."

"When? I want him dead now. I should have killed him years ago."

I paced my dressing room, thinking. "Maybe we can."

The noises faded as Tibby left the club. Wind whistled down the earpiece.

"How?"

"What if we could make him look like an informant and leave clues for the Princes to find, make them go after your stepdad." I stopped pacing and waited for her response. "He was on that list, remember? Let's use that."

Tibby paused for a moment. "No."

I froze at her blunt refusal. "No?"

"This was supposed to be mine. Mine and yours, everything is about the fucking Princes, and I just want us to do this. I need you, Nova."

I slumped onto the chaise in my dressing room. Where was this coming from? "You have me, Zenith. Always."

"Do I?" Her voice shook with emotion. Tibby wasn't much more emotional than I was, and this display was unnerving. I was failing my only friend.

"Yes," I growled. "Fuck the guys, Zenith. I'm coming over."

Tibby's laugh was hollow. "How?"

I started stripping, shoving the dress in the backpack and pulling on a pair of leggings and a black sweater. I tucked my hair up into a long, brown wig.

"Your lack of confidence in me is offensive. The guys might be monsters, but I'm a mother fucking assassin."

Tibby snorted. "What do you need from me?"

"Just get to the apartment. I'll meet you there."

"Already gone. Peace out, Nova."

I shrugged into the extra pair of army boots I had tucked under my vanity. I strapped on the backpack and checked the peephole. There was no one in the hall. No sign of the guys.

Tibby was right. I was getting sucked into their mind games and forgetting about what really mattered. Tibby lost her only family, and mine could still be alive. It was time for the next phase of our plan. I slipped into the hall. There was a fire alarm just outside my door, and the chaos would give me enough time to run. I flung myself out of the exit that led to the alley and ran like hell, staying in the shadows of other buildings.

The closest train station was only a block away, and the crowds would provide more coverage. I moved swiftly down the stairs and slipped onto a redline train just before the doors closed. Ty had found me so quickly before, and I still wasn't entirely sure what happened before he knocked me out and I woke up tied to the bed. I kept my eyes peeled for a hulking monster man covered in tattoos, but none appeared as the train shoved off.

The train was quiet, since it was so late on a weeknight, and I paced the car, keeping my eyes and ears alert. My earpiece was quiet, and Tibby hadn't checked in yet. I tried to remain calm, she could be offline for any number of reasons. The train stopped at Andrew Square, and I bolted out, running full speed to our apartment. My lungs burned as an awful feeling crept into my chest. I pulled my keycard from the backpack and slammed it into the front door, ripping it open and taking the stairs two at a time.

I typed in our code and shoved open the apartment door. "Tibby?"

My chest heaved, sucking down oxygen as my brain whirled. The apartment was dark. She wasn't here. No. She was fine, she was not hurt. I crossed the room, wondering if I should go back out there and look for her. The door opened and within moments I had a gun pointed at the intruder.

Tibby walked in, her eyes wide. "Holy shit," she breathed. "You scared the fuck out of me."

I dropped the gun and ran to her, wrapping my arms around her middle. "Me? Are you freaking kidding? I thought something happened to you. How did I beat you here?"

She hugged me back awkwardly before letting go and shutting the door. She shrugged and made a beeline for the kitchen, grabbing two water bottles. She tossed one to me and

I caught it.

"Well, the way you look, I'm surprised you didn't sprout wings and fly here."

I laughed, taking a long drink of the icy cold water. "Yeah well, Ty caught me so easily last time. Figured I'd do better."

"Well, you made it." She smiled, drinking down her water. "Now what?"

I made the right choice coming here. Getting away from the Princes was the right decision. The lust-filled fog was lifting.

"Now we dig deeper to find your stepdad. You're smarter than him ten times over, Tibby. I know you can find him." I turned to her, needing her to see the truth of that on my face.

She nodded but said nothing.

"Then we will get back to my hit list and we'll find my father and sister together. Any updates or movements at Vespertine Hall?"

Tibby shook her head. "Not that I can tell. A few lackeys coming and going, but no sign of the founders. And no weird stuff being transported out."

I nodded. "That's good news, I guess. I say we hit it this weekend. I'm ready to see it burn."

"What about the Princes?" Tibby asked, cocking her head and assessing me.

She had every right, considering I spent the last twenty-four hours getting very intimate with the four Obscuritas royals.

I sighed. "I won't let them get in the way of our plans. The last two days have been…strange. I'm not going to pretend I didn't feel some kind of connection to them."

I wanted to tell her more but I was scared of the things

I felt and I didn't want her to be disappointed. Falling for your mark was an amateur move. But even when I was their prisoner, things shifted. Watching the four of them together in their home, I noticed a bond. No amount of digging up dirt could tell me what I witnessed. The Princes weren't just bound together by this cult, it was something on a deeper level. The buzz of adrenaline running through my blood made me shiver. I took another swig from my water bottle.

"And Tibby, I get the feeling there is a lot more going on between the four Princes and their fathers. Nothing outright was said, but little things…" I looked up to see her watching me with a strange expression. My cheeks heated as if she read my thoughts about the Princes, my carefully orchestrated mask unveiled. Everything was getting mixed up in my head. "Tibby, I'm sorry I got wrapped up in them. You are my one and only friend. I'll do better. I will."

She nodded, her eyes shining, but still said nothing. I tipped the water bottle for another swig, and she launched herself at me, swatting the bottle out of my hand and causing it to splash on the floor.

"What the fuck was that?" I stared at her in shock and swayed a little on my feet. *What was happening?*

Tibby's face flushed, and her eyes burned into mine. That horrible feeling was creeping back into my chest.

"It's drugged." She whispered the words, and my heart stopped.

Cold dread spread through my body, and my words started to slur. "Why is it drugged, Tibby?"

"Laszlo Blackbyrn. He's coming for you. He knows who

you are. He found me, Sara. I-I didn't know what to do. He had my mother. And now she's dead anyway."

I stumbled back, feeling like all the blood was rushing to my head. "You…sold me out?"

Tibby choked down a sob. "I'm so sorry, Sara. I just…I didn't want to die."

I nodded, feeling significantly woozy. "Call. Andras."

Her eyes widened. "What? Sara, he's a bad guy. He's one of them."

"Call. Him. Please." I stumbled to the floor, my legs going numb.

I couldn't think right. Tibby. She was supposed to be my friend. My vision blurred as she scrambled for her phone. I heard her snapping at someone to hurry. My eyelids drooped, and my tongue felt thick in my mouth. Tibby's face swam in front of me. *Was I lying down?*

"He's coming, Sara. I'm so sorry."

I felt my body waking up before my mind could comprehend what happened. My limbs twitched, but my brain wasn't right. Everything was foggy. I had little flashes of memory. The wind whipping through my hair and…wings? It was the second time I had the strangest sensation of flying. I groaned loudly as my head pounded.

"Open your eyes, sweetheart," Andras commanded. His voice was barely a whisper, but it was more terrifying than if he'd shouted at me.

I slowly cracked open my eyes. Levi and Dev stood behind Andras, their arms crossed and faces furious. Andras wore his mask of cold indifference, but his eyes were alight with icy hot fire. My brain finally registered where I was: Andras's bedroom. And, once again, I was handcuffed to the bed. Only this time, my ankles were tied down as well. I was completely immobilized but I wasn't afraid. Not for myself, anyway.

"What happened?" I croaked, my throat dry as desert dust.

Andras arched an eyebrow at my quiet command. "You were drugged."

"Where is Tibby?" I demanded a little louder.

"Better question," Levi cut in, his easy smiles all but vanished, the daemon he kept locked down leaching out. "Where is Ty?"

My eyes widened, and I turned back to Andras, pleading. "Please don't hurt her."

Levi snorted. "Too late."

I choked out a sob. "Andras. Please don't. Please don't kill her. It wasn't her fault."

"She sold you out!" Levi exploded, his hands balled in fists as his blue eyes raged.

"What the fuck is going on, Sara?" Dev stalked closer to the bed and crossed his arms. He didn't seem as surprised, or even as angry as the others were, despite his words.

I sighed, closing my eyes. So Tibby hadn't told them everything yet. But she was alone with Ty. This was a fucking mess. I opened my eyes and stared back at Andras.

"I will tell you everything. Whatever you want. Please don't kill my only friend."

Andras watched me, assessing. Emotions warred behind his calm demeanor. He walked calmly around the bed, staring down at me.

"Tell us now," Levi growled, his fist slammed into the wooden bedframe, cracking it.

"Levi," Andras snapped. "Bring Sara to the basement."

CHAPTER TWENTY

Typhon

I pulled the soaked rag from the girl's face, and she coughed up water, her face blotchy as she sucked down oxygen. It was mildly impressive how much torture she could take. The British girl, Tibby or whatever, barely told us anything, and I'd had her locked up for a good eight hours. I was going easier on her than most because I knew Sara had a soft spot for her. And she did bring our girl back to us, after all.

Our girl. Adrenaline rushed through my veins as I thought about what she'd done. Sara left us. Ran away. Again. At first it was funny, and the excitement of the chase heated my blood, but then I lost her scent at the train station. I couldn't find her, and after about thirty minutes, the game took a sinister turn. When Andras got the call from some girl screaming about his father coming for Sara, time stopped and I nearly fell out of the sky.

Andras gave us an address, and Levi and I flew through the clouds to the apartment near Carson Beach. Levi broke the door down and almost killed the hysterical girl when he saw Sara passed out on the floor. I scooped up our pretty pet and placed her in Levi's arms, the only thing I could think to do to calm him down. Sara was an anchor for him, something precious to focus on instead of the daemon snarling inside his mind. I didn't trust him not to rip the pink-haired girl in half. Though, I did enjoy punching her in the face and knocking her out before we stole away into the night. The hair triggered several memories too. Tibby was at Noircoeur every night Sara performed. I was so wrapped up in my little vixen's presence, I didn't notice the sneaky little pixie hiding in plain sight.

Apparently, Laszlo Blackbyrn got to Tibby, blackmailing her to get to Sara. *But why?* Tibby wouldn't say more than that. The girl was tough and not even seeing her own blood dripping down her wrists would make her talk. I patched up the wounds before she could bleed to death, though. Sara would thank me for my thoughtfulness, I'm sure.

Heavy footsteps announced their presence before the door opened. Sara's heart beat rapidly, and I turned as she gasped at the sight her friend chained to the wall. The relief that filled me at seeing her warred with my need to strangle her for leaving us again. Levi set her on her feet, her wrists still cuffed together in front of her body.

She's fine, brother. She heals fast, Levi's words sounded in my head.

Without actually speaking, my brothers and I collectively dropped our barriers when we brought Sara and her friend back to The Towne House. The four of us needed to communicate discreetly while we interrogated the pink-haired spy. And sharing our thoughts on the situation was necessary. Dev didn't fully drop his mental shields because he's been a little prick recently, but he let us in enough to communicate.

Sara ran toward Tibby, and I caught her roughly around her pretty little throat. My thumb brushed against her racing pulse, and I tilted her head back, cutting off her oxygen as I stared her down. Her aquamarine eyes burned with defiance as she glared back at me.

"We need her to be coherent enough for questioning, Typhon," Andras snapped. "Let her go."

I snarled, dropping Sara. She doubled over, sucking in air, then quickly straightened and punched me square in the mouth with her cuffed fists. I was too shocked to make a sound for all of ten seconds before I laughed from deep in my chest, licking the blood from my busted lip. My dick hardened instantly for my naughty pet.

"If you wanted to play, pet, you just had to ask," I teased her, my daemon shining through my eyes enough to make a normal human piss themselves.

She glared at me, and I could see the fire inside her writhing, itching for a fight. I wished she would. Instead, she turned her back and went to her friend.

Tibby's voice was hoarse as she mumbled a few words in Sara's ear.

I stepped toward them. "Now, now. No more secrets or I'll have to get the rest of my toys out."

I released Sara from the handcuffs, rubbing my thumb over her reddened knuckles. The marks on her hands pissed me off. No one was allowed to cause her harm, not even herself.

I brushed the sweaty strands of hair from her face, and she attempted to bite my fingers. "I'm going to have to punish you for hitting me, pet. You hurt your hand, and I'm the only one allowed to give you pain."

Sara rolled her eyes at me and stepped in front of her friend protectively. "Fuck off, monster man."

Andras cleared his throat. "Now, *Sara*, you've seen your backstabbing friend. She's clearly alive. Speak plainly. If you lie, we will know, and Typhon will hurt your traitorous accomplice."

"Let her down," Sara demanded.

Andras crossed his arms, taking a seat in a metal folding chair. "No."

Sara crossed her own arms, glaring at him, and fuck if I didn't want to tie her up and fuck the brat right out of her. I prowled toward her, tracing my fingers down her throat.

She swatted me away, and I chuckled. "Let me tie her up, brother. She'd like it."

Sara's fist slammed into my gut, and I groaned, taking the pain and relishing it. I dodged her second punch, slipping behind her and bringing my knife to her throat while my free hand wrapped around her chest, pinning down her arms. She stiffened, but only for a moment. Her hand reached back and squeezed my balls, and my knife slid away enough for her to spin out of my grasp. I licked my lips, eyeing the line of blood on her pretty neck where the knife cut her.

Levi snuck up behind her and grabbed her wrists, shoving her arms to her sides. She reared back, headbutting him in the nose and dancing away when his grip eased. She ran toward her friend, ready to rip the chains from the walls, when in a blur of shadow, Andras shoved her to the wall, a lethal-looking blade resting over her heart.

Dev let out a strangled cry as the tip of the blade pierced her shirt and Sara hissed. I could feel Andras's daemon rearing up, and I rested a hand on his shoulder, bringing him back to us.

Take a breath, Andras.

"Don't worry, brother." I chuckled, keeping my voice light, trying to calm his daemon. "This is just foreplay. Isn't it, pet?" I glared at Sara, daring her to move as her eyes darted between mine and the devil with a knife to her heart.

"My name is Seraphina Nuriela Voldis Bronwen," she whispered.

Her sea glass eyes shined as she said the name. Was her skin glowing? The light disappeared so quickly, I wasn't sure if I imagined it.

"The missing daughter," Andras stated, his voice deadly calm. "And the skeleton key you were wearing?"

"My father gave it to me before he left me behind. Said it protected my mother's family's secrets. I came here for them. I know The Obscuritas have my father and my sister."

"Sara..." Dev's voice was broken as he stared at the girl with wide eyes.

She ignored him, her gaze locked on Andras.

Andras nodded, confirming her accusations. "And what was your endgame, Seraphina?"

Sara swallowed, but her face remained a hard mask, so unlike the sassy smiles and delightfully violent looks she gave us. "I'm going to destroy them all. Everyone who played a part in murdering my sister, my mother. Every. Single. One."

I chuckled, leaning against the wall. "Well this is certainly an exciting twist of events."

Sara's eyes snapped to mine, and I grinned.

"Your endgame is not so different from ours."

"Typhon," Andras growled a warning.

He stared at our girl, uncertainty clouding his gaze. But I could sense her truth. I believed her.

I shrugged him off. "We're all keeping similar secrets, brother. It doesn't matter what she knows now. She's part of this. She has been from the beginning."

"No," Dev cut in, his voice shaking with emotion. "I don't give a fuck who she says she is. She is not part of this. Because we aren't doing this."

"That's not your decision to make, Devon." Andras pulled his blade back from Sara's heart, finally in control again.

Sara stepped toward him, unafraid, and her boldness had my dick twitching. More than a siren, Seraphina had angel's blood. Or Lumens, as they called themselves. The daemon in me ached to taste it. Would she taste like sunlight? I licked my lips and followed her movements like the predator I was.

Her eyes darted between the four of us, and she exhaled heavily. "At first...the plan was to take you all out. I wanted your father to suffer. I was going to kill you first. So he would know what it felt like to have his family ripped away. But...I don't know if I can do that anymore."

Sara's gaze shifted downward, and Andras used the blade to tip her chin back up to face him.

"And why is that, sweetheart?" Andras whispered like a viper stalking its prey.

"Because," she whispered, her words so quiet, I strained to hear them. I could feel the others holding their breaths as we waited for her answer. "I...want you. All of you. I don't know what's happening. But I can't pretend anymore. I don't want to pretend anymore."

Andras dropped his arm, setting the blade on the table. "Unchain the girl. Lock her in the holding cell with food and water."

"She's not going to hurt any of you," Sara protested as Andras walked toward the door.

He stopped, turning his head to the side without looking back. "I know that, sweetheart. I haven't forgiven her for hurting you."

He quickly left the room. Dev followed after him, and Sara frowned at their backs.

I knew the stubborn prick would come around, though. He was in love with her and just too afraid to admit it. Levi shuffled over to the Brit and unhooked her chains. Tibby's legs gave out, so he carried her gently to an adjoining room. He set her on the bed before locking the steel door behind him.

Levi glanced at Sara and cocked his head, eyeing her like a hungry beast. "I'll grab her some food."

"Thank you," Sara whispered with a small smile.

Levi's lips turned up slightly, and he winked. He wasn't the type to hold grudges and he'd move past this bump in the road, as would the others. I was already over it. Lumen or not, my blood burned for this woman.

I strode toward her, and she looked up, ready to speak, then gasped as my hands cupped her face and I crushed my lips to hers. Her soft mouth parted in submission, and I growled, twisting my tongue with hers in a possessive kiss. She moaned, folding her arms behind my neck and pulling me down to her. I lifted her off the ground, and she wrapped her legs around my waist. Sara's body melted into mine, and I never wanted to let her go. She was a feral creature, sent down from another world to torment me. I shoved her against the wall, and her toned thighs squeezed my waist. I pulled my tongue from her mouth and trailed kisses down her neck, licking up the blood from the cut I'd given her. My dick throbbed at the taste of her, and my blood burned at the electricity shooting through my veins.

"Fuck, pet," I moaned, unable to hold back as my daemon shivered with need. "Just as I thought. You taste like heaven, like sunlight. I could suck the blood right out of you."

Sara coughed out a laugh between her moans, her hands in my hair pulling hard enough to sting. "You're such a monster."

"More than you know." I chuckled. "Although, I suspect you'll be finding out all our secrets soon."

She pulled back, her chest heaving. "Andras doesn't trust me."

Her eyes searched my face as she spoke. They were hypnotic, an endless sea of blue and green.

I shook my head. "The problem isn't that he doesn't trust you, but that he does. You've got him wrapped around your little finger, pet. Just like the rest of us. And it scares him."

"It doesn't scare you?" She nipped at my bottom lip, and I growled.

"I told you before, if you were to be my death, so be it." I fisted a hand in her hair, and she cried out as I tugged it back sharply, exposing her throat to me. "But if you ever, *ever*, run away from me again, little vixen. I will make it hurt."

Sara grinned, and her eyes lit with desire. "Give me your worst, monster man."

I chuckled, ready to devour her, just as Levi walked into the room with a tray of food. He arched an eyebrow and turned away, unlocking the steel door and delivering the sustenance to our prisoner. Sara unwrapped her legs and dropped to the floor, attempting to leave me behind, but I hounded after her. Levi came back out and locked the door.

"Is she…alright?" Sara asked, standing on her tiptoes to try to see her friend through the one small window.

Levi nodded, his expression distant. "She's sleeping. She'll survive."

Sara nodded, stepping into his personal space. Levi held still, tracking her every move, and I rolled my eyes. "Get over yourself, brother. She's not going to run."

Levi snarled at me even as he stared at our girl, his eyes searching. "Why did you leave the club?"

I stilled, waiting for her answer. He wasn't the only one pissed off about that.

Sara shrugged and refused to look either of us in the eye. "I just…I—" she stammered, before being interrupted.

"I made her feel guilty." The pink-haired girl's face peaked through the slot in the door, her voice still hoarse from my hours of torture time.

Sara shook her head in defiance. "No, it was my choice to go."

"No, Sara. You weren't even thinking about it. I saw you at the club. The way you were with them, the way they hung on your every move. Like some invisible string connected you all. And you *smiled*, Sara, a real smile." Tibby's voice quieted as she cried. "My head was all screwed up, but I couldn't take that from you."

I stared at Sara. Seraphina. My gorgeous little vixen. The hurt from Tibby's betrayal was plain to see on her face. Anger built inside me as I stared at her. It was probably a good thing the girl was locked behind a steel door. Tears welled in Sara's eyes as she pressed her face to see her friend through the small window.

"Is your mom really dead, Tibby?" Sara whispered.

The girl nodded. "I'm not sure of anything anymore. But I think The Obscuritas are behind it."

I stepped closer, resting my hand on Sara's shoulder. "Why do you think that?"

"Because the news of it happening just appeared on my computer. I tried to trace the IP but there was nothing. Just a one-off article popping up in my feed. I think they did it to fuck with me. Laszlo contacted me right after. And my memories… they're fucked up. Like I can't place them all in the right order."

Interesting. I sent the words to Levi. Our faces remained unbothered. *You think Laszlo is using mind control on her?*

Levi frowned. *Possibly. We need to track the last few months of Tibby's movements. See if we can find out how she actually connected with Laszlo. Something is definitely off.*

Sara slipped her fingers through the window. "I'm so sorry, Tibby. I'm sorry I got you into all this."

Tibby shook her head. "I'm the one who should be sorry. You're the only person I really care about, and I fucked that up too."

"I forgive you, Tibby. And those fuckers will pay for what they did to you." Sara's voice was low and menacing, and I fucking loved it. Our murderous little angel.

But I wasn't sorry for torturing the traitor. She almost cost me my girl. Andras would look into her connections with his father. Sara might be willing to believe Tibby, but I wasn't.

Sara turned to me, her eyes pleading. "Please. Does she have to stay in here? It's just—"

Andras's voice boomed over the intercom. "Bring Seraphina upstairs. Now. Leave the Brit."

Sara snarled, turning to her friend. "I'll be back, Tibby. I won't let them keep you down here forever."

The girl sighed. She looked exhausted. "It's alright. I'm going to eat and rest." She glanced toward me. "The big guy really took it out of me."

Damn, right. I grinned as Sara turned and swung her fist directly into my junk. My knees buckled, and I fell to the floor, cupping my balls when her fist snapped out again, busting open my lip.

I groaned. "How can someone so tiny cause so much damage?"

Sara grinned, and my eyes narrowed on my prey.

"Oh fuck." Levi laughed, scooping Sara over his shoulder and bolting for the stairs.

CHAPTER TWENTY-ONE

Sara

"Run faster, Levi!" I yelled out as he threw me over his shoulder and ran like the house was on fire. "Damn, being a firefighter is really working for you right now."

Levi smacked my ass with a laugh. I heard Ty roaring from the basement as Levi took the stairs two at a time.

"You better fucking run, pet!" Ty roared, and I was almost certain he sounded closer.

I smacked Levi's ass as he barreled up the stairs. "Yah, horsey, yah!'

Levi shouted a laugh. "Oh you're going to pay for that later, *diabla*."

We shot out onto the main level where Andras was sitting at the dining table, sipping vodka on ice. Levi whipped by him as Andras arched an eyebrow like a snob. I stuck out my tongue at him and grinned when his mouth twitched with a smile. The breath whooshed out of me as Levi tossed me on the couch, and I screamed when he pounced on top of me, burying me into the plush cushions beneath him. He nuzzled into my hair, biting my neck as his hands roamed down my waist. My skin heated, and I arched into his rough touches, threading my fingers in his shaggy brown locks.

"Don't ever do that again, babe. Ever," he whispered into my ear and bit down on my neck, marking me as his.

My skin tingled, and my blood began to sing.

"I won't," I whispered back, wrapping my arms around his neck, knowing it was true. Every minute I spent with the Princes made me realize how wrong it felt running away from them.

"Come out, come out, wherever you are, little pet," Ty growled, his voice rumbling like an angry lion. He rounded the corner, his eyes narrowing. I flipped him off and he snarled. "I'm going to whip your plump little ass raw, pet."

I threaded my fingers in Levi's lush, wavy hair and tugged hard. "Save me from the beast, fireman!"

Levi's laugh turned into a moan, and his breath tickled my skin. "What will you give me in return?"

He smelled like a lit match, and I craved the fire smoldering beneath the surface. I smacked his arm playfully. "You're supposed to be a prince, saving your princess."

"I'm no white knight, *diabla*," Levi whispered, his eyes heating with wicked intentions as he ground his hips into mine and pinned me more firmly beneath him.

"Fine." I huffed at him even as my body responded like a horny teenager. "One massage with a happy ending?"

Levi chuckled. "Deal."

Ty hovered above us over the couch. "Come out, pet. He can't save you now."

I smirked as Levi cocked his head, keeping me safe beneath him. "Sorry, brother. I really want to fuck her later so for now, you'll have to go through me."

"I'm swooning," I deadpanned.

Ty's eyes narrowed, and I screamed as he prepared to rip us off the couch, but Andras had to step in and ruin our fun.

"Enough," he snapped. "We have things to discuss."

I wiggled, and Levi's hard length pressed into my stomach. "Put your hose away, fireman."

Levi barked a laugh, leaning back and pulling me with him to sit in his lap.

I turned to Andras with narrowed eyes. "Yes, we do have things to discuss, like letting my friend out of her cell. It's your father who's to blame."

"For now, she stays in the basement." Andras sipped his drink, his stern expression saying that was his final word on the matter.

"Well, fuck that." I tried to shove off Levi, but he quickly snatched my waist, pulling me back and clamping a hand over my mouth.

"Hush. Daddy's talking." Levi chuckled.

His free hand reached under my sweater and massaged my breasts, and I yelped as he pinched my nipples through my lacy bra. Andras's lips twitched in amusement, his eyes zeroing in on Levi's roaming hands. Ty came around the couch and sat next to us. His rough hands gripped my thighs, and I started to reach for his cock.

"Levi, brother, if you don't stop groping her tits and making her moan, this conversation is going to turn into a fuckfest." Ty chuckled darkly.

Levi laughed, tugging my sweater off my shoulders and trailing kisses along my neck. "And that's a problem, why? I'm bored with this conversation anyway."

My skin felt so alive everywhere he touched me, and heat pooled between my thighs. I squirmed, needing friction to ease the tension building inside me. Would it always be like this? Would my body always react to these men like it does now? Or would the lust fade away over time? I hoped not. Being with them made me feel alive, even more than when I sang. It was a heady feeling, and I wanted to drown in it.

"Sweetheart." Andras's voice was filled with amusement.

I snapped open my eyes and found four sets of horny devils eyeing me like I was their next meal.

"Whatever fantasy is playing out in your mind, we're more than happy to fulfill it."

Levi's hand drifted between my thighs, cupping my pussy. "Fuck, babe. I can feel how wet you are through your leggings."

"What are you thinking about, angel?" Andras leaned forward, his eyes raking over my body.

I blushed, and Ty grinned like the Cheshire Cat.

"I like it when you blush, pet. So innocent. So corruptible."

I laughed. "I'm hardly innocent. It's just a lot for a girl to take in; you four prowling like wolves on the hunt."

"And you will always be the prey, pet," Ty whispered, brushing his thumb across my bottom lip.

I sucked it into my mouth, grinding my hips against Levi's hand as he stroked my pussy through my clothes.

"I was thinking about all of you," I whispered after releasing Ty's thumb from my mouth. "I've never felt like this…never even had—"

"Had what?" Dev asked, his eyes eager and needy, like my next words held the answers he needed to hear.

I smiled softly, glad he was talking to me again, particularly while two of his brothers teased me with fingers and lips.

I laughed, slightly embarrassed and…nervous? "Confession time. Before any of you, I always faked it with partners and I only ever got real release from toys. My first orgasm with a guy was with Dev. And then you three."

Levi grinned like a kid gawking at all the presents on Christmas morning. "Damn, Dev! I'm jealous you got the first one. Well done, brother."

"Is that true, angel?" Andras asked, cocking his head. "You've only had orgasms with the four of us?"

I nodded, shrugging. "Yeah. What's that about?"

Ty grabbed my hips and pulled me into his lap, away from Levi. I straddled his thighs and felt the press of his hard-on through his sweatpants. He fisted my hair and tugged me close, devouring my lips with his own. I leaned into the kiss, grinding my hips into his cock and moaning, the friction on my sensitive clit driving me insane.

"Ty, let her go." Andras commanded casually, and I broke the kiss to look at him.

"Why?" I panted, ready for more.

Andras stood, stalking toward us with a daemon's grin. "Because I've decided your punishment for leaving."

I pouted. "What? You know it wasn't like that. You heard what happened."

Andras nodded, unaffected. "Yes, and you still made the choice to run away instead of telling us the truth."

I scoffed at him, sliding out of Ty's lap and placing my hands on my hips as I stood. "It's not like *you* are Mr. Open

Book, Andras. All four of you have secrets too."

"If you don't accept the punishment, sweetheart, it's going to hurt so much more," Andras purred.

I shivered, debating whether or not I wanted to push him on this. I crossed my arms. "Fine. What's the punishment?"

"The punishment is two-fold. First, we're going hunting." Andras left the room without another word.

I turned to the others, confused. "Hunting?"

Ty grinned, his biceps bulging as he crossed his arms and towered over me. "Yes, pet. But don't worry, you're not the prey this time. My father is. Well, one of his men."

Whatever I expected him to say, that was not it. We were hunting one of The Obscuritas members? My mind spun as Levi grabbed my hand and tugged me after Andras. Dev said nothing as he followed behind with Ty. We marched in silence to the garage. The Princes pulled on their winter coats and grabbed several weapons from a locker just beside the door. Andras held out my leather jacket, and I slipped my arms into the sleeves.

"So what exactly is going to happen on this hunt?" I asked, unable to keep silent any longer.

Andras gazed into my eyes for several moments, his expression unreadable. He pulled out a cell phone, and I realized instantly it was mine.

"You received several messages from Ms. Audrey Kingston."

I frowned. "She's in my class. Why is she messaging me?"

I reached for the phone, but Andras snatched it away like an asshole.

"She messaged you asking for help." Andras gripped my arm and guided me to the Land Rover. "Apparently, her friend has hinted at some trouble with a teacher, and now the friend has gone missing."

"I don't understand. Why did she message me?"

Audrey and I only spoke a handful of times. She seemed nice enough in class, and we swapped numbers, but nothing I'd said led me to think she would contact me for help, especially for something like this.

Andras opened my phone and pulled up a screen. It irritated me beyond belief that he was looking through my messages, but there was nothing incriminating for him to find on that phone. He handed over the cell, and I quickly read the first message.

Audrey

I don't know why I'm asking you for help, you just seem like someone who can make things happen. The way you stand up to Andras in class and snap back. No one has ever done that. I don't know who else to ask.

I smirked, and Andras rolled his eyes, snatching the phone out of my hand.

"Audrey's family is not part of The Obscuritas, but my father has hinted at recruiting them. Her friend is in trouble and potentially being held captive by her teacher. The psychology professor in question is a member. And the missing girl, her name is Danielle Portman. She has no family in the area and got into Lesley College on grants. She is, well…"

"An easy target." Ty finished his sentence with a grim face.

He jumped into the driver's seat, and Andras helped me into the back. Levi and Dev followed, smashing me into the middle seat as Andras walked around to the front passenger side.

"Why would you guys give a shit about this girl? Especially when the professor is a member of your little cult." My tone was mocking, but I was genuinely curious.

Andras turned his body, and his furious eyes caught me off guard. "I do not, nor will I ever, support the torture and kidnapping of innocent men, women, or children."

His words forced memories of my sister and mother scream-ing as they died during that horrible ritual, and I snarled at him.

"Unless it benefits you, right? My mother and sister died for your fucking cult!"

"Sara…" Levi's quiet voice felt too loud in the dead silence after my outburst. He tried to take my hand, but I snatched it away.

Andras turned his back to us, and Ty drove out of the garage and into the daylight. The bright, cheery sun only angered me further. I wasn't paying attention to the roads as we sped through the city. Of course they had nothing to say to my outburst. How could they? The Obscuritas had no problem hurting people when it benefited them.

The rage was building inside me, and I needed to punch something. My skin felt hot and everywhere Levi's and Dev's bodies brushed against my own was torture. I bit into my tongue, drawing blood, just to keep from shouting.

Ty's eyes snapped to mine in the rearview mirror. "She's bleeding."

Levi snatched my chin in his hands and turned my face to his own. "Why are you hurting yourself?"

"Why do you care?" I sneered back.

His grip on my face tightened almost enough to bruise, and

I relished the feeling of pain. I needed it. My eyes burned as I held back tears for my continued failures to save my family.

Levi's dark-blue eyes softened as he stared back at me, his gaze piercing through the cage of ice wrapping around my heart.

"We were too young to understand what was going to happen that night. Too young and too broken down. The days leading up to that night, our fathers kept us apart. Starved us, tortured us. When it began, we were given drugs to slow our minds and bodies so we couldn't fight what was to come."

My mouth dried out as I listened to Levi's words. I didn't want to listen, didn't want to hear his side of the story, but it was impossible to turn away from him. I could see things from his point of view. A scared and confused teenage boy caught up in something so strange and violent. The others remained silent as he continued.

"When they brought the woman and the girl out, I knew something bad was about to happen, but I couldn't stop it." Levi swallowed, his eyes distant as he recalled the memory. "I will never forget the screams your sister made as she died."

Tears did fall from my eyes then. My vision blurred, and I sucked in a breath as I cried. Levi's rough hands cupped my cheeks as he brushed away the tears. He kissed my forehead with such care as the ache in my chest made me sob harder. Dev's hand squeezed my thigh, letting me know he was there too.

Andras continued the story. "When we woke the next day, everything had changed. We were not only powerful, but the four of us were connected, our minds linked. Our hearts were filled with fury at what our fathers had done. We vowed then that we would stop them."

"And why haven't you?" I whispered, unable to raise my voice as the emotions swirled inside me.

Levi brought his hands down and twined his fingers with my own. "Our fathers are more powerful than you can imagine and willing to destroy anyone who stands against them. Even their own sons."

Ty suddenly stopped the SUV, bringing the storytime to an end. "We're here. Let's go."

I brushed the salty tears from my face. I probably looked like shit, but for this situation, I didn't really care.

The neighborhood was obviously full of wealthy people. The homes were massive and spread out between perfectly manicured lawns. The professor's home was modern and dull, nothing cozy about it. I hated it. Ty stalked up to the front door and banged loudly. Andras came up the steps next and waited. A small window popped open in the wood door, and I tried to look around Ty's massive frame, but he kept me tucked behind him.

"Professor Lehmann," Andras spoke first, his tone clipped.

"Andras, ah…Mr. Blackburn. What a surprise," the man stuttered.

"Indeed. I have some news from my father," Andras lied, his voice even and professional.

"Oh of course. Come in." The professor stepped back to unlock the door.

As soon as he turned the handle, Ty shoved through and punched the man in the face. Blood spurted from his nose as he cried out in pain.

Levi and Dev remained protectively by my side as Ty

continued to beat the man until blood splashed all over the white, polished floors of the foyer. Andras crossed his arms and watched for several minutes before ordering Ty to stop.

Professor Lehmann coughed up blood and groaned, unable to move. He turned his head slightly to stare up at Andras, one eye swollen shut. "Why?"

Andras flicked an invisible piece of lint from his jacket and stared down at the man with disgust. "Because you deserve it. You're pathetic. Exactly the kind of trash my father would recruit, and the type of male I abhor."

Ty pulled out a blade, and before the piece of shit could say another word, the sharp knife was plunged into his heart. He was dead instantly.

I was glad of it, but still confused. "How do we find Danielle now?"

Ty wiped his blade clean on the dead professor's pants and turned to me with a grim face. "She's in the basement, locked in a meat refrigerator."

My mouth dropped open. "How do you know that?"

Levi threaded his fingers through mine and squeezed. "The night of the ritual, we gained abilities. One of them is reading minds."

My eyes nearly bugged out of my head, and my cheeks flushed. "You can read my mind?"

Ty grunted in frustration. "No, pet, we cannot. We think it's because of your Lumen blood. Daemons and lumens have many abilities and can also block out others more easily. Human minds are weaker."

I shook my head, absorbing this information. "I'm not

exactly a firm believer in all the daemons and lumens shit, but it's difficult to ignore. So, you needed my family or our lumen blood for your ritual?"

"Not our ritual, Sara," Dev cut in, his voice soft and his eyes sad.

I stared at him and thought of his father, who was one of them, but then murdered as well.

"So why does the stupid cult want me now?" I huffed.

My four daemons frowned, looking down.

Andras spoke first. "My father is always looking for ways to gain power and while he gained some through that ritual, he thirsts for more. And apparently it's you who can give him that."

I crossed my arms. "What about Michaela?"

Andras sighed and rubbed the back of his neck. I wanted to reach out and ease his stress for him.

Ty turned to Andras and spoke first. "Did you see that flash of memory before he died?"

Andras nodded, his concerned gaze meeting mine. "He's seen your sister. They were at some kind of cabin home."

My blood heated, and I rushed at Andras, smacking my fists against his chest. "Why did you kill him? He could've told us where she is! He could've hurt her!" I screamed, imagining the horrible things this sick fuck did to my baby sister.

He let me hit him again and again. He didn't fight me. Tears burned the backs of my eyes.

Strong arms wrapped around me from behind. Ty hugged me tightly, soothingly. I couldn't move. Andras stepped close and brushed the tears from my cheeks.

He held my face and forced me to look up at him. "He

never touched her, Seraphina. His memories were altered to forget about her. I assume my father used the professor to find her, but that's it. He never saw her again."

I whimpered in Ty's arms, the fight draining from my limbs. I wanted to hate them, to fight. But I believed him. Something deep in my soul trusted his words, and I couldn't ignore the feeling.

"*Belle femme*, I swear it." Andras caressed my cheek, his eyes searching mine. "Our fathers did not tell us about your sister being their prisoner. We only knew about your father. We were under the impression that he still searched for your sister."

I believed him. Something was shifting among the five of us, and with every secret revealed, my walls cracked further. The Princes were slipping past my defenses, drawing me out.

I nodded, accepting his words. "Alright. Fine. I think that's all I can handle right now. Let's go rescue Danielle and get the fuck out of this ugly ass house."

Andras nodded and turned, his face a mask as always. Ty followed him out of the room. Levi and Dev each clasped one of my hands and refused to let go.

I started to walk, but Dev stopped me.

"We don't need to go down there. Andras and Ty will bring her out. She's in rough shape." He swallowed and turned away from me as he spoke.

Blood pounded in my ears as rage filled my veins. "I wish the fucker was still alive so I could kill him slowly this time."

Levi squeezed my hand. "Me too."

We waited for them on the front porch. It only took a matter of minutes, and my heart ached for the broken, passed out girl wrapped in blankets in Ty's arms. Her straw-colored hair was dull and matted, but her face was unmarred. I imagined the rest of her body was not so lucky.

Andras clenched his jaw as he held the door open for Ty. He pulled out my phone and held it out. "Please let Audrey know her friend will be at St. Elizabeth's."

My fingers brushed against his as I took the phone. The connection between us hummed with so many emotions, some I didn't yet understand or want to acknowledge. I stared into his cold, handsome face. Andras might have worn his mask well, but I could feel the anguish rolling through him. This happened because of his father. I knew now Andras hated The Obscuritas Kings as much as I did.

His dark eyes were filled with unending fury, and in that moment, I loved him for it.

After we returned from our little hunting trip, Andras ordered me to shower. Alone, much to the disappointment of the others. I took my time, letting the scalding hot water wash away the yuck still clinging to my skin after being at the professor's house. It felt really good to save someone today. I told Audrey to keep me updated on Danielle's progress. The doctors told Andras she would survive, and her physical body would make a full recovery, at least. Levi and Dev waited in the car with me, because of course I wasn't allowed to go inside or be seen by anyone. The Obscuritas were everywhere. But Andras had connections at this particular hospital, and no one would alert Laszlo of the visit.

I stepped out of the shower and wrapped my clean self in the lush, navy robe Andras left for me. The bathroom door opened, and I looked up to see Dev holding out a glass of champagne.

"For you, my lady." Dev bowed with a smirk that brought out his dimples, and I nearly melted to the floor. He was so ridiculously gorgeous when he smiled.

I took the glass of champagne from him and stood on my tiptoes to kiss his cheek. "Thank you, kind sir."

Dev laughed. "I am anything but kind, but I will try for you, beautiful. Feeling refreshed?"

The champagne felt delicious as I sipped the bubbly liquid and nodded. "Very refreshed."

He turned toward the room and offered his arm. "Good. You'll need all your wits about you for what comes next."

Bees buzzed inside my stomach with excitement at his words. I was eager for a bit of fun after the emotional rollercoaster of the morning. Dev continued to tease me with hints of what was to come as he led me downstairs to the theater and gaming room.

Levi, Ty, and Andras stood around the bar, sipping various cocktails. They all turned when we entered the room. Three sets of eyes locked on my face, and I flushed with desire as we walked over to them.

"So, I suppose it's time for the second part of my punishment?" I teased, turning to Andras.

He smiled, and it was not the good kind. *Did he even have good smiles?* No, they were always wicked, and I think I liked it better that way.

"Bring her to the pool table, Ty." Andras gestured with his

glass in the direction of the table.

Levi and Dev followed behind as Ty scooped me over his shoulder, gripping my ass hard. His rough hand slid under my robe and up my leg. He dipped his thumb between my thighs and teased my bare pussy. I moaned and wiggled against the pressure of his hands on me.

"Do not let her come, Typhon," Andras ordered.

Ty laughed, moving his hand away, and I whimpered pitifully. My body was a bundle of nerves, and I desperately needed a release.

Ty dropped me onto wobbly legs and caged me in against the pool table. "Now what?"

"Remove her robe," Andras commanded, leaning against the wall like a smug bastard.

Dev watched as Levi and Ty stripped off my robe. My nipples hardened at the influx of cool air, and my pussy pulsed with need.

"So far I like where this is going." I smirked. I turned to Andras, and my face fell at the wicked delight in his eyes.

I realized they must be doing the mindreading thing, because without another word Ty lifted me up and shoved me on my back on top of the pool table. Dev and Levi came around with leather straps, pulling my hands and feet wide and tying them off to the legs of the pool table. I struggled against the bindings, but there was barely a foot of movement allowed in any direction. Andras came around the table, standing near my feet. His dark skin glistened in the afternoon sunlight shining through the room. His dark eyes captured mine. His large hand slid up my leg, caressing my thigh and giving me goosebumps with his gentle touches. I shivered and gasped as his finger dipped inside me, oh so slowly. I was close to begging.

"We're having a party tonight. And you will remain here, on this table, while we get ready for the event. You do not get to come again, until I say so." Andras continued to slide his finger in and out of my pussy, and I bucked my hips as far as I could move.

"We will bring you to that edge, over and over, as we please, but you will get no release, sweetheart. That is your punishment." Andras slid his finger out, and I nearly cried.

Ty chuckled, walking around the table. He leaned over my naked body and sucked my nipple into his mouth. I arched my back as his teeth grazed the sensitive skin. Fuck this was torture. He pulled away too soon, and I pouted.

I slumped back on the table. "Fuck all of you."

"You will, later, if you behave." Andras smirked.

I stuck out my tongue at him. "Not much I can do from here, is there? Do I even get to eat?"

"I've got something you can eat." Levi laughed, adjusting his sweatpants and making me grin. "Do we still get orgasms?"

Andras pondered that. "Yes. As long as Seraphina does not."

"Like fuck I will be getting you off when I'm being tortured like this."

Andras smiled like the devil. "Oh I think you will, sweetheart. I think you'll be so aroused you won't be able to think straight, and pleasing us will be your only release."

I squirmed at his dark promises and fuck I was so turned on it was starting to hurt. Levi shoved himself onto the table and nestled between my thighs. His hands were rough as his fingers slid between my folds, and his tongue lapped up my soaked pussy.

"Fucckk," I cried out, my hips bucking wildly as he fucked me with his mouth. I was so, so close, my clit swollen and sensitive, then he pulled away, and I screamed.

"Fucking shit, babe. You're soaked." Levi laughed, licking his lips.

Andras smirked like a fucking devil king. "Let's give her a little break, brothers. We'll bring you something to eat in a while."

"Fuck. I fucking hate you," I grumbled as my body twitched with burning need. This was a horrible fucking punishment. "I'd rather be chained up and bloodied in the basement."

"Oh we will do that too, pet." Ty grinned, flicking my nipple and making me shiver. "All in good time."

CHAPTER TWENTY-TWO

Devon

The thought of Sara tied up on the pool table was giving me a constant fucking rock-hard dick. Fucking blue balls. The cold shower didn't help much either. Her confession was driving me mad. I was still pissed about all the lying and the secrets. And I hated these guys who were supposed to be my brothers and this stupid fucking cult we were all messed up in.

But knowing that I gave Sara her first orgasm…fuck if it didn't make me feel like a goddamn king. I wanted to give her more. I wanted her all to myself. Forever. I shrugged into clean black sweatpants and paced my room. My body felt hot and itchy, the cotton rubbing against my skin making my dick twitch.

"Fuck this."

I pulled out my phone and opened the video feed from the cameras in the house. Andras gave each of us access to the app that monitored the cameras and controlled the intercom system throughout The Towne House. I pulled up the media room camera. Sara was staring up at the camera angrily, like she knew we were watching. She had the body of a fucking goddess. Her muscles were toned, and her curves soft. Her breasts heaved as she panted angrily. The piercing in her navel glinted, and the tattoos along her arms and down her sides made her look like a dark goddess of my very own wet dreams. The ache inside me grew too strong to resist. When no one else appeared on the cameras, I stalked down to the room.

Sara's head tilted up when she heard my footsteps. "Oh hey, Dev. Welcome back. Thought maybe you forgot about me."

"I could never forget you, beautiful. Even if I wanted to." I ran a hand through my messy, wet hair.

She frowned. "Do you want to? Forget about me?"

I sighed. "Part of me does."

Her face fell. I took the last few steps toward the table and tucked her loose hair behind her ear. She stared up at me with those piercing blue-green eyes. I don't know how I didn't see them shooting daggers at me through the colored contacts. It seemed so obvious now.

"Well, feel free to leave then," Sara snapped. "I don't need someone around who secretly wishes I was gone. Why don't you go back to your bar, Dev?"

"It's not that simple, and you know it," I growled down at her, bracing my arms on the edge of the pool table.

Sara shook her head. "No, it really is."

I grabbed her chin, forcing her to look at me. "I'm not leaving you."

"He says with a look of disdain. Fuck off, Dev."

She tried to look away, but I held firm and leaned in closer to her.

"I could never leave you, Sara. And I don't want to. I want you, more than I've ever wanted anything, and I don't want to share you with anyone else. I want to take you away from all of this and give you mind-blowing orgasms for the rest of our lives."

Sara's pupils dilated with desire, and her lips parted as I stared down at her perfect body with raw hunger. I leaned down and kissed her, consuming her fire. Her skin was soft and smooth. I traced the tattoos along her torso with my tongue, enjoying the sound of her moans.

"Fuck I need to be inside you," I snarled into her mouth. "I want them to hear you scream my name."

"You can't make me come." Sara gulped down oxygen. "Andras will punish us if we break the rules."

I rolled my eyes. "I'm not afraid of his punishments."

Sara laughed, and her own gaze filled with mischief. "Yeah, well, I am. If I have to go more than one day without orgasms, I might die."

I chuckled, leaning down and kissing her navel, nipping her soft, sensitive skin with my teeth.

"Dev," Sara whispered my name like a prayer, and I met her gaze. "Let me give you some relief."

I arched an eyebrow even as blood throbbed down through my dick. "You want my cock in your mouth, beautiful?"

Sara bit her full bottom lip and nodded. "Yes."

I groaned, reaching in my sweatpants and stroking the head of my cock. I didn't have the strength to say no, even if I couldn't fully pleasure her too. I dropped my sweatpants, and she eyed my dick hungrily.

"You are so fucking beautiful, Sara," I murmured as my dick swelled. I stalked around the table, pulling myself onto it, near her pretty head. I leaned back on my heels, and she tilted her neck back, looking at me with pure lust in her eyes. "Open those pretty plump lips, baby."

Sara licked her full lips, and I pressed the tip of my cock to her mouth. Her tongue licked and swirled over my slit, lapping up the pre-cum. I leaned forward, and she relaxed her throat, taking all of me in at once. I groaned, rocking slowly in and out of her mouth. Her back arched, and she tugged at the straps, locking her body in place. Fuck, I wasn't going to last very long. I leaned over her, rocking my hips as she took my cock like a good fucking girl.

I braced my hands on either side of her hips and dropped my mouth to her beautiful, pink cunt. She was so fucking wet. Sara moaned, and the vibration of it ran through my dick, forcing me to shudder with need for her and everything her body could give me. I pulled away from her pussy and leaned back again, rocking faster, harder, fucking her mouth. She whimpered, straining with need, and I groaned her name as I came hard in her mouth. I pulled out, not wanting her to choke, and let my cum spill onto her chest.

Her lips were swollen, and her chest heaved. It was a beautiful fucking sight to behold. I slid off the pool table and dropped a gentle kiss on her forehead. I snatched my sweatpants from the floor and was about to wipe up the mess I made when Andras's voice boomed over the intercom.

"Leave it."

I snarled, glaring at the camera. "You're being a fucking prick, Blackbyrn."

Sara laughed. "Like I give a fuck if his cum is all over my chest." She glared up at the camera. "Come down here and see how nice I treat you, asshole."

I moved to wipe her up anyway, but Sara shook her head.

"Leave it." Her commanding tone was as stubborn as Andras's and it made me grin.

"Whatever you say, beautiful. Are you cold?" I grabbed a blanket and brought it to the table but she shook her head.

"Nah. I don't really get cold." She winked at me, and my dick twitched like it was ready for round two. "Besides, I'm all hot and bothered right now. I'd rather have an ice bath than a blanket."

I laughed. "You're not like any woman I've ever met, Sara Braun."

Her smile faded, her eyes clouding with memories, and I swallowed, realizing what I said. She wasn't Sara Braun. She was Seraphina, daughter of Aurora, who was murdered by my father. My cult.

"Sorry," I mumbled, unsure what to say. I hadn't fully wrapped my brain around this entirely fucked situation. Every hour we spent together, more secrets spilled out. "Just so you know. I don't care what your name is. Or what color your eyes are. I will always want you. Always."

I turned away before she could respond. I was a coward. A fucking coward because I wasn't ready to hear what she had to say. I shot a text to the others, letting them know I was heading to the bar to pick up kegs and liquor for the party. I needed to get the fuck out of this house.

CHAPTER TWENTY-THREE

Sara

"H elllloooooo!"

I was so fucking bored. And hungry. No one had come down to play with me or feed me since Dev. I couldn't exactly tell time strapped to the table, but it felt like fucking years. The sun was still out, so it wasn't evening. Sunset was somewhere around 4:30 p.m. right now, so I'd been left alone for maybe an hour or so.

Dev's fucking cum dried, and my skin was itching like crazy, but at least my slut of a pussy had finally cooled down.

"Somebody come feed me. You said there would be food Andras! I'm dying down here!" I shouted into the silence.

Fucking assholes. I rolled my hips and tried to bend my arms and legs to keep the blood flowing and the sleepy tingles away. I slumped to the table, staring at the ceiling, and began to sing a feisty ZZ Ward song called "365 Days."

ZZ Ward had such a badass voice, and her songs were so catchy. I belted out a few more songs, choosing the best ones for pissing off boys. Footsteps bounded on the stairs, and I continued to sing, ignoring whoever decided to visit me. A shadow fell over my face, and a slim knife pressed to my throat.

"Hello, pet," Ty murmured.

I continued to sing as the blade bobbed against my skin.

"Feeling feisty, are we? I can work with that."

I finished the song and arched an eyebrow. "Oh yeah? Why don't you untie me, and we'll see how feisty I can be, monster man. Where's the fun in me being tied up anyway?"

He chuckled, lazily drawing the blade across my neck. "Oh, plenty of fun, pet. I promise."

I huffed a sigh. "You didn't even get to chase me. So you didn't really win anything, you know. Just a trussed up turkey you didn't even get to hunt."

He grinned, flicking his knife between my breasts and making my nipples pebble with desire. "And what a feast I will have with you, pet."

My breathing grew shallow as his knife slid across my breasts, the cool steel tracing my hardened nubs. Ty tipped up the blade, letting the sharp edge dance along my skin.

He leaned down, his lips brushing against my ear. "I wonder how delicious your pussy would taste with your blood on my lips, pet?"

I inhaled sharply, trying to hide my racing heart. *Fucking hell*, I was wet already. I willed my body to remain still even as I ached to move, to clamp my thighs against the pulse building inside me. Ty stalked around the table, toward my feet. His eyes dipped between my thighs, and he licked his lips, his gaze violent and filled with lust. My tits ached and needed to be touched, and I couldn't help but to pull against the leather straps holding me captive.

Ty chuckled. "Feeling restless, pet?"

"Fuck. You."

"With pleasure, siren."

Ty reached forward and traced the point of his knife against my bare pussy. I didn't dare move as I watched him tease and tempt me. He flipped the knife, holding the blade between his fingers as he twirled the handle along my stomach.

"What are you going to do?" I panted, unable to restrain my curiosity.

His wolfy eyes met mine, and his grin was pure sin. "Whatever the fuck I want, pet."

I swallowed, watching as he pushed the handle of his blade inside me. I gasped, my pussy clamping around it like a lifeline. He pushed it in further, stretching me, then slid it out again, over and over. My hips arched into his movements, my body craving more and more of this taboo pleasure.

Ty pulled the knife out and held my gaze as he licked the handle. He walked toward me and pressed it to my lips.

"Taste how much you want it, pet," he growled, and fuck if I didn't want it.

I slid my tongue along the hilt, tasting my own arousal.

Ty groaned. "Fuck, babygirl." He moved back to the end of the pool table and tugged my body toward him.

I cried out as my arms stretched tight over my head. Ty brought his blade down to the mound of flesh above my clit, and my breath caught in my throat as I strained to see what he would do next. The knife cut into my flesh, and I hissed in pain. His mouth came down on the bead of blood, kissing the wound. I shivered with pleasure, and his knife sliced into my inner thigh, so, so close to my pussy. My arms strained against the ropes, and I gasped as his tongue licked up the blood dripping down my thigh.

"Two cuts for the two times you ran away from me, pet," Ty murmured, his lips brushing against my clit and making me moan.

"Ty. Fuck. Please." I was fucking begging and *I. Did. Not. Care.* I needed a release, needed him to give it to me.

Ty chuckled, sucking my clit into his mouth, and I cried out as the hilt of his blade thrust inside me once more. He pulled it out quickly and shoved in again, lapping up the blood trickling around my pussy as his tongue swirled around my clit. Oh fuck, it was happening. I could feel it. Finally. *Fuck. Yes.*

"Enough," Andras snapped, leaning against the wall.

Ty's hands and mouth stilled, and I cursed like a fucking sailor at the fucking asshole. Andras's lips twitched with amusement. How long had he been watching us? I was so wrapped up in Ty and that damn knife I didn't hear him enter the room.

Ty pulled the blade from my soaked pussy, and I whimpered. I was so fucking close.

"Remove her restraints, Typhon." Andras commanded. He was always giving commands, and ninety percent of them made me want to punch him in the face.

Andras continued to lean against the wall like this was all incredibly boring for him as Ty used the blade he'd fucked me with to cut the leathers. Even after my limbs were free, I couldn't move. My muscles ached, and my body twitched with too much bottled up pleasure needing an outlet. Ty gripped my chin and kissed me roughly, my blood and pussy juices still coating his lips. He let go, winked, and walked away.

"Fucking assholes," I mumbled.

Andras shoved off the wall and moved toward me, his eyes shining with satisfaction. He no longer wore his signature button-down and fancy slacks. A fitted T-shirt hugged his muscled frame, and the hunter-green sweatpants looked exceptionally good on him. His arms were covered in tattoos, and I noticed the same weird runes I found on the others. He scooped me up in his arms like I weighed nothing at all, and I slumped against his warm chest.

"Do you have wings too?" I mumbled, my eyes drooping.

He laughed deep and low in his chest. "Yes, Seraphina. Black and feathered, like a fallen angel."

"Hmmm. Is that what you are?" I rolled my head back to look at him as he carried me up the stairs.

"No, *belle femme*. I'm a daemon in disguise," he purred.

I snorted a laugh. "Not a very good disguise."

His low chuckle vibrated through me, and my blood heated at the knowledge that I made him laugh. Andras pushed open the door to his room, then kicked it shut behind us and carried me into his bathroom. The whole room was hazy and full of steam that smelled like lavender and eucalyptus.

"Can you stand?" he asked.

I nodded, and he lowered me gently to the floor. I braced myself against his chest.

Andras pulled off his T-shirt and dropped his sweats to the floor. He grasped my hips and guided me to the oversized claw-foot tub. He lifted me effortlessly over the edge and stepped in behind me. My body melted into the simmering hot water, and I moaned. Andras sat behind me, his muscular thighs lightly wrapped around my own. His massive hard-on pressed into my lower back as his arms circled around my chest. I leaned my head back and sighed.

"Better, sweetheart?" he murmured, kissing my shoulder like the gentlest of lovers.

"Much better," I moaned, my body coming alive once more. "Just missing one thing."

I felt Andras smile against my neck as he kissed his way toward my jawline. His hand gripped my chin, turning my head toward his, and his lips touched softly to mine. I sighed happily, and his tongue pressed into my mouth, teasing me. His other hand drifted down my chest, pinching my nipple before he cupped my pussy. I moaned, and his kiss grew more demanding. He pulled away as he dipped two fingers inside me.

"Are you sorry for leaving us, sweetheart?" Andras whispered against my mouth.

I could barely register his words as his thick fingers curled inside me.

"Tell me, Seraphina." His words were a request, a plea. So different from his usual authoritarian tone.

"Yes, I'm sorry," I breathed, my body arching into his touch. "Say it again."

"Say what, angel?"

I moaned as his thumb circled my clit. "My name."

Andras devoured my mouth in a kiss that made my head spin as his fingers worked my body into a frenzy. He pulled back, his lips moving along my jaw, toward my ear. His fingers thrust deeper, and my hips bucked.

Andras growled possessively into my ear. "My dark angel,

Seraphina. Come for me."

I screamed as the orgasm burst through me like a fucking firework. I moaned and squirmed as his fingers curled inside me, drawing out my pleasure.

My body gave out, and I slumped against his chest as he circled me with his strong arms. I don't know how many minutes passed before Andras stepped out of the tub, carrying me out of the water. He set me on my feet long enough to wrap a fluffy robe around my body before scooping me back up and carrying me to his bed. I was a helpless waif as he tucked my body beneath the covers and fluffed the pillows around me.

Andras leaned down and pressed his lips to my forehead. "Sleep now, angel."

I mumbled some incoherent words before the darkness claimed me.

For once, I slept without any horrible dreams pulling me to life in a sweaty mess. I vaguely remembered all four of my men checking on me as I slept. Is that what they were, mine? I couldn't exactly pretend we were still enemies, or that I was a prisoner. Is it a prison if you don't want to leave? That shining light inside me was growing, and I could see it reflecting in their eyes. I could see the same light trying to fight its way to the surface inside them too. Something big was building, and once the light broke through, I knew in my soul there was no going back.

I sat up in bed, alone, and pulled a tray of food closer. I

lifted the metal lid, feeling like I was eating at some kind of fancy hotel. I sipped at the mimosa and picked up a piece of warm, buttered toast. Even the bread tasted expensive. I could definitely get used to this, even as I remembered Tibby locked up downstairs. The door opened soundlessly just then, and Levi strode into the room. He smiled, his eyes glancing down my body in the silk nightgown. *When did I put that on?*

"You look well rested, babe." He flopped down on the bed and snatched a piece of my toast.

"How long have I been sleeping?" I asked, grabbing my fork and shoveling delicious scrambled eggs into my mouth.

Levi shrugged. "Forever. I've been bugging Andras for at least an hour to let me wake you up."

I snorted a laugh. "What time is it? What's happening now? How's Tibby?"

Levi laughed. "She's fine. I made her a mimosa too, but don't tell him. And she has a TV down there. I think Andras is considering giving her a laptop. And it's like six in the evening. Our party starts at 8 p.m. Andras had all kinds of girlie shit brought in for you. Including new clothes."

My eyes widened. "Damn. Guess I need to get moving then." I looked around. "Where's all the new stuff?"

Levi winked. "In your room."

What? I frowned. "My room?"

Levi jumped off the bed and pulled away the tray of food. I plucked the mimosa glass before he could steal it.

"Yeah. Even though I don't plan on letting you sleep alone, ever again, Andras thought you might want your own space here."

I tugged on my fluffy robe, literally having no idea what to say. "That's…really nice."

Levi clasped his hand in mine and brought it to his lips. "Nah. We're not nice guys, *diabla*. Doesn't mean we won't treat you like a queen, though."

I smiled because despite their scary faces and tendencies to stab first and ask questions later, it was incredibly nice. "Lead the way, Fire Prince."

Levi arched an eyebrow. "Fire Prince?"

I shrugged with a laugh. "You're an Obscuritas Prince. And you're a firefighter. It just works."

He laughed, tugging me close and kissing me softly, his touch scorching my skin. "As long as I get to be your Fire Prince forever, call me whatever you want."

Levi led me through the house, down the hall to a small set of stairs. I stopped short. I'd never noticed these stairs, the door was always shut.

"I didn't realize there was a fourth floor here."

Levi's hand slid down my back, guiding me up the stairs. The circular stairs opened up to a bright, open bedroom, even bigger than the master suite Andras claimed. Windows dominated the room, and beautiful iron sconces adorned the emerald-green walls with warm light. A massive Alaskan King bed was cornered to my right. A beautiful canopy of dark-gray, sheer fabric surrounded the bed. There were floor-to-ceiling shelves half full of books, and I eagerly skimmed the collection. Levi opened two separate doors on the wall without windows. One led into a beautiful marble ensuite and the other into a massive walk-in closet stocked with dozens of shirts, pants, fancy as hell dresses, and designer shoes.

"Holy fuck," I gasped, perusing the beautiful clothes. "Seriously. Did you have this all setup for another girl you planned to take prisoner? Because there's no way you could do all this in the few hours I slept."

Levi laughed. "Andras is very persuasive. And very rich."

I smirked, stepping back into the bedroom to find Andras leaning against the doorframe. He looked absolutely stunning in an ash-gray suit and dark-green tie. His face remained emotionless even as his eyes raked across my body with a hunger that made me shudder.

"What do you think, *belle femme*?"

I walked toward him, completely unafraid of this deadly monster the rest of the world feared. I wrapped my arms around his neck, his own automatically reaching around my waist.

I kissed him, savoring the taste of his lush lips against mine. "I love it."

His lips twitched with a hint of a smile. "Good. I've picked out a dress for you. And we would like you to sing tonight, siren."

I grinned. "Oh yeah? Do I get to pick the songs?"

Andras smirked, and the tiny smile made my insides melt. "I assumed you would. Even if I tried to choose, I know you wouldn't listen."

I patted his cheek. "Yes, that is true."

Andras pinched my ass, and I yelped. "That doesn't mean I won't punish you for it later, sweetheart."

"We'll see." I spun out of his arms and dropped my robe to the floor. I felt Levi and Andras watching me like hungry lions. I pulled the silk nightgown over my head and dropped it to the floor as well, walking to the bathroom. "I need some girl time now, boys. Keep the mimosas coming, though."

Levi laughed as I winked and slipped into the bathroom to prepare. I stepped into the massive shower. Multiple shower heads surrounded me on all sides and heated floors warmed my bare feet; it was actual heaven. The water was instantly hot, and I leaned back onto the bench, breathing in deeply. My body still ached from being tied to the pool table, but I felt rested and buzzing with energy now.

I was curious about this party. And more than a little weary. If Laszlo Blackbyrn was hunting me, wasn't throwing a party a bit of a risk? Andras wasn't the type to do things on a whim, or without some kind of seven-layered plan. No, this was more than a party. It was a show of force. Andras was taking a stand. My mind whirled with the implications. If Laszlo found out who I was—officially—would he hurt my father, my sister? Or maybe he already knew? I needed to convince Andras to let Tibby work her magic and find out what was happening behind closed doors.

I spent the next hour and a half perfecting my hair and makeup. I was surprised when none of my new roomies bothered me, but it was also nice to have some alone time. I wondered which one of them guessed that I needed it. Andras was ridiculously nosy, so it could be him. But Ty was surprisingly perceptive. And Dev kept his distance for some time before finally showing me his own place. Even Levi took his alone time at the firehouse. Is this what grownups do in relationships?

A quiet knock on the bedroom door jarred me from my

thoughts, and I slipped on my fluffy robe before exiting the bathroom.

"Come in."

Andras stepped into the room, looking fucking edible in his gray suit. He wore a crisp, white shirt beneath and an emerald-green pocket square in his jacket. His lips twitched with the hint of a smile.

"Hello, *belle femme*."

Ty, Levi, and Dev filed in behind him, all wearing similar suits with emerald-green pocket squares. Ty's long, dirty blond hair was tied back in a low bun. His hazel eyes lingering on my body as if he could see straight through my robe. I shivered under his gaze. Levi grinned, his blue eyes twinkling with mischief. His shaggy, brown hair was still messy, and he brushed it away from his face as he stepped aside for Dev. Dev's smile was shy, his bright-green eyes searching for something in my own. Acceptance? Trust? I wasn't sure.

"All four at once? Damn I don't know if I'm ready for that." I smirked.

Levi let out that infectious laugh, and Ty snatched me into his arms with my wrists secured behind my back.

"Oh you're ready, pet. But we're not here for that."

"We've got time," Levi added, and Dev snorted, rolling his eyes.

"No, we do not," Andras clipped. "Guests will arrive soon."

Andras stepped into my oversized closet and reappeared with a gorgeous velvet gown, the same emerald-green color as their pocket squares. "For you, *belle femme*."

I slid my fingers along the soft fabric. "It's stunning."

"As are you, beautiful," Dev murmured. "With or without the dress."

I gave him a soft smile. "Thank you for the dress."

Andras laid the gown on my bed and pulled something from his pocket. He held out a tiny earpiece, and I frowned.

"What's this?"

"Another gift." Andras pressed the piece to my hand, and I pushed it into my ear.

"Hey, Nova," Tibby's voice rang out over the microphone, and I squealed like a little fucking girl.

"Tibby?! What's going on?" I turned my wide eyes to see all four men smiling, each in their own way, as they watched me.

Tibby's nails clicked against her keyboard. "Back in action, baby. A show of good faith between me and your little harem of devils."

I laughed. "Seriously? Damn, you must've been really persuasive."

Tibby's snicker vibrated through the line. "I just offered up free use of your vagina for life."

Levi burst out laughing, and I cocked my head in his direction, narrowing my eyes.

He tapped his ear. "I want a code name too."

I gasped as Levi's voice echoed through the earpiece.

Tibby snorted a laugh. "A concession. The harem gets earpieces too."

I rolled my eyes and turned to Andras. "I can confidently say that was your idea, oh fearless leader."

He grinned like the devil he was. "Of course, sweetheart. Tabitha has access to all of our security controls and she will be monitoring everyone at the party from her room downstairs. I've upgraded the state of the room to make it more comfortable for her. But for now, the best way to keep you both safe is for her to remain hidden."

"He's right, Sara," Tibby added. "If we're going to beat these fuckers, we need to work as a team."

"From what we can tell from movement at the manor, your father and sister are not there," Andras said quietly. "But I know where they will be. And we *will* help you get them back."

I felt the hot sting of tears welling in my eyes and rolled my neck, blinking a few times to force them away. Fuck, when was the last time I actually cried? I had so many emotions bubbling up and it was difficult to form coherent thoughts. These people who didn't owe me anything, let only their allegiance to my family, were willing to go up against the most powerful leaders of The Obscuritas. It deserved some fucking tears, damnit.

"Let's get this party started, shall we?" Levi gave my hand a squeeze, and I smiled at him, grateful for the segue.

I nodded. "I'll get changed and be right down."

Andras stepped closer, a blue velvet box in his hand. "One more thing."

He held out the box, and I took it.

I gasped at the beautiful display of diamonds. "Is this...a collar?" I looked up, and Andras's deep-brown eyes filled with a daemonic hunger.

His head tilted to the side as he appraised me, seeing the desire I was unable to hide. "Yes."

The blood rushed to my clit as I stared back at him and licked my lips. "Why?"

He pulled the box from my grasp and took out the diamond choker. "The answer is threefold." He stepped behind me and brought the necklace around, brushing my collarbone with his fingers. I shivered, heat flooding through me as his hands traced my throat. "One, because it will look stunning wrapped around your pretty neck. Two, because being collared will annoy you to no end. And three, because you *do* belong to us, and every fucker who attends this party will know it."

I swallowed audibly as he clasped the diamond choker around my neck. The metal was cold against my skin, a reprieve from the heat coursing through my veins. A predatory growl caught my attention, and I turned. My mouth dried up and my stomach was full of nerves as Ty stalked into the room, his gaze zeroing in on the diamonds at my throat.

He traced the collar with his rough fingers and a devilish grin on his stupid hot face. "You're ours, little vixen. And if you tried to refuse the collar, you'd get my hand wrapped around your pretty throat for the evening instead."

My own grin turned wicked, and I leaned into his touch. "I like your hand necklaces just as much, monster man."

Levi stepped in close to my side. He gripped my chin roughly, turning my face to meet his wild eyes next. "You're ours to torment, *diabla*." He placed a gentle kiss against my lips, keeping his mouth close to my own when he whispered his next words. "And ours to worship."

My body sang with pleasure at their words. I had nothing clever to respond with. The emotions tumbling through me were too much.

The four men left, leaving teasing kisses along my skin as

they went. My blood was singing with hope, and my heart beat with a light brighter than it had in over a decade.

I tossed my robe across an armchair and slipped into the dress. The fabric was incredibly soft and hugged my body in all the right places. The long sleeves wrapped my arms snuggly, leaving my shoulders bare. I found a pair of strappy gold stilettos in the closet. I glanced at myself in the full-length mirror just outside the closet. I went for a glamorous Marylin Monroe look, with black winged eyeliner and red lips. My silvery blue hair was curled in soft waves down my back. I looked fucking hot, thank you very much. I eyed the sparkling collar around my neck with too much feeling.

I turned and opened the bedroom door, finding Dev waiting for me.

His bright eyes went wide and his gaze heated, looking me over. "Damn, beautiful. You look gorgeous."

I blushed with pleasure, biting my lip and sliding my arm through the crook of his elbow. "Thanks, handsome."

"Would you two stop eye fucking and get down here?" Ty growled through the earpiece. "Bring me my pretty little pet."

"Nova, you look fucking amazing! You should wear that dress like always." Tibby laughed as Ty growled in frustration again.

I could hear music thumping through the house as Dev led me downstairs. The party was taking place on the first floor, where the theater room, bar, and pool table were located, and the garden level, including the courtyard, which was lit with twinkling lights and enclosed with heaters.

We passed waitstaff with trays of champagne and appetizers. Dev snagged us two glasses of bubbly while I sniped a caprese salad cup. I sighed with happiness as I ate the fresh mozzarella and juicy tomato. Rich people's food was on another level. I took Dev's arm again as he led me across the room.

Ty was playing pool with a couple of men I didn't know and one I did. I smiled at Dominic and he gave me a wave. Ty growled, and Dominic instantly looked away, even as Ty winked at me. I gave him the finger. I scanned the room and noted many curious faces glancing our way.

"Do you know these people? They're all staring at you," I whispered into Dev's ear.

"Like anyone would be staring at his ugly mug," Levi snorted down the earpiece, and I snorted a laugh.

Dev leaned down, his lips brushing against my ear. "They're staring at you, beautiful."

"The most stunning woman in the room," Andras murmured, pressing his hand to my lower back. "*Tu es magnifique, mon amour.*"

I winked up at him. Even in heels he was still so much taller than me. "*Merci, bébé.*"

Andras arched an eyebrow. "You speak French?"

I shrugged. "Very little."

"Enough to talk dirty?" Levi cut in over the mic, and I snickered.

I caught Andras's gaze before responding. "*Veux-tu me baiser ce soir, pompier?*"

His eyes blazed as Tibby laughed, and I caught Levi's frown across the room. "Please tell me that was dirty because it got my dick twitching already."

Andras smirked, pinching my waist possessively. "She called

you an idiot with a small cock."

I grinned, and Dev even let out a quiet laugh down the mic.

"This is going to be a good night." Tibby snickered, and we all grinned.

"Will you sing for us now, siren?" Andras asked, smiling down at me and making my knees weak. He was gorgeous when he smiled. "There's a small stage near the DJ's table for you. And your preferred antique microphone."

I flushed with pleasure, not remotely surprised Andras knew I had a favorite mic. He and Dev led me to the stage as crowds of guests parted for the two dark-haired Princes walking before me. They helped me up the short steps, and I whispered my request to the DJ. I decided to start the night with "Time of the Season," The Ben Taylor Band version. I liked the dark and moody vibe of their rendition of the Zombies song. There were cocktail tables scattered around the room, and beautiful people in gowns and tuxedos hushed their voices as the music swelled. I scanned the crowd and swayed my hips to the music, adding my own voice to the tune as I sang out the lyrics. I let the music carry me away, the base notes vibrating through my bones. I could feel the eyes of my men on me, and my blood sizzled with desire for each of them.

As the song drifted to its end, a round of applause went up from the crowd. The DJ took over once more, and I moved to step down from the stage when a hand reached out to help me.

I looked up and smiled. "James. Good to see you outside of the gym." He wore a black suit, shirt, and tie, and his hair was styled perfectly to finish off his pretty boy meets sinner look.

He grinned, and his caramel brown eyes twinkled with

mirth. His hand wrapped around mine as I held my dress up to avoid falling on my face.

"You too, killer."

I laughed at the nickname he'd given me after beating everyone's ass at the gym. He had no idea how accurate it was. Tibby cleared her throat, and I grinned.

"How are you?"

He shrugged, running a hand through his hair. "No complaints. Need a drink?"

I nodded. "Yes, please."

I let James lead me to the bar, where Levi promptly stepped in, tugging me close to him.

"Hello, James." Levi's words were casual, but his tone was cold and possessive.

I rolled my eyes and smacked his shoulder. "Don't be a psycho," I murmured, tugging the lapel on his jacket.

Levi dropped his mouth to my neck, nibbling my skin before bringing his lips to my ear. "But I am a psycho, *diabla*. Don't ever forget that."

"I'll go see if Ty wants his ass kicked in pool." James smiled, unphased by the hellfire burning in Levi's eyes. "See you around, Sara."

I waved and giggled as Levi wrapped his arms around my waist and snarled into my bare shoulder, biting down playfully and marking my skin.

"Get a room," Tibby muttered, her fingers tapping away at her keyboard.

"Gladly," Levi murmured, his voice sounding husky with desire.

"How will I ever get anyone to dance with me with a beast clinging to my back?" I laughed and tried to pull away from him.

Ty chuckled through the earpiece. "Quit playing with the cub, little vixen. We don't need Levi's beastie coming out tonight."

I huffed, rolling my eyes. I slipped out of Levi's grasp and skipped to the dance floor. I swayed my hips, dancing to the beat of the pop song. Eyes turned toward me with interest, but quickly turned away when they realized who I was, and who I belonged to.

I pouted as Levi sauntered to the dance floor. "No one will even look at me. How rude."

Levi grinned, his eyes full of fire as he gripped my waist and curved his muscular body into mine. "Because no one here wants to die tonight, *mi diosa*."

I smirked and slid my fingers around his neck and into his hair. "Pussies."

Andras cleared his throat over the mic. "Be careful, sweetheart. It sounds like you're inviting trouble."

"Me? Never." I pulled away from Levi and rubbed up against another guy before the possessive daemon yanked me back.

"Now I have to chop that guy's dick off, *diabla*," Levi murmured all too happily, twirling me around.

I wrapped my hands around his neck and stared up into his navy blue eyes. "Let's give him a pass, just this once."

Levi pulled me closer, his hard length pressing to my stomach. "And what do I get for being so generous?"

"A date with me. At the firehouse. I want to ride your pole." I winked.

Tibby snorted a laugh, interrupting. "As if you haven't already."

Levi kissed my cheek lightly. "It's a date, babe."

Andras's authoritative voice cut into our banter. "It's time for another song, siren."

"I have just the one." I smiled. "I might not be so great with emotional declarations, but I can sing them."

Levi led me back to the stage, helping me up the steps. He passed me a glass of champagne, and I gulped it down, coating my dry throat. I whispered my song choice to the DJ once again. A beautiful ballad called "Bound to You," sung by Christina Aguilera. She sang it in the movie *Burlesque* from a few years back. I loved rocking out to that soundtrack. This particular song was slow, sensual, and emotional. The last one, something I rarely was. I stepped up to the mic.

"This one goes out to a few very important men in my life." Because fuck it, let everyone know I was dating the scariest motherfuckers at the party.

The lyrics burned into my soul, cutting through the darkness to that light buried within. I might not be an open book, but the soul of this song matched my own. I scanned the crowd and found my monsters standing together, watching me with fire in their eyes. I let my own fire shine through, for them and only them, as the song built and built.

The music faded, and a hush fell over the crowd as I stepped back from the mic. My eyes remained locked on the men I… loved? Is that what was happening? My heartbeat thumped so loudly in the seconds of silence, I was certain everyone could hear it. The DJ's voice cut into the silence, praising the girl with the voice of an angel. Everyone began clapping wildly, and I realized he was talking about me. I blinked, breaking away from the hypnotic stares of my men. I dipped into a slight bow, as much as the dress allowed. When I looked up again, Andras was there, offering me his arm. He guided me away from the stage and toward the packed dance floor.

Andras tipped my chin up to meet his gaze, and his dark eyes captured my own. "Is that how you feel, *belle femme*? Bound to me? To us?"

I searched his eyes, wondering if I'd gone too far. But it was too late now, and I didn't want any more secrets between us.

"Yes," I whispered, licking my lips. "I can't explain it, but for whatever it's worth, I'm yours."

Andras's grip tightened to the point of pain, and I leaned into him, needing to hear his next words more than I needed to breathe. His eyes darkened, and his voice was deep and steady when he spoke. "It's worth everything."

His lips crashed into mine, and I opened up to him, teasing my tongue into his mouth. His arm wrapped around my waist as the hand on my chin traced my jaw and curled around the back of my neck, drawing me in. His mouth claimed mine, and I melted into his embrace. This dark prince was all mine. And I was his.

CHAPTER TWENTY-FOUR

Sara

I finished reapplying my lipstick in the bathroom mirror and stepped into the hall. I was using the bathroom on the third floor, avoiding the crowds on the main levels. A shadow dropped in front of me, and I almost yelped.

"Damn, Dev." I laughed, my smiling face quickly falling flat when I noticed his dark expression. "What's wrong?"

"Come with me," he demanded, grabbing my wrist tightly.

I hurried along after him, trying not to trip on my dress as my heels clicked along the hardwood floor. Dev aggressively pounded the code to open his bedroom door and pulled me roughly inside.

"Fuck, dude. If you wanted to get me alone you just had to ask." I smirked.

He didn't return the smile. His eyes were wild and his face grim. Something was definitely off. In two long strides he was in front of me and ripped the earpiece from my ear. He pulled out his own and tossed them across the room.

"Seriously, Dev. What the fuck?" I slammed my hands onto my hips.

He paced the room, glancing at me between angry strides. I stepped into his path, forcing him to look at me. "Talk to me."

"I can't stop, Sara." His voice shook with emotion.

I cocked my head, watching him. "Stop what?"

He paused, his eyes an endless storm of hunger and pain. "Can't get you out of my head. I'm craving you, needing you."

I took a tentative step toward him, keeping my voice calm. It felt like cornering a jaguar, and I tried to keep my heart from racing. "I'm right here, Dev."

He spun toward me, grabbing my upper arms, his fingers gripping hard enough to bruise. "It's not enough. It's never enough. I need more. I want to consume you, Seraphina. Every atom of your mind and body, I want it all for myself."

I swallowed, unsure what to say. He looked ready to commit murder or strip me naked and take what he needed. I had to stay calm. "I'm yours, Dev."

Dev's eyes lit with fire and he spun me around, shoving my chest into a wall and pinning my hands behind my back. I bit back a yelp of surprise.

"No. You're theirs." He spat the words at me, his hot breath tickling my skin.

What was this about? He didn't like to share? My mind was panicking even as my body heated under his roaming hands. "I'm still yours too, Dev."

He snarled, tugging at my hips and crumpling my dress. I could feel the seams beginning to tear and I decided to try another tactic. I turned my head and narrowed my eyes at him.

"Hey, asshole. You're ripping my new dress."

His eyes turned feral, and my mouth popped open as he pulled out a pocket knife. "Fuck your dress." Dev slipped the knife down my spine, cutting the dress clean in half.

I gasped and tried to turn around, but Dev shoved me hard against the wall as he used his free hand to drop his pants and pull out his hard-as-fuck cock. I licked my lips, and he tracked the movement like a predator.

"Dev, whatever you want from me, it's yours. I'm yours and you're mine."

Dev growled and ripped my thong clean off, the fabric pinching my skin as it snapped. He forced my legs further apart and slid his fingers between my thighs. "You have no idea what that means."

Suddenly his mouth was on my neck, and he bit down hard. I screamed just as his fingers thrust inside me and my pain faded to pleasure.

He lifted his bloody lips to my ear, and I cried out as he shoved a third finger inside me. My pussy clamped down on his fingers greedily, urging him on.

"I'm going to ruin you, Seraphina. I'm lost to this darkness, beautiful. And I'm too fucking selfish not to drag you down with me."

I could barely breathe as Dev bit and licked at my shoulder, as his fingers curled inside me, hitting that glorious spot and bringing me closer to the edge.

"I'm already lost in the dark, Dev. We're already in this together."

Dev groaned. Ripping his fingers out and gripping my hips, he shoved his cock fully inside me. I cried out, my body shaking with pain and pleasure from the sudden assault. I pressed my now free hands against the wall, trying to gain some control.

He snarled and lifted my hips to where my feet barely touched the ground as he pounded into me. I felt the orgasm building inside me like a fucking runaway train.

"You should run, Seraphina," Dev panted, thrusting harder. "Run before your soul is destroyed."

"My soul is burned black, Dev. Take it. I don't want it." I bit out the words.

Fuck. My body felt like it wasn't my own, and I poured every ounce of my soul into the monster owning me. Dev reached around and pinched my clit, and I screamed as the orgasm crashed through me.

"All we can offer you is pain," Dev groaned, his cock swelling as he spilled inside me.

He pulled out and stepped back, letting me crumple to the floor, my legs too shaky to stand.

I looked up into his hard eyes, so full of hate and pain. "Dev…"

Dev pulled his pants up swiftly and went to the door. "It's just too late."

He didn't look back as he slammed the door and left. I curled my legs up to my chest and pressed my back to the wall. My dress floated in front of me like a blanket, torn and ruined. What just happened? I barely recognized this version of Devon Parrish. He looked practically daemonic.

I stared at nothing as my body shook with spent adrenaline, my eyes blurring. I barely registered the click of the door as it opened. Andras dropped in front of me, his movements slow and gentle as he reached out to take my hand. Ty and Levi stood behind him, his face telling me he heard bits and pieces of the bizarre altercation on the earpiece.

"What happened, Sara?" Andras whispered the words like a soft caress.

I shook my head, and my eyes burned, tears threatening to spill over. "I don't know. Dev was…wild. His eyes were full of hate and pain. He's never fucked me like that."

Ty's growl rumbled through me as he stormed out of the room, most likely to find their brother and beat the fuck out of him. Levi's body was rigid, his eyes dark, and I swear his skin was sizzling as he snarled. Andras stood and turned to him, his tone sharp.

"Levi. Sara needs you. Take her to her room, now."

Levi blinked several times and sighed, his eyes full of pain as he looked down at me. His arms slid under my knees, and he lifted me gently from the floor. "She's bleeding."

"He bit me pretty hard," I whispered, nuzzling into Levi's warmth. "Something was wrong, he was different. So angry and sad."

"Ty will find him, Sara," Levi murmured as he carried me down the hall and away from the party below. Andras followed behind us quietly.

"Don't hurt him. He's already hurting. I think he was punishing himself. We need to find him. I think he might do something stupid."

Levi snarled. "He already has."

I shook my head, tucking it under Levi's chin. "No. Something very, very bad."

"We will bring him home," Andras murmured. "Tabitha."

I looked up at Andras, remembering I could no longer

hear the others.

Andras frowned, listening to whatever Tibby had to say. "Typhon, find him. Bring him back."

"Where is he?" I demanded, my voice finally returning to something close to normal. I needed to talk to Dev. He was hurting, and I knew I wasn't truly the cause of that pain. My spidey senses were tingling, but I just couldn't see what the missing link was.

Andras moved in front of Levi to type in the key code for my room and held the door open as he walked toward my bed. Levi sat on the edge, keeping me locked in his arms. His skin radiated heat, and it felt divine against my bare skin.

Andras cracked his neck and brushed his fingers along my cheek. "I need to return to the party. Certain people have arrived, and it is important I speak with them. We'll find Devon. Leviathan will stay with you."

I squirmed in Levi's arms, but his muscles wouldn't budge an inch. "I'm fine, really. It was just a little jarring."

"Levi is staying because he needs *you*, angel," Andras stated as he walked to the door, closing it gently behind him.

I turned to Levi, searching his deep-blue gaze. "What's wrong with you?"

Levi shrugged with a smile that didn't reach his eyes. "I have a temper. Having you in my arms reminds me to keep my cool."

"Nothing wrong with being a little feisty." I smiled, flicking his nose.

He laughed, his chest rumbling. "When I get angry, people and places tend to burn down."

"Is that why you're a firefighter?" I asked curiously.

Levi stood, carrying me into the bathroom. "Partly."

He was clearly leaving out parts of this story, but I decided to leave it for now. I knew these guys had secrets, my snooping with Tibby hadn't uncovered anything about him starting fires, though.

Levi released me to stand on my own and walked to the massive zero entry shower, turning on the hot water. I dropped the torn up dress to the ground and stepped inside, turning to see Levi undressing as well.

My mouth lifted in a hopeful smile. "Going to join me?"

He grinned, his eyes glinting with mischief. "As if I could resist, *mi diosa.*"

I let my gaze roam his massive, muscular body and the intricate tattoos. Levi definitely didn't skip leg day. I licked my lips, eyeing the thick, swelling cock between his legs. "Get in here, hot stuff."

He laughed, and the smile touched his eyes this time. "I like that one."

Levi stepped into the shower, his fingers brushing against my bare skin from my hips up my waist and along the curve of my breasts. I shivered.

His hands stopped at the almost fully healed bite mark on my neck. "You heal fast. Impressively fast."

I turned my neck toward the shower head, letting the hot water chase away the dried blood. "I've always healed faster than most. My own little superpower, I guess."

"Hhhmmm," Levi muttered, tracing his thumb across my bottom lip. "I think you're more powerful than any of us, Seraphina."

I smirked. "Yeah, I am pretty fucking tough."

Levi grinned. "Fuck yeah you are. Now sit on the bench like a good girl and let me rub you down."

I laughed, even as my body heated under his hungry eyes and quiet demands. I sat on the bench, scooting back enough to let my legs dangle over the edge. Steam filled the room, and I closed my eyes, breathing deeply. Levi moved between my legs, brushing a soaped up loofa along my shoulders and down my chest. His hands lingered as he gently massaged the body wash into my skin. The smell of eucalyptus and aloe filled my nose, and I sighed, content in that moment.

Levi's fingers brushed along my jaw, his lips pressed to mine delicately, almost as if he were afraid I might break. I reached out and tugged him closer, teasing his mouth open with my tongue. Even his kiss was slow and sensual, and I moaned happily. His hands palmed my breasts, massaging my skin and tweaking my nipples. I arched into his touch, and he sucked the hardened peaks into his mouth. His hands moved lower, gripping my inner thighs and massaging, his fingers moving agonizingly close to where I needed them.

"More, more, more," I panted, spreading my legs wider to encourage him.

Levi chuckled. "Are you wet for me, *diabla*?"

I moaned as his fingers slid between my thighs, my pussy slick with desire.

"Oh, fuck yes, you're soaked. I think I'll have a taste."

I blinked slowly, feeling utterly blissed out as I leaned back against the glass and Levi propped my legs on his shoulders. He dropped down and sucked my clit into his mouth, his tongue lapping up my arousal. He groaned, and the sound vibrated through me. I rolled my hips, giving him more access as his tongue dipped inside me.

"Oh fuck, Levi," I cried out as the orgasm washed through me and my body shuddered.

Levi lapped up the cum like an eager puppy, and I grinned down at the gorgeous man between my legs. He looked up at me through dark lashes as his tongue dipped inside my pussy. It was filthy, and I fucking loved it. I fisted my hand in his hair and shoved his face between my legs.

"More, hot stuff. Gimme more."

He chuckled, and I moaned as the sound shot through me. "Greedy girl."

His hand slid up my thigh slowly until his two fingers replaced his tongue. He dipped them inside me, curling them deep. My hips bucked because, yes, I was fucking greedy.

I gasped as Levi's thumb stroked down to my ass, massaging the tight hole as his fingers pushed deeper inside my pussy. His thumb pressed into my ass slowly, teasingly.

"You're so fucking tight, babe." He sucked my clit into his mouth as he shoved his thumb in further, and I moaned at all the sensations colliding. His fingers thrust in harder as he fucked me with his hand and his mouth. I slumped further against the glass as his tongue swirled faster against my clit.

I screamed, my pussy and my ass clamping down around his fingers as another orgasm pulsed through my body. "Fuck me."

"Oh I will, *diabla*." Levi winked, lowering my legs to the floor. "Can you stand?"

I huffed a laugh, using his thick arms to hoist myself up.

"I'm standing, which means your job's not finished, hot stuff."

He grinned, his eyes glowing. "Challenge accepted."

Levi moved to shut off the shower just as Ty barreled into the bathroom. My eyes widened at his haphazard suit and windswept hair.

"Did you find Dev?"

He grimaced, and my shoulders slumped. "No. But we will."

His eyes drifted downward, raking over my naked body glistening with water as steam continued to fill the room. "Care to distract me for a few hours, pet?"

I smirked, curling my finger in an invitation. "Come on in, monster man. I'm nowhere near finished for the night."

Ty smirked, a dark chuckle on his lips. "I can help you with that, little vixen."

Levi shoved open the shower door as Ty ripped his shirt over his head and dropped his slacks to the bathroom floor. His massive dick was already standing at attention, and I wrapped my hand around it as he crowded me against the shower wall. I stroked him slowly, sliding my nails lightly against the sensitive flesh and making him groan. I dropped to my knees in front of him and pressed my lips to his cock, slowly sucking him into my mouth. Ty fisted one hand in my hair as the other braced his muscular body against the wall. I sucked him deep into the back of my throat and hummed.

"Fuck, babygirl," Ty groaned, his grip tightening in my hair to the point of pain.

I relished the harsh touch after the overtly soft ministrations from Levi. I needed them both. Gentle and rough. Pain and pleasure. Ty's cock swelled in my mouth, and he pulled my head back. I looked up into his dark and depraved eyes.

"You look fucking beautiful with your mascara running and your lipstick smeared on my cock, pet."

Ty pulled me up and turned me toward Levi, who was sitting on the bench and stroking his cock as he watched us. Ty pressed close behind me and nibbled my ear as his hand wrapped around my waist and dipped between my thighs. He groaned appreciatively as I bit my lip to hide my whimpering.

"So fucking wet. You want more, little vixen?"

I nodded, and Ty chuckled, his breath making me shiver. He gripped my hips, walking me toward Levi. He lifted me up as if I weighed nothing and set me down to straddle Levi's hips. Ty pushed me down further, impaling my slick pussy on Levi's hard cock. I moaned as he filled me completely, rolling my hips as I adjusted to his thickness. Levi's hands moved to my breasts, squeezing and tweaking my hardened nipples. He leaned back further just as Ty pushed me forward, bringing my ass higher and closer to him. I lifted my hips, riding Levi's cock slowly as Ty brought his mouth to my ass, dipping his tongue into me.

I moaned loudly, because fuck it felt good. Ty's hand smacked hard against my ass, jolting me forward.

"Relax, pet. I'm going to fuck your tight ass while you ride my brother's cock."

"Oh fuck, please," I mumbled, barely able to form coherent words as my pussy clamped down on Levi's dick.

Ty lifted me up onto my knees and slicked his cock between my thighs. He shoved me back down onto Levi's dick, and I gasped as he moaned. Ty pushed me forward, spreading my ass cheeks and thrusting his dick inside. I screamed, and Levi caught my mouth with his own, swallowing the sound. Levi and Ty pounded into me roughly, syncing their rhythms, and I could do nothing but take it over and over.

"Come for us, pet," Ty growled and smacked my ass hard as he filled me up and Levi gripped my hips, steadying me as his hips moved faster.

"Fuck, oh god. Oh gods."

"No gods, *diabla*," Levi spoke a word with each thrust of his hips. "Daemons."

My fourth orgasm pulsed through my body, and both holes tightened with pleasure. Levi cried out my name, stilling inside me, as Ty snarled, thrusting harder and squeezing my ass as he exploded. Hot cum filled my ass, and I moaned.

I collapsed onto Levi's chest, and he held me close, peppering me with kisses. He leaned forward into an upright sitting position. Ty gripped my hips and lifted me off Levi's lap to stand. Both men used a cloth and loofa to wipe me down and clean up the mess between my thighs as I swayed on my feet.

"Still standing," I murmured, grinning.

Ty's teeth grazed my shoulder as he growled, and Levi laughed like they had a secret to share.

I let them guide me out of the shower, towel drying my hair a little and offering their arms to walk me back to the bedroom. Their secret smiles were starting to grate on my nerves. I narrowed my eyes, ready to punch them both, when we stepped out of the bathroom and Andras stood, waiting. His white shirt was unbuttoned, and I licked my lips, catching a glimpse of his dark, tattooed skin.

His lips twitched as he looked me over. "My turn."

My eyes widened as Levi and Ty chuckled. "Oh. Fuck."

Andras gestured to the end of the canopy bed, near the wood frame. I walked toward it, keeping my eyes locked with his.

"Now what?"

Andras stalked toward me, wrapping his fingers around my throat and kissing me deeply. His lush lips devoured my own, claiming me. He pulled away slowly.

"Arms up, sweetheart."

I narrowed my eyes. "Am I in trouble?"

He smirked. "Aren't you always? Now, don't make me ask again."

I rolled my eyes and lifted my arms above my head. When I looked up, I realized there were leather straps dangling from the top of the bed frame. Andras reached over my head easily and slipped my hands into the leather cuffs. He pulled the straps tightly, and my body stretched, my toes barely reaching the plush rug beneath my feet.

Levi and Ty moved to the bed, watching as I struggled in the restraints.

"Fuck you look good all tied up and helpless, pet." Ty chuckled.

I craned my head to the side to see him. "Why don't you come over here and I'll show you how helpless I really am, monster man."

Levi laughed as Andras moved back in front of me, gripping my chin to turn me back to face him.

"Eyes on me, sweetheart."

He pulled a small bullet vibrator from a silk pouch and laid it on the bed. Andras stepped back and finished unbuttoning his shirt, draping it over a chair. His pants followed, and I could see the bulge between his legs beneath the tight, black boxer briefs he wore. Gods, he was hot.

He dropped to his knees and lifted one of my legs over his shoulders. "I want you to come on my face, my dark, dirty angel."

My chest heaved as I nodded, mesmerized. Andras kissed his way up my thigh, dragging his tongue around my outer lips. He flicked his tongue lazily against my clit, and my head dropped back, as my body surged with pleasure.

Andras pinched my thigh, and I yelped, looking back at him. "Don't make me punish you for breaking the rules. Eyes. On. Me."

I swallowed, nodding as his mouth returned to my clit. Andras grabbed the toy from the bed and turned it to a low setting. He slid it along my pussy, and my body shook with pleasure. Andras swirled the toy around, letting it rest against my clit as his tongue dipped inside me. It took all of my strength not to close my eyes and drop my head. I stared down at the god between my thighs and screamed when my body couldn't last any longer. My hips bucked against his mouth as he dragged out the orgasm with his tongue.

Andras pulled away slowly with a lion's grin on his face. "Good girl."

He stood up and dropped his boxers, and my body shuddered at his massive cock. My arms stretched almost painfully as I hung there like a limp noodle.

"Holy fuck, I didn't know my body could do this," I panted.

"So. Many. Orgasms."

Andras pulled a small bottle of lubricant from another silk pouch and coated his dick, his lips twitching with a grin. "I think you've got at least one more coming."

I licked my lips as Andras prowled toward me, dropping the lube on the bed and wrapping my legs around his waist. He turned the vibrator up a level and pressed it between my legs. I squirmed against the vibrations. I felt hands on my back as Ty came up behind me, his hard cock pressing against my ass. *Oh fuck.* My eyes widened as Levi dropped to his knees between them, positioned directly beneath me. He winked as his teeth bit into my ass.

Ty grabbed the lube and coated his dick, then slicked his finger with it, dipping slowly into my ass. Andras pulled my hips forward and thrust his cock inside me, making me moan. He moved my body slowly as my pussy became soaked with desire once more. I gasped as I felt Levi's finger dip inside me alongside Andras's cock. Ty came up behind me then, pressing the head of his cock into my ass. I moaned loudly as Levi took the toy and rubbed it slowly along my pussy and my ass as his brothers thrusted deeper inside me. I was utterly helpless between them as my body hummed with so much pleasure it was painful.

Levi pressed the vibrator to my clit, and I cried out.

"You don't come until I say so, angel." Andras growled the command as his thrusts grew more needy.

Ty continued his slow pace as Andras sped up, and the dual sensations were maddening. Levi pulled the toy away, and I whimpered as the orgasm building inside me faded slightly. Ty fisted his hand in my hair, forcing my head back and kissing me roughly as he fucked me from behind. I heaved a breath as his lips released mine.

"Andras. Please," I panted, my tits bouncing in his face as they fucked me to within an inch of my life.

Andras nodded, and Levi returned the toy to my pulsing clit. I moaned their names, all of them, as the orgasm built inside my like a fucking hurricane.

"Come for us, angel."

I screamed myself hoarse as the orgasm burst like a dam inside me. Levi kept the toy pressed against my overly sensitive clit, and I cried out again and again until Andras and Ty stilled inside me simultaneously, their cocks swelling and pulsing with their collective release.

I whimpered as Levi removed the toy. Ty pulled out slowly, dropping a kiss to my shoulder.

"Keep your legs wrapped around me." Andras reached up and released my hands.

I barely had the strength to follow his command. He carried me to the bed, and my limp body sank into the soft blankets. Levi brought out a wet cloth and wiped the mess between my thighs once more.

"Time to rest, angel."

All three men moved to the door, and I whined. "Don't go. I know you gave me this big ass bed for a reason."

I smiled as I fell asleep surrounded by my monsters. Minus one. But I'd bring him back kicking and screaming if I had to, because these devils were all mine, just as I was theirs.

CHAPTER TWENTY-FIVE

Sara

"Wake *up*, sleeping beauty," Tibby howled into the air, jolting me from my relatively dreamless sleep. The lack of nightmares was almost more disconcerting than the actual nightmares. This time was different. I saw a single figure, over and over. I couldn't see their face because of a bright light shining behind them. And wings, this thing had wings. They tried to call out to me, but every time I tried to respond, I had no voice.

I rolled over, feeling around the big empty bed. My eyes snapped open suddenly. "Tibby! You're out of jail!"

She grinned, her eyes crinkling. "Yup. For good behavior. Who knew?"

I laughed, and she fell back onto the pillow next to mine.

I noted the empty room and lack of testosterone. "Where are the guys?"

"Andras went to a cult meeting, the bad kind. Levi went to the firehouse, and Ty is downstairs attempting to make breakfast."

I laughed, then sighed when I realized she left one name out. "And Dev?"

Tibby shook her head. "Still MIA."

I should have expected that. "I'm guessing he dumped his phone, or you'd track it."

She nodded. "He dumped it at the bar. I'm watching the cameras there too, just in case."

"So what's the plan for today?" I rolled out of bed, heading for the bathroom to brush out the morning breath and my very fucked hair. My muscles ached, and even the slut between my legs, Miss Mina, was surprisingly quiet this morning.

Tibby followed me into the bathroom, sitting on the edge of the clawfoot tub. "I've got footage to go through from last night. I didn't see anything strange, but after Dev took off I was kind of sidetracked. Oh, and your key thing is missing."

I spun toward her. "What? How?"

She shrugged. "I don't know yet. It was locked up with all of Ty's creepy torture toys and now it's gone, according to Andras. There are cameras everywhere so it's gotta be someone from the party working for the bad guys."

Andras was probably freaking the fuck out. Someone stole from his own home. Maybe the party was a bad idea. I went to the closet and pulled out black leggings and a cozy burgundy sweater. I slipped on a pair of fluffy slippers and followed Tibby to the kitchen.

The scent of sausages wafted through the air, and my mouth watered. We rounded the corner into the kitchen and found Ty at the stove, scrambling eggs. My mouth watered for a whole new reason as I took in his muscular, tattooed back. He wore low-riding, gray sweatpants, and his dirty blond hair hung loose and wavy around his tattooed shoulders. The dark-green, bat-like wings rippled across his broad shoulders as he cooked.

Tibby hopped on a barstool at the island. "Damn, cool wings, Ty."

I walked around the island to the beautiful, muscled man behind it, wrapping my arms around his waist. "Good morning, monster man," I murmured, biting his back playfully.

He growled, half turning, and gripped my throat, shoving his tongue into my mouth hungrily.

"I've been waiting for you to wake up, pet." He grinned, looking down my body. "I'm starving."

"TMI," Tibby yelled, making me laugh. "Just give me my food so I can eat peacefully in the dungeon."

Ty chuckled darkly, dragging his hand down to squeeze my ass. He dropped his spatula and gripped my waist, hoisting me up onto the island. "Stay." He returned to the stove and fixed a plate of food for Tibby, full of cheesy scrambled eggs and round sausages.

Tibby snatched the plate and made gagging sounds as she left the room. "I'll let you know if I find anything on the camera footage. But later we are having girl time in the theater room with *no boys*."

I laughed. "Deal!"

Ty shut off the oven and stalked toward me, placing his hands on either side of the marble countertop and caging me in. "I did not agree to this rule."

I shoved his chest, but he didn't budge. "Yeah well, I'm the boss around here, dude. Get used to it. Now gimme my breakfast."

Ty smirked, his eyes sparkling with the devil's intent. "Me first."

He grabbed my legs, hoisting them into the air, and I flew backward. He caught my head just before it slammed on the counter. Then his hands pulled down my leggings, revealing my bare pussy. That horny bitch pulsed as Ty stared greedily between my legs.

"If you insist," I panted, my hips bucking in his arms as he spread my legs wider.

Ty slid two fingers along my pussy lips and growled his approval. "You're so fucking wet, little vixen. And all for me."

I moaned as his fingers dipped inside me so, so slowly. My hips arched off the counter at his touch, and he took advantage of the angle, bringing his mouth down on my clit. All of the blood in my body rushed straight to my core as he licked and sucked the life out of me. His fingers moved faster, deeper. As his teeth grazed my clit, I cried out with pleasure. Ty slipped his fingers out and gripped my thighs as he shoved his tongue inside me. My pussy clamped around it, the orgasm washing through me as I came in his mouth.

"Oh fuck, Ty," I murmured, my body twitching with happiness.

He licked up my center and gripped my throat, pulling me forward and devouring my moans with his tongue. I sucked his bottom lip into my mouth hungrily, tasting my cum on him.

He pulled away slowly, smirking. "Now what would you like for breakfast, babygirl?"

I grinned. "Eggs and sausage."

Ty snarled, and I laughed. He brought a plate over to me, and I dug into it. I really was starving, and the food was delicious. Ty brought me a cup of coffee as well, and I moaned happily.

"This is the only way I want to wake up now."

Ty smirked. "That can be arranged."

I nodded. "Good. I'll consider returning the favor."

His eyebrow arched as he leaned against the counter. "Your sassy little mouth is going to get you in trouble, pet."

I rolled my eyes. "As if that's stopped me before."

A buzzing sound interrupted us, and Andras's voice crackled across the intercom. "Sounds like someone is looking for punishment."

I glared up at the cameras. "Aren't you supposed to be in a meeting?"

"Stepped out to make sure you weren't getting into trouble, sweetheart."

I smiled, blinking innocently. "Does that mean you don't think Ty can handle me on his own? Apparently we both need babysitters, monster man."

Ty growled at the camera. "Fuck off, Andras. I'll make sure she behaves."

"Try not to murder each other before I get home."

The intercom went silent, and Ty turned to me, snatching my almost-empty plate and mug of coffee and dropping them in the sink.

I pouted. "Hey. I wasn't finished."

Ty turned away from the sink with handcuffs in one hand and a knife in the other. My eyes went wide, and he smiled, a thing of pure evil. "Run."

He didn't need to tell me twice when he looked like that. I leapt off the counter, running for the stairs. I raced up and up to the third floor with Andras's room. I heard his office door click open and grinned, knowing Tibby was aiding me. I shut the door silently and backed into the closet. My ears strained, listening for footsteps. After about sixty seconds, I got bored and started to snoop. I'd never been in Andras's office. It was always locked. I couldn't see any cameras either, which meant he wouldn't know I was snooping.

The phone on his desk started ringing, and, since I was being nosey, I picked it up.

"Hello?"

"It's me." Tibby's voice was hushed. "Listen, don't talk. I've got eyes on all the guys, and you have a very short window. They have your sister at a warehouse, Sara. I tracked Dev there. They've been playing us this whole time."

My heart seized, and I wanted to scream as her words sank in. "Tibby…What are you saying? Are you sure?"

"I think they're all in on it to keep you occupied before they take you to their fathers. I caught your sister on a camera from the street corner. It's her Sara. And Dev went in too. The others aren't there. Levi is at the firehouse, and Andras hasn't shown up yet. Get away from Ty and go now."

I whirled around the room. Andras's office had a large window, but it would be a long jump. "I can't get out from here."

Tibby's keyboard tapped rapidly before she spoke. "Ty is in the gym. If you can get to the main floor, you can sneak out through the kitchen."

"What about you?" I whispered urgently. I couldn't lose her either.

"I'll sneak out too and grab a car. You get your sister free, and I'll be right behind you with the getaway car."

I blew out a breath, my heart cracking and darkness settling in. I didn't have time to feel for the men I opened myself up to, the men who betrayed me so deeply.

"Be careful, Tibby." I couldn't lose my only friend.

"You too, Sara." Her voice sounded nervous, but this had to be done. No time for second guesses.

I dropped the phone and rushed to the door, opening it as quietly as possible. I was no amateur and obviously knew how to be silent as I quickly descended to the first floor. I grabbed two sharp kitchen knives and slipped out the door. I didn't have an earpiece, so there was no way to call Tibby. I had to trust she would get to the warehouse safely.

I jumped on my bike and grabbed the hidden key. The engine roared to life, and I sped through the city. The warehouse was in a seedy part of town, and I could be there in ten minutes if I ignored traffic lights. I wasn't sure how long it would take for the others to catch up. Tears burned the back of my eyes as I recalled the pain and anger Dev directed at me at the party. Was he so mad because he fell for me before or after he betrayed me? I didn't understand. Flashes of all the moments between me and my men invaded my mind. How could I be so stupid? I let them become something more, refused to see them for what they were. Obscuritas fucking Princes. Bastards like their evil fucking fathers. My rage flooded my body, and I screamed at the world for the bullshit I fell for like a fucking idiot.

The warehouse loomed ahead, and I turned two streets down to park my motorcycle out of sight. The cold air did nothing to smother the fire raging through my blood, and I thanked mother nature at least for the overcast day. The dark clouds rolled in as I crept toward the warehouse. I found a side entrance and snuck in as quietly as I could. There was very little light due to most of the windows being boarded up. I slipped down a dark hallway and heard voices echoing ahead. I stopped short as the hall ended at the entrance of a massive open room. There was a chair at the center and someone tied to it with a cloth over their head. My heart raced. My sister was here, before me, after all these years of searching.

I scanned the open space. One guard stood at a set of double doors on the opposite side of the room. He faced away from me, so I slipped into the massive space, keeping close to the walls and in the shadows. The only light in the room shined down on my sister strapped to the chair. I pulled out one of the kitchen knives and, just before the guard turned my way, I sliced the blade across his neck. He dropped instantly, unable to call out before he died.

I grabbed his gun and tucked it into my waistband. There was no time to check for anyone else. I ran to my sister and ripped the cloth from her head as I came around to face her.

My face fell. It wasn't her. The girl looked up at me with wide, fearful eyes, her mouth taped over. She was roughly my age, but most definitely not my lost sister. Tears fell from my eyes, and I dropped to my knees as the doors opened and ten armed men entered the room.

They were dressed in black, and trained their weapons on me. Dozens of laser sights pointed directly at my heart.

One guard stepped forward. "Drop the weapons and stand up."

The girl tied to the chair began to shake, tears falling uncontrollably. She was just another lost girl. Like my sister, like me. It was all wrong. And I fell for the trap so easily.

"Did you hear me, bitch?" the dumb fucking guy shouted, and I blew out a breath to steady my nerves.

I closed my eyes and let the rage burning through my veins take root. This is where I thrived. I would get my vengeance. One way or another.

I stood, slowly. "I heard you. And my voice will be the last thing you hear before you all die."

I aimed my gun and shot out the light above us, plunging the room into darkness. I knocked the girl over, hopefully saving her from a bullet, as I raced toward the men. The idiots were shouting and easy to find. The first two died quickly. I snatched their guns and fired shot after shot, taking them all out as they fired aimlessly into the dark. My breathing remained even as I cut them down. I listened for their screams, relishing in the pain I could give them before I stopped their stupid heartbeats forever.

Two men remained. They called out to each other in a panic, searching for the door to leave the room, and the devil in me laughed at their fear. I crept up behind one of them, slamming my knife into his exposed throat. Blood splattered across my face. I was covered in gore. He dropped to the ground as his life force drained away.

"Please," the last man pleaded in the dark. "I have a family."

I laughed, and it sounded hollow and terrifying. "So did I."

I ran across the room where I heard his voice. His gun fired, and I almost stumbled as a stray bullet grazed my arm. I kept running until I lept at him, smacking his gun away and stabbing his chest with my knife. He screamed. I pulled it out and stabbed him again. His groans turned wet as the blood gushed into his lungs, and I stabbed again and again until my arms grew weak.

I dropped the knife and hung my head, the silence deafening. The creak of a door echoed into the room. I snatched up the dead man's gun and turned, ready to fire. Light poured into the room from the open door to reveal the monster before me.

"Seraphina?" Ty's voice was gruff as he spoke my name so quietly, as if he didn't want to spook a wild animal.

I pointed the gun at his head. "Don't fucking move," I snarled at him, but he didn't listen.

He moved anyway, opening the door wider to let in more light. His eyes surveyed the carnage.

"I told the guys we had nothing to worry about. Our girl could handle a few assholes." Ty grinned, and I wanted to scream.

"What the fuck are you saying? You did this. My sister isn't here. It was a trap. Dev…the others…" Tears blurred my vision, and I shouted at him. "You fucking did this!"

I couldn't see his face clearly, but his voice was low and steady as he raised his hands in surrender. "Seraphina. We didn't do this. Who told you that? Is Dev here?"

I shook my head, refusing to believe him, and inched closer to him. Ty's eyes widened as he saw me fully, covered in blood and training the gun on his heart.

"Lies. She saw him here. He's somewhere. Did they send you in first to subdue me? Thought I would be worn out from the fight by now? Guess again."

Ty frowned, shaking his head. Our eyes locked, and his widened at whatever darkness he found in mine. He dropped to his knees.

"Babygirl. This wasn't us. I swear it. We haven't seen Dev. Andras thinks maybe our fathers got to him somehow."

"I don't believe you!" I raged at him, my arms shaking and my heart falling to pieces. "Tell me where my fucking sister is or I will fucking kill you, Typhon!"

Ty leaned back on his heels, his arms wide in surrender. "Then kill me, Seraphina. I will die for you, if that's what it takes. I don't have her. We don't have her. Slit my throat and put a bullet in my heart if you don't believe me."

I stomped toward him and pressed the gun to his chest as I stared into his eyes. His beautiful hazel eyes stared back at me with sadness and love. Fucking love. I swallowed as my mouth dried up, and angry tears spilled over again and again. I dropped to my knees, hard, the pain unfelt in that moment, the gun still aimed at his heart. We stared at each other for an endless moment.

Ty slowly brought his hand to my face. He cupped my cheek, his thumb wiping away blood and tears. "My heart is yours, Seraphina. Take it."

My mind was exploding with uncertainty, and I wanted nothing more than to believe him. I needed to believe him. I dropped the gun and sagged forward as the adrenaline faded. Ty caught me in his arms and pulled my face to his, kissing me with such ferocity I thought my heart was going to explode. He pulled my hair to the point of pain, and I dragged my nails down his arms, making him bleed. There was nothing beautiful or romantic about our joining. It was dark and raw, and I needed the pain. I bit his lip hard, and he growled, tugging my hair harder, making me yelp as he ripped my head to the side.

"Mine," he growled before biting my neck, and my pussy pulsed with need for more.

"You fuckers couldn't wait for me?"

Levi's sudden presence made me jump, and Ty released my hair. We stood and turned toward Levi.

A shot rang out, and my eyes widened as Levi suddenly dropped to the ground. Dev stood behind him, gun in hand. Levi slumped to the floor and the silence was deafening for all of two seconds.

Ty roared in fury and ran at Dev like an angry bull. Dev brought the gun up, and a second shot rang out. Then another. Ty dropped to his knees and cradled his stomach with a groan.

My brain couldn't comprehend what was happening. Dev shot them. I stared at Levi, unmoving with blood pooling on the concrete around him. And Ty at Dev's feet, trying desperately to move. I started toward him, but stopped when Dev suddenly turned the gun on me.

"Don't move." His voice was cold and distant. The sound stopped my heart. "I tried to stop this. Tried to get you to leave with me. But none of it mattered anyway, and this is how it has to be."

"Dev, what the fuck are you talking about?" I took a step toward Ty.

Dev didn't respond, just watched me, cold and unfeeling. I kept going until I reached Ty. He was on the ground now, and I cupped his cheek as he had mine moments before. His eyes opened and he looked terrified.

"Get out of here, Seraphina," he mumbled the words, pain searing across his face.

I shook my head. "No. I'm not leaving you."

Dev pulled out a second weapon, and I heard more voices in the distance. "You are, actually."

Ty growled. "I'm going to fucking kill you, Devon Parrish."

Dev shrugged. "Not today."

I looked up at Dev, my heart hurting and shame coloring my cheeks. "You did all this? Why?"

Dev's mouth turned into a grim line, and his eyes clouded with anger. "Same as you. For revenge."

He lifted the second weapon and fired. A dart slammed into my chest and knocked me back. I felt the drug coursing through me, numbing my body. Dev walked forward and stared down at me with unrecognizable eyes. We stared at each other until the drug took hold. My eyes closed, and I couldn't hold on any longer. My last thoughts focused on the one I needed most. My mother.

CHAPTER TWENTY-SIX

Andras

I buried a third knife into the dart board, hitting the bullseye, and dialed Devon's phone again. The call went straight to voicemail, and I almost screamed my rage. Almost. I was close to losing it. My phone rang, and I answered immediately.

"Where the fuck are you? And where is she?"

Ty knew exactly who I meant. Our girl. The beautiful, stubborn, sinful woman who waltzed into my life and turned everything on its head. When I had her in my arms again, I was going to spank her plump ass raw. And then have Typhon string her up in the dungeon I now paced.

"I've got her scent. She's close. Levi is across town but not far behind. Have you found Tabitha?" Ty's voice was diluted by the rush of wind, but I could hear him enough to understand.

"No." I shook my head and started to fill the duffle bags with weapons. "She isn't here, and her scent disappears outside the house. She must have been picked up. Something feels wrong about all this, Typhon. Have you heard from your father?"

Ty growled down the line. "Not since yesterday morning. Something is definitely wrong. He sounds restless and edgy. I can always tell when he's lying, Andras. I'm at the warehouse. I hear fighting. Get here now."

The call disconnected, and my heart raced. I should've known this would happen. I thought I was being prepared. The party confirmed our allies within The Obscuritas, and we were close to making a stand. For Sara and her sly little friend to suddenly disappear the next morning, it wasn't right. I recalled the look in my father's eye when he spotted Seraphina on the dance floor at the ball. She looked exquisite in her navy gown, but it wasn't her beauty Laszlo was admiring. I knew then what I refused to acknowledge. She was the one he was searching for. And with her blood, he would become unstoppable.

I hauled the bags of weapons over my shoulder, heading for the garage and tried Levi's phone. Straight to voicemail. I was beginning to hate voicemails. I tossed the two bags into the Land Rover. My phone rang out in the silence, and I frowned at the blocked number.

"Who is this?" I demanded, knowing it wasn't going to be good.

"Catch you at a bad time, son?" The deep voice of my father halted my steps.

My heart raced. He never called me directly. "What do you want, Laszlo?" I jumped into the driver's seat and started the engine. This was very, very bad.

"You will join me in North Carolina. We have found the girl. It's time." Laszlo Blackbyrn sounded practically giddy. He had Seraphina. Which meant Ty was in trouble too. "I have them all, son."

His words nearly stopped my heart. "What are you saying? Enough of the riddles."

Laszlo growled, and a lesser man would've cowered at the

sound, but I was trained by this man. I was accustomed to his moods.

"Seraphina is mine. Typhon and Leviathan are on their way to me as well. You have traitors in your home. Spies among your friends. Did you think you could outwit me, boy? You are nothing but what I have made you. The longer you take to follow my orders, the greater their suffering."

The phone went dead, and I let loose the scream of rage I'd held back for decades. My blood turned cold, and the windshield shattered as the glass froze. I was quickly losing control of my senses, my power. My world.

I took several deep breaths and tried to gain some control. My father might think he held all the cards, but I was certain he didn't know everything. I sent out several texts in rapid succession, then tossed the phone to the ground and smashed it to bits with the heel of my shoe. I would go to my father, as he demanded. But I would not be going alone. I would save my brothers. I would save Seraphina. If I had to burn the entire world down to do it, so be it.

ABOUT THE AUTHOR

S. D. Paine is a writer of fantasy and romance of the dark and paranormal variety. She loves a good plot twist and creating morally gray characters. She reads constantly, and cannot function without at least two cups of coffee. She lives in the Midwest with her family and a small horde of adopted dogs and a crazy cat.

ACKNOWLEDGEMENTS

There are plenty of people I could name drop, but I'm not the touchy-feely type. When chatting with a friend about writing and how I wanted to get this book written and published, they offered the most basic and profound advice–just gotta do it. Seems silly, but it stuck with me until one day, the book was written and ready to be shared.

Thank you to the amazing bookish friends I have made along the way as my author journey took flight. Sending all my love to the best betas and ARC readers ever! You all rock!